THE SILENCE OF
THE SHAGGY RUG

THE SILENCE OF THE SHAGGY RUG

Daniel Jacob

First published in 2021 by Redshank Books

Redshank Books is an imprint of Libri Publishing.

Copyright © Daniel Jacob

The right of Daniel Jacob to be identified as the author of this work has been asserted in accordance with the Copyright, Designs and Patents Act, 1988.

ISBN 978-1-912969-24-1

A CIP catalogue record for this book is available from The British Library

Cover and book design by Carnegie Book Production

Libri Publishing
Brunel House
Volunteer Way
Faringdon
Oxfordshire
SN7 7YR

Tel: +44 (0)845 873 3837

www.libripublishing.co.uk

Dedicated to:

LXX

And to the generations of perfidious parliamentary plunderers whose predilection for piggishness made penning this publication possible.

In the Bleak Midwinter

Lord Archibald Penley Crooke-Wells wasn't the front runner in desiring to add weight to Marjorie Trembel's already sagging innerspring mattress. But he was the first of an archaic English coterie, the hereditary rich, to seek her hand in marriage. This age-old minority group safeguard their penchant for perpetuation by intermarriage, mutual greasing-of-the-wheels, and a cherishment of class solidarity. Therefore, despite being twenty years his junior, and lacking any sentimental attachment, she'd agreed to the merger and its breeding presumption.

On her twentieth birthday in nineteen seventy, Marjorie became Lady Crooke-Wells, née Trembel, when she and Archibald were conjoined in wedlock.

* * *

After ten years of mutual monotony, another Christmas nailed to the William IV mahogany chaise longue in their claustrophobic four-floored, five-bedroomed Georgian house in Bloomsbury, failed to find favour with Marjorie. Yuletide festivity was to be in the Caribbean with offspring, Rodney, Tristan, and Cuthbert – Nanny of course in tow to take the irritation of parenting from Mummy's shoulders.

They'd not be penned at the departure gate with the package-peasants, who, for a few hundred pounds, would soon blight quaint Spanish fishing villages with booze, brawls and bingo.

The luxury of a coddled Concorde flight was but one manifestation of her raison d'être for marriage to Archibald. If their Louis Vuitton monogrammed luggage – cosseted comfortably in Concorde's baggage compartment – could sneer, it would have. For glissading five miles above – and faster than a bullet from a bolt-action Purdey – they would land nearly six hours ahead of the basement bargain bags of the masses dumped in the hold of the galumphing Jumbo below.

Although grave bound for well-nigh eighty years, it would've thrilled Louis to know his latest luggage was winging its way for three weeks of sumptuousness at the Club Royal Columbus, Barbados.

* * *

Christmas Day, and the sun was intent upon impelling the temperature beyond thirty degrees. Nine-year-old Rodney had struggled hard, but Nanny's determination had prevailed, and she'd piled oodles of sun cream upon his pale podgy body.

The morning had been ace as he'd spent tons of time breaking the legs off the bleached remains of starfish on the seashore and hurling them into the surf. After lunch, whilst Nanny had dragged his younger brothers, Tristan and Cuthbert, off for their afternoon scream and nap, he'd settled on digging in the soft pink sand of Crane Beach. He didn't mind playing alone for that was the same at home.

When he'd started the undertaking, Rodney perceived creating castles as a great pleasure for he possessed a good imagination. But, after a time, he found that the task was becoming more and more problematic. The mediaeval edifices kept collapsing as the soft dry sand was not the best construction material. He sat staring discontentedly at the lacklustre turrets and towers. Even the moles that regularly burrowed in the croquet lawn at home would have scorned those he now surveyed.

Peeing in the sand brought forth no benefit. 'I'm probably lacking a thirst quencher', he thought. Undeterred, he ordered Joseph, the beach lounger man, to lug loads of water in a plastic bucket from the outdoor shower. Only then did the fortifications measure up to his satisfaction. Taking a breather to admire his labour, he was outraged to see that, despite all the donkeywork, within minutes the turrets became as parched as their predecessors, foundered and flopped.

Exhausted from toiling in the hot sun, he gave up castle construction and adopted instead the excavation of a crater. The plan was to dig a deep hole, then position fan-like palm leaves from fallen fronds over the pit, and to camouflage them with a bit of sand on top. Upon completion, he would lounge against the trunk of a coconut tree casually sipping Cola whilst waiting until someone fell into his mantrap, then delight in the consequent kerfuffle.

It was a pity neither Tristan nor Cuthbert were there. It would be joyful to see Nanny sprint to save one of them from being buried alive, and it would make his efforts worthwhile. If that puny four-year-old whining mongrel Cuthbert perished in the pit, it would be ace. Yes, ace as he was the smallest and it would've saved lots of sweat not having to make the hole so deep.

While it was not difficult to detest both brothers, it was Tristan who was the easiest. Despite being two years younger he was taller, and a hideous limelight-seeking show-off. Seeing Nanny stroking his haystack blond hair was as puke-worthy as watching her force-feed Cuthbert. That very morning, she'd put only a smattering of sun cream on Tristan. Then, although he'd spent all morning in the sun, he still didn't look anything like a tomato when she'd dragged him and Cuthbert off to rest.

Meantime, in their absence, to cripple a normal-sized person meant the crater had to be deep. He measured this by standing in the hole and digging until his belly button was level with the rim. Excavating with a plastic spade made construction jolly hard work. The heat and toil took its toll and Rodney became thirstier than he remembered ever being before, his mouth as dry as the sand at his feet.

Daddy had gone to get himself a drink from the Swashbuckler Beach Bar ages ago and Rodney thought he also deserved one after slaving so hard. The sand was as hot as the coals on a fakir's fire as he scampered over to the bar with his toes burning to blister point.

Upon arrival, he found it deserted and sat waiting for what seemed to be like an everlastingness, which annoyed him as his plan was to complete the excavation with all haste. It was important to get it finished, so when someone fell into the hole, sprained an ankle or, better still, got carried away on a stretcher, he was there to watch. But if Nanny had by then taken him to dinner and he missed the tortuous screams of agony, it would put a damper on his entire holiday.

On a previous occasion, when his favourite drink had run out, the bar lady went to the room at the back to get one for him. She might be there, he thought. Rodney poked his head around the door and there she was, and so was Daddy! He was buttoning up the front of her shirt; it had sprung wide open revealing that she wore nothing underneath.

Seeing Rodney made Daddy jump out of his skin and rush to the door. Bending down with his face within an inch of Rodney's, Daddy said he was helping the lady because she had a sore hand and couldn't hold the buttons. He gave Rodney a one-pound note saying not to tell Mummy because Mummy didn't like Auntie Aryanna, and Daddy would thrash the living daylights out of him if he ever uttered a single word about it.

Rodney thought doing up the buttons must have been as exhausting as burrowing in the sand because Daddy's face was so red and sweaty. Auntie Aryanna's hand improved like greased lightning for, when Rodney raised his eyes to ogle at the contents beneath the shirt, it was with disappointment he saw she had done all the buttons up. Until then, Rodney never knew he had a black auntie living behind a bar on a beach in the Caribbean. Neither Mummy, nor Daddy, had ever mentioned her before. Musing, he wondered if it was because Mummy didn't like her.

From that moment on, Rodney loved his new auntie, and Aryanna was a beautiful name. She must have been just as surprised to find out a little white boy from England was her nephew, and made up for every missed birthday their separation had elicited by giving him as many ice creams, cold drinks and sweets as he desired. Poor Auntie Aryanna's hand gave oodles more problems, for Rodney noticed Daddy helped her quite a lot during their three-week vacation, and also gave him more one-pound notes.

Although he'd only had a brief glance, he rather liked his auntie's bosoms. Other than Mummy's, and Nanny's little ones, and the wet-nurse's – Daddy called her the Jersey cow – he had never seen any others and the two black ones were particularly ace. I'll tell Lysander what a black titty looks like when I get home, he decided – Lysander being chosen because he was Rodney's only friend and no doubt had never seen a white one, never mind two blacks.

While Rodney was at the bar, Mummy's already sienna-tanned skin was being bombarded with sufficient ultraviolet rays to keep a covey of Consultant Dermatologists as rich as Croesus. Her portable radio's bent aerial was also being bombarded, but with radio waves transporting carols from a cathedral in England. The enormous minster, she surmised, must be as cold as a harlot's heart and the choir was appropriately singing her favourite carol, *In the Bleak Midwinter*. Tears trickled from the corner of her eyes as the beautiful rendition caused the spirit of Christmas to come upon her. Then the added irritation of the acrid brume from her Passing Cloud cigarette incited a cloudburst, which gave rise to mascara junketing down her cheeks.

For years, she had loved this laconic Christmas song; it never crossed her mind that the opulent and hedonistic lifestyle she led might be at odds with her reverence for this treasure of religiosity.

Believing coconut and pineapple would settle the morning's vodka; Mummy placed her fourth post-luncheon Piña Colada on the side table and – with eyes smarting from the acrid fumes – she attempted to stub Raleigh's revenge into the turtle-shell ashtray. The sight of the shell brought a cataclysmic event to mind, resulting in a fresh wave of tears.

The why and the wherefore of the reaction was that on Mummy's eighth birthday, her fifteen-year-old cousin Tracy was staying the weekend. Tracy, who'd been born again, twice, did what St. Francis would have done if he were alive, she'd set about saving mink from unscrupulous breeders who turned the creatures into coats worn by her mother. When taking tea with Mummy one afternoon, Tracy had learnt that they kept the Chinese oolong leaves, used to make the beverage, in a nineteenth-century French tortoiseshell caddy. She'd determined there and then to also save such reptiles. So, deciding that Marjorie's pet, Terry the tortoise, wouldn't end up as a comb or trinket box, she sought to return him to the wild. Pretending to feed the reptile a piece of lettuce, she kidnapped him. Then, with no idea of the difference between a turtle and a tortoise, she launched him into the middle of the duck pond, just below the croquet lawn.

With Tracy singing *Born Free*, little Marjorie had watched helplessly as, with his neck fully stretched like a snorkel, and, she thought, mouthing 'help', Terry sadly sank. Her brother, Magnus, rushed to the house and donned the snorkelling set he'd received the previous Christmas. Then, as he bolted back, his goggles steamed up and the flippers got caught in the croquet hoops, delaying him. Despite manning a belated search of the knee-deep murky water, his efforts failed. They never recovered Terry's remains.

The combination of Terry's final moments, the cigarette smoke and her favourite carol prompted Mummy's eyes to fill with tears. With that, and her intoxication, she didn't spot the glass of Piña Colada and her hand sent it flying, the contents flooding the radio.

Unlike the designer of Mummy's tummy, who had taken the frailty of mankind into consideration, Mr No Do-Woo of Sky High Radio Inc., when designing his wireless, did not anticipate that a barricade against a Piña

Colada ingression on a sandy sun-soaked shore in the Bahamas might merit his consideration. Mr Do-Woo's creation evidenced its lack of resistance to the assault by puking smoke from several sub-miniature components. The electromagnetic waves, that'd run the gauntlet with millions of rivals equally eager to rush down Mummy's twisted radio antenna and have their voice heard, in a flash found their onward passage stymied. Rossetti's heart-wrenching masterpiece surrendered and fell silent in the fourth stanza, just when the organist detached to play the F major and the choirmaster showed the required diminuendo for the choir to sing *Kiss*.

And from that tear-jerking moment Mummy set her sights upon Rodney becoming a chorister boarder with a cathedral choir.

* * *

After the holiday, and faster than the executioner's axe had cleaved Sir Walter's craving for a fag, she applied to several cathedral schools; all replied to an absence of vacancies, one even implying she should have put Rodney's name forward at birth. She sent a letter of apology for not having had the foresight to register him before her own pubescence.

But amongst the pile of rejections was one ray of hope. A note from a school said, although they had sufficient applicants for the next intake, she could give them a ring to discuss other possibilities.

Upon telephoning she learnt that if a Charitable Benefaction, as they called it, of the right magnitude was forthcoming it could open the door to an interview. Mummy, never a filly to falter and fall at the first fence, declared whatever anyone else was offering she would up it by ten, no, make it fifteen per cent. The school settled on a non-refundable deposit of twenty-five per cent of the benefaction, thereby circumnavigating the application deadline faster than a political promise, and Rodney was on the list of the would-be warblers.

Although of a high standard, the halls of knowledge were a little less prestigious than those of the others she had considered. Nonetheless, Mummy was ready to bend over backwards, a position she was quite familiar with, to make sure of Rodney's acceptance, no matter the monumental disbursement.

'Charitable benefaction!' Daddy raged. 'Bloody blackmail! I won't have my son growing up a choirboy; it's a prelude to entering the fairy kingdom.' But Mummy had her ways.

To conquer her lack of knowledge pertaining to the goings-on in churches, she thought watching films showing nun's habits was the obvious route for laying the groundwork. *The Sound of Music* provided most of her education on the subject. After viewing it five times, she felt capable of writing her own book on the nunhood. The Abbey scenes were just what she needed as they highlighted how an aura of peace, calm and tranquillity was at the heart of cathedral life.

But, being honest, seeing the film so often made the ending no less painful. It wasn't Maria von Trapp's fault, but that Mummy, when aged fourteen, had fallen off her Shetland pony and was left frightened of heights. So she'd give a miss to the very thought of scaling mountains, traversing the Alps, yodelling between verses of do-re-me whilst herding a bunch of whining kids and a pubescent step-daughter in love with a Hitlerjugend postman. But even worse was the husband strumming a few E minor chords on a guitar while being pursued by a group of Nazis hell-bent on dragging the plucker off to command one of the Führer's gunboats. If she'd been forced to choose between scale and sail, when the sailor was searching for his crampons she'd have buried his boots, lidded his lederhosen and turned the troubadour over to the press-gang.

The Nun's Story was another source of inspiration that guided her choice of apparel and elegant demeanour. The film featured a tubercular vestal virgin with glamour, elegance, poise and serenity. These qualities, Mummy knew, she exhibited in abundance, except for the cough. . . oh, and virginity, also not forgetting the occasional lapse in serenity. She was well-versed in whole slews of whimsical ways that gave rise to a sweat, but playing Jane in the jungle with a turned-on Tarzan would be unthinkable.

To make the right impression when visiting the school, a new outfit was needed. Paris was the place to buy a frock, therefore she and her personal shopper, Linda Lefeuvre, devoted a delightful week in the French capital to deciding upon the correct dress for evensong. Believing Coco Chanel was the ultimate couturier for black dresses, they selected a calf-length with long sleeves. The design flattered her curvaceous figure, while providing modesty and elegance in the positions they imagined she might find herself. Clothes shopping in Paris, Rome, or anywhere, was always fun, but finding that particular dress brought with it insurmountable pleasure.

After the purchase, they had a sandwich lunch and Belgian coffee in a chic café near to the Passage Alombert. Linda agreed with Mummy that anyone who maintained money could not lead to happiness had never discovered the perfect frock on the Rue de Passy.

On the plane back to London she read a do-it-yourself book, *How to Conduct Yourself in Church*. It revealed that a head covering, called a chapel veil, whilst not obligatory, was considered mandatory by some High Church clergy. As it was crucial not to put everything in jeopardy for the sake of a bit of lace, she would purchase a black chapel veil.

Although it was some years since wearing her wedding dress, she still adored it. Embellished with Nottingham lace, the dress was the best part of the wedding day or, for that matter, any subsequent day, and so she commissioned the same lacemaker to create a mantilla.

Upon its completion, she travelled by train to the Queen of the Midlands, as the residents call the city. The lacemaker placed his masterpiece upon her head; its beauty had to be seen to be believed. The skilfully understated gold embroidery lifted it from pretty to perfection. No wonder royalty uses Nottingham lace, for it made her feel quite regal, and would sort out any fossilised clergy. Chatting to the lacemaker, she learnt that the bright clear water filtering through hunter sandstone and used to wash the finished product, was what elevated Nottingham lace to its position as world leader.

After leaving his tiny studio in the thousand-year-old creative area known as The Lace Market, she had time to spare and walked past the Council House to the nearby city centre. There she spotted a sign to the Castle and Robin Hood.

It was but a short walk to the foot of the fortress where the bronze statue of the arboreal thief stood. Mummy considered it paradoxical that the citizens of Nottingham (notorious for its crime rate) embraced a villainous charlatan as their hero. Cast in bronze and surrounded by his miniaturised gang of cutthroats, the overweight, and without doubt uncouth, personage of Robin Hood wore the wrong hat and garbs. It was disappointing, for he was not portrayed as in the old Hollywood film; she loved the early romantic movies.

Hollywood had created Robin as handsome and affable, not short and fat. But then, how could émigré brothers called Wonskolaser from Poland, living in America, have any knowledge of Robin Hood? Changing their name to Warner and having Errol Flynn on the payroll changed nothing for the better. It was they who had influenced her, and the rest of the unsuspecting audience, into believing that Robin was not a thieving malefactor, but a moustachioed Tasmanian rascal with a phoney English accent. Perhaps the bronze image was correct, and he had been short and fat, for after all he was a local boy so they should know. She spotted that the drawn longbow had no arrow. Had some reprobate robbed the robbing rascal Robin?

Another visitor to the scoundrel's shrine was a frail elderly gentleman leaning heavily on a walking stick. When he tripped on the damp moss-covered cobbled pathway, Mummy leapt to support the dear old soul. The fellow's knees trembled like Mungo Manley's had when he took her behind the gardener's shed. He'd been her first, and as clumsy and uninitiated as she. The old fellow croaked, 'Thanks very much dear, only been out of hospital two days. I'm still feeling dizzy, it's my blood pressure you know, won't get no better.'

After a few moments with Mummy's support, he caught his breath. 'Saw you looking at the arrow, often gets stolen, tourists, or drunken youths,' he wheezed. 'They'll change it from bronze to fibreglass then it won't get nicked. There're lots of thieves around.' He paused for a wheezy inhalation and phlegmy cough. 'Won't be the same, can't have a plastic dart can yer?' She agreed that a modern material was incorrect, but the Warner Brothers wouldn't care. He asked who they were. She was getting bored, so responded by saying they were just friends for whom attention to detail was unimportant.

After viewing the replicas of Little John, Will Scarlet and the remaining band of brigands, she couldn't miss Friar Tuck, played in the film by an obese American with a frog-like voice. The old man asked her to help him to a bench where he would sit and wait for his wife. Mummy asked if she was shopping.

'No, gone to the chiropodist, can't see her toes no more.'

Mummy commiserated. 'Cataracts?'

'No, fat! Can't bend over no more,' he said, before convulsing.

Saying goodbye, she departed with a wave.

It was but a five-minute downhill stroll to Ye Olde Trip to Jerusalem, the antediluvian tavern hewn into the same sandstone hill that filters the fine-lace-making water. The sign above the inn proclaimed it a stopover for the Knights and foot soldiers that'd travelled in 1198 with King John's Crusaders to battle the Saracens: a journey without a return ticket for many.

Standing at the bar, she ordered a drink of the local ale. Granules from the hewn sedimentary-rock ceiling fell constantly onto the counter. She speculated that nigh on 800 years before, Richard the Lionheart and Robin's band of outlaws drank there, not at the same time of course. From time to time the evil Sheriff, on his way to extract taxes from the poor, probably rested on this spot, while threatening the landlord to hand over a free beer.

Nearby Robin's statue, an information board pronounced Sir Roger de Mortimer had once revelled in the facilities of the fortress. After having the king killed, the errant Knight-errant not only took over the country but also his majesty's French widow's assets. On a cold October night, the late king's son then cantered through the castle caves and, ne'er a knock, bounded into his mother's bedchamber and routed Roger from his repose. Tied and gagged, the randy noble was dispatched to rot on a rope at Tyburn. The information sheet said he and his mistress were now two of many residential ghosts romping the ramparts. Perhaps Roger had also enjoyed sustenance where she now stood, in-between his 'hey derry down derry dildo' sessions.

Placing the drink on the counter, the barman requested the remittance. She went through her handbag, but to no avail; her purse had gone. How dreadful!

'I'll come back in a minute, me duck. Yer alreet, just take yer time,' the barman said, placing the beer under the counter, for, whilst Mummy didn't appear to be a gulp-and-galloper, you never knew. It had happened that clients went without paying.

The barman's local friendly term of endearment, 'me duck', would have raised a smile under normal circumstances, but losing her purse was perplexing: Where had she last used it? The realisation soon dawned. The elderly gentleman who'd told her that crime abounded, he must have stolen it. She thought of hightailing after him, but no doubt the debilitated beggar had vanished faster than a wig in a wind. She fumed. While angry with the robber, she was more furious with herself. Out of respect for his age and feeble physical shape, she had assisted the pilfering plunderer, but never again. From now on the aged can help themselves, she decided. If I were to come across one astride a mobility scooter with a flat battery on a flooded plain, I wouldn't give a single volt. Not even if they offered to pay. I mean, what else is there to expect in this current criminal climate.

A seedy fellow, wearing a dirty raincoat, observing her distress, stepped forward, and asked if he might help. Without waiting for a response, he called the barman, paid for the beer, and slithered closer to Mummy. 'Ey up me duck, sup up, me car's just down the road. It's the red Allegro, shall we do the business thar?'

Men frequently propositioned her, but never in such a coarse manner. Smiling she parted his raincoat; his excitement was apparent. But all notions of nooky were snuffed when the amber brew cascaded down the front of his trousers.

Smiling, she winked, and walked.

* * *

Upon her return to London, she'd taken stock. Both the mantilla and dress were perfection, so the next item was shoes, and the only place in the world to buy them? Italy. And there was only one way to start her seven-day jolly jaunt – in a sumptuous Wagon-Lit Art Deco carriage on the London-to-Venice Orient Express. Then, once there, the elegant Piano Nobile in the Dorsoduro district on the Grand Canal was the place to stay. Breakfast would be on the balcony, where the view of the Academia Bridge lit by the morning sun would be gorgeous.

Six days later she pulled out of London Victoria Station. The men on the train buzzed around her as bees an Elvish honeypot. She toyed briefly with a Bulgarian businessman until his wife interrupted them. Then it was fun flirting with the Russian Ambassador to someplace she'd never heard of, but it became problematic after his umpteenth vodka.

When bored with flirting, she joined a sprinkling of writers and artists arguing for a new world social order, where everyone would be equal. They offered her a crystal flute of Champagne from one of the five best available at the bar. A painter of contemporary art, whose work she knew but loathed – judging it to be more vulgar than a bidet – was the most vociferous. The injustice of society was his burden; that was until he slid from the footstool onto the deep pile carpet in an intoxicated stupor.

She preferred dining alone and had refused the proffered overtures of candlelit evening repasts from both the Russian rascal and the bulbous Bulgarian – whose wife had retired early. Mummy was well aware they wanted to have her on their pudding list.

The bar emptied as patrons left to prepare for dinner, leaving her alone with the Russian. The diplomat's stage of inebriation was at maudlin; the understandability of his accented English as measured on the international crapulence scale of one to ten, stood at eleven.

Between sobbing and further shots of vodka, he delivered the tragedy of a home-alone wife.

'When the Politburo inform me of my ambassadorial appointment, my wife Galina was at first happy for, as ambassador, I receive a Lada motor car. Her friends were very envious for as well as the three forward ones it also had a reverse gear. We had so much fun showing off to her friends by driving backwards up Tverskaya Street. But her joy soon wore off, and she decided not to accompany me as she said leaving her friends was too painful. So many friends: there must be at least a dozen in the bread queue alone, if you add the baker it's thirteen. He was very kind, in one week he give her five small barley loaves, she break them up to give away.

'Also, there are those good comrades waiting by the dock for the fishing boats to come into port. One bitter morning, we woke to find that rats had eaten all the food in the apartment. Mercifully, a comrade fisherman traded two small fish for a rusted razor blade my wife could no longer use. Two small fish I ask, but you can't expect miracles. We decided the effects of her leaving would be heartbreaking for far too many others. If Galina stay at home and I take up my position unaccompanied, there be only one person miserable: me. That is why I travel alone.' He then broke down, wailing.

Mummy cradled him on her shoulder for some sobbing minutes. Not wishing for her Givenchy top to get tear stained, she was about to raise his head when he bolted upright.

'Madam, I come from St. Petersburg. Oh, dear, I mean Leningrad. My city is renowned for the long summer nights; there are times when darkness never falls. Have you heard of them?'

'Mr Ambassador, do not worry. There are no microphones here, we're alone, let us call it St. Petersburg. And yes, of course I've heard of them. Your White Night Walks are world-famous.'

'Thank you madam, I love my city,' he looked left and right before whispering, 'St. Petersburg. To escort a creation as charming as you on a White Night Walk would be the greatest privilege for which any man on earth could wish. I implore you to grant me the honour before we dine.'

'Mr Ambassador, under ordinary circumstances it would be a joy to take a stroll with you. However, as we are whizzing along a railway line at eighty kilometres an hour, through the alpine regions of heaven knows where, it is with the greatest sadness I have to pass on your kind offer, perhaps some other time.'

'Oh dear, it was not my purpose to cause you sadness.' Another vodka chased the last. 'If it is your intention not to be my companion, madam, I will proceed alone.' He stumbled to the carriage door, opened it and stepped out. The door slammed shut.

No reason to beat one's breast came to mind, as Mummy strolled through for dinner. Several rejected suitors had declared suicide to be their only solace, but, until now, she couldn't recall one who'd done the deed.

The dining car shimmered with candlelight. It pleased her to see that they had set the table for one; she disliked it when they removed place settings after she'd sat down. It was as if she was being shamed for daring to be alone. The folded napkin on the white tablecloth and the impeccable silver tableware delighted her, without a doubt the work of the chichi waiter.

The sommelier recommended a Bourgogne Pinot Noir. Never a wine snob, she believed life was too short to worry about matching food and wine. Unless it was Champagne, she almost always drank red. 'Drink to enjoy', was her view.

The *amuse-bouche* and hors d'oeuvre were superb, but she abstained from the entrée. After a zesty lemon sorbet, the *plat principal*, Chicken Suprême with celeriac, chestnut and truffle, was delicious. Warm chocolate pudding, a favourite since childhood, she rated as outstanding. A Passing Cloud cigarette with a cup of spicy Ethiopia

Genika coffee, relaxation, serenity: she was ready, now, for sleep.

A single carriage on the Orient Express was at a premium, but she disliked sharing with strangers. Three years before, when travelling north for a Highland fling, she had opted to share a double sleeper as such a short journey was not worth the single subsidy. The other occupant couldn't speak a word of English, and her body hair was comparable to that of the Hebridean Longhorn on the many posters inviting the world to visit Scotland. But, in the end, it was her rendition of Wagner's 'Ride of the Valkyries' – performed with farts, snorts and snores – which made sleep impossible and drove Mummy to proclaim, 'If forced to choose between a bewhiskered Brunhilda or a hairy haystack, I'd go for the latter.'

Now snuggled beneath the cool sweet-smelling sheets thinking at least in Italy she was free from being accosted by unsavoury characters; that ne'er-do-well in Ye Olde Trip being fresh to mind. The occasional tweak on the buttocks only emphasised her desirability in a country she loved like no other.

Italian men are so captivating. An informal luncheon followed by a nap until four; woken with a soft kiss on the cheek and a whispered, '*Andiamo a fare un giro*'. The invitation, to stroll with other lovers in the main Piazza and then to mingle in the narrow streets, was irresistible.

A fleeting smile would bond strangers, while, around each corner, another café with chairs and tables in the street provided an opportunity for a further cigarette and a drink, or two. Italian men are adorable: always suave and refined with a jumper tossed across the shoulders, dark hair curling over the collar, brown brooding eyes deep set in an olive skin. Even preparing a humble plate of pasta or grinding black pepper over Carbonara would be accomplished with feeling.

At a fashion show in London she had met Luca, and an invitation to join him for a weekend at his holiday home in Griante followed. The opportunity to take up the offer arose when Archibald was overseas, on business he said.

With Luca 'a quickie' could never be in the back of a clapped-out rusty Austin Allegro parked half on the pavement. For him, it was a two-hour hair-raising Champagne drive, in his adorable red Zagato Spider, from the Bergamo Airport to his holiday apartment. From the balcony she could see the village of Varenna on the opposite shore of Lake Como. At his recommendation they caught a ferry for the brief, but scenic, trip.

A group of noisy British tourists was the only negative part of the journey. When off-loaded from their coach, they jostled and pushed their way onto the boat as if an impending Mount Vesuvius eruption was on their itinerary.

A woman, thinking Mummy was Italian, asked her in a loud clipped northern manner reserved for addressing foreigners, 'Do they 'av broth on t' ferri?'

Mummy, not wishing to have any discourse, responded, 'Sorry I don't speak English.' It satisfied the wretch, who didn't comprehend the reply being in her native tongue.

At Varenna, they strolled past small fishermen's houses lining the steep cobbled alleys, with steps and slopes in profusion. Whilst wending their way to the Villa Monastero, Mummy purchased a superbly crafted belt from a tiny leather shop in Contrada dei Sarti.

Luca had his arm around her waist as they explored the wondrous botanical gardens, contemplating the good fortune of the monks who had once inhabited such a gem.

Close by was the Villa Cipressi, which was last on their list before they meandered back to the ferry terminal. While waiting for the boat, they paused for refreshments at Bar Bellissimo overlooking the tiny stony beach. Mummy's legs and feet were sore from the unusual exercise, but she relaxed as a warm breeze caressed her skin.

A handsome young man – truthfully, a youth – was sitting on a stone wall a few metres from their table. She held his gaze long enough to be considered flirtatious. A slight smile over the top of her Campari dispatched a corresponding signal of interest. The sound of shattering glass startled Mummy as glasses and cups crashed upon the Sassuolo tiled patio. It was Luca, who had leapt to his feet sending his chair flying whilst chastising his rival.

At first, the youth feigned innocence but, with bravado emboldened by a glance from her, reciprocated with equal ferocity. But, as usually happens in Italy, as fast as tempers flared so calmness rebounded. Luca and the youth shook hands, patted each other on the back and tummy, both apologising for the misunderstanding. A bevy of patrons clapped; passers-by, having enjoyed the impromptu drama, resumed their strolls. The coach party of British tourists, fearing they would lose their position in the queue, had watched from a distance; anxious to be back on time for the evening meal of Pappardelle coi Fegatine di Pollo with chips, or mash, and peas.

The bar owner declared that if it had been he escorting such an enchanting lady, he might have acted in the same fashion, but admonished the inexperienced young fellow for his indiscretion, saying, 'She is a he, when she is with he!' But added, 'If I were younger, I may have flirted myself.' There was lots of laughter when his wife playfully smacked him on the head. Refusing reparation for the breakage, the proprietor joined both men in a free drink and presented Mummy with a rose.

Returning to the apartment, they'd dedicated the rest of the afternoon to fare l'amore. After an early meal they'd sat under the stars drinking Prosecco whilst enthralled by an open-air production of Respighi's La Boutique fantasque. 'Italians are so distinctive,' she'd often told her friends. 'What suitors they are! Never boring.'

Dear Luca, such a sublime lover, she mused. As an expert on the topic, she stood by her position that they were better lovers than the heel-clicking Germans, the vulgar Americans, or the overbearing self-opinionated English. How dissimilar Luca was from her husband who, after their angry exchanges, skulked and scowled – not a word for days, sometimes weeks, never making up, sliding back to passionless boredom.

Free from the German gas generator's Wagnerian recital, Mummy slid into sleep.

* * *

Venice! Inspiration flows from every alley and gutter, it's incomprehensible that any artist worth a pinch of pigment hasn't painted at least one Venetian scene. It's a pity mosquitos eclipse the number of tourists at this time of the year, she thought, trying not to scratch her arms, while strolling through Dorsoduro.

Stopping at a small café teeming with laughing boisterous students, young and animated as only they can be, she ordered a coffee, enjoying the carefree youthful banter. Although an easy twenty-five minutes walk to the elegant Carina Boutique, which sits beyond the arch with the clock atop on the narrow Le Mercerie, it being hot and crowded, she hopped onto the Line 2 ferry.

Barbara da Vechia, the tall chic owner, had known Mummy for many years, and so greeted her in the way Italians greet old friends, by continuing the discussion where they'd left off months ago. They spoke of Luca, Marco, the Russian Ambassador and, briefly, Mummy's husband. She felt quite sad because Barbara had not had a new relationship since Mattia returned to his wife after she'd received an inheritance.

Donning the Chanel dress, she told Barbara the occasion for which she needed the shoes. It took but a few minutes before Mummy was proffered a pair with a one-and-a-half-inch heel. They both felt them to be perfect, other than for the jewelled bows; the alteration hand removed them and attached gold buckles. A good decision; they were far better suited to black.

It takes time to say farewell to a friend in Italy, be it one who has just detached four hundred pounds from your credit card, but they would no doubt soon see each other again.

She'd settled for plane in preference to train for returning to England. As it wasn't a Soviet Airline, no one would jump out.

When trying on the outfit at home, she recognised something was missing. An air of reverence to match the gold buckles and strands in the mantilla was required. After searching high and low, she found it in the window of a tiny second-hand emporium in the Portobello Road: a gold cross with pearl beads. The ancient dealer asked far too much for it. Offering less, she scolded him for making money out of a Christian artefact. He said he was Jewish and, as a Christian, it was she who ought to be ashamed for taking bread from the mouths of his children who had suffered at the hands of gentiles like her for centuries.

To crown it all, one child was a struggling dentist who needed support while extracting himself from a difficult marriage. Mummy was filled with pity, paid the full price and donated an extra twenty pounds to help the tooth fairy.

The well-worn necklace was exactly what she wanted; it alluded to her being a regular church attendee and matched the buckles on the shoes. Unaware the dear little necklace was, in fact, a rosary, she was now fully prepared.

Deeds Not Words

It was November when Mummy and Rodney headed for a day at the Raby Cathedral School. They were met by a fellow a few years older than Rodney, who introduced himself as Tarquinius St John Cholmondeley-Fetherstonhaugh, although he told them to call him by his Latin appellation, Aulae Praefectus.

'Just in case your Latin is rusty, it means head boy. I must say, you're fortunate to have gained me as your guide. Lottery, you could've had a duffer instead.'

From his pompous claptrap, Mummy gleaned his task was to attend to them and impart his unbiased views on the school's outstanding amenities as shown by his own admirable tutelage. Knowing that the school's plan was to extract eighteen thousand pounds a year from her husband's bank account, plus a large Charitable Benefaction, it was obvious this twerp, whom she renamed Prattius, was part of the plan.

He blathered on about the meritorious educational results being a consequence of the academic facilities, average class sizes of fifteen, and high-quality tutors. 'My results clearly demonstrate this. The only area where I didn't achieve an exemplary result was the humanities, but they are of little value.'

What a surprise that is, Mummy thought.

Both she and Rodney found the tour of the classrooms, language laboratory, art studio and science block boring.

The music conservatoire, with pupils in the soundproof rooms rehearsing their chosen instruments with orchestral backing tracks, was the best part. Prattius spoilt it by telling them he was lead violinist in the school orchestra.

'I have AP,' he added. 'There're only a few people in the world with it.'

'Oh, what a shame! Is it terminal?' Mummy asked, hoping she didn't sound joyous.

'It means Absolute Pitch. I'm sure you know it by its more common nomenclature, of Perfect Pitch,' he advised her, putting the emphasis on, 'you'.

Mummy considered telling him she knew it by its other nomenclature, of absolute prick, but, with effort, refrained.

Leaving the building, they entered the quadrangle and walked to a weathered oak door ensconced in the Tudor walls. It provided access into the library. Mummy allowed her feet to touch the deep red-and-blue cut-pile wool carpet with trepidation, lest her shoes soil the school's coat of arms woven within it. She glanced at Rodney's footwear lest he contaminate the carpet with mud from the quadrangle. With rows of floor-to-ceiling bookshelves, the library held more books than Mummy imagined any academic institution required. Her obvious appreciation cued Prattius to, once more, blow the school's horn.

'Over twenty thousand publications, many first editions,' he crowed, and upon passing row upon row of mahogany desks, 'We're gearing up for computers and are top of the supplier's list to get them.'

It made no sense to Mummy, and she was thankful when they left the silent refuge of engraved enlightenment.

While the indoor facilities were boring, both Mummy and Rodney found viewing the outdoor ones even more tortuous. The hockey and rugby football fields ruined her day shoes as they sank into the turf. Rodney found nothing of interest: frozen feet and misery were all he experienced.

After the wretched muddy sods, the 'all-weather' athletic track was next. Prattius pronounced that at age twelve he'd run the mile in five minutes and two seconds.

'That was below the world record for my age, but if the coach had taken care in tying my laces and if the wind wasn't against me, my time would have been better.'

It was no revelation to Mummy that Prattius was the captain of the rugby, cricket and fencing teams. However, conflicting polo schedules made attendance at hockey impossible, which meant they were only a mere third in the league.

'Wouldn't be in that state if I captained,' he said, and then apologised for not taking them to see the County-standard cricket field. 'Don't want your shoes ruining the pitch, do we? The pavilion's right next to the Olympic-sized heated indoor pool and saunas.'

I don't give a toss, Mummy thought.

'It all adds up to a jolly sporting environment,' Tarquinius pronounced, as he finished the facility visit by leading them to the indoor fencing, tennis and squash courts. While walking away from the sporting amenities, he explained that there was also a fine sailing club, then whined, 'But, we have to travel twelve miles in the school bus to sail.'

Mummy asked, expecting a laugh, 'Why not bring the sea closer to the school?'

'Not possible, we sail on a lake.'

In the foyer of the King's Hall, Prattius announced he was certain his tour was superior to any given by the other escorts.

'Just one further detail to present to you,' he said, ushering them to an illuminated granite monument, perhaps three metres high, upon which was a sculpted figure of Atlas bearing the heavens on his shoulders. Beneath the figure were the chiselled words, Acta non verba. It was a memorial to those former alumni who had reached the zenith of society. While the monument predated the suffragette movement by many years, Mummy wondered what the Old Boys in the nineteen-hundreds had thought when gazing at the suffragettes' rallying cry above the all-male list. If anything like Prattius, they were certainly a bunch of pompous boors.

Prattius, said, 'That's my grandfather', and pointed out Major General Lord Charles Tarquinius Peregrine Cholmondeley-Fetherstonhaugh of Bentwitch, Cdr. LH, ORB, KBE, KCH. The name, engraved in the polished granite, took up three lines.

As the sound of the school song, Audere est facere – To dare is to do – emerged from the hall, Prattius stopped rubbing out the letters 'KFC' that a vandal had scratched into the granite after the name of his illustrious forebear and sprang to attention, placing his right hand where normal Homo sapiens hearts abide.

'Shush,' he spat, lest even a bird dared sing.

With the song finished, he bid them 'Tempus edax rerum' and departed, allowing them to prepare for the next part of their visit.

'What did he say, Mummy?' Rodney asked.

'Something about time. He thinks he's clever, but we know he's a pain in the backside, don't we?'

'Daddy calls it, "arse",' Rodney said.

'Well, he shouldn't, it's not a nice word. But that boy is one. Now, although the tour was tiresome, it was a necessary torture to get you a placement here.'

While deploring Tarquinius' verbal diarrhoea, she embraced the architecture, history and tranquillity of the place. It was the conspicuous wealth, like claret oozing from a leached vein, she found most appealing. Rodney will look back with nostalgic pride at his privileged schooling, she thought, and treasure every moment of the pomposity and ostentation. She had no intention of allowing any of her children to end up in state schools, where class sizes of fifty and more were commonplace. In a year or two, if inflicted with a state education, they'd end up in dreadful comprehensive schools.

Lady Georgia Winthorpe JP told Mummy she'd heard at her Parish Council meeting that state schools were selling sports fields and playgrounds to developers. It must be correct, Mummy thought, because Georgia is on the Board of Governors of a state school and her husband is a developer.

She couldn't think of a reason why Rodney shouldn't enter this ivy-covered entrance instead of a derelict rundown building described by the government as a place for mass education.

Next on their agenda was evensong.

A Shot in the Arm from a Maid

Other than the infrequent oddities of burials and weddings, Mummy did not attend church. But she knew her diligent collecting of a-thousand-and-one ecclesiastical snippets would be more than enough to impress the archbishop.

There was to be academic entrance examinations, but, from her observation of friends' children who'd entered such places, if intelligence were the prerequisite for admission, they would be uninhabited. Only two qualifications presented any form of barrier for entry: wealth and class.

Evensong was where she and Rodney would be at their pinnacle. The plan was to crush the competition by deploying the information she had religiously assembled. Rodney's destiny was in her hands. She'd sown the seeds of success, now it was time to harvest the hay. Sorrow was all she felt for the other candidate choristers as they stood no chance. Her dream of being stretched out on the beach in Barbados listening to Rodney sing 'In the Bleak Midwinter' on the new radio she had purchased was growing ever closer. The next task was to make ready for the service.

To facilitate preparation, the school had provided parents with private facilities.

The brochure, or vade mecum as Aulae Praefectus had pompously designated it, informed them that, '*If selected, for scholarly activities your children will wear Top Hat and*

Tails, while for other pursuits, the apparel called Formal Change is mandatory'. Mummy, for whom parsimony was preposterous, had pre-empted any preconditions of acceptance and purchased all the gear which, at two hundred and fifty pounds, she felt a snip. The underwear was a regulation vest and boxer shorts; his were a size greater because, 'They must be loose fitting in case they check to find out if your testicles have dropped.'

Rodney was despondent and so sat sulking, dressed in the complete Formal Change outfit as if he'd already been selected. What a horrible day, and how stupid he looked in a get-up that Mummy said was as ancient as his great-grandfather whose picture hung in the hall. The starched double-round detachable collar was most uncomfortable, and the comic he was reading was rotten.

Mummy's smart business suit, chosen for the academic and sports facilities tour, lay in the dromedary leather garment carrier from which she had removed tonight's apparel. A charming French Assemblée nationale député admirer had given her a vintage Louis Vuitton Italian train case which was ideal for cosmetics. She placed it on the small table below the browned-glass mullioned window. Rodney could smell she was doing her nails.

'Dammit! I've dropped the nail varnish remover.'

A similar experience at home had clearly demonstrated if left on varnished wood for more than a second it acted like a paint stripper and so, using a handkerchief, she wiped the liquid from the quarter sawn oak boards. Luckily the residue on the hanky was sufficient to remove the red varnish from her nails.

Her beautician, a lovely young man called Cyril, who lisped, had advised her upon what make-up to wear.

'The frock is crying out for an aura of understated mystique. My suggestion is a gold smoky look for your eyes; it'll complement the black dress. If I were you, I would use this French rouge lipstick over a Parisian infusion cream base. Your skin is impeccable, so this super smoothing powder will leave it matt and perfect for just a touch of lipstick as a blush.'

She followed his advice, and had to admit the image in the mirror was even better than she had hoped. Covering her head with a disposable protector hood, she lifted the dress from the hanger and slipped into it. Removing the hood, she was more than thrilled at what she saw; it was a dream come true.

'I'm sure the bishop will go bonkers when he sees this. What do you think, Rodney?'

He showed no interest, or offered any opinion as that was how Mummy always looked before leaving him in the care of Nanny.

The last stage of evensong preparation had arrived. The mantilla in place, she hung the mother-of-pearl beads around her neck, ensuring the battered gold-plated pectoral cross sat between her ample bosoms. It conveyed a sense of sainthood, which was just what she wanted the vicar, or archbishop, to see, a perfect mother and child, at ease, and in harmony with such an esteemed establishment.

Getting ready had been hard work as achieving such lofty standards was pernickety, but she believed success lay in proper preparation. The time having flown, Mummy took Rodney's hand and, dropping the bags off into the car on the way, dashed to the adjacent cathedral.

Arriving at the west door, they entered the huge narthex leading into the nave. She noticed the other parents were already seated. The clip-clop echo of her shoes upon the stone slabs fractured the funereal silence; she'd never heard footsteps so loud. Every eye watched her wobbly progress across the uneven flagstones. The ogling men were, without doubt, more appreciative of her image than were their spouses. A woman nudged and insisted her husband 'Stop gawking,' while declaring loudly, 'Tasteless.'

Plonking herself down onto an oak chair, Mummy was surprised to see how other parents were attired. The woman next to her wore trousers that'd be more at home on her gardener, and she had trainers on her feet! Glancing around it was clear the rest looked no better. Everyone should know evensong requires solemnity, the book described it as 'One of the greatest treasures of the Church'. Their faux pas advances Rodney's future, she thought. A bishop is no fool, or he wouldn't be in charge of the monks, so he'll soon spot my obvious breeding. The others? Plainly laughing stock.

The architectural magnificence was stunning; nothing could ever have prepared her for this. The columns alone were amazing, so high they could touch heaven. To her, it was akin to a full-rigged man-of-war, its bow having traversed the tempest of mankind's frailties and follies for one thousand two hundred and fifty years.

Thousands must have sat on this same spot, polishing the oak with their fidgeting wool-covered posteriors. What problems, loves and hopes had they brought as baggage? Had they come seeking solace by listening to overlong senseless sermons and the lilt of Latin chants? In times past, before somebody thought up a fiendish torture instrument called an unpadded oak chair, had people stood? The uncomfortable seat was, without doubt, designed to make certain that slouchers sat upright. Was hers the first bottom to sit on this seat and dream of their child being a chorister? Touching the battered gold-plated cross on her chest, she decided that Rodney was to be her sacrifice; he'd be God's new choirboy, that should do it. Kneeling, eyes closed, she crossed herself the way Audrey Hepburn had in the film, and gave thanks that the pins and needles in her bum had subsided.

Rodney was wondering: Had intergalactic invaders built the place? It's ancient, so they could have. Maybe the pillars and arches represent the spaceships that had delivered them from their planet where they were dying due to a lack of oxygen. Or had asteroids rained down upon their heads in ever-increasing showers? Was a spacecraft their only way of escape?

If they started the engines now, it'd be cremation for everyone. Perhaps burning in hell was being sizzled by the rocket exhaust flames. He'd ask Mummy later.

It wasn't the roar of rockets that broke their reverie, but that of the organ. Out of the ranks of the five thousand one hundred and forty-eight pipes, the keys from the triple manual and pedal keyboard ordained that those bursting into life would be to glorify Gustav Theodore Holst's, 'Cranham'. The choir then filled the air with 'In the Bleak Midwinter' and it wasn't even Christmas.

Mummy sobbed into the handkerchief she'd used to clean the nail varnish from the floor. The hanky now contained the narcotic-inducing compound, methyl methacrylate. Oblivious to Rodney's embarrassment, Mummy snivelled and sniffed throughout the carol's rendition. God had spoken! Her dream had come true: this school, the choir and cathedral. It was Rodney's destiny, which she'd dreamt of on the beach in Barbados.

She placed her hand on Rodney's head, he pushed it away not being used to public displays of affection. The choir sang the final word, 'Heart', ritardando diminuendos, as directed by the choirmaster, their intonation perfect. Feeling as if she were in space, Mummy kept the hanky pressed against her nose to absorb the torrential tears.

The rendition was so enthralling and stimulated even more sobbing and many blinks and snuffles before she could see through the downpour. Thereupon, a blinding light filled her eyes. Was it a flashback to the tanning-bed in Thailand, when a so-called 'Beauty Therapist' forgot to fit the goggles? Or could it be the phenomenon being reported in the press that occurred in a Big Top circus tent run by an American evangelist. It said that when he put his hands upon someone's head they saw bright lights and fell to the ground babbling gobbledegook, and were born again. The photograph in the paper of the whopping great canvas tabernacle had brought back happy childhood memories, for the name of the original circus stood out on the faded canvas. It was the one to which her daddy had taken her.

However, she wasn't Thai tanning, or under a Big Top, so was it preparation for being converted? Hope not, she thought, as she considered holiness could start when tampons went out and incontinence pads came in, so now was not the time. She was far too young to give up life's pleasures, or to keel over and ruin a Chanel dress. There was only one reason she was enduring her bum going numb on a hard seat, it was to get Rodney into the choir. Hugging, loving and forgiving were not part of the plan. Nor was annoying others by proclaiming how 'blest' she was, neither would she stop eating meat and walk around as colourless as a corpse. As for seeking forgiveness whenever a carnal thought crossed her mind, impossible! She'd be on her knees for eternity, even – heaven forbid – finishing up a saint. Intolerable! Hence, if it's a rebirth, there had been ample opportunity to inform her on the activities list, with a 'No Thank You' tick-box. Born again? Out of the question. But the light was dazzling.

As her eyes readjusted, the source of the illumination was plain: it was flooding from a stained-glass window in the nave. As she gazed in wonderment, the glorious blaze metamorphosed into a figure. She blinked away the tears; it was Joan of Arc astride her charger, but what the devil was she doing here?

She knew it was The Maid of Orleans for she had seen her in Paris. Not the real one, she's dead, but the massive bronze effigy of Jehanne la Pucelle on the Avenue Cesar Caire. The sculptor had depicted the right foot of the majestic horse striking the sacred earth of France, leaving no doubt as to its task of conveying its rider into sainthood. Nobody could miss her if they passed Saint-Augustine Church. Mummy had spent ages looking at her; she'd recognise The Maid anywhere.

It was even more of a shock when Joan spoke. 'Heaven helps those who help themselves. I am with you,' she called out. It was nice to hear directly from the glorified soul and thoughtful of her to use English for, as a saint, she would definitely have known Mummy refused to speak French, unless in an emergency, as was the case when last on the Paris Metro and a nasty one-legged garlic-reeking fellow in a scruffy raincoat with a medal dangling demanded money. Telling him to go away as his accordion playing was abysmal and not worth a sou was to no avail. Being French, he just persisted. But *foutre le camp* resulted in him trying to trip her up with his crutch. Other commuters rushed to give Mummy a helping hand, but took his side when learning she was a *Rosbif*.

Kicking his crutch away, she ran and leapt onto her waiting train leaving the crowd to pick him up. As it careered away, she looked out of the carriage window and saw he had two legs; one was strapped up. The beggar must have seen the film where a, so-called, one-legged man was determined to kill De Gaulle. The last view she had as the train plunged into the tunnel was of a female commuter bashing him with a baguette. Joan must have watched over her on plate-forme trois.

While Mummy, still under the influence of methyl methacrylate, was preoccupied with Saint Joan and the prospect of an unplanned conversion, the Dean introduced Lady Lorelei Montagu-Innes, Chair of Governors. Lady Lorelei explained how the school spent their benefaction. Towards the end of her litany, she said, 'Whilst we rely upon our maker for many things, heaven helps those who help themselves. I am with you tonight to tell you of an example of its use. The new state-of-the-art sodium-vapour floodlights were switched on this evening for the first time. We are so excited. When you leave, I am sure that you will be amazed by how brilliant the floodlit cathedral looks. And', she pointed to Mummy's window, 'behold the famous stained-glass window in the nave depicting St George, see how wondrous it is with light streaming through it.'

Every eye turned to look at the window that Mummy's eyes had never left.

After Lady Lorelei had finished, the Dean announced they were to have a few minutes of meditative silence before moving to the next part of the programme. The hushed congregation sat in reverence. Meanwhile,

Mummy reasoned that Joan would know that most of England consisted of state educated individuals who just about managed elemental English and, hence, would not comprehend French. But Joan, being a saint, must know that she was public school educated and able to speak her language. So, since The Maid had had the decency to speak English to her, she would reply in French and cried out, 'Merci Joan, Dieu nous aidera! Avoir une bonne bataille.'

Startled, the congregation – to a body – gaped at the weird woman waking them from their moment of sleepy meditation. Rodney, as always embarrassed by his mother, asked why she was yelling. She explained, 'Joan of Arc and I have had a chat. Well, she did the talking, and confirmed that you will enter the world of Angels. So I said to Joan, thank you for telling us, I hope you have a good fight. Isn't that wonderful news?'

'Who's she?'

'Joan of Arc, silly! The Maid of Orleans. Oh, never mind, sit still and pray for something.'

'What shall I pray for?'

'Listen Rodney, don't be difficult. Pray for anything.'

Closing her eyes, she faced the light with hands clasped in the way she envisaged The Maid must have had hers just before being bound to the post and barbecued to a cinder. The light from the window highlighted the coagulated mascara, tears and Parisian skin infusion cream.

From the gloom of the quire a figure materialised. Lit from behind, it ambulated toward the nave where they sat. Rodney, with his eyes and mouth wide open, watched the thing traipse up the aisle. It justified his earlier notion that aliens once occupied the earth. Was the thing moving toward him magnetic? He considered it conceivable for he couldn't take his eyes away from the sinister shape as its long shadow moved closer, ever closer. The apparition was now surrounded by a halo of light and looked creepy, if not ghoulish.

Nanny had taken him to see a film about intergalactic interlopers. After the invaders' spacecraft had landed on earth, it seemed as if they wanted to download a mobility scooter for, from underneath the rocket, a ramp was lowered to the ground. It took a moment or two, but then a hideous creature with spindly arms and a funny-shaped head appeared. Rodney had watched through half-closed eyes as it descended the ramp on skinny legs in time to weird music played on an organ. Then, he had battened down his eyes until a nudge from Nanny told him the safety of the film credits had arrived. He decided to use the same tactic now.

Mummy had no qualms and was looking forward to meeting the priest, monk, or bishop who was walking up the aisle. Her preparedness would not leave her wanting. The statute bequeathed by The Maid was 'Heaven helps those who help themselves'. It determined her to be the first to come face-to-face with the ecclesiastical dignitary and, by doing so, make the greatest impression.

When the shadowy figure was still a good way off, she went in at a full gallop as would a filly out of a starting stall in a maiden race. Skidding to a halt, she flung herself at his feet and, seeking his Episcopal ring, took his warm wrinkled right hand in hers. The startled fellow was so taken aback, he froze to the spot. Not finding the artefact, she switched to the left and discovered only a gold wedding band, and so kissed that instead.

Looking into his face, her wish had become a reality for a gentleman as old as the dust on the floor, sporting a flowing white beard and deep brown eyes, was standing over her. He was just as she imagined God to be: incapable of a debauchery of any kind.

She looked into his eyes. 'Bless me, Holy Father, for I have sinned, and it's my first time. Hail Mary!'

Taking her tenderly by the hand he helped her to rise and, with his breath warm upon her cheek, whispered, 'I'm a tour guide dear. If you need the Roman Catholic Church, it's on St Magdalene Street.'

Mummy explained she was a parent.

A concerned look crossed his face, 'Are you changing to take the tour?'

'No! Why should we change?'

'It is because we will go into confined passages and narrow spiral staircases. We said in our letter that you must wear clothing that is appropriate,' he said, looking at the somewhat forlorn boy next to this strange woman. The child brought to mind Little Lord Fauntleroy, a book with wonderful illustrations he'd read in his childhood.

Mummy had assumed 'appropriate' meant for evensong, as she had no recollection of a cathedral tour being on the cards and thought he had misplaced his anxiety.

'We're wearing the oldest clothes we have and it's always been my intention to donate them afterwards to an Indian orphanage.' Thinking back to *The Nun's Story*, she added, 'They'll wash them in the Congo.'

Choosing not to discuss geography, he called the parents together and said that the first part of the tour was to be in the crypt. He led them to the spiral staircase in the retro quire.

Fearful of tripping on the rough-hewn stairway, Mummy put Rodney in front. As neither she nor Linda Lefeuvre had envisaged her potholing, the tight Chanel skirt had to be hoisted halfway up her thighs before she could descend the well-worn sandstone stairs. It was only with Rodney's help that she reached a dusty corridor, twisting its way narrowly into a large damp crypt.

The guide explained, 'The winding labyrinth is a reminder of the twists and turns in life. Although our earthly journey will be tortuous, we all head to the same God-centred destination. Other cathedrals have turned their crypts into small chapels but – I hope you agree with me – it is better left as a burial vault, more historical.'

Horribly gloomy, needs a team of damned good cleaners, was Mummy's opinion.

To Rodney, it confirmed what he had suspected: Upstairs were the pillars dedicated to the rockets that carried life to earth, while this subterranean chamber was a mausoleum devoted to the memory of the brave individuals who sacrificed their lives to take care of the launch. The tunnels represented the supply chain, ferrying fuel for the motors, while the short pillars the engines used to thrust the rockets on their intergalactic journey. It would not surprise him if there were other artefacts in the silo honouring the doomed mission-control personnel. Now he knew for sure that churches were monuments to space travel.

The winding passageways with wet floors brought to mind the time Mummy took him and his brothers on a popular pirate theme-park ride; Daddy wasn't there. They had queued for ages behind a group of Japanese visitors. One, a short man with a white flag on a stick, herded the rest using an incomprehensible language. Rodney was surprised anyone could understand him.

Boarding the boats was similar to the ski lift in Saas Fee where he had enjoyed winter sports, just once, with

Daddy. They moved slowly so that people could hop on and off. Most of the Japanese group got into the first boat, while he, Mummy, and his brothers joined the rest of the Japanese in the next one. Although the front craft was tethered to theirs, the man in the lead boat kept the flag held high to make sure his charges wouldn't get lost.

Gliding out of daylight through a cave entrance, they entered an enchanting paradise. A placid winding river carried them through a realistic world. Meandering, they passed castles, palm-lined beaches, shipwrecks, treasure chests, sinister jungles and a multitude of romanticised swashbuckling scenes.

He remembered the animated buccaneers singing out from their little electronic hearts, 'Yo ho, ho, a pirate's life for me'. Then there were robotic willow warblers whistling, psychedelic parrots spouting, and cows, goats and sheep mooing, braying and bleating in time to the music. He recalled thinking that the boat was very slow and it would be better if the water was rougher, but it was still top-notch.

As they reached the stone bridge where the pirate captain waves his cutlass at you, Mummy was seasick. While she was retching over the side of their oarless rowboat, Cuthbert, who was standing on her lap, fell overboard into the river. There was panic. Screams were in Japanese, German, English and American, one pleading for a lifebelt.

Mummy told him later that a New York Wagnerian contralto, with an unfortunate wide vibrato, had burst into *Nearer Thy God to Thee*. Rodney had not heard her singing, for he, having just learnt to swim, dived overboard to rescue his younger brother, but his head had bashed the floor. Lying prostrate and dazed, he saw the boat ran on wheels and rails: it wasn't a boat – the water was only two inches deep – it was a fake to make them think they were floating. No wonder it was smooth. A siren screamed as emergency lamps blazed, replacing the subdued theme lighting, and the armada of rowboats halted.

The glare of floodlights ruined the whole experience, particularly for the children who screamed and cried as they now saw the wires and mechanical bits used to deceive them into loving the audiotronic avatars. The Japanese flag bearer stood up, wrapped a red-and-white hachimaki around his forehead and, waving his stick in the air like a wakizashi sword shrieked 'Banzai'. He then herded his charges off the boats, leading them upstream to seek sanctuary in the plastic jungle.

Some of the remaining parents were shouting and cursing Mummy, except for the Brits who were forming a compensation committee amid the dying cries of the animatronics. Massive doors were swung open and the cavernous hanger-like structure was awash with dazzling sunlight. Armed security personnel entered, and escorted Mummy with her brood off the ride, to jeers and boos from other patrons.

Rodney received four stitches to a head wound, two aspirin for the pain, and the determination never again to be a Good Samaritan.

His daydream of the pirate ride ended with Mummy taking his arm as the group continued its exploration of the cathedral. It was boring. There were raised coffins, fallen masonry and wet floors. Raised coffins! Holy whack! Excitement mounted. He'd almost missed them. Memorials to mission-control personnel who had sacrificed their lives to save others. He'd counted on seeing them.

Mummy found it troublesome to struggle through small passageways in a tight dress and heaved it up. Navigating the narrow circular staircase to the vaulting was even worse and, no doubt, ungodly. Neither the passageways nor the staircases had been as harrowing as ascending the ladder leading to the bell tower. It was here that her acrophobia came to the fore as her legs turned to jelly and refused to budge beyond the first two rungs. A stalwart figure stepped in and offered to help. The beast had a dollop of dolly by groping as he shoved her before him. While her dress was raised higher than the flag on Buck House, the repulsive rotter announced to everybody, 'What a splendid view there is up here.'

After the tour, Mummy felt drained, and disconsolate because of the state of her dress. Even Coco, who must have devoted hours stitching it together, would not recognise the tatty ruin. The Venetian shoes that had elevated her by one and a half inches had also let her down. The left heel was an implant between sandstone slabs in the crypt, while the right, bent at an oblique angle, required Mummy to break it off and convert the shoes to flats.

The torrents of tears prompted by hearing her favourite carol sung in the magical surroundings of the cathedral, coupled to imagining Rodney singing *David's City* a cappella were together emotionally painful enough. But the visit from Joan was the last straw, prompting a deluge not dissimilar to a Mandalay monsoon. Added to that, she had been required to scramble, to clamber, to climb under and over and up the military-style assault course they called a tour. Her bedraggled appearance bore testament to its exacting nature.

If the lisping beautician, Cyril, could see the state of her make-up, it would have catapulted him into a tiz-woz. For sweat, snivel, creams, powders and potions had unified, mutating Mummy into the doppelgänger of the camouflaged Soviet sniper, Major Lyudmila Pavlichenko. The *People's Paper* reported that Lady Death, as they called the sharpshooter, alone dispatched more Germans to Valhalla than had the entire French army on the Maginot Line.

Rodney whispered that she'd smudged her make-up: Mummy slipped into a dark alcove and vainly tried to repair the damage by wiping her face with the hanky. Looking out from the gloom, she saw another bearded fellow in sweeping robes approaching. This has to be at least the archbishop, or one of his monks, she thought. Waiting until he drew near, she leapt from the shadows prostrating herself at his feet.

The man was terror-stricken! Although never having met her in person, he was positive she was The Countess Dracula.

Neither he, nor his wife, had the slightest forethought and did not pack a clove of garlic into his pocket when preparing for work, garlic being a decisive means to repulse vampires, so they say. Plunging a wooden stake through the bloodsucker's heart was another method of vanquishing a recalcitrant Transylvania traveller, but there was neither stake nor hammer handy. He felt for his cross, another form of protection, but discovered that it was beneath the robes. Then, the apparition spoke!

'Bless me Father, for I have sinned, and this is my first time, or at least the first time with you, although it's the second time today, but never mind. Hail Mary, once again. Oh, yes, I have a list of my sins, except I left it at home, but I can remember some.' She'd locked the list in a drawer in case her husband read it; there were things it was best he did not know.

Recovering his poise, the gentleman stepped back and addressed the rest of the group. Mummy was left seeking Rodney's help to get up from the bitterly cold stone floor and return to her seat.

'Good evening, I am Dr Quinn Markinswell, the musical director.' Motioning toward Aulae Praefectus, Tarquinius St John Cholmondeley-Fetherstonhaugh, he went on, 'Our Caput Chorista has the truest pitch I can recall hearing for at least the last twenty-five years.'

The woman next to Mummy whispered, 'That's Latin, it means head chorister. He's my son, such a delightful child, and everybody says he has an outstanding voice.'

Mummy's reply was a little louder, 'That adds up, he'll have the same voice for life you know. Without balls, it'll never change.'

As the woman opened her mouth to respond, the musical director continued, 'Tarquinius will take your boys to put on their liturgical choir robes whilst you return to your seats. Please remember they are singing as a taster and not a test.'

After the choir and potential choristers had departed, he began again. 'We sang *In the Bleak Midwinter* because most people know it and it's not too difficult to learn. It gives me pleasure to say it is on our Christmas album, now in the throes of completion. We will take orders later for the CD, and before dispatch Tarquinius will sign each one.'

Christmas album! How wonderful, Mummy thought. That's the one Rodney will be on. But how can it be in the throes of completion without him? Must have been a slip of the tongue, I'll order it unsigned, Rodney can autograph it afterwards.

Tarquinius led the boys into an anteroom where they changed into the mediaeval costume. He told them that they would wear this same regalia at the six services a week and half an hour before each service in preparation. Rodney found the starched white ruff was even more uncomfortable than his shirt collar.

Dr Quinn Markinswell popped back in and said, 'You will devote many hours learning to read music, play a musical instrument, master voice projection, correct breathing, and stage performance. As a distinguished choir, we travel and perform worldwide, seeking perfection in all we do. There are only five places available, so I expect all fifteen of you will do your best. Right! Do you have any questions?'

'Will we travel to Barbados?' Rodney asked.

'No!'

Pity, Rodney thought. It would be great to see Auntie Aryanna again, or with honesty, her titties, as they would enhance his growing bedtime fantasies.

'I will return to your parents,' Dr Quinn Markinswell said. 'You are lucky enough to have Aulae Praefectus to lead you in a short rehearsal, after which you will accompany him to the quire.'

Following the departure of the musical director, Tarquinius stepped forward and said, 'I have paired each of you with a chorister whom you will follow and sit next to when we return to the stalls.' He placed each applicant next to a choir member, except for Rodney who was left unpaired. 'You', Tarquinius pointed at Rodney, 'will stand behind me.'

It was just his luck to be stuck next to Tarquinius, the entire thing was not sounding great, but how was he to escape? After a moment's consideration, a plan emerged. Tell Mummy he'd felt his testicles drop. No, say somebody else had heard them plunge as he was putting on the ruff, and – a masterstroke – adding that the extra-sized underpants had provided no support, allowing them to plummet even further. That should give her a guilty feeling. Yes, and then add what a surprise it was that neither she, nor the congregation, had heard the thunderous clang, nor his cries of pain, for that matter.

But, upon reflection, travel is better than a classroom, so why not tour first, after which, expulsion? That was it! Enjoy a tour or two and then get evicted. He would put his heart and soul into being selected for the choir. Despite his misgivings, he enjoyed the rehearsal and after twenty minutes they filed into the cathedral.

Oh, how wonderful my boy looks, thought Mummy. It was as if a cherub had descended from heaven for a photo shoot. In her mind's eye, they featured her little angel on the album cover. She could see it now: Rodney's face aglow from the flickering flame of the large candle held in his delicate right hand. Bright green holly sporting glistening red berries would surround him and two pink-bodied cherubs, plucking their harps, will float overhead. The rest of the choir was in soft focus, unimportant, indistinguishable, for added interest only, quite unnecessary accoutrements. She gave him an encouraging smile as if to say – she'd read it somewhere – well done, my good and faithful son. He nodded.

The choirmaster announced the boys were ready to sing. 'This is not just for fun, but for them to gain confidence when they undergo their singing tests.' He turned to the boys. 'How thrilled you and your parents must be. Put your heart and soul into it.'

During normal occupancy, the choir stalls were brimful, but with the extra incumbents they were jam-packed. Rodney found it excruciating, so elbowed Prattius for space.

Prattius whispered, 'Move over you little runt.'

Rodney, trying to listen to the musical director, mistook the word 'runt' for a far worse one, and pushed Tarquinius off the pew onto the floor. Tarquinius rose and bulldozed Rodney, ramming him forward and bashing his nose on the stall in front. Rodney lunged at his assailant, screaming, 'You featherbrained prick.'

The musical director rushed over and, most unfortunately, received a blow on his nose that Rodney had destined for Tarquinius. Dazed, and with blood spurting from his nostrils, he tried to steady himself by grasping at a candlestick fastened to the end pew. His weight wrenched it from its base; it fell from his hand and shattered as it struck the flagstone floor. It was Ming dynasty, an irreplaceable gift from King Henry VIII to the cathedral.

In the turbulence, the musical director's score of *Cranham*, a gift from a secret admirer to Herman Goring, fell to the floor, floating in a slight breeze before settling against the Jurassic limestone wall.

When the Ming gift crashed to the floor, the still burning candle rolled, as would a Double Gloucester on Cooper's Hill, coming to rest against *Cranham*. As the flame touched the tinder-dry parchment, it was reduced to ashes but not before the ensuing flames licking up the wall had ignited a priceless tapestry.

The wall hanging had remained unmoved for over four hundred and fifty years: another benefaction from Henry. The smoke from the burning artefact sneaked into the vapour detectors – provoking them to alert the emergency services – and also activated the high-pressure water mist protection system.

Rodney was, by now, astride the cowering Tarquinius.

'I beg you, please don't spoil my looks, hit me anywhere but not on my face,' the snidey turd snivelled.

Mummy leapt to her feet, screaming, 'Give the weasel a whack from me.'

'You should be ashamed,' Tarquinius' mother, the wife of the man who had fondled Mummy's backside, was shrieking. 'Your son's nothing but a common hooligan, hitting my Tarquinius. If that ruffian damages his bridgework, I'll sue, you trollop.'

Mummy shouted back, '*Vos adipem vetus bos*.'

'Don't you dare call me an old cow,' the woman screeched.

It pleased Mummy that her smidgen of Latin, even if not correct, was comprehensible to the baggage, and continued. 'And tell your husband to keep his hands off my arse. Mind you, it's obvious why he prefers my backside to your lumps of drooping whale blubber.'

Red faced, and with her raging shrieks lost in the cacophony of the raucous ringing of the alarm bell and cries of others rushing to get out, the woman whacked her spouse across the face.

Sirens grew louder by the second and water mist had soaked Mummy through to the skin. Rodney still in his quirister outfit ran to her, leaving the bewailing battered Tarquinius on the quire flagstone floor. Hand in hand they dashed through the Gothic arch to the car park. After a brief look back at the recently installed exterior lighting, they zoomed off, barely missing a collision with an arriving fire tender.

Mummy couldn't blame Rodney, as her dislike for that horrible Tarquinius had mushroomed when he said his grandfather was Major General Lord Charles Tarquinius St John Cholmondeley-Fetherstonhaugh of Bentwitch. A Liberal Peer!

Either you are right or left-wing. Wishy-washy Liberals who can't decide upon which side of the bed they must sleep are boring, was her opinion.

Her dream of Rodney as a warbling cherub had turned into a hallucinatory nightmare, as the rejection letter described their visit.

Foot Note

Dear Reader,

It would be remiss not to report upon the state of affairs following the chaos at the cathedral.

As the Dean said at the time, 'There are no words that can express my thanks to the firefighters from the ten tenders in attendance that contained the blaze before the entire place went up in smoke.'

One should not underestimate the financial cost of restoring the catastrophic structural damage. Of the five million pounds required for restoration, one thousand one hundred and fifty was raised by public donation; Lord Archibald Crooke-Wells claimed back his fifty-pound act of philanthropy from his House of Lord's expenses. It took five years to complete the repairs, so that today Raby Cathedral, the adjacent Gallows Inn pub and the first flushing public toilets in the north-east, circa 1952, are easily missed when one whizzes up the M1.

The musical director suffered no ill effects from the fire or from the assault upon his nose. But, on medical advice, took early retirement as his sanguivoriphobia therapy was unsuccessful, his fear of vampires never departed. Responding to the advice of an expert on vampirism, he surrounded his house with a hedge of holly and hawthorn as the jugular junkies despise such plants. A small vegetable plot was dedicated to growing garlic, both the hard and soft-neck varieties, as they provide a year-round protection.

Most days he spends in solitude, carving wooden stakes in the small garden shed.

* * *

It'd also be a dereliction of duty to continue the sorry Crooke-Wells saga by glossing over the loss of such important artefacts as the candle holder, tapestry and the manuscript of *In the Bleak Midwinter*.

By their actions, the Crooke-Wells' deprived future generations of feasting their eyes upon what were manifestations of Tudor history.

Thanks to a handful of archivists the following information is presented.

An Itchy Codpiece

From the writings of, O renomado historiador Português, Professor Paulo Fidalgo Escudeiro Marinho Agostinho Eustaquio Teixeira (1763–unknown).

King João III of Portugal had received the Ming candlestick as a gift from Canton in China. Under the orders of Governador Afonso de Albuquerque, a Captain Fernão Pires de Andrade had delivered it with a note from the Emperor, but as the message was written in Guānhuà, the King couldn't discern a dicky.

João had a long-standing grudge against the Chinese. After attending a fandanguillos class he'd eaten a Peking duck takeaway. For four days thereafter, he'd been perched on his privy tortured from the trots. So from that, and thinking the candlestick ugly, he'd stuffed it in a cupboard.

He was well aware that Ming, the Great Son of Heaven as he had claimed himself to be, had of late flooded the market with cheap Chinese junk – manufactured for hoopla stall prizes – while imposing import levies on Port and other merchandise. To top that, the bugger was executing Portuguese merchants and had lifted the head off his ambassador, all on the ruse that a few sailors had bought girls to take on board their ship.

'Confound the man. He fails to understand boys get fed up with boys,' João had said.

Meanwhile, his ambassador to the English court had told João that Henry had made known he was to be married.

'Yet again!' Queen Katharina of Castile exclaimed. 'What, prithee, shall we send him?'

'No idea,' said João. 'Henry really is a compulsive nuptualist and I've run out of ideas. What say you Katie?'

The Queen, clued-up on João's dislike for Henry, proffered, 'Rather than another toasting fork, what about the candlestick? You know, with that load of Chinese junk in the cupboard?'

João agreed that a worthless piece of pottery from China was the perfect retaliation for Henry having sent him a woollen codpiece as a birthday gift, knowing full well he was allergic to wool since recovering from the Spanish disease, and it'd make his crotch itch. King João's ambassador to Henry's court reminded him that Henry loathed the Chinese even more than did João, because of the oriental suit of armour sent as a birthday gift by the self-styled Lord of Ten Thousand Years.

'You might recall, my Liege,' said the ambassador, 'that Henry thought it strange as it wasn't his birthday, and sent the birthday card attached to it to the Fu King Chinese Takeaway in Windesore for translation. It turned out that it was Ming's birthday, and he was following an old Chinese proverb, 'On birthday better giving than getting'. Henry's court suspected Ming was sending a free sample to get them to buy Chinese armour for their knights. But, as Your Majesty is aware, the English import their armour from the Swedish company, International Knights Expandable Armour. They receive it in kit form for local assembly and it's adjustable to fit any knight.

Other than a few missing nuts, bolts, wrongly drilled holes, occasional rust and incomprehensible assembly instructions, the supplier is quite adequate therefore there is no requirement for another. Given this, they placed the Chinese armour in Henry's war room. It was a talking piece, interesting, but a useless bit of oriental handiwork, far too small and lightweight for any Englishman. Henry then sent a letter of thanks in Gaelic.

'Henry at the time had joined forces with Ferdinand to sort out Louis XII. The battle was a catastrophe if ever there was one, for it seemed Louis knew every move the English army was to make. After defeat, Henry was enjoying a game of chess and a chat with Lord Suffolk in the war room where they'd blueprinted the bollixed battle plan. To hold onto his head, Suffolk had let Henry play well, so being material-up he'd just traded off his Queen when a scratching noise came from the suit of armour. Lifting the visor, Henry found himself eyeball to eyeball with an Asian face.

'Leaping out of his skin, he'd screamed, "Great cullions and ballocks; there's a Chink in my armour!" Sure enough, Ming had installed a spy in Henry's court. The armour was rice papier mâché painted to look like metal. The spy had kept himself alive by eating the armour – his method was as ingenious as his being there in the first place.

'You see, my Liege, the Palace employed a rat-catcher, one Charley Trapper, who had a cat that was lame. An ancient Chinese proverb says, "When rats infest the Palace, a lame cat is better than the swiftest horse". The lame cat, being unable to move around, stayed in the war room.

'Inside the armour the spy kept a Chinese rat, and when they discussed the invasion plans the spy wrote them on rice paper torn from the armour, which he fed to the rat.

He then fed the rodent to the cat together with the seed of Chinese mallow, a strong laxative my Liege. The cat digested the rat which had digested the war plan, but it defecated because of the mallow seed. The cleaner threw the faeces, with the undigested paper, out of the window. A Chinese spy engaged by Louis collected it and hid it in a jar disguised as Black Bean Sauce.

'On his way to take the battle plans to the French ambassador, the courier was hungry and called in at the Fu King Takeaway for a Chinese, but accidentally left the jar on the counter. On the eve of the battle, Henry's generals placed an order for Beef in Black Bean Sauce to stave off their hunger. The Fu King Chef, thinking the jar was sauce, stirred the excreta, with the battle plan, into the saucepan.

'They lost the engagement, Your Majesty, because the commanders all ailed with the backdoor trots and were unfit to command. My Liege, Henry was so angry he returned the spy in four flat packs, with assembly instructions in the Welsh language.'

João rolled on the floor with mirth and guffaw, hardly able to dictate a congratulatory note which he then read to Queeny,

Lief Henry,

Congratulation on yet another marriage, prithee find a Ming candlestick, 'tis mine own most prised thing, other than mine woollen codpiece you give me. I lavish it upon thee to further fetter our friendship. I also enclose a bombard of port; it goeth well with a bite of cheese.

Most wondrous wishes,

Jo

Henry's reply to João:

Lief Jo,

Thy wonderful favour is most unexpected. I hast putteth it on the mantelpiece in the lounge at Windesore, it matches the curtains well. The bombard of port was excellent with a bite of Stilton. Telleth me Jo, doth thee still weareth the same bawbling codpiece? I hast a new one, the firsty one didst stinketh to high heaven. Mine new one is the biggest one in England and the very envy of every male.

The ladies-in-waiting of the court behold it with great fondly.

Thy mateth,
Henry

A Game in Bed

Talebearer Scribe to Henry VIII: Athelardus Digby Beaurepaire.

(Ref 278 Se Candelstæf, Inventory lower library Windsor.)

Upon receiving a candlestick from His Majesty King João III of Portugal, Henry considered the gift to be hideous and unsuited for public presentation. But, not wishing to cast it aside – as Jo might pay a visit one day – gave it a fair trial and ordered it fixed in his bedchamber.

And so it was on a raw, freezing, two-dog night in February, the Mistress of the Bedchamber had lain out only one comfort greyhound on Henry's bed to provide warmth and to feed the fleas.

'How can the stupid woman think just one undernourished tyke enough to provide a sufficiency of warmness on a night such as this?' he ranted through chattering teeth. 'It won't be just the career of Mistress Bedchamber that'll be foreshortened when I declare her de trop; she'll be the first to be axed.'

His gaze had fastened upon the ugly shapeless candlestick in which the flickering Clock Candle was resting at an annoying angle, making telling the time almost impossible.

As far as time-telling goes, you can't hold a candle to the Swiss, even if they do short change you by drilling holes in their cheese, was his opinion. However, his cold feet, a shapeless candlestick, and a drooping candle posed a conundrum.

Do I not have a wife somewhere who might arouse me, and keep me warm on a night as cold as this? I know, I'll call Bessie. So, he called his daughter Elizabeth to attend his bedchamber.

Upon arrival, after booting the dog off the bed, she pushed the flea-ridden cur over and snuggled next to him, 'Did you want me for something Daddy?'

'I was looking at that shapeless candle holder, with the candle that won't stand erect and thought to myself, I think I may have lost a wife along the way. Do I still have one?'

'Sometimes, Daddy, I think you're going daft forgetting so many things. Yes, you have a wife.'

'You know, I was almost certain I did, what's this one's name?'

'You ought to remember her, Daddy, but I'll tell you what, let's play a game.'

'That sounds marvellous; it's been so long since I played any games in bed.'

Elizabeth spoke forebodingly, in the manner that her father used when sending a wretch to the Tower. 'Mr Henry Tudor, are you ready to play, This Is Your Wife?'

Henry's excitement was mounting. 'Oh, what fun! This is Your Wife – how do we play?'

'You must listen, Daddy. I will ask a question and if you can't think of the answer, I will give you a clue. Are you ready?'

Henry nodded.

'Mr Henry Tudor, tell me, who was your first wife?' She paused, while Henry thought.

'Give me a clue.'

'Right, this is your first clue. At three, she was betrothed to your brother.'

'Which brother?'

'Daddy, don't be silly, you only had one. It was Uncle Arthur, the Cornish Welshman. Okay, I'll give you your next clue. Five months after their wedding, your brother died.'

'Did I kill him?'

'No, whatever made you say that? You belittle yourself, always taking the blame. You didn't chop off his head, he just died. Right, here's another clue. After he died, you married his widow. She was your first bride and her name was Catherine of. . .?' Henry remained silent.

'You're as daft as dog chasing his tail, think of the herb tarragon,' said Elizabeth.

'Oh yes, that's right. Her name was Tarragon, no, it was Aragon. That's it! What happened to her? Did I chop her head off?'

'No silly, I'll give you a clue. The Pope refused to annul your marriage.'

Now Henry was into the game. 'Ah yes, I remember. I hung a priest or two and pinched all their cash.'

'Yes Daddy, that's right. But don't forget you also started your own church and what did you...?'

Henry butted in, 'I annulled my marriage!' 'Clever Daddy. Few men would think of that. Right, now we come to your second wife. Who did you then marry?'

Henry sat in silence.

'You are a silly old sausage; you married my Mummy!'

Henry shouted jubilantly. 'You're right! I remember her. Where is she?'

'In heaven, you sent her to heaven. You chopped off her head,' Elizabeth laughed. 'She was Anne Boleyn.'

'Great Scott! You say I sent her to heaven. Why? Why did I do that?'

'It was because you wanted a new wife. So, Henry Tudor, who was your third wife? I'll give you the clue, ready, steady, now: You could. . . see more. . . in Mummy's lady-in-waiting.'

'I know, I know! Don't tell me. It was Seymour, wasn't it? Yes, Jane Seymour.'

'Oh Daddy, no wonder you're the king. You are a clever dick.' She hugged him, 'Oh dear, why are you crying? Please don't cry, Daddy.'

He wiped a tear from his eyes. 'Jane was a lovely girl. Died giving birth to my son, I loved her so much.'

'There, there. You are such a sentimental soft-hearted old sod, aren't you? I sometimes wonder if you chop off a few heads just for bravado, you know, to show off to the boys. But I know you're an old softie.

'Now, after Jane became a ghost you were very lonely so you looked around for comfort, and – wait for it – this will be the final question for tonight. Ta te rata ta ta taaa. That's the sound of a trumpet. Here's the question. Henry Tudor, into whose arms did you fall?'

Silence.

'Come on, Daddy, it was Anne of. . .? It rhymes with thieves and,' pointing to the ugly shapeless candlestick, 'it looked like that.'

'By Jove, I've got it! That's who it reminds me of. It's – what's her name? – the German bint: Anne of somewhere, or other. . . That's it, it was Cleves; she's the one I forgot to remember. What's happened to her? Did I send her to visit your mother in heaven?'

'No, Daddy. She's upstairs, locked herself away, been there for years, covered in cobwebs I wouldn't wonder.'

'Good heavens! I'm not surprised I'd forgotten her. I mean, to have a wife in a closet's not-much-cop, can't keep me warm. Tell me dear, if I can find her, what do you think I must do?'

'Well, as you couldn't recall having a wife, you may not remember how popular she is with the commoners, and don't forget the Krauts. You know how they love penalties; I wouldn't put it past them to impose a few. If you have her decapitated, even with a modicum of decency – say with a sword instead of an axe – the Bosche would bash the bulwark and, aided by the Parish peasants, they'd plunder and pillage. Look Daddy, as head of the church you're the man at the top. To keep all and sundry happy, annul the marriage, put the bag in a residential retirement home in the country and instead of her, why not have another dog in the bed.'

'You know what, that's right. My golly! Pity you're a girl, you'd make a good king. I'll tell everyone that the Hun and I never had it away and, to make it convincing, put it round she's my sister and a jolly good friend. Brilliant! Lucky I got rid of the Wops and started my own church. Come to think of it, I've still got your mother's old castle. It's free, going spare, so I'll give that to the Flanders Mare. She can live there and grow cabbages in the garden. With that off my mind now, I'll be able to sleep.'

Elizabeth yawned and looked at the Clock Candle standing at a precarious angle. 'You're so right Daddy, that is a horrible candlestick, can't even tell the time.'

'Pleased you think so. Thought it was just me. I'm going to get rid of it.'

'Sorry Daddy, must go, I'm very tired.'

'Tell you what, bid the guard to pop two beagles on the bed; they'll be warmer than that gaunt greyhound.'

'Night, night Daddy' she called as the door was closing.

'Thank you for helping me. Night, night. Oh, I nearly forgot to mention it. . . please don't try smothering your brother again. That wasn't very nice.'

'I won't. Night, night, Daddy.'

Now they'd sorted the missing spouse problem, he could set his thoughts upon what to do with the candlestick. If he didn't wish to have a nocturnal reminder of his shapeless wife, he must jettison the junk. He could dump it in the moat, but if Seb were to come over for a weekend he'd have to drag it back up. I know, he thought, to the glory of God, I'll give it to a church. No, Jo would expect something grander than a mere church.

Henry recalled that just last week he'd ordered a Roman Catholic cathedral to be ransacked and a couple of monks to be strung-up. Certainly that'll be in need of redecoration. So, the following day a courtier wrapped and took it to the Raby Cathedral.

Disburdened of Ming's monstrosity, it was time to mark the annulling of his own marriage to the virtuous vestal virgin. For lying about the German's beauty Henry made whoopee by cleaving Cromwell's head from his body. He then commissioned an immense wall hanging from the greatest tapestry artist of that period, Barent van Orley. It was to be nine and a half Rhenish Rods square. The Flemish weavers would use silk, wool, silver and gold thread.

Believing that being unfettered from marriage was much the same as the Israelites being freed from slavery, he chose a scene of the patriarch, Moses, leading his people to liberty; Henry was the model. Later someone told him that Barent was a flaming Flemish Romanist and reasoning, mistakenly, that being a Romanist meant he was a Catholic, gave the tapestry away to Raby Cathedral where he'd gifted the candlestick.

And so, on Friday morning the 13th day of March in the year of our Lord fifteen forty-two, it being a time of great floods, Archbishop Octavian Foljamb called for the cathedral sexton. 'Putteth this rubbish in a dark lodging in the quire where twill not beest seen, it being another unwanted gift from Henry.'

Wir sind in der Scheiße

(US Army Archives, Reich Marshall Herman Goring)
(British Intelligence, Section 24 leaked redacted material)
(Rabe Cathedral Archive Register)

To accompany *In the Bleak Mid Winter*, Gustav Holst composed a melody he called *Cranham*, now one of the nation's favourite Christmas compositions.

The musical director's score, containing Holst's painstakingly hand-written notations, was believed to be the one used by the composer when conducting the carol at its very first public performance in 1906, in the presence of King Edward VII. It is not known how the score came to be in Hitler's hands, but was rumoured to be a birthday gift from – *(redacted)* – around 1937, or 1938.

Adolph's mistress, Eva Braun, although more accomplished as a skater than a pianist, entertained the Nazi party hierarchy at the mountain retreat Berghof with her rendition of the song. Its beauty always made Goring cry. Whilst in the middle of a particularly poignant rendition in January 1943, a messenger arrived and handed Hitler a sealed envelope. Its content read:

'*Priorität – komma – Mein Fuhrer – komma – Wir stecken in der Scheiße – komma – die Schlacht von Stalingrad ist verloren – komma – Grund: trostloser Mittwinter – Punkt – Mit freundlichen Grüßen – Punkt – General Paulus.*'
(British Military Intelligence translation: We're in the shit,

battle of Stalingrad lost, reason, bleak mid winter, best wishes, General Paulus.)

It struck a chord with the Führer for, although his astrologer, Karl Ernst Krafft, had told him not to believe in the unscientific nonsense of omens, he flew into a rage declaring, 'Das ist ein schlechtes Omen!' Ripping the document from the piano, he threw it at a still sobbing Goring, who put it inside his jacket – it was never played again in Berghof.

A Lieutenant Butch Barovsky III of the US Army found the document amongst Goring's private possessions and gave it to his driver, who was a musician, skilled as a jaw's harpist. The driver, unable to read music, exchanged it for a comb and tissue paper offered by a British Tommy, Bert Bunter, an accomplished pub pianist. He realised its importance and sold it to Raby Cathedral where his mother was a cleaner. It was irreplaceable.

Into Daddy's Hands

Rodney found it challenging to recall warm memories of Daddy. Sometimes after Nanny had tucked him in, Daddy would sit on the bed and tell a story. The character Scrooge was his favourite. His version was more of a lecture, for it illustrated his frame of mind. Despite having heard the tale several times, Rodney was never bored, for it brought a brief moment of intimacy.

'Now look at that twerp Bob Cratchit. If there was ever a lesson in business management, it's *A Christmas Carol*. You see Rodney, he's got an inkwell and a feather with which he scratches a living by keeping Scrooge's books. There's nothing expensive, no high-tech tools; perhaps a ruler to draw the next straight line, but nothing else. No air conditioner, or fancy lighting, just one miserable candle and, as for office furniture, the wretch has to stand at a high table all day and half the night before hobbling home to his hovel. Now Rodney, the next bit is very important so listen carefully. Cratchit gets the going rate for his work. Although it's perhaps at the low end, don't forget he had agreed to it before he started. Even so, the ungrateful henpecked worthless bounder sees himself as underpaid and persecuted.

'So here's the picture: due to the poor lighting conditions Cratchit's nearly as blind as a Samson socket. He can't afford to purchase a second-hand crutch for his kid, and he's so worn out that Tim, as tiny as he is, is too heavy for him, so his wife has to carry the urchin on her back. What then does Scrooge do?'

'He buys them a present, Daddy.' Rodney knew Daddy's version of the story well.

'You're quite correct my boy, that's what Scrooge does. He buys them a present. Anyone would think the old boy's gone soft. But no, he hadn't lost his marbles, had he?' He always paused for effect at this point, and Rodney shook his head in agreement.

'You see, my boy, Scrooge had lain awake all night formulating his plan. The man's a bloody genius. On Christmas morning, he's in bed waiting for the moment when the first smidgen of light breaks through the grime on his windows then, as fast and as sly as a fox, he's out in the smog-sodden dawn looking for a turkey. A turkey, I ask you! A bloody oversized grouse!

'He's had one bad night's sleep and a couple of phantom visitations – which can happen to anyone. Perhaps he'd been trying to sleep on a full stomach, who knows. Anyway, tell me Rodney, why did he wait till Christmas morning to buy the bird?'

'Because the shops are shut, Daddy.'

'Exactly. You're right, he's not daft; he knows all the shops are closed and anyway the best birds would have been gone long ago. But, being clever, he found a street trader with just one turkey left, nobody else wanted it. Why do you think that was?'

Rodney was very excited, 'It had died of not eating, Daddy.'

'Beyond any doubt, my boy, well done. That's right, it had died of malnutrition. You must remember the right words: malnutrition is why it'd died, it was a heap of emaciated skin and bones, and so Scrooge gets it cheap.'

They rocked with laughter. Rodney loved Daddy's stories.

'Then off to Cratchit's hovel he goes, where he presents them with the skeletal carcass that's so devoid of meat there's not enough to fill a decent sandwich, never mind make a meal. What do the ragamuffins do?'

Rodney shouted with glee, 'They all fall down, Daddy'.

'No Rodney, that's *Ring a Ring of Roses*, which is about how the poverty-stricken rat-infested illiterates died of the plague, but you're nearly right. You must pay more attention. I'll tell you what they did. They did what the rest of the down-and-outs do; they fall on their knees crying out their gratitude. That is, with the exception of Tiny Tim who knew that if he got down on his knees he couldn't get back up, so he jumps for joy on one leg.'

The image made them chortle.

'Then they all sob and cry, thanking their lucky stars because Mr Ebenezer's had a couple of hallucinations in the night.' Daddy always paused and sat back at this point.

'See Rodney, Scrooge's not yielded a penny in back pay for the years Cratchit's toiled. Nor if the weasel wishes to warm his skinny arse will he find solace from a freshly installed central heating plant, there's only a candle for comfort. He doesn't offer to fund life-transforming surgery for Tiny Tim's ailments, or a tube of glue to fix the tyke's crutch, nor does he pitch in and pay for Cratchit to pick up a pair of specs as compensation for his loss of vision. No, my boy, he's not that stupid.'

Daddy would draw on his cigar and blow circles of smoke for Rodney to poke with his finger.

'Despite their so-called "good fortune", the Cratchits are still in poverty and always will be; it's what they're born to be. Now, you see Rodney, Scrooge hasn't suddenly gone soft. He's made a mint from years of cheap labour and all its cost him is an anorexic turkey and a very small pay rise. You might ask what about the rest of the workers? No mention of them, is there? No hint of an across-the-board deal, or Christmas fare, for the rest of the ne'er-do-well's, is there?

'I am convinced his real plan was to get rid of Cratchit in the New Year, without notice, or any redundancy payment whatsoever. That's the way I'd do it. Let 'em pull the wishbone, then leave the Cratchit brood to languish in their intoxicated euphoria whilst picking at the skinny carcass of the dead fowl before they have to boil the bones for soup. Then, just when they think he's a hero, send them packing. Scrooge was a genius.'

Mrs Cratchit boiling bones always made Rodney roar, a signal for Daddy's departure and a 'Good Night' as he closed the door. Rodney would have loved a kiss on the cheek like he got from Nanny.

After leaving Rodney's bedroom, Daddy would speed off to the Cullinan Gaming Club where he spent his abundant free time. Membership of this exclusive quasi-political gentleman's society was strictly governed by nomination from an individual who was already a member. Given the outrageous shenanigans in which members were engaged, a wise rule was that their progeny could not hold membership until their daddy's demise.

On one such an evening, shortly after his wife's unfortunate visit to the cathedral, Archibald sat in his club mulling over the ridiculous fiasco of Mummy trying to turn Rodney into a fairy, and had put his foot down to any further attempts. His son would follow in his footsteps. First, off to Eton, thereafter a humdinger of a time at Oxford; Classical Archaeology was what his father had chosen for him as it proffered just a chance of a pass. Rodney was no brighter than he, so that might also be okay for him, but he'd see.

After scholastic failure Archibald had joined his father's City of London company, climbing quickly to the summit. At twenty-five, he became head of sales, marketing, and personnel administration, but, wisely, not finance. 'On merit!' His father had told the disgruntled longer-serving staff members. 'Take it, or bugger off,' was the response to a number of malcontents too old to find employment elsewhere.

From childhood it had been instilled into Archibald that you don't have to be clever. If you've money, you just employ some clever sod who's studied real subjects and has the brains to make you even richer. It was obvious!

Birthright was what it was about: it decreed some were destined to be beasts of burden, while others ensured that the creatures were yoked and got on with the job. Above those were people like him, with wealth enough to pay as little as possible to ensure that both parties got on with the dreary drudge of bringing in more means.

His father had always maintained any company worth its salt, needed two Members of Parliament as 'political doormen', and he'd persisted in this wise practice. 'Don't bother with Liberal Whiggamores: too many principles, not worth a tinker's damn, live in a dream world. Must have one adviser from the governing party and one from the opposition,' his father had advocated.

The ones his father had employed were long dead, so Archibald had selected two new leeches that, like him, were as crooked as corkscrews. Each declared they'd spend a maximum of four hours a month advising his company. In reality, a lunch and a couple of phone calls sufficed.

Of course, it was all above board, as the *Parliamentary Members Declaration of Interest* showed. The remuneration they received for being available for four hours a month was twice the annual salary his father paid some of his full-time employees. Then, on top of their parliamentary salary and expenses, one hired his wife as a researcher and the other his mistress as a secretary. They raked in more by advising two other companies whilst delighting in a plethora of freebies.

A number of senior MPs were members of the Cullinan Gaming Club, and Archibald noted most were descended from politicians. It seemed when an MP retired, invariably his son would go into the House to continue fighting the same battles the old boy had fought. His conclusion was that both the House of Lords and Commons were bailiwicks of reticulated nepotism and cronyism, well worth buying into.

Rodney, in Daddy's opinion – being too thick for much else – was particularly suited to the undemanding life of a Member of Parliament, and he would see to it that the boy followed the route.

Bartholomew de Clare-Smythe, MP, was on Daddy's payroll and, under Daddy's initiative, they set a strategy code-named Rodney's Elevation.

He would go off to Eton, thereafter Oxford to read Politics and Media Studies. Daddy didn't want him to read Archaeology, in case the twerp passed thus showing him up. After university, he would do a stint as an unpaid parliamentary junior assistant to De Clare-Smythe, who would certainly be in Parliament for life as his seat was as safe as his Cayman Island account. After a spell as a junior assistant, a period in the Party Research Department would be followed by time spent 'working' for a friend, probably the one who ran a media company.

De Clare-Smythe had friends in very high places and so, after consulting them, he had in mind a *safe seat*. By the time Rodney was ready to enter Parliament, the present Member for Upper Norton would be willing to step down for a fee that wasn't too substantial, and Rodney would be the incumbent.

To ensure all things were in place, Daddy would purchase a flat in the constituency and would rent it out until Rodney was ready to take occupancy. After moving in, he'd show his nose in a pub, or two, thereby becoming a local, so to speak. There'd be photo shoots on a dismal night with Rodney trying, without success, to modestly shield his face whilst delivering blankets to the homeless, or serving soup to the down-and-outs from the back of a Salvation Army mobile kitchen. De Clare-Smythe suggested they have him sleep rough for a couple of nights to show solidarity with the homeless.

'We could run a cable through a shop doorway to an electric blanket to keep him warm,' said De Clare-Smythe.'

Daddy had baulked at that in case it rained and Rodney was electrocuted before Election Day. 'Rather,' he said, 'pack him off to Calcutta and get him photographed helping Mother Teresa bandage up a leper, or two. That'd help, wouldn't it?'

De Clare-Smythe thought that in the mainly right wing, anti-immigrant, white constituency of Upper Norton it'd be judged as negative. After days of deliberation they'd put together what they considered a spot on long-term plan that'd enable Rodney to display himself as a worthy parliamentary candidate.

Of course, as Bartholomew de Clare-Smythe had pointed out, for the doors to open really wide there would have to be even more regular donations to the party, as well as appropriate disbursements to the local party agent, and his administration costs would increase significantly. Daddy said it was fine; he'd increase his donations and also give some to the opposition. His own life peerage had been purchased in that manner.

While outsiders might think it irrational to scheme so far ahead, it's clear the privileged classes have, for centuries, maintained their position by proper planning. It keeps the system going. Nothing left to chance, Daddy thought, as he took Rodney aside to tell him of the final plan and to ensure they were bowling on the same wicket.

'Look, my boy, we both know you're as thick as a fart, idle and useless, but you won't find my proposition a handicap. Firstly, I don't want you working for me, so the best course of action is to get you into something where brainlessness won't make you stand out from the crowd. You're going into politics where intelligence, freethinking and honesty are downright dangerous – you'll fit the bill nicely. There are two academic options, my boy,' Daddy had said, almost kindly. 'Option one is you'll attend the John Balliol Academy for Boys in the Scottish Highlands, with the school motto, *Laborare perituri.*'

Rodney enquired as to what that meant. Daddy looked on the brochure. 'It means Die Hard', he said. 'I've been up and had a look at the facility and think it will be most suitable for you.' He then described the daily regime.

'At five in the morning it's hands off cocks, on socks, followed by a quick five-mile bash over the boggy heather moors. After that there's a brisk cold-water shower in the open-air ablution block, overseen by the director of sports who doubles up as the cook. Any lazy laggards receive a whack across their spotty pink arses with a size eleven plimsoll. Thereafter, water for the cookhouse is collected in an iron bucket from the Bailoch Burn which is about a fifteen-minute walk away, if you hurry. This fatigue is selected from those with a lower scholarly predilection. Breakfast is a plate of salt porridge made by the cook with the water from the burn.

'The cook is huge: was a Glasgow stevedore and quite used to lugging bloody great sacks of grain around. Nevertheless, whilst having a quiet drink in a Gorbals bar, a woman's drink was knocked over. Apparently, the creature screamed, 'ye dobber', and followed it up with a Glasgow Kiss.'

Rodney asked, 'What's a Glasgow Kiss?'

'It's a head-butt. Often happens in Glasgow; part of the school curriculum,' Daddy explained. 'The untreated broken nose brought on rhinorrhea and a continuous nasal drip ensued.'

He went on to tell Rodney about the cook's other attributes. 'Superb athlete and a Highland Games Champion Stone-Putter and Caber Tosser. The title of Champion Tosser was undisputed until the results of a routine drug test showed he was pregnant. Pregnant! How can a bloody great muscle-bound tossing Jock be pregnant? I'll tell you how. A physical examination showed that he was a she. Hard to tell though, but perfect as the school's director of sports and catering services.

'I tell you, Rodney, I watched her, him, or whatever, prepare breakfast. Not a sight I want to see every morning! The wind was biting, and the snow was falling – well, not falling, it was a blizzard and as cold as a fart in a corpse. Hard to believe, but there she was with sleeves rolled above sweaty tattooed biceps just as if it were summer. Her huge clenched fist gripped the thistle-carved wooden handle of the iron spurtle as she stirred the gruel clockwise. You see Rodney; the Scots are infested with superstition and the twerps never stir anticlockwise lest Satan slip into the gunge. But, you know what? There's not a demon who'd ever risk even inserting a finger, never mind bathing in the mush. The mixture became so coagulated that stirring it made her bulging muscles comparable to bloody melons, and she was sweating like a heifer in heat. The nasal drip, slaver, and sweat, joined before dribbling from her hairy chins to turn the gruel into a state beyond circumvolution. Neither the Three Bears, nor Goldilocks, could have stomached it, but the Scots love it, stuff themselves like the ravenous ruffians they are. It's the insatiable appetite for porridge more salty than the Red Sea that does for Scotsmen. A Jock's life expectancy is five years less than an Englishman who eats cornflakes encrusted in more sugar than a cane cutter cuts in a day. Questions?'

Rodney could only think of one thing, 'Do they get up later on Sundays?'

'A little,' Daddy replied. 'Instead of a run they allow you to stay in bed for fifteen minutes longer before outdoor physical exercise. Then, after forgoing porridge in favour of a slice of plin breid, it's two hours of Calvinistic jollity at the Presbyterian Kirk.'

He paused, looked Rodney in the eye, and said, 'The choice is yours. Die young in the Highlands, or off to Eton? Decide now.'

Forever Chained

To the relief of his tutor, Mortimer Meskill, Daddy had Rodney shipped off to his alma mater when reaching thirteen, leaving only Tristan and Cuthbert for him to grapple with.

Telling who was the most distraught, Nanny or Rodney was out of the question, so within minutes of setting off to Windsor, the chauffeur closed the privacy glass divider between him and the wailers.

Between sobs, Nanny told Rodney that Mummy had sent her love with the message he would enjoy Eton. There was no word from Daddy as he was away on business in Kenya, or the Keen-Ya Colony, as Nanny still called it.

Upon arrival, he failed to fight off the sturdy arms of the Matron that prevented him from tearing after the coupé as it sped down the drive, with Nanny waving through the rear window.

It took a short time before he found a downside. They had made him share the dorm with a detestable boy. The loathsome creature's family was poor and thus forced to beseech the school's charity for a bursary. At least it enabled him to gain a proper education and to live alongside the upper class. The fellow had hailed from up north, so his English was oft unintelligible. The worst part was the obnoxious maggot's constant declarations of how blessed he was, the pious pauper. Blessed! Feeling blessed is contrary to reason if you don't have a halfpenny or two in your pocket with which to scratch your arse, how blessed can you be?

One night Rodney thought he had a cold because his eyes watered. The little dick said, 'Are you homesick?' Homesick! Sanctimonious twerp. And then, without a by-your-leave, the sky pilot's scrawny hands were upon his head and the pretentious prat was praying for him. He didn't need prayers. It was a cold, or something in his eye; it often happened when he thought of Nanny.

On the whole, Eton was a haven of affluence, jam-packed with, if not clones in a physical sense, duplicates in wealth, speech, and pretension. He rejoiced in school life; everybody accepted him as if he were a bearing in a race that safeguarded the future of their class. There were counterfeits in the quadrangle, nouveau riche, and a pauper or two, who, like sky pilot, were being educated by some busybody do-gooder. But one utterance from their lips immediately exposed them as impostors and they were left to their own sort.

Other than his abortive attempt to escape from the clutches of Matron, his first confrontation with a member of staff involved the sports master. The brute dragged Rodney from his afternoon nap and demanded he run in the freezing rain like the rest of the twerps. Being ordered around by a man whose wage was being paid by his Daddy! Rodney told him where to go and didn't voluntarily engage in any future physical activities.

He guessed it was the man's dislike of him that resulted in his selection as a substitute in a boxing tournament. It was against a band of hooligans from a local state school. Eton's star boxing champion went down with a cold, so the teacher said. With hardly any preparation Rodney found himself in the dressing room with the sneering sports master wet sponging his sweating face, and that was before the tournament had even started.

Why they expected him to become a target for a lump of leather was a mystery. Backing out was impossible, as all his friends had cheered him on.

They helped a fellow back into the dressing room and laid him on a bed for examination by the doctor. Rodney thought he recognised him but couldn't be sure because of the blood. It sent not only Rodney into a swivet but also signalled it was his turn to enter the arena.

The walk to the ring was long and lonely. The sports master's steady push blocked any chance of escape and guided him to the blue corner. As he stepped through the ropes, his chums' cheers grew louder than the booing from the opposing school. Sitting on a low stool, he saw that in the opposite red corner was the other school's champion. The beast stood flexing his muscles and bobbing his head from side-to-side and shadow boxing in the pretence that he was already thrashing someone. Schoolboy! It was a shaven-headed thug who looked more like an escaped convict from Dartmoor than a youth. The referee called them to the centre of the ring to shake hands. The felon looked Rodney up and down, smirked, displaying gaps where front teeth once resided between tawny incisors. A mean-looking bit of dung if ever Rodney had seen one.

Seconds after getting back on the stool, the bell rang. With the clang still pealing' in his ears, and the sports master attempting to unglue Rodney's backside from the stool, the swivel-eyed swine leapt from his corner, streaked across the ring and delivered a whack to his whiffer. Before the agonising pain had even checked in at his cerebellum, he hit the canvas and stayed, refusing to get up even after the count of ten. Dizzy and demoralised, he lay in what seemed a deluge of blood. Through the pain came the sounds of jeers and boos from schoolmates and the opposition alike, and the vision of the sports master's smiling face.

But his friends soon forgave him and the illicit drinking after watching a boat race or game of rugger, continued. The camaraderie, almost love, was something he had never previously experienced.

He adored joining the other fellows in singing the school song. The sixth verse was his favourite. It declared they would be chained together for the rest of their lives. He oft sang it in the shower. It was marvellous.

Adhering to Daddy's instructions, he created a circle of influential acquaintances with both pupils and parents. Unfortunately this required spending many weekends on their estates, annihilating fowl, pheasant, and fox. This aspect of unifying his relationships he found abhorrent. Blood sports made his stomach heave. It wasn't the gore, the feathered creatures circling the ground whilst attempting to flap shattered wings, or foxes screaming as the dogs ripped the flesh from their bones that disturbed him. It was the climatic miserableness. One such episode was when his father, again, accepted an invitation for him to attend a long weekend shoot at the Le Pelletier's estate in Yorkshire. A cold, probably flu, was developing, which caused journeying anywhere beyond Cambridge even more nauseating than usual.

Upon arrival at the rural seat, they informed Rodney that Fairfax Forbe's brother, Quigley, was in charge of the entertainment. For the evening, it was to be drinking and laying odds on the direction of a card or two. The tomfoolery was still going an hour after midnight when, feeling under the weather, and knowing that they'd shortly be demanding him to vent pheasants, he called it quits. After all, he was up fifty pounds.

It seemed only minutes since his head had touched the pillow, when a manservant roused him. Not an inkling of daylight filtered through the heavy curtains covering the Palladian arched window. Jerking back the blinds made no difference, for outside it was as black as a Whitby Jet.

Then, with jolly badinage, for which he held no truck, they herded him into a frigorific wooden shooting-brake. He was then cast about while they towed the springless Victorian cart with a cacophonous diesel tractor to a bleak windswept moor.

A traipse followed across frost-bound plants and Jurassic clay with toes freezing and fingers throwing in their lot by becoming benumbed. By good luck, they didn't ask him to act as a walking-gun. He hated the solitary chore of hiking in line with the beaters. That assignment was to shoot any game flying away from the shot. 'Ta frit', 'aven't got t' moxie', was how the flat capped peasants had jeered at the escaping birds. Rodney considered them more intelligent as they had a better chance of survival from his shotgun than the fusillade of five-thousand size six pellets waiting in ambush.

The last occasion they had enlisted him for the task was also up north. Then the hired-hands made known their views of him by scoffing at his lack of proficiency to pepper a pheasant. The estate labourers in the south never laugh at a miss, they know their place.

To cap it all, it was on those same moorlands that an incident sowed the seeds of his lifelong germaphobia. They were going from drive three to four with his next allocated peg of six when, unexpectedly as he thought his bladder was like the rest of him frozen, he'd an urge to relieve himself. While doing so in the heather, Sir Layton Pinyon, the owner of Pinyon Fine Foods of Knightsbridge – by appointment to you know who – stood alongside and, peeing on his hands, said, 'Warms them up, gets the blood moving.' Then, after wiping the top of his brandy flask with a hand he'd just warmed up with the contents of his bladder, offered him a sip of brandy. Even though the assembled dignitaries had created the cream of society from their appendages, touching anything handled by another member of the shooting party, eventually almost by anyone, left him nauseated. He never again placed an order, not even for the famed Japanese Wagyu fillet, from Pinyon's Fine Foods. At the end of the shoot, as he'd oft seen, beaters buried the bodies of dozens of carcasses. He knew not the truth but had heard that game with more holes than the pips in a pound of pears could cause death from lead poisoning, so making the corpses good-for-nothing.

He suffered in silence as the discomfiture was essential in furthering his future political career. He did what Daddy decreed with as much enthusiasm as a sore shoulder, and a bruised cheek from the twelve bore recoil could muster.

* * *

After Eton, he scraped his way into Oxford to study Politics and Media, just as Daddy had planned, and, upon his father's instructions, joined as many debating societies as an active social life allowed.

Having the right connections is what counts in life, and those are what had enabled Daddy to call in favours from friends who pulled the required strings to furnish Rodney with an invitation to join the small, snobbish, male-only two-hundred-year-old Bullingdon Club.

Members of this notorious and unofficial Oxford sodality not only become lifelong friends, but also support one another in both political and business circles. Bullingdon is open only to the wealthy and privileged. Membership enables them to spend their idleness behaving in a manner that, when in positions of power, they will pontificate about and legislate against. The mandatory club uniform of a sky-blue, ivory and dark-blue tailcoat, a mustard waistcoat, and dark-blue tailored trousers cost more than the average worker earns in six months.

'On one occasion,' Daddy boasted, 'a few of us were as drunk as fiddlers and trashed one of the best restaurants in the town. We instructed the owner to add the damage to the bill. We'd gone prepared and paid cash. Great fun.'

He and Rodney roared.

'What's prosperity for if you can't show it off? The totties adore nothing more than a man who's got money and moxie, except one who's also earned his badge of honour by spending time in a cell for drunken high-jinks.'

As instructed, Rodney became a member, and, as Daddy had before him, of another Oxford institution, the old Etonian Gridiron drinking club, thereby also establishing lifelong relationships.

While slow on the uptake of theory, he was quick to learn practicalities. Politics wasn't about looking after the needs of the people; it was about locking verbal horns, exploiting language to one's own advantage, understanding government, and using clever words to stay in power. Understanding what you were doing was not a necessity; one only needed to appear to know what one was doing.

As Daddy had taught him, principles and conscience must be handled with caution as they are irrelevant, if not dangerous. As for morality, it plays little part. What counts is not being caught. With fancy footwork, a smooth tongue, and a measure of weasel-like cunning woven with a sanctimonious veneer, you can fill your pockets, and anyone else's you wish. It was obvious that the recompense for sweating coal miners, cotton pickers, sugar-cane cutters, or any form of hard labour for that matter, never leads to the workers' wealth.

Although academic learning was boring, Rodney loved the social life. From the lectures, he committed little to memory and had not considered reinforcing the gaping holes in his understanding of tutorials by opening any of the prescribed reading material.

He completed his formal education with a Bachelor of Arts in Media, having just scraped through on a recount, but had failed Politics. Neither he, nor Daddy, were concerned, for – far better than any degree – he had matriculated with the attributes they felt necessary in the world of politics: be careful of having too much concern for conscience, benevolence, hard work, facts, ethics, morals, or the dignity of others.

After university, with Daddy at the helm, assisted by De Clare-Smythe, things went swimmingly. They followed the plan for Rodney's Elevation *'verbatim et litteratim'* – as it would have been pronounced by the prick Prattius – and Rodney entered Parliament as the prestigious Member for Upper Norton.

Rodney Crooke-Wells MP

After nineteen years as an MP, by bending the malleable Expense Rules, Rodney was a proficient plunderer of taxpayers' treasure. In addition, he'd harvested a small kitty in an offshore account, of which a scant amount bordered on legal.

Like almost every member in the House, he'd experienced a couple of cans of worms, such as the expense scandal which had rocked the boat. For a few weeks it was tin hat time, keeping his head below the parapet before carrying on as usual. During that period, the saintly newspapers were downright tiresome: wailing and wallowing in a quagmire of moralistic rhetoric. But, like all things in life, the allure of cash silenced the saga. When the next sensational headline failed to add a penny to the proprietor's Tax Haven pension, it was 'All quiet on the Westminster front'.

Rodney and the rest said sorry to the electorate, 'We've learnt by our mistakes.' They set up a commission to report back in a few years when memories had faded and rewrote the rules with fresh ways to fiddle. (As the Namib scorpion stings and devours its mate, so the MPs bided their time. They got their own back by setting up an inquiry into newspaper behaviour. Quid pro quo was the belief held by both publicly posturing pugilists.)

Of course, before tonight's dinner he'd used the private dining rooms many times for buttering up prospective donors: it was but one of the plentiful perks his position proffered. Tonight's was a bit unusual in as much as there were no shady deals on the menu. This evening's little bash, with his brothers in attendance, was intended to celebrate dear old Mummy's seventieth birthday.

When arriving for dinner, he was met by the Commons' doorman who'd handed him a note with a sealed envelope from Mummy, it read, '*I won't be attending as something came up this afternoon. Open the accompanying letter at dinner, it explains everything*'.

Fancy the poor dear being unable to show up to celebrate such a monumental milestone, he thought. Never mind, not many birthdays left for her; we'll just have to make the best of it. Nonetheless, it is strange... I wonder, what could prevent her from enjoying her own birthday party? And, what does, 'Something came up' mean?

MPs trying to impress business associates, or foreign donors dithering with their donation, used the impressive private dining rooms as one would a magnet, and they were always in demand. Securing the room for the evening had taken months of jolly hard work, not to mention the backhanders. His PA had managed it against the odds, performed wonders, bless the little treasure, and for what? For Mummy to cancel at the last minute and for his lazy good-for-nothing brothers to be late, already fifteen minutes, useless sods!

It would be annoying if Mummy had preferred to go off with some of her fossilised friends for a celebratory rave at the Women's Institute. A cup of tea, followed by a sniff of nasal decongestant, two arthritis tablets, and a swing to Jerusalem? Probably not. She'd not do that.

The note didn't say she was ill, but the letter might. Whatever the reason, it's most disagreeable, damned annoying and far too late to cancel dinner. He looked across at the smiling face of the worthless wazzock of a waiter. Despite his protests to the catering manager, they'd lumbered him with an agency worker whose English was unintelligible.

'Unwanted, from a cancelled dinner,' the catering manager had declared. 'Sorry sir, but I need the permanent staff at a Prime Ministerial dinner.' Bollocks!

The whole evening was turning into a shamble: not the jolly soirée he and his PA had planned. While waiting for his brothers to arrive, Rodney checked the menu, made his choice, and gave short shrift to the lame-brained waiter by sending him scurrying off to polish cutlery and glasses at the service table.

He sipped the fine Champagne. It had a silky ethereal feel on his lips after which the tiny bubbles exploded, caressing his taste buds as if with a silken feather. Well worth the seven hundred pounds a bottle, he thought. The House of Commons own label was fine for everyday drinking, but he'd felt, a Grandes Marques Cuvée would be more befitting the celebration and had it ordered in. Against all expectations, the brainless waiter opened the bottle without doing a Horatio on him by taking out an eye. The fool at least knew how to remove the muselet and cork with the tiniest gratifying pop.

Needing something to lift his spirits, he contemplated his years in the House. The Honourable Rodney Crooke-Wells, MP; a grand title that carried an exalted ring to the ear. Membership of the oldest Parliament in the world was marvellous, it brought prosperity, influence and a bucketful of eye-watering benefits.

Elections were stressful; even explaining the platform upon which he stood was irksome. Especially when talking to those young idealistic, lefty, bearded, sandal-cloven morons who'd read and, damn them, understood the nonsense. Then, using their superior knowledge, wasted his time nitpicking and arguing the toss, knowing full well they'd never vote for him, no matter what. Manifesto! The leaders call it The Legislative Platform upon which we will govern. Unintelligible trash, tripe and trumper penned by a juvenescent panjandrum at the central office with more probiotic yoghurt than hair sticking to his top lip. To the electorate it's as clear as a dog chase on a foggy day in Dagenham and, what's more, after the election the bunkum's binned.

He looked at his watch and muttered, 'Bloody lazy buggers, will they ever get here?'

The waiter rushed over. 'You call, sir?'

'Bugger off.'

He blessed the day when they elected him Member of Parliament for Upper Norton. What a haven of peace. Residents of its leafy-tree-lined suburbia came from the affluent classes. In Upper Norton's world of plenty, the morning rush hour is the 4x4 SUV taking a child five hundred metres to the school. Right outside the playground gates, the council thoughtfully provided double yellow lines for such vehicles to park. They save dear little Sebastian from reducing his girth by unnecessary exercise. The hectic flow of traffic lasts on the underside of thirty minutes; thereafter, the most significant danger to life and limb is being bowled over by a deranged fossil astride a mobility scooter.

As their MP, it was a pleasure to knock on the doors of such people, often resulting in, 'Come in old chap, time for a Gin and Tonic?' or 'Shall I see you at the club next week?' No need to solicit their support, it was more rooted than Cromwell's wart.

If the party announced a policy to euthanise the elderly, they'd be queuing for a shot, even plunge the needles in themselves. Not Henry Franken, the chemist – he'd kick up a fuss. His golf club membership hinges upon the old crones exiting with a cornucopia of pills and potions in a shopping trolley.

It is unfortunate but, similar to a Bolshoi ballerina's hidden bunion, nothing is perfect and some Upper Norton suburbs were stomach-churning for they housed a breed of person more likely to steal the pencil in the polling booth than to place a cross. But, even if they voted for his rival, their choice made not one iota of difference to his being returned. His agent, however, was a stickler for democracy and demanded he rang their Westminster Chimes doorbells. In the 1980s this class of person, with a seventy-five per cent reduction gifted by the government, had bought their council houses. In addition, they then filled their pockets with discounted shares in British Gas.

The powers had anticipated it would mutate the masses into moneybag capitalists. Some hope! Euphemistically called the Working Class, they were and would forevermore be the Welfare Class. He remembered standing in front of what had originally been a white uPVC door and thinking he needed a crystal ball to foretell what lurked behind the grime. It was a yelping white miniature Scottie held by a woman, who looked seventy but was probably fifty, shouting, 'Stop it Molly, the man doesn't want to play.' Play! If deciphered by a canine cryptologist, the fleabag was snarling, 'I'll rip your throat out if this old hag releases me.'

As the door had opened at number 25 Queens Chase, a liberated stench akin to crushed dungwort, no doubt euphoric at its escape, in nothing flat found refuge in his nostrils. A fat bow-legged urchin goggled at him, while sucking the teat of a bottle filled with a red sugary liquid. Then, an overfed tatterdemalion piece of baggage propped herself up on the plastic door jamb, stuffing potato crisps into its mouth. He'd had a hard day, and the noise generated by the constant crunching and teat sucking overwhelmed a croaky explanation of his take on the party's health policy.

Most nauseating was even the thought of physical contact with such people, but in the name of democracy he had to shake hands. After touching them, or their doorbells, he used two hand gels, each guaranteed to kill ninety-nine per cent of all germs – combined he hoped they would dispatch every parasite to purgatory.

At their first meeting, his constituency agent didn't mince his words. 'Even if the party was to choose a dry-nosed primate, we'd still get a twelve thousand majority. And', he had added, 'the incumbent would swing in the Commons bar alongside the rest of the barrel of monkeys. So, keep your nose clean, gibber, preen and nod as required, and you'll be the member for the Upper Norton constituency for as long as I want you there.' Rodney noted the threat and ensured the agent had no complaints.

What a farrago of archaic rules he'd had to learn when first entering The Honourable the Commons of the United Kingdom of Great Britain and Northern Ireland in Parliament assembled. But, over time, he had come to love them. Smiling, he recalled being advised not to wear a suit of armour in the Chamber and, before entering, to hang his sword on the silk loop provided on his coat hook. He also realised a distinct feeling of superiority and smug satisfaction in pointing out the rules to new members who made foolish gaffes in etiquette.

It hadn't taken him long to grasp that the commoners considered his office to be of high esteem and that it provided a multitude of astonishing sweeteners for his kitty. Tables magically appeared in overbooked restaurants and best seats for sold-out West End theatres found their way into his pocket, often free.

The local family doctor had a three-week wait for appointments, but a mention of his name brought a same-day consultation. Upon arrival at the surgery, he always insisted on waiting for his turn and ensured those around him knew who he was. 'Our MP uses the NHS,' they would say, and he could then proclaim in the House how brilliant it was, although he used his private medical aid more often than not.

The Commons Register of Members' Interests showed him to be an adviser to three companies. He understood little of their activities but his income, for a maximum of two and a half hours each per-month, totalled sixty thousand pounds a year. Oh yes, and the annual donation of twenty-five thousand, plus his salary and other expenses, was a good start. The other perquisites were almost endless. However, his agent's words were never forgotten, 'Keep your nose clean!' This he had done – almost.

He recalled that it was an ex-colonial, an American he thought – what was his name? Lincoln? Yes, that was the chap. The colonials had named him after an old English town. It was that fellow who'd said, 'A statesman is he who thinks in the future generations, and a politician is he who thinks in the upcoming elections.' What absolute tosh and codswallop, as the latter was obvious to anyone, and why not? Life was short. Grasp opportunity by the forelock, was his mantra.

The highlight of his political career, unto the present, was two years ago when Downing Street had selected him to ask a planted question at the weekly jollification known as Prime Minister's Questions, or, as the press call it, Panto Time.

To Rodney, being chosen to ask the P.M. a question was most prestigious, requiring him to be as sharp in his application to the task as the favoured blue-winged olive nymph on his trout line. With television cameras in the House, he knew when he stood to speak his image would orbit earth with a caption beneath declaring his name and that of his party. It was, therefore, beholden upon him to ensure everything be perfect. He had heard that some in America watched it every week thinking it to be an idiosyncratic English comedy series. He'd always thought foreigners strange.

With only eight days to prepare for the big day, there'd been no time to lose. After a measure of vacillation, he'd felt his Savile Row blue worsted suit would be spot on for the occasion. He'd have it spruced up. As a master tailor and a cutter had, between them, spent more than a hundred hours assembling the masterpiece, plonking such a work of art into an oversized washing machine reeking of chemicals, to swill around with 'Made in Bangladesh' synthetic rubbish, was not on. Neither was having it flattened under a thundering great steam press that provided not an iota of a distinctive finish.

Rodney had a Knightsbridge valet service collect his suit for sponging and pressing. One hour with an eighteen-pound goose iron, a wet cloth, and the back of a wooden brush was the key to achieving the desired finish. While his shoes would be unseen, they, nonetheless, also went for coddling to spic-and-span: a snip at fifteen pounds. Added to the fifty-five for pressing the suit it might appear over the top, but claiming back through 'Expenses' was effortless.

When said and done, getting ready for such an auspicious occasion was comparable to a judge donning a wig and gown. The apostles of the law leave any predispositions they might have had in their earthly clothes. With the wig and gown in place, they metamorphose into arbitrators of humanity, leaving fear, prejudice and earthly identity in the changing room.

He knew what would happen when he raised his backside off the green-leather bench: the opposition would whoop and howl like hyenas fighting for their dollop of flesh from the warm twitching corpse of the wildebeest. Wearing the correct bib and tucker would impart an air of authority, raising him above the scrummage. From a lofty height, he'd observe the noisy rabble in their off-the-peg, hang-like-rags rubbish, probably stitched with crowbars in Dhaka. True, most would find five thousand pounds for a suit extravagant, but his would outlast their rubbish, and them. He thought Shakespeare was spot on with, 'For the apparel oft proclaims the man.'

If money wasn't for life's little luxuries, what the deuce was its purpose?

He ordered a new shirt from Jermyn Street; no need for measurements as the shirtmaker kept his cut patterns. One felt superior knowing that the imprint of one's body rested in perpetuity within the sapele mahogany drawers alongside those of many famous dignitaries, both past and present. A Jermyn Street drawer was akin to having one's crypt in Westminster Abbey: a sepulchre to the great. He might be resting between Lloyd George and, say, Lord Elgin, or, heaven forbid, squashed between Oscar Wilde and his boyfriend, Lord Alfred Douglas. He hoped not the latter. He'd get his PA to inquire with whom he shared space, just in case.

Sleep had been elusive the night before the big day, so an early start provided ample time for preparation. Hours were spent in front of a full-length mirror perfecting posture, gesticulations and intonation to emphasise the important points of the question. A written copy was in the coat pocket for he had no wish to make a fool of himself fumbling for words. One hour before he was due to take his seat in the Chamber, he told his PA to hold all calls as he was to get dressed. The moment of glory was drawing nigh, no need to rush.

It was unfortunate that whilst pulling the trouser zip up he'd trapped a wee bit of the shirt in the fly. Although only a smidgen of the finest white Giza cotton peeped out, it would be clear to all, particularly the television cameras. After an annoying and stressful period spent trying to release the captured material, he called for his PA's help. She'd tried wrenching the zip up and down, but achieved not a millimetre of movement. 'We need fly-spray,' she'd chortled, receiving a gruff response to her playful repartee. Rodney had been in no mood for such flippant nonsense.

'Sorry, I'll get closer and have a look,' she said, hoisting her skirt up and getting onto her knees in front of him. It was most distressing. He was not a master of his time and must not be late taking his seat. Anxiety and the physical effort of fighting the zip took their toll, for, like a fox in a chase, his face became florid and streamed with sweat.

'Please hurry,' he urged.

'Don't worry, it's moving,' she said, gasping for breath at the exertion.

Holding the trousers above the fly with one hand, she gave a few yanks with the other. Her efforts were rewarded as a hard tug released the shirt from entrapment.

As the zip zoomed downwards, it caught Rodney's willy causing him to throw his head back and shriek at the excruciating mutilation of his manhood.

'It's come,' she squealed with delight, apathetic to his pecker's impalement.

'Ayup! Was it grand, lad?' The odious voice was that of Rodney's opposition 'pair', for the uncouth blighter had slithered into the office without a by your leave.

(Rodney, as did other MPs, had a 'pairing arrangement' with a member of the opposition party. Under the scheme, if either wanted to skive off for a game of golf, or have a baby, by a gentleman's agreement the other abstained from voting, thereby maintaining the status quo in the House.)

Whilst Rodney was rubbing his painful pecker, his 'pair' was ogling his PA on her knees with her skirt halfway to paradise holding his fly zipper.

She exclaimed, 'I was pulling it down!'

Rodney burst out, 'I was trying to get it up!'

'Up, or down, just thought I'd pop in and say have a grand time, but it looks as if you've already 'ad one.' His snide laughter continued long beyond the door clicking closed.

'Great Scott! I hope he didn't think. . .!' exclaimed Rodney. He detested the snivelling, rat-arsed, silver-tongued, ferret-legging, goat's pizzled piece of dirt, with a wit darker than a nauseating Pontefract cake. Glancing at his watch, he said, 'Got to rush.' With his tool tingling from its entrapment, he finished dressing.

While collecting the shirt, his PA had purchased a five-fold self-tipped Bombyx mori silk tie as a gift to celebrate the occasion. It added an air of quality and matched the party colour. 'Good luck,' she whispered when pecking him on the cheek after ensuring the tie looked perfect.

What a treasure she is, he thought, I'll have to give the dear girl something later.

Taking his seat in the Chamber, he listened to the meaningless hogwash and poppycock that is the prelude to the double-talk called Prime Minister's Questions, or PMQs.

He looked across at his opposite number: the tyke was puckering his lips and making crude gestures causing Rodney to blush and sweat like a copulating Jersey bull. As a distraction, and to gen up on his question, he removed the note from his coat pocket.

It read, '*Dear Sir, we have cleaned your suit and hope it meets with your satisfaction. If you have any complaints, please contact me. Have a good day, Gloria.*'

Oh, no! His hands flew from one pocket to the next: not a fleck of floss, the pockets were as empty as an election promise. Searching the floor and bench produced diddly zilch.

He thought hard. Surely after all the practice he could remember it. 'Does the Prime Minister think?' No, he can't think, the Prime Minister never thinks.

He had to remember. It was imperative. Something to do with the economy? 'Does the Prime Minister believe?' No, confound it! That was not right. Oh, good grief, how does it go? If the damned shirt tail hadn't got stuck in his fly, or his dick ambushed by the zip, this'd never have happened. What the devil was it about? Yes, it was to do with the economy and the National Health Service.

'Order! Order! Questions to the Prime Minister.' Mr Speaker's voice boomed, its reverberations comparable to a twenty-one-gun household artillery cannonade.

'Number one, Mr Speaker,' cried a government backbencher.

Bugger the other questions. Where the devil was his?

The rule at PMQs is anyone wanting to ask a question must 'Catch Mr Speaker's eye' by bobbing up and down. This meant Rodney had little time to refresh his memory of the question for, from the start, he had been up and down more times than a whore's drawers.

Other questions had passed, and then Mr Speaker called 'Mr Rodney Crooke-Wells.'

Unfortunately, as if by Pavlovian response, he'd stood up but, instead of remaining on his feet, had sat back down. Above the rowdy laughter and derisive catcalls from the opposition benches, the thundering haughty voice of Mr Speaker boomed out his name once more. 'Come Mr Crooke-Wells, it's your turn. Let your words fly.' The House roared and Rodney looked at his smirking nemesis; the rat had spread the word of his demise.

He rose and, as if the canonical hour had arrived, silence descended upon the gathering. Taking a deep breath, gathering as much composure as nerves allowed, he desperately tried to remember the question.

'Thank you, Mr Speaker.' He cleared his throat. 'Will the Prime Minister. . . or my Right Honourable Friend, agree with me. . . or does he?' Rodney fell silent. All eyes were upon him – the odd snigger breaking the silence. What the devil was the PM supposed to agree upon? Ah, yes – he remembered. 'What I mean is, does he agree with me that the best way to raise the economy is by carrying on the high health standards of my constituents and not abandon them as the party opposite do if they were us?'

Rodney sat to tumultuous shouts of 'hear, hear' ringing in his ears from his own side of the House whilst the opposition hurled derision at his delivery and the insensibility of the question. When back on the bench, he remembered where he had put his question paper; it was in the pocket of his monogrammed shirt. He took it out to read, '*Will the Prime Minister agree with me, the way to raise Health and Social Service standards to even greater heights is to continue following his long-term plan of rebuilding the economy from the shambles he inherited from the party opposite?*' Oh dear, his biggest day, and he'd got it wrong.

The PM, meanwhile, was staring at his notes and speaking to the Chancellor, both shaking their heads and looking towards where Rodney would have been had he not slipped down as far as he could go. There was chaos in the House; feigned laughter and derision filled the Chamber.

'Order, I will have order,' the Speaker had shouted above the noise and then mocked a recalcitrant opposition backbencher. 'Mr Finch you are an over-excitable individual. You must stop larking about and getting so ruffled, calm yourself, or you'll fall off your perch. I want to hear the Prime Minister's reply.' Turning to the PM, he roared, 'Prime Minister.'

The PM rose, 'Mr Speaker,' and looking towards Rodney said, 'my honourable friend is right. Under this government, satisfaction with the National Health Service is at an all-time high. It is imperative we continue rebuilding the economy which has risen like a phoenix from the ashes left by the party opposite. We will continue to reduce the financial deficit whilst maintaining the funding to build our public services to even greater heights.'

The opposition erupted once more, hurling ridicule and derision upon Rodney's performance. The jeers were a painful reminder of his first and last boxing match when at Eton. At least in Parliament members of his own party tried to lift his spirits by patting him on the back. 'Well done old bean,' one declared, but without doubt they were mere lip servers. It was his forty-seventh birthday and asking the PM a question was like the cherry on the ice cream sundae Nanny had always bought him on his special day. She never forgot.

'Ayup, oos a chuffy gawby then,' his opposition 'pair' crowed in a loud voice. The hideous northern dialect made it sound even more scornful. The mirth from the rat's 'Comrade' clique made clear that they loved the put-down. Rodney's dealings with the axed miner were ample enough to know he was being called an arrogant fool.

If the subterranean turd-shovelling mole had called him a rat, or a blackguard, he'd have had to apologise to the House. But the cinder shifter knew chuffy gawby wasn't in the parliamentary rulebook and was free to be used without the Speaker pouring wrath over the utterer and seeking a grovelling apology.

No doubt the ghastly little man was still furious with Mrs Thatcher for closing the pits and putting a stop to the free coal he and the other idle skivers had enjoyed. But, to give credit where credit's due, although the gargoylean Neanderthal had a chip on his shoulder there was no wood on top. He was an intelligent, articulate and dangerous political adversary whose Yorkshire accent slipped easily into English in the Stranger's Bar. Not for him the ghastly

Brown Ale drunk by his kind up north, he imbibed subsidised eighteen-year-old Speyside single malt whisky. The merits of the Pre-Raphaelites and the Hudson River School were his favourite topics and, rumour had it, the man had used his redundancy to trot off to university and gain a first-class honours degree in maths, apparently keeping it under wraps in case it damaged his rotten reputation.

Britain still needed coal, but did he and his fellow moaning miners show any thanks that, instead of them breaking their own backs, it'd be their Russian comrades, and others, who'd deliver the required millions of tonnes? No, none of them expressed any gratitude to Maggie for providing them ample time to burnish their bugles and ham it up with the colliery brass band. They've not even praised her for dishing out their dole. Problem is, idle minds are the devil's playing field – not that there're many fields where they come from, more like slag heaps. Ungrateful, that's what they are.

The working classes fail to grasp that those of the upper crust don't vacate their mummy's wombs with the aid of silver forceps, or gallop out of passion valley astride a field hunter, and are certainly not sprinkled with gold dust in place of baptismal water. People, like Daddy, had worked damned hard to sustain the coffers, although somewhat depleted since their heyday of the Atlantic slave trade.

He checked his watch again. . . another fifteen minutes had passed. Brothers! Damned nuisances.

Only the other day, he was reminded of Daddy's inherited fortune and his eventual inheritance when a debate was held on modern slavery. He condemned it, as did every other member as, 'Damned barbaric', and the Atlantic slave trade as, 'A stain upon the nation's history', and all that stuff and nonsense. But, like him, many owed their status and present-day living standards to the fruits of subjugation and serfdom.

If slaves still cut the cane and tended tobacco fields, would we waste valuable parliamentary time debating obesity, rotting teeth and cancer? He thought the answer was 'certainly not'. Historic servitude is what had purchased status and power, and neither he, nor anyone else he knew, gave a tinker's cuss if the masses had to masticate chicken tikka masala on nicotine-stained gums.

Many of the Palladian-style mansions where he'd spent weekends owed their existence to bondage. Even the silver plaques beneath ancestral portraits in the long corridors bore testament to the fact that money carries you up the tree of life. Nothing's new under the sun. Say what you might, was his opinion, without the slave trade a catastrophic depletion of inherited wealth would have blighted Britain. It'd be brimful with dingy dwellings overflowing with riff-raff. There'd be no private forests packed with pheasants to shoot, or rivers awash with trout, or lawns to sit on at garden parties.

As if by doing so it would hurry the blighters along, he glared at the door and then, again, checked his watch: eleven more minutes overdue.

Oxford had hardly jammed his intellect with wisdom worthy of reflection, but the study of one of Britain's greatest Prime Ministers had stuck like a barnacle on a boat to his grey matter. His tutor had reasoned that if modern military commanders gave the eagle eye to the Chinese General Sun Tzu (whose last victory was two thousand years ago) he would be required, as part of his university curriculum, to delve into the skulduggery of past political icons. Knowing that his family had a connection, if somewhat loose, with William Gladstone, he'd chosen him as his subject.

Although Gladstone was a country bumpkin, he was, nonetheless, a dignitary who Rodney aspired to mimic: a man with fancier footwork than a covey of Celtic *céilí rinceoirí*. His involvement in the Slavery Abolition Act of 1833 proved him worth a gander. In Gladstone's time, MPs received no salary for their services; this kept the working class out of Britain's Mother of all Parliaments. William's father, Sir John Gladstone of Fasque, was a wealthy Scottish merchant and slaver who financed the expensive lifestyle of his offspring partly from the proceeds of vassalage, as did many of his peers.

The abolitionists, understandably, had a battle royal on their hands when hawking their views through Parliament. The philanthropic prats must have known it would never be child's play as many Parliamentarians not only owned the slaves, but were also in the pockets of wealthy planters. They held shares in plantations and in the ships carrying the human cargo. Their vested interest was the status quo.

Slavers weren't stupid, and so, when seeing the tide was turning, at the pivotal moment they sought their own emancipation aided by a dollop of hugger-mugger. Forty thousand of them plotted to hold the nation to ransom and plunder the Royal Mint. Included in their number was Sir John Gladstone of Fasque and his friend and confidant, Rodney's great-great-grandfather, the Very Reverend Quinton Bartholomew Crooke. He had no hyphenated Wells.

The Very Reverend's diaries – now family heirlooms – had many entries relating to abolishing the Parson's ownership of slaves and the ensuing misery should he lose his property, as the enslaved were called. Rodney had found it quite a plod getting through the scrawl for, not only was it crab handed, but – what with working only on Sundays – the vicar also had stacks of free time to witness his woes, so the script rambled as, no doubt, had his sermons.

The pretty Suffolk village of Wood Hollow was his benefice, where he lived together with his wife, Elizabeth, and their five children. A family portrait proved her dowry was far more attractive than her physical demeanour, it being short and sombre. Another period picture showed the enormous three-storey rectory, described in the diary as the grandest property in a village where five hundred souls lived in thatched cottages with walls painted a Suffolk pink – obtained by combining whitewash and pigs' blood. A watercolour painting of the property presented towering wrought-iron gates giving entrance to a sweeping tree-lined drive leading to a neo-Jacobean manse, the benefaction of a wealthy wool merchant who had considered shrinking his bank account preferable to a sackcloth cilice. One might say the merchant built the regal manor upon the back of Suffolk sheep, while the incumbent reverend built his earthly riches upon flagellated slaves.

While most of his ancestor's promulgations were boring, with slathers of ecclesiastical poppycock, a few bits were quite riveting. One diary entry described how an abolitionist, carrying a banner asking 'Am I Not a Man and a Brother?', had confronted the vicar outside his own church, on a Sunday of all days. The rampaging altruistic twat had denounced the cleric's slave ownership. But the representative of God in Wood Hollow gave the protagonist short shrift by quoting Genesis IX, the curse of Ham, as being proof enough of the admissibility of slavery.

The reverend wrote: '*It did cause poor Prudence Ro-Herring, spinster of the Parish, to be so overcome with the vociferous nature of the unwarranted confrontation that she did stagger from the gravelled path and slumped quite faint upon the soft grass.* It went on to say, *Harvey Fisher, widower of the Parish, administered hartshorn, so enabling Prudence to regain an upright position.*'

How lucky his ancestor wasn't a Methodist, for, as the diary said, the narrow-minded bunch from the holy club had banned their clergy from slave ownership and, unbelievably, also from alcohol. His great-great had written, '*Better an Anglican than a Methodist, but better either than a celibate Catholic*'.

The mediator between God and the village folk had purchased, with his wife's cash, insufficient slaves to be a member of the upper plantocracy who counted their 'property' in the thousands. However, as a man of the cloth he was an important member of the group, for his pre-meeting pious prayers imparted a beatified legitimacy upon their altercations with the abolitionists. The seating plan at the meetings elevated him next to Sir John, a status unmerited by his relatively meagre slave ownership. Even so, according to the dedicated devil dodger's diary, he would be bankrupt if the notions hawked by the anti-slavery apostles became law.

Rodney broke out in a sweat, while reading how close his ancestral doorstep had come to impoverishment. If the ranting of the do-gooders had prevailed, he might have been living in an awful little hovel packing wine gums in a sweet factory.

He gave thanks for the Bible thumper's fortitude, while sipping the Champagne. Checking his watch, he cursed his brothers, and scowled at the smiling waiter.

Emancipating half the African continent and lugging the buggers back across the Atlantic would have cost a fortune, Rodney gleaned. But, he sensed, that within the rambling journals the Rev had perceived a glimmer of hope, even if as dim as the taper used to light the Easter candle. The sermoniser's writings described how the plantocracy and their Parliamentarian fellow-travellers, had sought a way to keep the cash, appease the abolitionists, and, importantly, retain Rodney's inherited place in society. Why then, Rodney had asked himself, did his ancestral pulpitarian, and most other slavers, defect and become almost fanatical abolitionists?

An entry recounted how the proliferation of hostilities to their fair trade had got quite out of hand, but the diaries gave no inkling of a capitulation. Another note, a few weeks later, had two words: 'Slave War'. War! It became obvious from a later diary account what was to transpire:

'London Friday 10th. Had dinner with Members of The House, some fine fellows from the West India Regiment attended as observers. The army, it seems, has worries about emancipation, they've bought more slaves than the planters. They stick the coffles in red uniforms and, heaven forbid, give 'em guns with orders not to shoot their officers. Although Major General Lord Wetherston Lochwater be in great pain from The Gout, he declared – If we can't beat 'em on the battlefield we must ambush the lobcocks and bobtails in the swamp as we did the fuzzy-wuzzys. My advice? Outflank the enemy, by bowing to their wishes and agreeing to give up our property, but only if Parliament provide commensurate compensation for our losses.'

To the delight of the slave owners, Honourable MPs, and Lords, The Slavery Abolition Act of 1833 flew through Parliament faster than the whack of a whip. This was a fair shake for the Rev, Sir John and also for William as it meant he would eventually get his cornucopia of cash and the devil dodger would bag a bundle whilst, with a pious countenance, he could denounce slavery from the pulpit.

Parliamentarians, of whom many were slavers, voted to pay compensation for the loss of their 'property' and that of their friends at a rate they themselves set, the Bill passed on a vote. The payout to release the slaves was so enormous that the Exchequer hadn't the wherewithal and had to put up taxes and raise a loan from Mr Rothschild, who – not, yet rich enough himself, – raised more from others.

Everyone was a winner? Well, almost. For, Rodney had roared with laughter when realising that the debt was so humongous that the British taxpayer wouldn't pay it off until the year two thousand and fifteen. And the simpletons were even now paying exorbitant entrance fees to visit the stately homes that they'd been purchasing with their taxes for over one hundred and eighty years.

Brilliant! Be careful what you wish for, ran through Rodney's mind.

But there was a twist to the tale. Never to miss an opportunity, along with the compensation they voted to keep their slaves for another six years and to rename them as Apprentices.

After that time was up, the slavers sent the Negroes packing in favour of low-paid indentured Indians. The ex-slaves, with no kudu to capture or plots to plough, starved, and their dreams of sunsets over the Serengeti were but a nightmare voyage. Beyond the horizon; beyond possibility; beyond dreams; beyond hope.

The diary noted grudgingly that it had been a hard-fought moral victory for the elated abolitionists. It also noted Sir John Gladstone bore the grief of losing his 'property' of over two thousand five hundred slaves with a cash payoff of over eighty million pounds in today's legal tender. His son William must have walked on water, with the abolitionists off his back and his inheritance saved.

Rodney's ancestral harp polisher, the diary noted, at the present going rate received more than two and a half million for his 'property'

Without the moral encumbrance, the vicar re-invested his recompense in the East India Company, it being exempt from the Act.

Rodney smiled when he thought of the ingenuity of the contrivance. The Very Reverend Crooke, without a Wells, and the other slave-owning cohorts, had set a trap and zapped the abolitionists.

'Strike first, as the Chinese General said, that was the key'. What shrewd men were Gladstone and the cleric.

Checking his watch again, he muttered his displeasure.

His thoughts turned to the House of Lords which led his mind back to when he had to share the dorm with that detestable boy at Eton. There was a similarity between the child and his subterranean nemesis in Parliament: the runt had also hailed from up north, or was it Ireland? Either way no person in their right mind would have believed it, but that insufferable born-again holier-than-thou turnaround collar was now a suffragan bishop. A Bishop! On the path of righteousness to the Lords Spiritual: a seat in the House of Lords, no less.

No sign of the sods, flashed through his brain and the hands of the watch had hardly moved. 'When the devil will they arrive?' he said aloud. The waiter wavered, but remained at the service table.

While he wouldn't say no to a knighthood – Sir Rodney has a certain ring – it should only be a stepping stone for elevation to the regalement of the House of Lords, as that is what he'd often considered desirable. How he craved to place his ample derrière upon the red leather upholstery alongside the other titled nobles and emulate Daddy, the late Lord Crooke-Wells of Mountdick. There were many worse things in life than ending one's days as a Peer of the realm, all things considered.

It was so absurd. The ermine-collared scarlet robes; he'd use his father's old one with cheaper rabbit skin painted with black dots. Batty but British. The surrealistic spectacle of the Gentleman Usher of the Black Rod launching an assault on the Commons door requesting their permission for him to enter, it always raised a smile. How many other nations would consider televising a man wearing breeches and ladies' black tights, bashing on a door with an old wooden stick? Only the British would see fit to summon elected leaders to an unelected Chamber in such a bygone manner; and there to hear an unelected monarch read a speech he, or she, hadn't written. No one else in the world! But then, the rest of humanity hasn't the good fortune to be British or, better still, English. Only those so born could display such ridiculous idiosyncratic behaviour and not be incarcerated for insanity.

The Gentleman Usher of the Black Rod, Sir James de Hout Pennington – a lickspittle fruitcake in pantyhose if ever there was one – is tasked with summoning MPs to attend the Lords Chamber for the State Opening of Parliament. It's on that grand occasion that the green-eyed monster of envy becomes all-consuming. Upon arrival, the MPs must stand peering over the heads of the robed layabout Lords who get paid a tax-free daily allowance, expenses and luncheon for squatting on red upholstered benches listening to the Head of State. And then what do they do? Bugger all!

A Lord's life with the commoners looking over his head was his pre-eminent target. He imagined how he'd turn around and smirk at the bow-legged shit-shovelling ex-collier. What a wonderful dream!

Although remembering little from lectures at university, he thought Herbert Samuel's views came straight from the horse's mouth, 'The House of Lords must be the only institution in the world kept efficient by the persistent absenteeism of most of its members.'

It was not his plan to upset that apple cart. There'd be enough sweat giving a daily nod to the other old farts, clocking-in for the three hundred quid a day, then morning coffee, a spot of subsidised breakfast, and a casual read of the free newspapers. After which, it'd be time for a brief cab ride to the Cullinan Club, whose membership he'd continued since his father had gone for a permanent sleep. There he could look forward to luncheon while observing the cash rolling in from his investments and the non-executive directorships of, say, ten companies and City institutions. That was the nirvana to which he aspired.

The abundance of banknotes that Daddy had stuffed into the party coffers hadn't lifted him through the plunderbund of the honour labyrinth, a life peerage was all he'd got. So, when he reached the end of the rope, the title had died with him.

How wonderful a hereditary peerage would have been, he'd have become the greatest Mountdick ever. In the interim, he thanked his lucky stars for his present position, but hoped to achieve elevation before the insufferable suffragan bishop.

He looked at his watch, his anger rising by the tick. Mummy not coming, Tristan and Cuthbert late, those two are more than irresponsible, it was appalling luck to have them as brothers. Bloody layabouts!

'Llamedos!' he exclaimed. It was a secret word Daddy had taught him. They often said it in front of Mummy who never knew it was sod-em-all backwards; she thought it was a Welsh pleasantry.

Dear Book Worm

The sorry saga of Rodney Crooke-Wells and his rise to prominence has been told. As discombobulating as you might have found that to be, it is not the end.

Being members of the hereditary rich, the Crooke-Wells have, unlike the Great Auk – which three Scotsman made extinct because the ginger jobbies couldn't tell the difference between a penguin and a wart-covered crone when they murdered it – a partiality for permanence. Therefore, not wanting to be things-of-the-past they have joint tenets to produce as many offspring as possible. We now turn our cogitations to Mummy's second offertory to the survival of the sub specie – the rotten rich.

Meet Tristan.

The Lives and Loves of a Linseed Lancer

They blessed their second child with the names Tristan Peregrine Crooke-Wells.

Mummy chose the first name after The Hon, Tristan Longshafter, who, although of German descent, she adored. It was but a brief period since he'd been not so honourable when bedding her while his wife was away visiting her mother and Archibald had gone by plane to play polo in San Paolo. Peregrine was the name of her maternal grandfather.

Mummy's gynaecologist, Doctor Ludovic Labuscaigne, fixed the birth date of the 9th of August as it was spot on for both parents.

She was very fond of Ludo, a very close member within her inner circle, for he always had a contented demeanour as, she'd found, had most of his trade. The date of birth gave Daddy two days to show some interest, while still having time to zoom off to the Scottish moorlands. It was the start of the grouse-shooting season. The day known as the glorious twelfth was always a jolly time for the shooters, if not for the five hundred thousand birds weighted down with lead.

From Mummy's viewpoint, it could not have been more perfect. Matilda Rutherford-Tate had employed a wet-nurse for a year to feed her son, Cecil. As soon as she'd finished Cecil's last lactation, the buxom lass from Burnley took root below stairs in the room next to Nanny's. Then, over the next twelve months, she served gallons of nourishment as an around-the-clock rent a teat for Tristan. When her contract ended, he'd become so attached to the girl that Mummy extended the agreement and Tristan became even more bonded to the boob, an addiction that would steer the course of his life.

In the Crooke-Wells household, it was rare for both parents to be in the house at the same time, unless throwing one of their frequent dinner parties. So, for Tristan, Nanny performed the role of parent absentia, an arrangement not unusual within their circle. He was unsure who he loved the most, the wet-nurse, Nanny, or Mummy? He thought he might love the one daddy called Jersey cow more than any other person in the world, along with Mummy that was, or Nanny. Mummy always popped in to say goodnight before going out; he loved the lipstick on his cheek although he said he didn't, and also the whiff of her perfume that'd lingered.

After finishing home tutelage at age thirteen, Tristan was shuffled off as a boarder to Rugby School and warbling Floreat Rugbeia with the rest of the prepubescent favoured few.

The school's founder was a tradesman who had garnered a fortune from supplying pickled eggs, onions, baked beans and curry powder to the Virgin Queen, Elizabeth Gloriana. While hard to believe, he was but a shopkeeper – a grocer if you will – much the same as Margaret Thatcher. But this earlier purveyor of perishables, one Lawrence Sheriff, had been just that wee bit more unhinged for it transpired the fellow suffered from a congenital infirmity: a deluded social conscience.

(For good order's sake, the Queen Elizabeth referred to, is the same so-called Virgin Queen who decapitated her cousin Mary and anybody else who mentioned her pocked white-leaded face, rotten teeth and fetor oris. The reason Sir Walter Raleigh, of bicycle and fag fame, introduced tobacco into the Royal Court was for it to function in much the same way as an air freshener would today: to cloud her foul farts.)

In 1567, Lawrence Sheriff changed his profession. Leaving the rat race, he took one last gulp of London's putrescent air before becoming an astronaut, and being launched into space on a celestial cloud. Being as dead as one of his baked beans meant he had no use for his fortune. But, having foreseen such an occurrence, he was savvy enough to draw up a Last Will and Testament.

When sitting in the solicitor's office having his ramblings read, the family was quite shocked to learn that they were to get zilch. It turned out that the lamentable lunatic had bequeathed his sizeable bank balance to the setting up of a free school for local male malefactors. Lawrence's insanity was obvious to the world, but in particular to his peeved, penniless progeny. So, the hopeful heirs did their best through the judiciary to put an end to the maniac's deranged recorded ramblings.

Unfortunately for them, a judge as batty as the trafficking tradesman foiled their attempt at fingering the fortune by declaring the fool to have had a complete set of marbles. It goes almost without saying that every imbecile constrained in an asylum was, compared to that Justice of the Peace, of sound mind. But because the law had spoken – even if by a buffoon – the wants of the Will were carried out and Rugby School was founded.

It took time for common sense to find a voice, but a blue blood spotted the direction things were heading, and so sought a way to keep out the swinish multitude. Upon his advice, the school plonked for an entrance fee enormous enough to ensure paupers need not apply.

One has to be mindful that were it not for Master Sheriff, Thomas Hughes – the scribe of the Tom Brown twaddle – would never have made a fortune writing rubbish about an ex-scholar thanking his headmaster for thrashing him. It is beyond belief how anyone can assert, 'It had been the kindest act which had ever been done upon him and the turning point in his character', after being thrashed. What absolute tommyrot!

A good thrashing had in no way, shape, or form, altered Tristan, not an iota, other than to make him more careful about getting caught. Even then, many of his ill-fated acts resulted in a well-deserved shellacking. Tristan always asserted there was no rational reason for Tom Brown – an offensive little coprophagous dung beetle if ever there was one – to become the hero, while poor Harry Flashman was vilified for trying to uphold what was dear to society and had made England the greatest power on earth. If we had more Englishmen like young Flashy, we'd still have an Empire and would not be prostrating ourselves before those who hitherto had kowtowed at our feet.

Rugby has an enviable history of turning out bucketloads of Britain's most celebrated heroes, but a failure in its half a millennium history was inevitable. (A fact needing no reiteration is that no matter the time spent, or energy expounded, polishing a dead pig's pizzle will make not an iota of difference. It will remain just that, a dead dick.)

And so it was that Tristan, having received more polish than almost any other pizzle in history, was still a humongous disappointment to Daddy. Rugby should have given him a good leg-up in life, but it was not to be. He left school with educational results unprecedented in their mediocrity, even inferior to those attained by his now hero, Harry Flashman.

Finding employment was difficult. His devil-may-care temperament was not one that engendered confidence in anyone sitting in an employer's chair. Good fortune led Daddy to convince a friend to give Tristan an unpaid job in his City office. Rather than Tristan being remunerated, the reverse was true: Daddy coughed up what they described as an internment fee.

It took little time to display a level of clerical incompetence in order that no one in the place entrusted any form of serious work to him. Between making copies for the typists and having another brew, his life in the office was boring.

To ease the tedium, he photocopied his pecker with a fake ruler lying next to it: the inches were only half what they should have been. He distributed a copy to every female staff member. It shocked most, but not the elderly tea lady who felt stirred as she sat gazing at it in her little kitchen, while sucking on a dunked Ladyfinger biscuit from boardroom meeting leftovers. The image was a reminder of Norman, a flame of her youthful years. It was a surprise how the feelings she thought had dried up so long ago, caused her cheeks to glow and a delightful shiver to run down her spine.

Tristan felt it was deplorable that they fired him without a by your leave ceremony, or compensation of any kind. Although unpaid, he had expected a small pecuniary settlement, something to see him through to his next allowance. It was a puzzlement. . . how had they known it was his member imprinted upon unsigned white paper? With modesty, he surmised one or other of the girls must have recognised it, and recalled that mailroom Jane had been more impressed with his endowment than the rest.

Daddy blew his top. 'You useless twat! How can you get fired from a job when you're not even an employee? Not so long ago, I'd have dispatched you off to the colonies. It would've been the Raj for you – just another lazy, incompetent civil servant looking after half a dozen munshis, or chaiwalas. That's all you're bloody fit for, a cursed clerk in Calcutta. But, as we've abandoned sanity and given India back to those inept natives to bugger up, it's the army for you my boy. You're off to join the rest of the good-for-nothing sods who can't find work in the real world.' Daddy had never been one to mince words.

Not even Tristan could comprehend how he had scraped entry into the Royal Military Academy Sandhurst. Could be Daddy knew a general, or two. Maybe, it was Mummy? But more astonishment was to follow. Despite three reprimands – one being on C/O's orders for being so unfit that the sword was too heavy for him to carry on parade – he completed the training. His physical condition, and other setbacks, meant he was back-termed twice; hence the forty-four-week course lasted fifty-four.

At the midpoint, they required him to nominate a first and second choice of the Corps for which he considered himself suited. He'd contemplated an infantry regiment, but even in peacetime that's where danger lurks. It stands to reason, if one psychopath is being trained to kill another psychopath, accidents will happen. Also, there's all that foot stamping when pratting about on parade causing ankles and feet to swell, not to forget having to tote a cumbersome ceremonial sword. The final decider was that officers no longer blew Hudson whistles, or joined the fisticuffs with Webley six shooters, they've now to heave heavy guns like common foot soldiers. The infantry would be the last thing he'd ever join.

As many paintings depict, a Dragoon officer's uniform's dandy, but the days they hopped on and off a horse with a blunder dragon and sabre became extinct at Mons in nineteen fourteen. British High Command then found that thirsty nags were no match for Spandau water-cooled machine guns whizzing rounds off at five hundred a minute. How times have changed; nowadays a Dragoon's world consists of being roasted in a tin can while sniffing petrol fumes, sweaty armpits and the gunner's arse.

The Military Police, whilst not top of the list for any one of the other Sandhurst fellows, was on his, having garnered knowledge of the role from the film, *The Longest Day*. It was easy to figure out that the job was simple and safe. Like a policeman on traffic duty you stand at the crossroads directing the troops to the battlefront for slaughter and when they struggle back through the mud, point the way to the canteen, field hospital, or graveyard. Okay, there would be downsides, such as shooting malingerers and cowards, but he'd be up to that. Oh yes, life as a military policeman would be without doubt the safer option, and they wore a wonderful dress uniform, so he opted to be a Red Cap Officer.

His second was the Royal Army Medical Corps, or the Linseed Lancers to anyone who has ever felt a prick whilst in their hands. In choosing the RAMC as his alternative, he was being as shrewd as Eve's serpent; for it was incomprehensible that those in command of such matters would consider the Royal Army Medical Corps a suitable beneficiary of his enlistment.

Tristan's only anatomical knowledge was home-study gynaecology, which he'd addressed with vigour from early in life, but, aged fifteen, circumstances had forced him to take a breather.

Whilst in the middle of swotting up on the ins and outs of the matter in hand with cousin Fenella, her wretched fiancé, Caedmon Cockfoster, had, without a by your leave, barged in and halted his revision. First Cockfoster had thrashed him, then Daddy joined in the Donnybrook and everyone blamed him for the broken relationship. So, it figured that with not a mite of medical savvy, his candidacy for the Military Police was secure.

Thinking back to the *Charge of the Light Brigade*, or even worse, *Isandlwana*, one could not conclude that the British military were natural custodians of soundness of mind. It was, nonetheless, astonishing when they appointed him a Medical Support Officer in the Royal Army Medical Corps. He was both amazed and disappointed to be assigned a Lieutenant Linseed Lancer, but determined to make the most of the opportunity.

At least it was a unit safe from having to put your life on the line. There'd be endless mess dinners. He'd be attired in an eighteen-century dress uniform with idolising young girls clinging to his arm, desperate for his attention. On top of other jollities was the prospect of playing polo and squash, and enjoying utopian evenings of bridge.

But, even before his backside had touched a padded office chair, he was shocked to find himself dispatched to Scotland for Initial Training. The first part of his course was in 'Auld Reekie' as known by the locals or, by those fortunate enough not to have been born there, Edinburgh. But, despite the place swarming with Scots, his stay was more enjoyable than he'd anticipated.

There was an abundance of opportunity to dawdle on Princes Street keeping an eye out for the many red-haired beauties who unashamedly flirted with him. After bedding his fair share of the lasses, and watching Scottish television with subtitles, his understanding of the dialect became second nature. What had spurred Tristan into watching Scottish television with subtitles engaged was that soon after arriving in Edinburgh he'd felt tired, so spent an afternoon performing Egyptian PT. Upon awaking, he'd seen an Italian football captain being interviewed on the television, his English was impeccable, but then the Scottish captain gave his views on why he'd lost the game, 'Mah gang did thair best bit whin ye speil th' ref 'n' th' ither gang thir's na hawp.'

Later on, wanting to miss yet another deluge on a miserable Sunday afternoon, he and a bonnie lassie had dived into a museum on Chambers Street. On display was a historical photographic exhibition of Newhaven fishwives. Well-known for their fortitude, they looked wet, frozen stiff, and bloody wretched in their long woollen dresses and petticoats with great baskets of fish on their backs. It seemed beyond one's wildest dream that, in such a loathsome climate, any man would don a skirt, but Princes Street was full of retail merchants making their living selling tartan apparel. The pavements heaved with tourists. Men from every nationality under the sun jostled as they sought proof of a Scottish forebear, thus entitling them to wear a dress and escape from accusations of being closet queens. Of course, the ever-canny shopkeepers gleefully plucked the unwary would-be haggis bashers off the pavement and into their emporiums.

A shopkeeper's tout once grabbed him by the arm and was frog-marching him into the shop, but by then being well-versed in the vernacular he gave short shrift to the assaulter.

'Ye Scots prick, fin' someain else tae pit oan a body ay yer glaikit skirts.'

Although evading their clutches, he held Edinburgh shopkeepers in high regard. The deftness with which they extracted cash from the loose wallets of tourists was without parallel. The famous Harry Handcuff Houdini could not have accomplished it with any greater dexterity, he thought, observing the green stuff gallop, pell-mell, out of a patron's pocket into the peddlers' sporran. It was easy to imagine 'Manfred von Mandelbaum from Munchen' being shepherded into an emporium. The lederhosen-clad loony loser would Schuhplattler to Ein Prosit through the doors, but beyond the portals the canny Scot would spring the trap. Twenty minutes later Manfred would emerge with the ink still wet on a scroll confirming they had certified him as another member of the Clan MacDick. Regaled in full Highland dress, his blond hair under a polyvinyl ginger wig and gleaming new ghillie brogues reflecting in the puddles, Manny would march off playing Scotland the Brave on his Pakistan-made bagpipes.

Wizards, absolute geniuses!

All things end, be they good or bad. Tristan was sorrowful to leave the red-haired lassies behind but, even worse, were his Orders. He had to undertake battlefield casualty evacuation training; and under live fire. That was not in the plan! Further, it wasn't to be in Edinburgh, where the sun occasionally glimmered upon the globetrotters, but on a Ministry of Defence island next to Cape Wrath. The Isle was at the tip of Northwest Scotland where the boggy moors were as wet as a teenager's dream and as bleak as the silence in a coffin. Robbie Burns, the Bard of Ayrshire, must have had it in mind when he penned the immortal words, '*dark as misery's woeful night*'.

Fare Thee Weel, Thou First and Fairest!

(Robert Burns)

Upon his arrival those wise utterances, *'dark and woeful'* summed up Tristan's view of the training grounds. The nearest civilisation, if you could call Inverness civilised, was a five-hour trek away by boat and buses. Robbie's cautionary words about a girl from Inverness – *'The lovely lass o' Inverness, Nae joy, nor pleasure, can she see'* – failed to portend it to be a playground worthy of an excursion by any red-blooded fellow.

Practical Enlightenment, as they called it, took place on a day when the contents of sullen slate clouds spewed torrential rain upon a muculent mist clinging to a bleak grey moor, and summer hadn't even ended!

Tristan stood freezing in the driving rain, with a handful of junior officers and two dozen other ranks, being briefed on the planned revelries. The major, whose moustache and hairy eyebrows matched his khaki uniform, had a cloth band tied around his arm declaring him to be Chief Marshal. His clipped upper crust accent was not dissimilar to those of the officer classes in World War II films.

'Your task is to jolly well go into tha battle zone where you will find injured men, and even an injured totty, or two. Our make-up artists have applied some bloody horrible wounds, made me sick I can tell ya, so you'll apply a trauma wound dressing and move him, or hah, to safety and thence to ah field first-aid station. Now chaps, remember the words of that famous American, General Douglas MacArthur: *"Whoever said the pen is mightier than the sword never encountered automatic weapons."* Be aware, there will be loud explosions and live ammo from bags of ghastly ordnance, so keep your heads down, don't fancy having any accidents, goodness me no. Jolly good. Well, go forth and save the wounded, bring 'em beck against all the odds. You'll be issued with a Red Cross armband to wear, so the enemy knows yer a – what's the name? – yer know what. Dismiss.'

'Totty!' Tristan's ears had picked up on the word. So, amongst the cheerlessness, a snippet of good news: not only injured men but also skirt. Things could be on the up. He considered his orders. In a nutshell, they required him to find an 'injured' squaddie, drag the chump off the very realistic battlefield, while some rotten barbaric sod potted at him with a hideous semi-automatic rifle, or machine gun and threw bombs around the place. Not only that, but they demanded he stick a Red Cross advertisement on his arm heralding his being weaponless, and would not – even if shot at, blown up, or worse, perforated with a beastly bayonet – be able to reciprocate. Bloody preposterous! They must think him off his rocker. This was not the vocation he had contemplated, or for which he had enlisted. All in all, it sounded detrimental to health and well-being, far beyond what any sane person, whose purported mission was the preservation of humanity, should be expected to endure.

As an officer, Tristan felt he had a moral obligation to stay alive. Logically, if dead, there'd be no one to send the rest to get killed or, after the battle, to dress up all fine and dandy with rows of medals and proclaim how glorious it was to die. It seemed the dead were reticent to articulate on the merits of their condition, unless they planned to start a religious movement. No, sacrificing oneself seemed a complete waste of time. Having established dying held no part in success; he laid out his battlefield strategy. First, find a piece of totty with, hopefully, play-play chest wounds. Then, having assessed the injury, apply a dressing and thereafter find a hideaway to pass the day out of harm's way; a simple but perfect plan.

He moved into the search area and soon fell into a crater with sides of slimy mud and a well of urine-scented water. After extracting himself, he clambered over barbed wire and took a header into a trench. It was hell. Bullets whizzed overhead and thunderflashes, smoke, and even phosphorous grenades exploded all around. He steered clear of the 'injured' male soldiers who were screaming as if seeking roles in B-grade movies, let them rot.

His objective was a gentle totty with perhaps the lightest of whimpers; but the search for a piece of skirt was taking forever and a day. As he plunged into yet another boghole that would have made a Turkish squat toilet smell balmy, he felt more dispirited than a eunuch in a harem. Slithering up the slimy side, his thoughts turned to how happier he would be with his Purdey loaded, at the ready to blast the arse out of a grouse or two.

On the crater's rim he paused and looked around at the quagmire of a shell-holed landscape. He concluded that even grouse, as stupid as they are, would rather divert to an alternative landing strip than chance a go-around and still get shellacked crashing on this shitty taxiway of a disgusting hellhole called a wet infantry training ground.

The lashing rain had turned the already bleak terrain even bleaker. It was now a cold, obnoxious swamp that the Scots, not known for their discernment, would still call 'hame'.

The bleakest of God's towns on the bleakest of God's bays, was how one of the famous sons of Scotland, Robert Lewis Stevenson, described his home in Scotland while attempting an escape to America. It was in that bustling New World city he suffered flashbacks of his earlier life and found therapy in penning the euphoric story, Dr Jekyll and Mr Hyde. Then the poor fellow found that even New York was too close to 'hame' so set sail for Samoa where he eventually found eternal rest under 'the wide starry sky'.

In the misty gloom, Tristan spotted what he'd been seeking: a bit of skirt sprawling in the mud. A gambol in the goo will see you on your way, my girl, he thought rushing, as fast as the boglach would allow, lest he be beaten to the totty. The sight of the injuries inflicted upon the wretch were so realistic that they made Tristan heave, but, even worse, it flabbergasted him to see that it wasn't totty but a ginger jobby in a kilt. A quick assessment decided him that it was abundantly clear the tosser was a lost cause and would soon be dead. The film *The Longest Day* again sprang into Tristan's mind. 'Now listen, Jock, I'll give you an imaginary shot of morphine so you won't notice any pain and then drag you back for burial.'

The man responded, 'Whit ur ye sayin?'

Tristan removed a flask from his coat and took a swig of Scotch, it helped him speak in the vernacular. 'Cannae ye ken Sassenach ye hielan boaby? Ah said seen ye'r sa badly injurred ye wid die anyway sae ah will juist drag ye back fur burial.'

The man pleaded for a nipper-kin of Tristan's toddy, saying, 'Geeza a dram!'

Tristan laughed, 'A dram! Ye cannae! Wi' yer wounds it would leak thro' the bloody holes!' And he set about dragging the worthless half-wit back.

Explosions assaulted Tristan's ears with thunderflashes exploding to the left and right, while the crack of rifles sent their projectiles zinging dangerously close to him. Dragging the Gay Gordon by his webbing through the slimy sludge was backbreaking. For what seemed an eternity they were in and out of ditches and trenches, or entangled in barbed wire. Meanwhile, all the ungrateful malcontent dead-weight wounded warrior could do was to whimper and whine. The barrage of thunderflashes and phosphorus grenades intensified causing carnage to his eardrums and, facing extinction from the live rounds winging overhead, he stopped in a sodden pool of mud for a rest. A further swig of whisky was most welcome.

Why the devil am I here? he reflected. It's worse than dreadful, it's the bottomless pit of purgatory. Another hit by Robbie Burns sprang to mind: Drumossie moor, Drumossie day a waefu' day it was to me!

Just listening to himself recite the lines left him feeling more wretched. The snivelling wretch of a Jock Juggin dressed in a ludicrous multicoloured frock wasn't helpful, as the barbed wire kept hooking the wool making lugging the laggard difficult, and the nitwit did diddly-naught to mollify the nightmare. Until recently, Tristan thought only tasteless individuals wore such fancy dress, but here he was dragging a red-haired gruel-gobbling Highland dick, garbed in bloody wedding wardrobe, through such wretchedness. He decided to seek the man's assistance.

'I know they told you to act as if your injuries make you incapable of assisting yourself, but can't you at least help me? Surely sanity should take precedence over stupidity?'

The Jock asked, 'Whit ur ye sayin'?'

'Forget it!' Tristan responded, taking another sip from his flask. It's been the devil's own luck to find this one, he thought. Perhaps if I sat the fellow up someone might shoot him, but that would mean dragging the body back. What happened to the totty? The major said there were female casualties. Other lucky devils are probably mud wrestling as I wallow here.

'How long have you been in the infantry?'

'Whit ur ye sayin?'

Tristan took another swig and used the vernacular, 'Hoo lang hae ye bin in th' bloody army?'

The Jock responded, 'Fifteen years.'

'Why did you join?' said Tristan.

Seeing the man's eyes glaze over with miscomprehension, he changed into the indigenous lingo again, 'Wit gart ye sign up for?'

The Juggin answered, 'Tae learn a trade.'

'To learn a trade is it? Better that than staying on the dole I suppose. What's yer trade?'

'Machine gunner.'

'Machine gunner!' Tristan blurted out. 'A bloody machine gunner ye say! That's a guid trade fur a Saturday nicht in th' toon centur.'

'Fowk respect me,' the Juggin said.

'Aye, ah bet thay dae,' Tristan added, resuming his tugging and hauling of the infantryman through the quagmire. It took but a few more minutes before the Scottish rat of a toss-bag's wretch became entangled in barbed wire again. By now the artificial battle wounds applied by the military make-up artists had turned into blood-soaked reality.

'Mah shank, mah shank ye'r hurting mah shank!'

'I say, I am sorry old chap if I'm damaging your leg. Soon have you released, what, what!' Tristan mocked.

Despite his efforts, it was futile. The more Tristan struggled to free him, the more ensnared the Jock became. His sporran and the oversized safety pin holding the picnic blanket around his waist had become entangled in the spiky wire. It was when Tristan tried one last tug that the man fell upside down, and gravity caused the pleated plaid to lift. Tristan was then confronted by a naked sallow crotch, somewhat resembling an insipid plucked chicken thigh camouflaged with curly ginger hair. Ignoring the shrieks, he tried to extricate the man from the spikes, but the ginger groin acted like a magnet to the ferrous thorns. The arrow-shaped barbarous fangs masticated upon his pelvic girdle; his screams not dissimilar to those of a Pan troglodyte.

'Mah baws, mah baws, canny mah baws!' the man shrieked.

'You ungrateful self-centred sod! Have you not seen the state of my clothes? You've ruined my kit. I'm as freezing as a harlot's heart, soaked as a sewer rat and all you can do is to think of yourself. If you wore a pair of drawers like the rest of humanity, the barbs wouldn't have skewered your ballocks!'

But despite Tristan's continued struggle, the moaning gnashnab's head became entangled.

'Mah heid, mah heid! Be cannie ye Sassenach dobber, yoo'll pull ay mah heed an aw as mah baws.'

'That's it! That's it! First, I'm an English bastard hell-bent on pulling your idiotically piddling balls off. Now it's your bloody head!'

Tristan changed to the vernacular, 'Tak at ye slimy piece ay cuddie jobby,' and gave the useless featherbrained curd a slap he wouldn't easily forget. 'Ye volunteered ye Scots pillock, ye kin crawl back intae yer nook oan yer ain,' doling out a farewell wallop.

'Don't lea me tae die ye Sassenach bas,' were the final screams Tristan heard from the snivelling struggling drag queen, ensnared headfirst in barbed wire.

Even without the hindrance of the malcontent, he squirmed at a snail's pace through the filthy fog and oozing sludge. The ever-present danger of lethal projectiles made his progress seem longer than dawn breaking on a Scottish winter's morn.

* * *

But, back in his quarters, solace arrived in a glass of the only decent thing to come out of Scotland, other than grouse and bonny red-haired lassies. *Old Pulteney*. It was, in his opinion, the finest whisky to have passed his lips. It took but a few drams to purge the purgatory and revive his devil-may-care disposition.

Before going to the mess for evening drinks, he made sure to leave a measure of Jock Juggins blood on his face. With an added touch of tomato sauce, the mirror displayed handiwork that any military make-up artist would be happy to sign. Upon arrival in the bar, the other junior offices were aghast at the blood upon his personage. Brushing it aside as, 'Oh, it's nothing, all in a day's work,' and feigning the sycophantic la-di-da accent of the chinless turgid toads, he took no time recounting his discovering of an injured soldier.

'Salt of the earth, that's what he was, goodness me! I'm awfully sorry to say, but they unwittingly shot the poor fellow, through the thigh don't you know. When I came upon the chappie, ne'er gave a thought to him being a Scot and treated him as I would one of us. Seeing the wound, I stuck my ring finger in the hole ta stem the flow of femoral claret, the bullet was easy to find, still hot, pulled it out.'

Triumphantly, he held his finger aloft with tomato sauce clinging to it. 'The wretched devil was in spiffing pain, screaming to high heavens. Begged me to put him down, out of his misery – done it a few times with field hunters, don't you know. One ends their misery if one can. To him I replied, 'Can't do that, my good fellow.' I said, 'You're not an old nag, nor ready for the knacker's yard, you're English – well almost. Be of stout heart; up you come my lad.' And I lifted him onto my shoulder and carried the miserable chap just a few miles – I imagine it be less than four, at the most five, or six – to the field hospital.'

He sipped his drink; his audience hanging enthralled upon his every word.

'Goes without saying, dodging live rounds wasn't easy. Had to stop twice, under fire, to administer a precordial thump to treat the unfortunate fellow for ventricular fibrillation' – he thought he had heard that in a lecture. 'Was a bit anxious. Thought I'd lost him once. Just about to bury the poor soul, when I said to myself: Try one more time. And he came round. We made it and that's all that counts, don't you know.' He looked to the sky as if giving thanks to some greater being who had provided a small measure of help and guidance.

A sycophantic admirer deferentially speculated, 'One has to say, Tristan old chap, you doubtlessly saved the poor man's life.'

Others nodded in agreement.

Tristan said humbly, 'Oh, one doesn't know, can't say. Probably saved his leg, but well, to be honest, the doctors mentioned something about his life.'

They rapturously celebrated his fortitude, clapped him on the back, shook his hand, while praising his courage, heroism and endeavour in saving the man. Accepting the celebratory drinks offered, Tristan responded with the greatest modesty he could muster, 'Any of you would've done the same, no matter the man's station in life, or even his nationality.'

In the mess on the following day, while enjoying a Gin and Tonic, he heard fellow officers talking of how they had volunteered for a search party the previous night.

'Out seeking a lost soldier,' they said.

Tristan had no recollection of a call for volunteers and, anyway, Goddess Nyx had spotted his inebriation and offered her solace of a dreamless sleep.

'Chalky White found the man in the early hours of the morning on the boggy moor,' reported one fellow.

'A Private, Cameronian rifles,' agreed a deep voice.

Someone else piped up, 'Chalky said the barbed wire had entangled the hapless chap upside down, can you believe it? Apparently, his bare testicles had been the main attraction for midges all night.'

'And his head was nearly under the mud. Hardly alive, delirious,' declared another.

Someone else said, 'Rambling incomprehensibly, according to the medical orderlies.'

Yet another, 'I know a male nurse,' Tristan suspected as much, 'and when they took the fellow into hospital, he was in an advanced state of delirium.'

'That's true,' added Lieutenant Xavier Bellevue. 'I was the orderly officer last night. Took his statement, as best

I could, though couldn't understand a word, so I wrote it verbatim. Tell you what, I'll read it to you. Not good with languages but shall do my best.' He took the paper from his pocket. 'Here goes, chaps. He says, "*A rotten Sassenach bas boaby skelp me 'n' left me tae die. Th' dobber left me wi' mah balls as a naked bairn fur midges tae feed oan aw nicht.*" That's it! Absolute gibberish, beyond comprehension.'

Tristan thought Xavier's enunciation excellent and asked, 'May I read the man's words please?' Xavier handed him the paper. After reading, he placed it in his pocket, closed his eyes, and sobbed with uncontrollable grief, 'It was me, and I'm sorry chaps. I confess it was me. I left him there all night. It was I who nearly killed the poor fellow.'

The lieutenant, a friend of the male nurse, put his arm around Tristan. 'There, there, my old son. Surely you can't be to blame, you saved the other one.'

'I am guilty,' Tristan lamented, removing the man's limp arm. 'It was me what left him. If the rain and mist hadn't been so skew-whiff, I might have observed the poor chap. I could have carried him back. After all, I had a spare shoulder. Didn't I?' The fantasy of his own words brought tears to his eyes, and he sobbed convulsively.

But his fellow officers would have none of it and voiced their opinions vociferously.

Lieutenant Danforth Jackshaft stepped forward, 'I'm sure I speak for every man here, even the whole of humanity,' he looked around at the smiling faces, 'when I say, I mean, we all declare, well done old chap. You are an exceptional and faithful servant of mankind. What a cracker! No one could have done more; you're a spiffing hero who deserves a medal.' They roared, bashed their glasses and fists on the tables, shouting, 'Hear! Hear!', and spontaneously sang, 'For he's a jolly good fellow.' Amid the applause, were cries of, 'Victoria Cross.'

Dismissing their adulation for as long as seemed decent, Tristan finally succumbed to the endless free rounds of Gin and Tonic.

When he was as drunk as a jumbo on marula fruit, the fawning worshippers hoisted the heroic charlatan above their heads and toted him off to his quarters to be bedded down for the rest of the day and night. He awoke when a thumping good chunk of the following day had passed.

The Jock's 'Service Complaints Form JSP 831' that Tristan had pocketed was deposited in the camp's septic tank with the rest of the crap.

For a Canter on a High Horse

After completing his training, he was posted to the south of England and there became a member of an admin team of non-medical staff shuffling doctors and nurses around the globe. 'Eeny, meeny, miny, moe.' Tristan considered the four names in front of him and decided, without malice aforethought, upon 'meeny'. Captain Berrycloth.

He signed the papers that would consign the youthful captain to an unaccompanied desert posting for two years.

Looking through the file, he noticed the official photograph of the handsome officer, and noted a wife and two young kids, and he mused that they would keep the little lady busy while the boss lives it up in the dunes. Although the plot was by now vague, he recalled that as a child Nanny had read to him about the French foreign legion, it was a book called Beau Geste. A smile crossed his lips as he fitted the captain into the story. Berrycloth was the medical officer of a desert fortress under attack by hundreds, if not thousands, of Arabs. The Welsh quartermaster had done a runner, taking the medical supplies which he'd flogged to a Frenchman who'd sold them to the Arabs. Despite his not having even an aspirin, the doc tried his best to save the wounded, even using a length of rubber pipe, taken from the braking system of an old truck, to give his own blood for transfusions to a dozen or more. But, notwithstanding his ingenuity and dedication, the entire garrison, including his brothers, were dead. He was the sole survivor facing a continuous onslaught upon the British bastion. A fine fellow if ever there was one, ripped the Red Cross from his arm and raced around the fortifications propping up the deceased soldiers.

The Bedouins – or were they Tuaregs? It didn't matter – couldn't believe their eyes. Day after day they'd been shooting the infidels, but were still facing the entire British army on the ramparts. Captain Berrycloth continued sprinting round the stronghold faster than a Cassowary's kick, pulling the triggers on rifles held by his dead comrades. Hundreds, no, thousands, of charging Arabs, slain by one man, Doctor Berrycloth. After the depleted enemy had surrendered, the weary physician would then sit on his haunches in a Mesopotamian black tent with the now friendly Bedouin chieftain. A Nubian slave girl, dressed in almost nothing, would flick off the flies while feeding him on sand-covered sheep's eyes and sticky dates. She'd then serve him the first decent cup of tea he'd had for weeks, because Jock Juggins had poisoned the Fort well by peeing into it. The captain would return to Blighty, get a VC, thank Tristan for his posting, and put his wife, who Tristan in the interim had had an affair with, up the spout for the third time before being promoted major. Tristan sat back and thanked his lucky stars he wasn't going to a similar rotten place, Nubian slave girl or not.

There is no craft more antediluvian than that perfected over millennia by the British Tommy. They call it, skiving. In no time flat, Tristan became a grand master of indifference to any industrious labour. Not only did he polish to perfection those commonly practised skills of idleness, but rediscovered several ancient techniques considered lost. In short order, he identified chameleonism and skiving to be as conspiratorial as promiscuity is to

STIs, as illustrated in the ghastly films he'd been forced to watch during training, with the warning from the MO, 'Don't want you down with crotch crickets, or the clap.'

He'd been in the post for four months with not a lumen of his superior's spotlight falling upon him. If, heaven forbid, a famishment for work had entered his grey matter, it really would have been more exhausting finding himself an endeavour, never mind carrying one out. In times of peace there's nothing to do. It's obvious: conflicts keep an army busy and provides fame for its commanders. Military heroes would be unheard of, and, if it were not for war, no MCs, VCs, Bars, or scars. So, what does the army do with soldiers when they've got no one to kill? Simple, they invent things. That very day, Unit Orders: Part One: 2.3. said, '*There will be a tour of the establishment by a Middle Eastern potentate,*' etc.

Despite the date being one month hence, it required preparation, and would give a small measure of work to Tristan who would tell the sergeant who would direct the corporal who would bawl at the lance corporal who would scream at the privates to clean up the place.

After which Tristan would inspect the work, tell the sergeant that he wasn't happy, and so on, it could take days or even weeks to complete. The climax of the visit was to be a cocktail party in the officers' mess.

Tristan looked forward to wearing his rarely worn full mess kit. When dressed in such attire, it was essential to have the correct accoutrement clinging to your arm. The choice of a frame had oft upstaged many a work of art. He recalled the Hunt Ball six months before at Nutsfield Manor when cousin Casper had had a pretty filly clinging to his arm. She was about the correct height, had a splendid figure and would round off – but not draw attention away from – his image. Calling cousin Casper elicited the girl's telephone number and her calling card being posted to him. Casper said she was quite a goer. Although Tristan had never met her, he knew the family and decided she'd be his escort. On dialling the number, her mother answered, so Tristan asked her to tell the daughter of the date, and where to meet him.

Upon reflection, it was a touch of narcissism that gave Tristan a thought. Protocol decreed junior officers would be introduced to the visiting camel herder, so he decided to learn a few words in the desert dweller's lingo. How marvellous! The other officers would not only salivate after the delightful filly, but be jealous of his prowess when he spoke in the potentate's patois; just a smidgen would suffice. Within days of his order, an Arabic audio course arrived. With stacks of time on hand, and aided by a pair of headphones he'd pinched from the telephonist's desk, he began learning the language, finding it more enjoyable than he'd expected. Within two weeks his linguistic abilities had far exceeded his expectation, and there was even time left for more study.

On the day of the Sheikh's visit, Tristan thought how much easier it'd be if he had a fag, like the insect creature he'd called Bugsy at Rugby. Servants made life less burdensome, but sanity had given way to lunacy and the army had abandoned the fine tradition of an officer's batman. Not having a manservant meant he had the wearisome task of laying out his own uniform on the bed to make sure he'd forgotten nothing. Marcella dress shirt, silk bow tie, tight-fitting navy-blue barathea trousers with a cherry maroon stripe, maroon vest, dark navy-blue doeskin jacket with maroon lapels decorated with the distinctive Rod of Asclepius insignia, black socks and handmade patent leather George boots. For the outfit, the tailor had charged three thousand pounds to Daddy's account.

When dressed, he marvelled at the glorious image in the full-length mirror. Viewed from every angle, the reason for his magnetic appeal to women was obvious.

Striding from his quarters, he threw back his shoulders and, with head held high, proceeded to where his escort, Penelope Ponsonby-Pierson, would await his arrival. Penelope's mother had instructed her well, for she was just where he had declared she should wait: on the bench beneath the lilac tree at the entrance to the mess. Such a lucky girl, he thought. With no apologies for being late by nearly twenty minutes, a quick kiss on the cheek had been her reward for patience. 'You look dashingly handsome,' was her response. 'Yes, the colours suit me somewhat,' he acknowledged, leading her by the arm. She and a friend had spent hours trolling Mayfair before purchasing her dress from a small understated fashion boutique. There was no resentment at not receiving any accolades from her beau as she, too, considered herself lucky to be invited to enjoy his company for the evening, and her mother had winked and had said he was a good catch, so she must look after him.

The Victorian-period mess comprised a large dining room, smoking lounge, library, games' room with card tables and a billiard table with carved elephant tusk balls. The junior officers and their invited female partners were assembled around the games area, drinking whisky, gin, and vermouth, served from jugs carried around by lower-ranked white coated squaddies, whilst senior officers entertained the Middle Eastern guest in the library.

Penelope was from the south-coast Ponsonby-Piersons, pleasant and pretty but, like the whole family, as thick as flies around a cow turd in a midsummer meadow. She thought he looked slim and dashing; the costume much the same as worn in films she'd seen about the Raj. The prospect of spending the night with him was most exciting. Perhaps he'd wear bits of his uniform in bed. Harold the Household Cavalry officer had, but she'd drawn the line at spurs and breastplate. It was gratifying to see Tristan's outfit had no such bits of sharp stuff.

The room was stifling and the ancient ceiling fans did little to disperse the cigar and cigarette smoke. Spotting that the other ladies in the group had cast aside theirs, Penelope removed the shawl that her father had demanded she wore, 'for the sake of decency', he'd said. Her mother had whispered to dump it when she got there. It wasn't the low-cut dress but her pair of gravity defying pearlescent orbs with pendants of perspiration twinkling in the light that riveted Tristan's peepers. The other gals were envious for, with barely a peek, theirs were put back under wrap leaving not a tad of tittie touted. She was far more stunning than Tristan recalled and, like rutting Suffolk stags, the other fellows now vied for her attention.

The speed at which the glasses were refilled had resulted in Penelope's rapid inebriation, hotly pursued by Tristan's. Soon the whimsical jokes and banter that had previously raised a polite smile became risqué, and accompanied by raucous laughter.

It was nigh on seven forty-five when the Commanding Officer brought the swarthy, youthful, white-robed figure into the room. The men fell silent and sprang to attention.

Tristan remarked, a scant too loud, 'Lawrence of Arabia's arrived chaps.'

Penelope found it as hilarious as only a drunk could and, throwing her head back, whinnied in the manner of a mare meeting a mate in the covering yard. Sadly, the action induced a nauseous reaction and, staggering to the open window, the very well-tended herbaceous borders received an unwelcomed discharge. The delightful Hummingbird Hyssop and Summer Phlox were the most affected, as they at once drooped under the weight.

Upon her re-entry, it was plain for all to see that her ample left hooter had slipped anchor and popped from its moorings. The room fell silent. All eyes were upon her, or rather upon her appendage; the men ogling and the women turning green with envy. The Sheikh showed a particular interest in the visage of a burqa-free boob. Confronted by an unshackled Charlie, the blue bloods turned into an unruly run of Sockeye Salmon. Several gallant officers sprang to her aid and were fighting amongst themselves to manhandle her honker into its depository. Many hands make light work – or is it too many cooks? – whichever, she continued to whinny, thus foiling their fumbling.

Seeing things were getting out of hand Tristan legged it over to the robed figure and bowed slightly and placed his right hand upon his heart saying, '*As-salaam 'alaykum, masaa al-khayr*'

'*Wa 'alakumas-salaam*,' the potentate responded.

Taking Penelope's calling card from his pocket, he passed it to the Emir and then, continuing in Arabic, Tristan said, 'She's a nymphomaniac and that's her phone number.'

The Sheikh looked at it, 'Thanks, she's got a great pair. I'll contact her. Known her long?'

'No, this is the first evening,' said Tristan. 'She's a friend of my cousin's, but, as you say, an impressive pair of hooters.'

The Sheikh laughed, and they passed a few more pleasantries.

Touching his heart once again Tristan said, '*Ma' al-salāmah.*'

Having said goodbye to the Emir, he nodded to the stunned CO and strode back to his quarters with anonymity forfeited for a canter on a high horse.

The next morning, his twentieth birthday, began cheerfully enough, even more pleasantly than normal. Before breakfast, he had trounced a sweaty overweight captain, having him run around the squash court like a one-legged man in an arse-kicking contest. Then, following a shower, his breakfast had been extraordinary, scrambled eggs on top of two kippers. Although it made him burp and produced several regurgitated meals for the rest of the morning, it was delightful. Wandering to his office, he found a single birthday card. It had a racing car with a bottle of Champagne on the front; the typewritten note said '*From Mummy*'.

A little later the major dropped into Tristan's office for a 'chat'. Beneath the mountainous smokescreen of papers kept on his desk for just such a situation, Tristan submerged the crossword within two flickers of the CO's eyelids.

'Well, morning Crooke-Wells. I say, who was the young lass in the mess last evening?'

'I'm awfully sorry, but to which of the young lasses do you refer, sir?'

'The one with you, the lovely gal, she was feeling a bit off.'

'Goodness me! Are you referring to the one who uncovered her knocker, sir?'

'Of course she's the one I'm referring to. The one with you.'

'Me! Awfully sorry, but the lovely gal ain't known to me. I thought she came with Lieutenant Breckinshaw.' He was a pompous contemptible rat whom Tristan loathed, an excellent reason to give him the problem. 'Can't say she's my type, sir, prefer 'em with a spot of intellect, don't you know. Far too vulgar, can't have a totty take her jugs out in public. Goodness me, no class. But you know what, sir, it was an admirable evening.'

This seemed to satisfy the old man who said that His Highness had been most amused and considered the young woman to be exquisite. 'Tell me, old chap, where did you learn to speak Arabic? It was absolutely top hole, I have to say.'

With as much modesty as he could muster, Tristan said he knew only a smattering, just a few phrases, as he'd spent a scant few moments reading up on it. 'Not fluent at all. My Russian's better, but Mandarin's always been one's favourite since Mummy read me Chinese Nursery Rhymes.' He spoke neither language. Nanny was the only one to read him rhymes and she was very English, believing anyone born north of London was foreign.

The CO seemed impressed. 'What did His Highness and you discuss?'

Tristan explained the Sheikh and he shared an interest in the poetry of Omar Khayyám, from his early years before he became commercial.

'The Moving Finger writes; and, having writ, moves on,' quoted the CO. 'Sorry to say, old chap, I don't know any more. I suppose being an Arabic scholar you'll know the rest?'

Tristan had heard the drivel before, but had assumed it to be a Shakespearean ditty; it sounded like the rubbish he wrote. Thinking hard, he said, 'It's almost impossible to translate this particular piece into English without destroying Khayyám's intent. I will therefore complete it in Arabic.' He cast his mind back to lesson one of the American-produced, Jerabek's Arabic for Travellers in Thirty Easy Lessons, he hoped it was correct. '*Hal yumkinuni tanawul kubin min alquhwat faqat min fadlik, 'atamanaa lak ywmaan seydaan.*' Placing his right hand over his heart, he looked wistfully at the CO, who'd just heard, 'May I have two cups of coffee please, have a nice day.'

'Well, that was smashing, so, ah, so lyrical,' the CO said. 'Yes, that's what it is, it's lyrical. You must be jolly well-pleased being enabled to communicate in such a manner, goodness me. You say his name's Breckinshaw? I'll keep an eye on him, must go, carry on.'

Upon the major's departure, Tristan unearthed the crossword from beneath the camouflage in double quick time, wanting to complete it before luncheon.

It was unfortunate he had not read Omar's quatrain – As for honour and fame, let that brittle glass be dashed to pieces against the earth – as it pretty well summed up the rest of his military career.

Later a telephone call distracted him from the clue for twelve down, it was his Commanding Officer. He said that he was in an important meeting, and Tristan must go to his house where he'd find documents, marked confidential, on the study desk. They contained information he needed. When found, he was to call the CO back. His wife wasn't answering the phone.

'She'll be in the garden, tell her to call me, to let you in,' he'd said.

Twelve down: Something precious in the Chamber? Got it: Amber! He wrote it down before departing.

The motor-pool sergeant, highly suspicious of young subalterns driving military vehicles, but having no drivers available, reluctantly supplied a soft-top Land Rover and directions to the house. The NCO was wise to be cautious, for Tristan broke almost all military driving regulations and public highway laws by tearing the arse out of the domain as he cleaved a path through the countryside. Pheasants, rabbits and muntjac, all reluctant to play Dunlop Derby, were sent running for their lives.

After dispatching two of the clueless creatures into zoological Xanadu, he reached the house: an isolated and rather imposing converted barn. His yank on the heavy rusted chain provoked a far-off bell to sound. He stood waiting, but nobody came, a second and third yank yielded the same result. As the major had been adamant Tristan must call him back, he considered there to be a measure of urgency.

Following the path into the rear garden he saw a woman, doubtless the major's wife, lying on her back wearing only earphones and an eye mask. 'As naked as a Norfolk dumpling', is how John Day would have described her, thought Tristan, for she was a wholesome-looking filly, pleasingly plump. He couldn't say it was a second glance, for he had not taken his eagle eyes off her once, but upon further examination 'filly' was incorrect. This one's more in the manner of a ripened Norman Cob. That extra morsel of weight made her unlike the raw-boned malnourished twig insects who'd been his companions of late.

After a few minutes of ogling, he beat a retreat to the Land Rover where he sat honking his horn. The noise must have entered her reverie, for a head soon poked around the side of the house. She strolled over, draped in floral chiffon, and confirmed she was the major's wife.

'Lieutenant Crooke-Wells, madam.' He introduced himself holding her hand, and eyes, for just that bit longer than needs be. He explained why the major had sent him.

'I'm sure you understand,' she said, 'but I must confirm it with my husband. Please wait.'

Returning after a few minutes she said, 'I'm sorry to keep you waiting. Security is a pain, but I had to make sure. Come I'll show you to the study.'

Tristan had a good view of her rather shapely rump whilst being led to the study.

'You know what he requires, so please excuse me if I leave you to it,' she said.

It took but minutes to find the information and then to call the major from the phone on the desk. The task accomplished, he called out to say he'd finished.

The wife popped her head around the door. 'I was just about to have a glass of iced lemonade, its home made, make it myself, would you care for one?'

'Rather. . . on a jolly hot day like this, I do fancy. It'll be delightful.'

'Take a seat on the terrace and I'll bring the drinks out,' she said.

They sat chatting, or at least she did, asking many questions, including how old he was. He said, 'Twenty-two today.' It sounded worldlier than twenty. He estimated her as a bit older than dear Mummy. Looking around, he expressed his admiration of the garden and house.

She responded, 'But you've only seen the study. Would you care to see the rest? I'm sure you'll find it top-hole.'

'Absolutely,' he said.

As a CO's wife had influence over her husband, one wrong word could risk her stymieing his career and have him shuffled off to an isolated wilderness, such as the desert with Capt. Berrycloth or, even worse, back to Scotland.

'Come,' she said leading him to the sunroom with its huge windows through which Tristan viewed green pastures, spreading out seemingly forever before touching the sky in a seamless vista. 'Exquisite. Smashing view,' was his response.

'Let me show you our snooker room. It's my husband's favourite, it's a man's room,' she said, leading him by the arm. 'I'm sure you'll love it.'

She was correct. Although windowless it was a magnificent central feature of the property. Tristan ran his hands over the polished-oak antique billiard table supported by eight carved octagonal legs.

'It's an antique dating from eighteen twenty, made by the same craftsman who supplied Napoleon when he was incarcerated on the island of St. Helena,' she told him.

'It's brilliant,' he said, feasting his eyes on it in admiration. Six antique pendent billiard lamps were equally impressive, above which oak beams soared seemingly ever upwards until vanishing into a vast pitch-dark chasm.

'Do you play snooker?' she asked.

'We play billiards in the mess, but I prefer snooker.'

'I also prefer snooker. Shall we have a quick game? Algernon won't play with me anymore.'

Tristan had heard senior officers referring to the major as Al. . . but Algernon! That's a snort. He checked the time and thought it a spiffing idea as he could still get back for lunch and a nap.

Using the mahogany triangle, he first set the fifteen in the racked group, ending with the cue ball in the baulk half circle. Turning around, he was astounded to see she was now more naked than when he'd first spotted her on the lawn, for the earphones and eye mask had been discarded.

'Happy Birthday, big boy.'

Wasting not a second, she threw herself upon the snooker table where Tristan, his cue quickly chalked and ready, set about what was, after all, his forte in life: coital callisthenics. The balls were soon flying with arms and legs flailing like the sails of a windmill on the Dordrecht Dijk. With a couple of backspins on the baize and a bounce off the cushions she'd almost reached the maximum break of one four seven, but potted white a little early.

A roar in Tristan's ears drowned her squalls, squawks, and squeals, as rough hands grasped his sweating buttocks uprooting him like a sapling from a swale.

'Algernon! You're home early, dear,' she gasped, lying prostrated and panting upon the green baize. Tristan thought the olive hue matched her rather beautiful eyes.

The CO bellowed, 'What the hell are you doing on my snooker table?'

'Terribly sorry sir, but not to worry, it's not much of a dog's dinner,' Tristan blurted out. 'Shan't take long, sure it'll clean up just like fancy new.'

'Put ah sock in it, you stupid fellow. I'm talking to my wife,' the major declared angrily, turning back to her. 'I thought we had a damned agreement.'

'Agreement! What agreement? It's what-oh for you to bring your boyfriends here, but I mustn't have my amusements, must I?

'Not here, nor with one of my officers. Jolly bad show,' he bawled.

'What about my frocks?' she screeched.

Turning to Tristan, she said quite matter-of-factly, 'I had two cracking dresses, both new, I looked at them this morning, he's so fat he's ruined them, and my underwear.'

At Algernon she shrieked, 'I know you think you look dishy in my clothes, well, let me tell you, you don't! You're a shapeless lump of fat shit.'

'I'm fat! I'm fat! Why don't you go and have a butcher's in a looking glass? If you fancy looking at a bit of blubber, jolly well go take a gander at yourself,' he bellowed.

Tristan, feeling he couldn't allow such ungallant comments to besmirch a lady, chimed in, 'I say old chap, have a care for what you assert. Well-padded, I'd suggest, but not fat.'

'Mind your own business,' the major shouted. 'If I consider her fat, she's bloody obese.'

'And you're as boring as bat shit,' she screamed.

Tristan thought the spectacle of her standing stark naked while exchanging vociferous altercations was exquisite as her body wobbled delightfully. Feeling that as they'd imparted ample information to offer him a 'get out of jail free card', if required, he dressed and hot-footed it from the house.

After resting, and an early dinner, his final thoughts before dropping off to a peaceful night's sleep were how lucky it had been to find such a game old bird on his birthday. A cut above any gift he'd ever received and, what's more, hard to recall if he'd ever had a more cracking canter. It was a pity Algernon got home early for, after catching her breath, he was sure she'd have been up for another gallop, or two.

The next morning just as he reached the clue for eight across – A Priest from the East – a call came for him to go to the major's office. A knock on the CO's door elicited a quick and cheerful response to enter. Tristan marched up to the desk, stood at attention and saluted, his salute was waved away.

'Forget the formalities old chap, take a seat if you will.'

Tristan feeling insolently brazen used the major's first name. 'Can I help you with anything, Algernon?' he said, sprawling across the chair.

The CO smiled. 'Now, old bean, we're both men of the world and one needs to ask for your understanding. It's about yesterday's palaver. The boss, that is Sandra, wasn't feeling herself.'

Tristan knew it to be a fact as he'd had that joyful task, but it was nice to know her name was Sandra; he'd try not to forget it.

'Sometimes she gets carried away, does frivolous things, it runs in the family, don't you know,' he continued, 'her mother's just the same.'

'I say, Algernon, sounds spiffing, a game old banger, is she?' Now versed in the qualities of an experienced older woman Tristan was keen to consider all such opportunities. Not eliciting a response, he continued, 'Now, look you here, old chap, if I could just get away for a spot of furlough, I'm jolly sure well on nigh every detail would be consigned to oblivion, or as close as it jolly well needs be, almost certain it would.'

'How long do you suggest your memory requires?' the CO asked, taking the leave form from his drawer.

'Ah, shall we say two weeks?' Tristan paused. 'But, just in case of flashbacks, or PTSD, how about three?'

The CO obligingly granted Tristan three weeks leave.

At his Brighton hotel, a most delightful girl, Irena from Slovenia, serviced both him and his room. As lovely as she and Brighton were, after a week he felt quite down in the dumps. It seemed ridiculous to waste time savouring ice cream cones in Brighton when a knickerbocker glory, with a plump, succulent strawberry atop the cream, awaited him. So, with the recent fun and games still in mind, he curtailed his leave and zoomed back, looking forward to more spankingly good rumpy-pumpy with dear old roly-poly Sandra.

* * *

From thenceforth it was a life of easy duties and keeping Sandra on orgasmic cloud nine, a task he was to enjoy many times a week for she was insatiable.

In no time his escapades were common knowledge. Fellow officers deplored and envied, in equal measure, his swaggering devil-may-care attitude that had replaced his initial goal of anonymity.

It was a gloomy freezing Wednesday in November when the CO ordered officers and men to enjoy an afternoon of excruciation that he labelled Active Sport. There were three choices of torture to which one could add a name. An eight-mile cross-country run over frozen fields, icy streams and barbed wire fences, dressed in a cotton vest and shorts. Have one's shins, teeth and brain shattered with hockey sticks. Or revel in being thrown onto rock-solid soil by a twenty-stone prop who'd then spread his arse across your broken nose and cauliflower ears. Tristan had opted to use his 'get out of jail card' by getting Algernon to sign a Form D149/ES (Excused Sport). Far better an afternoon with Sandra.

The drive was pleasant enough and, fully aware of the possibility of their demise, the fauna hid amongst the fallen leaves and thicket, so allowing his Land Rover to hurtle past unhindered.

Upon arrival, there was no cause to pull the doorbell chain as Algernon had provided a key. Sandra was waiting at the bottom of the stairs wearing only a smile and chomping at the bit. With greetings given a heave-ho, they vaulted upstairs to the set aside bonk room bed.

Tristan found her an extraordinarily attractive woman, the wrinkles on her pink buxom body only added to his desires. It was disconcerting, but when apart he missed her. Okay, she wasn't a spring chicken, but perhaps he was even more than fond. Was he in love? She forty-five, or thereabouts, and he, not yet twenty-one, but she was gorgeous. How could Algernon, or any man, have no desire for this lovely woman? 'He prefers young men,' she'd disclosed.

The hors d'oeuvres offered by the pert youthful things crying out for his attention had become a thing of the past; Sandra was now the only woman in Tristan's life. The recent months for him had been a course in eroticism, a time of intoxication from his explorative ardour. Now that Algernon was off the hook enjoying his own unconventional lifestyle, it had liberated her to indulge in whatever concupiscent activities after which she lusted. Whilst maths was Greek to Tristan, he figured this had to be a perfect equilateral triangle if ever there was one, it was ecstasy.

Lying exhausted and saturated with perspiration, the sound of the doorbell aroused them from their post-coitus catnap.

'It'll be Algernon home early, damned nuisance. I told him not to forget the keys. Stay at attention big boy I'll be back soon,' she said, throwing on a housecoat.

Tristan heard the stairs creak as she descended. Muffled speech infiltrated the carpeted old wooden bedroom floorboards and thereafter creaking announced her return. At least she didn't take long, he thought, as he prepared himself for making whoopee one more time before returning to the mess for dinner.

'Hello sir. Having a rest, are we?' one of two Redcap corporals said as they stood staring at Tristan's naked body. The silent one smirked, turned and called out mockingly, 'He's up here sarge, ballock naked! Our sergeant wants a word with you. . . sir.'

A large plain-clothed man entered the room, removed an identity card from his pocket and showed it to Tristan, announcing, 'Sergeant O'Toole, Special Investigations Branch. . . sir.'

The fellow's nose was as flat as a right-eyed flounder. What were once called ears were now pale, gnarled and jugged bits of flesh. Doubtless, it was repetitive percussions during shindigs with drunken squaddies that'd created this surrealistic work of art. It wasn't any patronising words that laid bare the man's contempt, but the derisory leer that provided Tristan with what the snivelling pig's-pizzle thought of him. Whether a raw recruit, or major general, he considered all and sundry as just another pound of crap covered in skin. Without removing his eyes from Tristan's, he snapped, 'Corporal Richmond, get your arse downstairs and watch the old bird.'

Tristan knew members of the SIB wielded powers far beyond their rank and could cause even the most senior officers to wilt before them. This character was no exception, as he stood with his eyes fixed upon Tristan's genitalia.

'Now Mr Crooke-Wells. . . sir, what a silly little thing that is, rather disconcerting. So, if you don't mind, put Wee Willie Winkie back under the sheet as I find the sight of that appendage rather disturbing. You've got a lot of explaining to do and we don't want that thing coming between us, do we. . . sir?'

'Explaining! Confound it, man. I'm a Commissioned Officer. You'll stand to attention and address me in a manner befitting my rank. Why the devil have you entered this room when I'm trying to take a nap after my cross-country canter?'

The sergeant turned to the corporal, 'Did you hear the officer? Put your feet together, he's resting 'cos he's been on a run.'

'That's better,' Tristan said, feeling in control. 'Now Sergeant, you'll explain yourself.'

'I am sorry. . . sir, but as you see, although I'm standing to attention, as requested, I need not do any explaining because that's what you'll be doing,' was the scornful reply. 'So, sir, now we are at attention, I'll carry out my responsibilities.

'Lieutenant Tristan Peregrine Crooke-Wells, I am here on behalf of Her Majesty the Queen, bless her and long may she reign, to arrest you on suspicion of collusion in the misappropriation of government property and funds.'

'Peregrine! Is that a real name, sarge?' piped up the corporal. 'Your old man must 'ave hated you,' he snickered.

'Under arrest! What the devil? Misappropriation! That's a slanderous accusation, the sort of thing that could give a chap a bad name. I don't understand what you're spouting about old sport. Okay, I've bagged a few bits and pieces; hasn't everyone? You must also have done in your time, a pair of handcuffs for the missus, magnifying glass for the kids to fry ants, perhaps fingerprint ink, we all do, don't we?'

He thought hard. What had he nicked of late? Then realised what this was about. 'All right, I want to make a clean breast. You're right, it was me, I nicked the bottle of frightfully awful gin from behind the bar, it was me what done it gov. You won't need thumbscrews, or the rack. Oh, yes, I confess and I ask you to take into consideration a packet of cigars I bagged at the same time. It was in Scotland, I'd just saved a man's life, while under fire. Yes, that was it, of unsound mind, shell shocked, and blind drunk! But, if that's not it, I can't for the life of me think of anything worth warranting an arrest. If it ain't that, I'm without a clue of what you're spouting.'

'Well. . . sir, no, it's not about a bottle of gin, or the cigars, although I have noted your confession, we'll talk about those later, sir, when we get to the barracks. Corporal, cuff and watch this officer whilst I get a blanket. If he tries to do a runner, or attempts to jump through the window, shoot him.'

'Shoot me! Are you a stark raving loony? Jump through a bloody window! We're on the second floor, I'd kill myself,' said Tristan.

'Often happens. . . sir. See, men like you got nothing to lose,' the sergeant responded as he left Tristan sitting on the bed under the eagle eye of the corporal.

Moments later the sergeant reappeared with a grey army blanket, 'Wrap this round you, sir.'

'No, I won't, why the devil can't I wear my uniform?' Tristan fumed. 'Bloody nonsense, army blankets are scratchy, they make me itch.'

'Well. . . sir, I can understand your reticence about the irritation, it's because they're pure merino wool, even the sheep what grows it find it irritating and beg for a trim. Comes from Australia, we send convicts, they send wool. Now, the reason I can't let you wear your uniform is because of Her Britannic Majesty needing it for evidence. So, it's going into an evidence bag, but if you don't mind, I'd rather not touch your underpants. Would you mind picking them up and placing them in yourself? Corporal, collect and put in the rest of the officer's uniform.' He tossed Tristan a grey army blanket. 'Put that round you, its fair bleak out there, wouldn't want you to get your pecker frostbitten, would we?'

With the blanket around his naked body and handcuffs on his wrists, he was led downstairs where he found Sandra sobbing. The poor dear's plump bosoms were heaving in time to her sobs. It was quite discombobulating for Tristan, who turned to the sergeant and asked, 'May I have a word with her before we go?'

'Just a quick one,' was the reply.

Tristan turned to Sandra, 'This is an ace balls-up. What the devil's happened?'

'It's Algernon,' she said, sounding quite frantic. 'They've arrested him.'

'Arrested! Good heavens, why? Caught wearing a dress on parade?'

She burst into tears and was incoherent.

The corporal led Tristan away for a freezing ride in an open-sided Land Rover. Upon arrival at the camp, Tristan was incapable of walking, his body was frigid and needed the SIB sergeant to half carry him to his quarters. It was a surprise to find Breckinshaw in his room. 'What the devil you doing here?' Tristan mumbled through blue lips and chattering teeth.

But it was the sergeant who answered as he removed the handcuffs, 'You will be questioned later Mr Crooke-Wells. . . sir. In the meantime, the charges you face are serious enough to call for you to be confined to your quarters. I selected Mr Breckinshaw from a huge clutch of your fellow officers who volunteered to be your escort. He will be present with you at all times, including any visits to the toilet, and, incidentally, sir, better get dressed,' he sneered, and left the room.

Breckinshaw slouched in the chair, gloating. 'They'll pwobably hang you, old sport.' He could not pronounce the 'r' in words and continued with one of those annoying sayings, 'If you fwy with the cquows, you get shot with the cquows.'

Tristan knew the addle-brained twit was wrong, for even assassinating the monarch was not a capital offence in Britain and, as he still didn't know what they supposed him to have done, neither did Breckinshaw. While Tristan was getting dressed into decent civvies and was starting to warm up, the idiot continued, 'All the chaps are on about you and the major's wife, don't you know.'

Tristan told him in no uncertain terms to mind his own business. But he wouldn't keep quiet, 'Sowwy old bean, buht the other chaps say you, the major and his wife are members of ah wotten wussian spy wing! Is it so?'

Tristan ignored him. The SIB sergeant returned about an hour later, Tristan thought he was looking rather crestfallen.

'They won't be questioning you. . . sir. Well, not about the misappropriation of funds and property. The major's statement of confession exonerates you. From his account, it's clear that he and his wife carried out the crimes alone.' He paused. 'But I am instructed by a power way beyond my comprehension to understand, sir, that a colonel from the Adjutant General's office is coming all the way from Whitehall tomorrow morning and wishes to 'ave a little chat.'

'Are you joking? A senior officer coming from the War Office about me nicking bloody foul-tasting cigars and a damned awful gin from the mess. Has the army gone barmy?'

'Can't say if the army is of unsound mind, no can't say that, but you must admit a court-martial might consider your nicking from the bar and screwing your Commanding Officer's wife,' he looked at his paperwork, 'she's confessed it to having taken place on the snooker table, to be activities covered under section twenty-four.'

'What the devil's section twenty-four?'

'Section twenty-four. . . sir, is to do with scandalous and, or, fraudulent conduct. What they call Conduct Unbecoming an Officer. Who knows, maybe we'll be meeting again after the colonel's visit, don't you think? And sir,' the sergeant sneered as he voiced his parting shot, 'keep your flies done up.'

'Sod off!' Tristan yelled, while kicking the door shut.

Upon the sergeant's departure, Breckinshaw expressed his opinion once more. 'I say, jolly spiffing old chap, they dwopped the sewious charge of helping the major to pwunder. I told the other chaps you were innocent. Twumped up charges, that's what they were, gwoodness me. Pity about the Adjutant General though, pwobably come to nuffing, don't you know?'

'I don't give a diddly-squat for your opinion, you turgid tit,' Tristan said, and walloped him on the whiffer. The yellow cur harefooted it from the room keening like a Killarney banshee, the blood fair flowing from his beak.

I'll dine in the mess tonight just to show the blackguards they can go to hell, Tristan decided. Although it was a freezing November evening, he resolutely donned his best bib and tucker and, with the tune of Colonel Bogey whistling softly on his lips, he marched to the mess. Passing the spot where Penelope Ponsonby-Piersons had awaited him, he recalled that it wasn't that long ago her rather super hooter had slipped anchor and made the others envious. Striding through the mess portal, he heard talking and laughter, but as he stepped into the dining room, it went as mute as growing grass. If the owners of the scowling faces had just trodden into an elephantine turd, they couldn't have looked more disgusted. The only spare table was in the far dark corner; his confident stride crumbled into what seemed an endless skulk.

Upon his being seated, the air was again full of jabber. The sullen waiter plonked a dinner down without a by your leave. With withered confidence, Tristan resolved not to speak out about the fellow's demeanour. He found the other diners' boisterousness unnerving, so sat within his solitude picking at the cold, tasteless food. Sneaking out would be impossible, and so, to prolong the time before having to face the gauntlet, he nibbled the tiniest measure of the meal.

It was an urge to urinate that commanded him to break free of the invisible shackles that bound him to the chair; a prompt return to his quarters was vital. As he rose, the others fell silent and glared as they had when he'd entered. When traipsing across the dining room, an annoying squeak from his left shoe broke the silence. Breckinshaw stood and orchestrated an embarrassing handclap, which overwhelmed the squeak. Even seeing the cretin's snout hidden beneath a whopping great plaster didn't make amends. The humiliating sound of glee his undoing had caused made his disposition as bleak as a necrotic corpse.

That night, Morpheus decided Tristan was not her cup of tea, so slumber eluded him, and the following morning he felt exhausted. While he'd been humiliated last evening, he was determined to deal with the snivelling dullards. He resolved that if there was any repetition of the nonsense, he'd turn up his nose to the blighters and to hell with them.

At breakfast time, he stalked into the mess with a boldness that belied the nauseous feeling of sycamore seeds circling within his tummy. A hush descended, matching the previous incident. Faces that in the past had smiled, were now smirking, elated by his downfall. A grimacing caricature now replaced Tristan's usual smug grin. He quickened his stride to a free table, but before his backside had touched down, another officer came and sat on the opposite chair. 'This table's taken.' Upon moving, Tristan received the same reaction. Upon his third move the officer stated, 'Crooke-Wells, you're not welcome in this mess.' Tristan stood, staring at the assembly before shouting, 'I'd prefer to gnaw on a dead leper's leg than eat with a bunch of green-eyed gobemouches like you!'

Whereupon he strode out, with catcalls and hand-clapping tied to his footsteps.

At eleven o'clock, without a knock, his door opened. Glancing up from the crossword, he spotted it was a colonel. 'I say old bean, the clue is The Fantastic Mr Fox, four letters, and the second one is A, got any suggestions?'

'Mother,' the colonel replied.

'Don't be a chump, too many letters.'

'I've spoken to your mother,' he said. That stirred Tristan into action. He hadn't considered anyone would discuss his plight with Mummy.

'My name is Colonel Farquart Pishorn. You will address me as sir and I will call you Tristan.'

'Yes, sir,' Tristan responded. The man sounded more fatherly than had Daddy.

'Now Tristan, your mother thinks you are as dumb as a bagful of hammers and as much use as a blank lottery ticket. I believe love tempers her analysis.'

'One can't say you are incorrect, sir,' Tristan responded.

'Just shut up! Stop talking like a snivelling nincompoop and listen to me.' The colonel spoke with a quiet reserve that Tristan found unnerving.

'Unlike most people whose brains are between their ears, yours show every sign of being housed within your scrotum as an integral part of your balls. You are a muddleheaded nitwit who's got himself into a damned awful mess. Your Commanding Officer is in custody, as is your lady friend – a woman old enough to be your mother. Both are on multiple charges, including theft of army property and, in the major's case, cavorting with male prostitutes on military property. What do you say to that?'

'Gosh, that's dreadful,' replied Tristan. 'Male prostitutes? I say, not on, sir.'

'And the theft?' the colonel asked.

'Oh, yes, and theft, as you say. I don't suppose that's zippy either,' Tristan responded.

The colonel continued, 'Did you never consider how a major could afford such a palatial home?'

'No sir. Never crossed my mind.'

Why should it? Tristan thought. His father might have been rich.

'It never crossed your mind, not for a second that it was strange? Such a huge house on a major's salary?'

Tristan didn't respond.

'Look, my dear fellow, I'm here for your mother. I've known her for years: a cherished friend, a very close friend. It's she I want to help. A fine woman. . . oh yes, very fine,' he paused, savouring his words. 'As I was saying – where was I? – oh yes, there're two ways we can handle this.'

'You won't send me to the desert, or back to Scotland, will you, sir?'

'No! Don't want another Arab revolt on our hands and there'd be an outrage from the Scots, no, that'll not work.' The colonel said, 'Look old chap, I can call the Provost Marshal, great friend of mine, and have you incarcerated until a trial, on charges he and I will conjure up. You'll be put away for. . . shall we say, ten to fifteen years. Or you can resign your commission and bugger off today. What's it to be?'

Tristan considered the situation before responding. 'May I keep my mess kit, sir?'

Kismet

Soon, above Tristan's quagmire of failures, his forte in life was to become apparent: he was a born linguist. The nub of his gift had surfaced when that whiff of Arabic enabled him to swagger in the officers' mess. But a fortuitous meeting with a Bedouin belly dancer – labelled Buthaynah bint Al-Bishi from Buraydah – in a beit al-share in London's Soho, was to be the turning point of his remunerative linguistic Kismet.

* * *

In Tristan's opinion, it was a fluky misfortune that stymied his promising military career, but Daddy still cut off his allowances and declared him to be a 'ne'er-do-well rapscallion'.

With skills as barren as a bald Inca orchid, finding work was out of the question, leaving no alternative but to cadge from a pitiful bunch of charitable acquaintances. Just that morning, one so-called chum had tossed Tristan into the street for reaping a favour proffered by the rotter's girlfriend.

The season of goodwill had swaddled mankind, but had passed him by as fast as a fiddler's fingers' fiddle his fiddle. Yet again, his companion was pecuniary paucity with the inevitability of homelessness.

Feeling as dank and dark as the depressing weather, a dispirited Tristan stood out front of Ricci's Gentlemen's

Revuebar (Members Only) gawking at photographs of dancing girls displaying their attributes. How gloriously graceful they were in their artistic poses, with bodies veiled in little more than flimsy feathers plucked from now-naked ostriches. There was naught for him here, except past remembrance.

Not one hour before, he'd bagged two pounds twenty-seven, a metal washer and a black plastic button by begging outside The London Dorchester with a ragtag stray dog on a string beside him. The cardboard sign around his neck declared him to be a blind ex-serviceman, but he had frittered his facade when a comely girl placed money into his hat.

In retrospect, shedding sunglasses to chat her up was unwise, for it required a sprint to put distance between him, her husband, and the bobby who had intervened.

In the dim light, Tristan was still staring at the feathered females when a man, wearing a trilby and a full-length beige trench coat with the collar pulled up, approached him and said, 'You appear to be a young gentleman who discerns the artistic side of life. Want to see a good show? Free entry.'

With only the takings, minus the discarded washer and button, from his recent career as an ex-serviceman destitute of vision, a free show sounded spot on, and so he followed the man. The destination was but a scant distance through shadow-puddled streets in London's Soho district. They stopped at a black studded door which exhibited resilience sturdy enough to repel a barrage from the King's Troop, Royal Horse Artillery. A flickering red neon sign above the entrance proclaimed it to be the British Middle Eastern Sporting Club. Posters of young ladies attired in less trim than plucked poultry in the

Smithfield Meat Market adorned the wall, making the girls at Ricci's Gentlemen's Revuebar appear on the verge of angelic.

The man pressed the bell push, a grille opened, and Tristan saw he was being gawked at by a pair of eyes sunk within puffy brows. As the metal grid snapped shut, the grating of a bolt being drawn back assailed Tristan's ears in the manner of chalk upon a board at school. In contrast, the door swung silently open and an elephantine fellow wearing an evening suit, looking like it was made for a manikin, allowed just enough space for Tristan to squeeze past into the black interior.

Turning to thank the trench-coated guide for his kindness, Tristan found him gone. The door slammed shut and his new host rasped, 'Down them stairs, and frew the door is where the girls is.' Tristan noticed that something had shaped the man's nose to resemble the Special Investigation Branch sergeant's; without any doubt not re-engineered on the sports fields of Rugby.

With no handrail to help descend the steep steps, Tristan leaned against the dirty wall. A door at the bottom of the stairwell opened into what appeared to be an ill-lit tent in which several girls, divested of almost any form of garment, sprawled upon large garish cushions lying in a disarranged jumble on tawdry rugs. Sacking covered the walls, while wooden poles held up a black canvas canopy. Scattered around were several Shisha Hookah pipes but, although the place could hold maybe twenty, he was the only patron.

A fellow wearing evening dress with curly lapels, and a red fez, was loitering behind a bar. Upon Tristan's entrance, the man put a record on a small gramophone causing atmospheric Arabian music to emanate from the machine. Tristan had received such a record player on his eighth birthday: it looked like the one now playing except Nanny had kept his clean and it hadn't clicked and jumped tracks until Rodney had bent the needle.

The barman sauntered over, gestured for Tristan to sit on a cushion and snapped his fingers. Two of the ladies came over and the man retired to the bar.

The girls snuggled up to Tristan who was now excited as both were curvaceous and wore little to naught beneath the gossamer-thin material. Arabian dancing girls? How enchanting, Tristan thought, as he stroked the shoulder of the one with the biggest knockers. He whispered Arabic into her ear, 'What do they call you, my little rose of Sharon?'

'Ayup Roy! We gota queer 'ear,' she called to the barman.

The barman came over: 'You got a problem, mate?'

Tristan explained he was only eliciting the lady's name in Arabic.

'Oh, one of them, are ya? A bleeding foreigner! Well, talk to 'er proper. She's an exotic bint, not used to ruffians, especially them what's not native here, so watch yer lip. What ya drinking?'

Tristan knew he had just over two pounds in his pocket, so plonked for a small beer.

The tiny glass of light-brown liquid delivered to Tristan tasted unlike any beer he had ever imbibed. 'What in goodness name is this, barman?'

'It's the 'ouse special. Arabian beer what we imports from Mecca,' he said passing the girls Champagne glasses with bubbles rising from the liquid in them, and asked, 'Wanna see a girl what dances?'

'Gosh, rather,' Tristan answered.

The barman put on a different record, then from behind a curtain one of the most graceful girls Tristan had ever seen emerged and held him spellbound. There were many so-called belly dancers flapping their fat in Soho clubs, but this gossamer-clad enchantress performing the ancient ritual of preparation for childbirth fair took his breath away. The two girls, feeling his rising excitement, snuggled even closer; he caught the sweet scent of cachou and lemonade on their breath.

After three minutes and thirty seconds, the magic passed with the sound of a clicking stylus. As the dancing girl moved to the curtain, Tristan called out in Arabic, 'You are exquisite and I love your dancing.' She smiled and vanished.

The barman returned, and said, 'Did you call for a nuvver drink?'

'No thanks. I was just telling the gal how much I loved her dancing. Sorry old chap, no time to imbibe no more, must dash, got to find a pillow for the night, don't you know. It was first-rate, yes, top-notch. I'll recommend it to all my friends. Thank you for your cordiality, girls. May I have my bill, please?'

'The management is pleased you enjoyed it, sir. Won't be a minute with your itemised account,' Fez said, and went to the bar. Returning, he handed Tristan a scrap of paper.

'Great Scott! What the devil's this? Twenty-two pounds! I had less than half a pint of beer. You've made a mistake.'

'Let me have the bill again, sir. An inaccuracy may have occurred, it do 'appen when I'm busy. Ah yes, sir. You 'ad one Arabian Mecca beer, two glasses of finest French bubbly for your lady friends and a private exotic floor show. Oh yes, you're right, sir. I do apologise, I see the mistake. I forgot temporary membership of the club, it's 'a nuvver five quid.'

'But,' Tristan said, 'the man outside Ricci's Revuebar told me it was free.'

'A man at Ricci's Revuebar you say, sir? I don't know about no revuebar man.' He turned, and called out, 'Cyril, do we 'ave a comedian what's on at a revuebar called Ricci's this week?'

A voice from the gloom responded, 'No Guv, there ain't no one.'

Tristan looked into the shadows from whence the utterance had emanated. There was now a monstrous fellow thwarting his exit by barricading the passage with a palisade of muscling fat.

'Well there, sir,' said Fez. 'We don't know no one what is at Ricci's, therefore, I suggest you pay up like a good boy.'

'Well, I don't have twenty-two pounds and that's that.'

'It's twenty-seven, with temporary club membership, sir.'

Tristan slipped easily into colloquial English, which did not appease the situation.

'Well my good fellow, twenty-two, or twenty-seven, you must whistle for the wind 'cause I ain't got either. It's two quid, or nowt!'

'Credit card? We takes all major ones except American Express and Diners Club, sir.'

'I don't have a credit card, apart from which I never ordered drinks for your girls, they came and sat here at your instruction and upon their own volition,' Tristan responded.

The barman spoke to the girls, 'Are you accompanying this gentleman?'

The one with the bigger boobs replied, 'No, we was sitting 'aving a cuppa tea and a pleasant chat about the church service last Sunday when 'e called us over to talk about matters of the cloth, he says.'

The other one joined in, 'Said he was from the Salvation Army, he did.' The other girl agreed, and continued, 'And he plied us with alcohol, so he did, and then touched my tit.'

'Are you saying this man of the cloth assaulted you, madam?'

'Yes,' she said, pointing to her right one. 'He toyed with this titty.'

Tristan exclaimed, 'That's a damned lie! I know a right tit when I feel one! It was the lefty, and it was you what planted it into my mitt.'

The barman again addressed the gloom, 'Did you 'ear that Cyril? This pervert was on the way to Ricci's to lech at ladies wiv no clothes on, but instead came 'ere for a freebie and assaulted our young lady guest by laying 'is hand on 'er Walter Mitty.'

'Shall I call the Lilly Law?' the man rejoined, with a measure of joviality.

'No,' the barman said, looking at Tristan. 'We don't need the fuzz. Just come and beat the crap out of him.'

In a flash Tristan saw the state of affairs was bang on the button of being perilous, for he spotted Cyril lumbering forward in the manner of a Sumo entering the rice-straw dohyo. So, what to do? He'd garnered snippets on strategy from watching Japanese wrestling on television and considered opening with the favoured yorikiri, or oshidashi, moves. But, as the frightful monster drew closer, it was as plain as pikestaff there was only one move at his disposal, hara-kiri. So, not fancying that, he fell to his knees and begged for mercy.

His pleadings fell as silently as dandruff upon Cyril's cauliflower ears for, without a smidgen of compassion, the brute plucked him from the cushion and propelled him through the air as if he were a Cornish Hurling ball.

Before ricocheting off the hessian-covered wall, Tristan's body jounced excruciatingly, twice, across the concrete floor. Prostrated and pulverised, he squinted through tear-filled eyes as the gigantic shadow cast by Sumo Cyril, ambling towards him, blocked the dim light. Terrified, he jammed his eyes shut, like when Daddy pretended to be a bogeyman, and tried to push away the hand that grabbed his shaking shoulder, 'Please, I beg you, don't whack me again. I'll ask Daddy to send all I owe and more, but please don't hurt me.'

But it was a gentle Arabic voice, whispering, 'Hurry, this way.' It was the belly dancer.

With the girl's help, Tristan raised his aching body to its knees and followed her behind a curtain, then through a door it concealed. With not a second to spare, she slammed and bolted it shut to the shouts and hammering from Sumo Cyril.

'Follow me,' she said, running up a flight of stairs.

Unable to move, Tristan lay at the bottom feeling as if Cyril had busted every bone in his body.

The girl ran back down, 'You must hurry. We have to go into the alley at the back of the club. Quickly, they will come around from the front and trap us.'

Although a great struggle, he managed – with her help – to mount the stairs and reach a small landing with a door. They exited into an unlit, dingy, dead-end alleyway filled with industrial-sized waste bins. Far-off streetlights and muted traffic noises showed it was some distance through the murk to the road. It being obvious that Tristan could not walk at a sufficient speed to beat Sumo Cyril's arrival, the girl slid a bin lid open. 'Hurry, get inside. You hide, I come back later,' she said, and helped Tristan scramble headfirst into the metal container, she then slid it closed.

Every tourist, rodent, and stray tyke in town knows there is an abundance of Chinese chow chophouses in Soho. Tristan had oft eaten in this oriental district of London; Dong Po Braised Pork was his favourite. But being thrust headfirst into the rancid remains of heaven-knows-how-many unfinished meals from the Ho Lee Fook restaurant made his stomach heave. Gaining a footing on the bin's slimy sides and base was impossible and so, up to his neck in noodles, in freezing silent darkness, his stomach heaved.

A minute later came the muffled sound of voices: it was Fez and Sumo Cyril, also a girl's voice. Had they caught his saviour?

'Open this one; it's closest to the door.' He recognised Fez's voice and heard a thud. 'Make sure he's not hiding inside.'

Taking a deep breath, Tristan plunged below the swill. A retching stomach made the act easier said than done. But intestinal fortitude, and the fear of Cyril sending him hurling down the alley, came to the fore, as he wallowed beneath the congealed cuisine.

No light or sound penetrated the gunge. Although not knowing if anyone was still there, bursting lungs forced him to erupt to the surface whistling like a Japanese ama, except, instead of a pearl between his lips, he had half a cashew nut. Thankfully, the bin was in darkness and as silent as the embalmed Tutankhamen.

Feeling safe, he attempted to take a gander outside, but could find no anchorage for freezing foot or finger, and so floundered in the superfluous fast food.

How long they had him trapped he knew not, for his body and mind were by then benumbed. The only respite from his ordeal occurred when, without warning, he was deluged with a bucket of warm wonton discharged by a Chinese kitchen hand too short to look in, but even that had now nigh on frozen.

Maybe he should bang the bin and bellow, ask Cyril – no beg, beseech, Cyril – to end the agony. At least being battered would be better than freezing to death in Chinese chow. Floundering in the slimy slop caused it to release monosodium glutamate and ammonia fumes which filled the steel tomb causing him to slip into and out of delirium. He had no notion of how long it had been since the bint had incarcerated him in the bin and then done a bunk.

Without warning the lid slid back and a blazing light exploded into his eyes and he screamed, 'I give in, get on with it, clobber me, put me out of my misery, I've had enough.'

But, realisation! He was already as dead as a duck in a Hangzhou soup dish, for the voice of an angel had fallen upon his ears. Thank goodness, he was clocking into the Promised Land where pain would be a thing of the past. A ditty his wet-nurse used to sing when he nibbled on her knocker resonated in his ears, so he joined in, 'Yes Jesus loves me, Yes Jesus...'

'Shush, it is I, Buthaynah.'

Tristan didn't know the name, but the sound of her voice was as gentle as the bells upon a belly-dancers' belt. With relief, he croaked, 'The dancer?'

'Yes. I help you, it is safe.'

She hoisted him out of the oriental banquet like a boot from a bog.

Standing frozen in the alley and shaking like a gallowed man, he felt her wrap a blanket about his shoulders.

'Come, I take you home,' she whispered.

Rigid as a rancid rat, he could not stand upright but with her support hobbled towards the dimly lit street. After peering around the corner, she led him to who knows where, for the rest of the night passed without his recollection of anything other than warmth returning to his body.

On the Up

The blanket beneath which he was ensconced was snug, but itchy.

A quick exploration to ensure Moby Dick was still in residence proclaimed his nakedness.

Cleaving his eyelids open, he was greeted by dimness not dissimilar to an entrapment he'd dreamt of last night. In his dream, a brute of a chef, akin to a Sumo wrestler, had tossed him into a giant Chinese wok, and he'd emerged as Kung Pao chicken. It had been a horrific nightmare unlike anything that'd previously disturbed him.

After a few blinks, his surroundings became a little clearer. He was in a Lilliputian room, almost devoid of furniture. The glow of a bare bulb dangling from the ceiling lit bare walls bedecked with floral paper, torn and with a finishing touch of multicoloured mould.

A voice as soft as a downing feather fell upon his ear.

'It is I, Buthaynah. Would you like tea?'

Although excruciatingly painful he turned, it wasn't a dream, for it was the dancing girl.

'Yes, please.'

While pouring the drink she asked in Arabic, 'How are you feeling?'

Responding in English, he replied, 'Not too well. Where am I?'

'Why do you speak English when you can speak Arabic?' she asked.

Apologising, he explained he'd learnt only a little.

Passing him the warm drink, and there being no chairs, she sat on the edge of the single bed.

'How did I get here?' he said.

She described what had transpired, explaining that he was not the first to have been so caught and, with modesty, her part in his escape. The horror flooded back leading him to realise she'd downplayed her role; the gentle kindness of her actions was as touching as was the disregard for her own safety.

Looking around she said, 'I am sorry, I can afford only this tiny room. The house is full of people like me with no papers.' Seeing his quizzical look when he sipped the tea, she explained, 'It is black sweet tea called Saiidi. I hope you will enjoy it.'

'It's excellent, but what about the club, you'll not be returning?'

'No matter, the pay is little. They told me I would dance classical Egyptian Raqs Sharqi, Baladi, but make me dance to keep dirty old men happy.'

'I say, I hope you don't think of me as dirty, because I was unsullied until you dunked me in the swill. I was off to the ballet but, blow me, I trotted down the wrong stairs, was quite taken by surprise when you popped on stage, expected the Bolshoi.'

From her glazed look, it was clear she'd not grasped a thing he'd said, and he was sorry he'd allowed himself to speak so stupidly, his normal swagger was not appropriate. He'd not met anyone who'd shown him such kindness before.

'Buthaynah, where are my clothes, please?'

She pointed to a pile in the corner, folded as Mummy's housekeeper would have.

Seeing his surprised look, she said, 'I had a little money so while you slept I took them to the laundrette; they are washed and dried. There are no facilities for such things here.'

'You spent your money washing my clothes?' Her tenderness humbled him even more.

From a small suitcase she took out a poster and showed it to him: it was in Arabic and described her as, Danse Orientale. 'People brought me to England on a contract which was worthless. There was no money. They wanted me to entertain men privately, but I am a skilled dancer. So, I ran away, but they have my passport, and I have no money to go home. I work in small clubs for little money.'

'Tell you what,' Tristan said, 'we can do something together. I'll find the work. You and I live here and you give me a few pounds from your income. How does that sound?'

He spent the next six months introducing her as 'The Queen of Saba, Danse Oriental' to London's swankiest clubs where the opulent members paid annual fees equal to half the price of a new home. She was a sensation.

Commensurate with her income, they ascended several layers of lodgement from vile to horrid before being ensconced in elegant. Their arrangement came to an end when a wealthy Middle Eastern businessman also sought Buthaynah's favours.

Tristan and she parted company as good friends. Although he'd had no shortage of women, she was unlike anyone he'd ever met. Full of gratitude for the Arabic lessons, he was even more so for the lessons in pelvic undulation. These were most helpful for when lumbago, amongst other things, became an irritant later in life.

* * *

The money he had saved, plus a tidy parting gift from Buthaynah, was soon frittered away, and he fell into the bosom of an attractive, but elderly, widow. It was fun while it lasted, but he was slung out by a solicitous son who considered him a gravedigger.

He'd enjoyed learning Arabic, but had never dreamt of studying Russian until, once more on the bones of his backside, by good chance someone he'd met through Buthaynah introduced him to an ex-Soviet KGB Colonel, now a Russian oligarch, named Dmitriy Nikolayevhich Ripitov.

The colonel had 'inherited' several oil fields, steel works and an international property portfolio as a benefaction from the fall of the USSR. Dmitriy introduced Tristan to his plump wife Svetlana, who – although nothing about her was small – told Tristan to call her by the diminutive Sveta. Unbeknown to Sveta, Dmitriy was paying Tristan a small fortune to keep his 'Churchkhela' (Sweet-sausage) happy, while he toured the world in his yacht, accompanied by Mayra, a twenty-five-year-old charango plucker from Piura in Peru.

Concealed from Dmitriy, Sveta was also paying Tristan a smaller pecuniary perquisite, but with an added nuptial bonus, and accommodation. As she spoke little English, he had to learn Russian post-haste, but didn't mind for, although having high mileage on the clock, she was a game old boiler. The set-up was even more ideal than roosting with the belly dancer, for his sole obligation was amatory. He had found that Shangri-La was not in the far away east, but in Mayfair.

After nearly a year, on a sunny Sunday morning in June, Sveta was busy in the second bathroom painting her toenails; a task foreshortened as she'd lost the nail on her left big toe to frostbite. The painful experience was a consequence of Dmitriy and her sharing a Siberian all-inclusive package holiday, with the compliments of the Union of Soviet Socialist Republic's Council of the People's Commissars.

As a child, she'd yearned to be a ballet dancer, but was too fat, too short, and without rhythmic talent. The People's Commissariat for Education and The People's Commissariat for Labour took her desires into consideration and selected her, aged six, to become a shipyard general worker when she reached the age of fourteen.

Loving ballet music, in particular Tchaikovsky's, she'd had her door chimes programmed to play the finale of the 1812 overture, complete with the cannonade. A high volume was necessary because the riveting machine she'd operated in the shipyard had impaired her hearing.

Tristan was still in bed snoozing when the thunderous reverberations of exploding Blomfield nine-pounders accompanied by the ear-splitting clanging of the Kremlin church bells shattered the peace. Checking his watch and seeing it was only ten fifteen, he thought it most unusual to get a caller at such an early hour. 'You answer the door, Sweety,' he called out in Russian. There was no reply, and the cannonade again rattled doors and windows. 'OK, don't bother. I'll get it,' he said petulantly, while putting on a white monogrammed knee-length bathrobe. Upon opening the door, he was confronted by a short thin man swathed in saffron-coloured robes, his head as bald as a cue ball – nary a wisp of hair – and his grubby feet clad in leather flip-flops. Looking down Tristan saw that in his right hand the fellow held a rather schoolmasterly leather briefcase.

'Not today thank you, we're Jewish,' he said, closing the door.

Sveta called out, 'Who is it, my love?'

'Jehovah's Witness,' he responded, but, before he could say anything further, the finale of the Tchaikovsky fifth – hell-bent on sowing the seeds of downstream hearing impairment – once again blasted his tympanic membrane. With increased rancorousness, Tristan threw open the door, ready to confront the reptile and tell the spindly creature where he could stick his Watchtower. The insect held his hands together as if in prayer and moved them to his forehead, and then he bowed.

Sveta had, by then, arrived and stood next to Tristan.

The man lifted his face and spoke in Russian, 'Hello Sweet-sausage.'

Both Tristan and Sveta exclaimed, 'Dmitriy!'

Sveta said, 'What has happened to you? You're so thin, and where's your hair, eyebrows and beard?'

'May I enter, my dear?' Dmitriy asked.

'Yes,' both Tristan and Sveta harmonised.

They sat on the couch, while Dmitriy squatted cross-legged on the floor.

Sveta said, 'I am sorry, my dear,' nodding toward Tristan, 'it's not how it looks. He was just fixing the electricity.' As the words crossed her lips, she realised how stupid she must sound. Unless, that is, she could convince her husband that Tristan was a naked submersible electrical engineer repairing the underwater lights in the swimming pool they didn't have. For, she noted, the short dressing gown showed his lack of underwear.

Dmitriy waved her apologies away, 'Don't worry, my love. I know about him. I couldn't leave you behind feeling lonely while I sailed around the world in my yacht enjoying life, could I, my little Sweet-sausage? Please forgive me, my dear, for paying this fellow to keep you happy. It was wrong of me, something for which I will forever seek your forgiveness.'

Sveta said, 'But it was I who paid him to keep me company, while you worked so hard on your yacht, travelling the world on business to keep us in a life of contented happiness.'

Tristan changed tack as things gained a pace or two. 'What's to do Dmitriy? Draped in old curtains because lost your togs? Tell you what, old chap, you whiff, and your feet don't look too good.'

'Yes, what's happened, my dearest love?' said Sveta. 'You're as thin as a Siberian larch twig, haven't you been eating properly?'

Dmitriy looked from one to the other, and said, 'I have taken the Bodhisattva vows.'

'What does that mean, dear?' asked Sveta.

'Russian Freemasons?' queried Tristan.

'No, I have become a monk.'

'A monk!' They both exclaimed.

Tristan asked, 'Is that why you're kitted out in rags, reeking like a rat's fart?'

Sveta touched his scalp. 'Why has your lovely hair and beard fallen out?'

'And your eyebrows, what's become of them?' Tristan piped up.

Dmitriy gazed into Sveta's eyes, murmuring, 'The Venerable Dharma Teacher Lotus Wailing.'

Reaching out, she patted his hand. 'Now what's that dear? I'm sure with rest, whatever it is, we can soon sort it out.'

'It is what I am called, Sweet-sausage. I am no longer Dmitriy Nikolayevich Ripitov, I am now The Venerable Dharma Teacher Lotus Wailing. I journey on the long road seeking enlightenment. May the rains come in time to deliver a bountiful harvest.'

Chipping in, Tristan asked, 'You've changed your name – to what?'

Dmitriy replied, 'To The Venerable Dharma Teacher Lotus Wailing. I'm a Bhikkhu.'

'You mean a berk,' scoffed Tristan.

'No. I am an ordained Buddhist priest. A Bhikkhu means beggar, so I will now live off the alms from other charitable souls.'

Tristan thought hard, but didn't recall the Russian word for a tosser. 'My dear fellow, or should I say The Venerable Dharma Teacher Lotus Wailing, done a bit of begging in my time, but feeding on scraps of free fodder ain't the way for a millionaire to eke out an existence. What's become of you?'

'I sense you mock me, so I will respond to my wife. You may listen if you wish.'

Turning to Sveta, Dmitriy said, 'When my yacht slipped out of London's Canary Wharf and headed down the Thames to the sea, I confess to you, my love, I was off to enjoy the bountiful things I thought this world offered. I had wealth beyond the imagination of any mortal soul, but above all my wealth I had you, my precious little Sweet-sausage, awaiting my return.'

She smiled and kissed him on his shiny new head, 'Am I Mrs Venerable?'

'We will come to that later, my dearest,' he replied.

Tristan noted that the charango plucker had slipped into obscurity.

Sveta smiled, and Dmitriy continued, 'I will tell you about all the wonderful things that have happened to me. We sailed from London Docks to Cape Town and from there to the Maldives after which, with fine weather, we got under way for India. Requiring victuals, we berthed in Matara; it's at the bottom of Sri Lanka. After loading supplies, we journeyed on, and now, my little sausage, it is here the story gets most exciting.

'It was calm for the first twenty-four hours but then, even though the weather forecast predicted fine, a vicious storm overwhelmed us, with enormous waves crashing over the decks engulfing even the helipad. We lost the helicopter overboard. I was terror-stricken, but the captain assured me there was no danger as my yacht could deal with a force ten tempest and the stabilisers could handle the rough seas.

'While the captain gave me every assurance he was in control, I felt more than a little sick as the roaring seas tossed the boat around. The tumult raged from one day of seasickness to the next, but then a miracle occurred. While strapped into the seat next to the captain's chair on the bridge, with a bucket close by, I noticed the radar showed we were passing the Sri Lankan coast, although nothing could be seen as we were blinded by the storm. Even with the high-powered infrared AN/PVS number twenty-two universal night sight binoculars you stole from the tank and gave me for my birthday, I could see naught through the lashing rain and spray. Then, my love, just when every crew member thought it could not get worse, we saw a great fish; it was the size of a Malyutka-class submarine. Now, you may believe it or not, but we were dumbfounded for it rode the waves in the manner of a long-haired surfer in Sochi.'

'Oh, a Malyutka,' Sveta swooned. 'Was it like a Polushkin series fifteen with the longer periscope?'

'Yes, my love, just the same.'

'How wonderful, Dmitriy – I mean The Venerable Dharma Teacher Lotus Wailing.' Sveta kissed his head, and said, 'You know how much I love Malyutka submarines, for did I not scrape more rust and barnacles from their bottoms than you have from yours, my love?'

'My sweet little Sweet-sausage,' said Dmitriy, looking into her eyes. 'I too will neither forget the forward torpedo tubes, nor the shape of their beautiful bulbous bodies. When you were just sixteen, and I was your comrade supervisor at the 82nd Ship Repair Factory Murmansk, was it not my pleasure to pin the Loyal Order of the Red Banner of Labour upon the thin blue material covering your left breast?'

'You took so long to attach it, my love. I'm sure you were as excited as I, Dmitriy – I mean The Venerable Dharma Teacher Lotus Wailing – for I will never forget how you trembled trying to get the rusty pin through the material. You pushed it so hard that it penetrated my flesh, leaving the medal attached to my breast for a week. When the wound became infected, it was only at the insistence of the comrade doctor, and your kindness in giving me two hours off work, that they surgically removed the medal. But, my dearest love, I didn't care, and I still carry the scar with pride as a token of your love. The other comrade scrubbers were as green as bilge water with envy.'

Tristan butted in, 'When you two have finished with your feelings of fellow fondness, get on with what happened next.'

'What happened, my cherished one,' Dmitriy said, ignoring Tristan, 'was that the creature struck my yacht with its gigantic tail, and we spun around faster than your Riga washing machine.'

'You're saying in the middle of a storm which nobody forecast, a giant fish struck your yacht with its tail and spun you round like a spin dryer! That's hard to swallow,' a chuckling Tristan said.

'Well, whilst the Riga was not a fast spinner, it revolved – with small loads. So, yes, it's true. I feel you are again laughing at me, Mr Crooke-Wells, but the captain confirmed that the impact of the fish crashing into the boat caused centrifugal forces so great that it damaged the steering gear, and destroyed both radio and radar. The damage was so severe we could sail only where the broken rudder would allow; it was as if we were under the control of a greater being. It was a seventy-five-metre yacht capable of sailing through Antarctic ice, so you can understand it was remarkable that a fish could destroy the steering gear, not to mention electronics, most remarkable. We were jubilant when, after three days of despondency, we made land.'

Sveta sighed and clasped her hands to pray. 'When the tempest showed no mercy, leaving you to flounder in the savage seas, thank goodness God lavished his love by cradling you in his gentle arms above the turmoil, my dearest.'

'Strewth, that was a quick conversion! Marx said religion's an opiate for the oppressed, not the opulent,' Tristan quipped. 'And tell me, where did you land?'

'Colombo, in Sri Lanka,' Dmitriy said. 'We made it into port with no time to spare for as the boat touched the quay and the ropes were being tied – the whole steering mechanism fell into the ocean. The marine-engineering divers were amazed that the vessel had carried us to Colombo, so grave was the damage. All agreed our getting into harbour was an act of divine intervention. After inspection they told us the spare parts and a new helicopter would have to come from America and repairs would take months to complete. The choice was to wait in Sri Lanka, or fly home. Divine superintendence guided me to stay. The owner of the boatyard had a friend with a taxi and, upon his advice, I went inland away from the heat to a very nice hotel in the mountains, in a town called Kandy.'

Tristan said with derision, 'Not the Big Rock hotel was it?'

Sveta squeezed her husband's hand, 'Take no notice of him, my cherished gem. While I do not really believe in the opiate of the people, I thank heaven you found a haven with no cannibals who eat human beings, therefore enabling you to come home safely my love. It was most fortunate you didn't end up in the manner of Mr Jonah, another opiate who I do not believe existed, and occupied a fish's tummy. At least you had a decent bed in which to rest your weary body, my dearest.'

'Stroke of luck getting into port,' Tristan added. 'But lady luck wasn't on your side when you think about it, old bean. That entire ocean to swim in and a bloody great sardine gets itself filleted on your propeller.'

'Divine superintendence,' stated Dmitriy. 'It was divine superintendence.'

'Let's get this right: an elephantine fish bashes into your boat. It can't be steered and you end up in the middle of nowhere, and you call it divine superintendence?'

'Yes,' said Dmitriy.

'That makes little sense,' Tristan continued. 'Divine superintendence would be if a trawler had caught the fish, cleaved it into fingers before it could hit your boat and cause God all that extra work in saving you.'

'I feel you are a sceptic,' said Dmitriy, 'so I will tell Sveta the full story later. But for now an abridged version will suffice. Whilst in Kandy, I went to see the Sri Dalada Maligawa.' Seeing Sveta's face go blank, he explained, 'It's the Temple of the Sacred Tooth Relic.'

'And what is the Temple of the Sacred Tooth Relic?' she asked.

'My love, when Siddhartha Gautama, who is known as Buddha, died in India, a tooth was found in the ashes of his cremation and it was venerated. Then there was a war, so they took the divine relic to Sri Lanka for safety and held it in Sri Dalada Maligawa Temple in Kandy. It is said whoever holds the relic will govern Sri Lanka. The Temple has great security; I can liken it to entry into Lubyanka prison when I visited you – although I saw no rats. They guard it very well. The priests carry out rituals every day, but on Wednesdays there's a special service called Nanumura Mangallaya at which the monks clean the relic with oils made from flowers and spices.'

'Dental hygienists?' Tristan said.

'That is most irreverent, Mr Crooke-Wells. I will continue relating the story to my wife. My love, after they have used the oil to cleanse the tooth – and this part of the story is important so you must pay great attention – the priests distribute it to the devotees because they believe it has healing powers.'

Tristan was even more bored and so chipped in, 'Tell me, Dmitriy old boy – sorry, The Venerable Dharma Teacher Lotus Wailing – but what's that to do with you?'

'Well, if you wait, I will explain. As a tourist, I went to see the ceremony, after which I was standing outside the Temple waiting to cross the road when a young thug tried to grab an elderly woman's handbag. Seeing the struggle, I ran to help and managed to snatch it back. The ruffian then ripped the watch from my wrist and ran off. It was not the Rolex you gave me my love, but a fake I had made by a Swiss master watchmaker to fool thieves. I returned the bag to the owner who, with great joy, grasped me in her arms. As you can see, my Sweet-sausage, it was divine superintendence for me to be there to intervene.'

'A guardian of the helpless, my dearest hero,' Sveta sighed.

Tristan broke in, 'It was Lady Luck who put you there, that's what I'd say.'

'But,' Dmitriy continued, 'it doesn't conclude at that point. No, there's much more; this was but the start of an astonishing pilgrimage.' Sveta squeezed his hand, and they looked into each other's eyes, as he continued. 'When you hear the rest of the story, my sweetness, you will understand being divinely shepherded to the shores of Sri Lanka was not where the wonderment ended. An earthly paradise was to be my future destination.

'After returning the bag, I found my hand to be damp with a sweet floral fragrance which I wiped with my handkerchief. I suppose I was distracted for, without thinking, I stepped off the crowded pavement into the road and, to my horror, saw a tuk-tuk taxi careering toward me.'

He looked from one to the other to make sure his story was falling on fertile minds. Sveta was gazing into his eyes, and he knew she'd marvel at the rest of his tale.

'Now, my dearest snowflake, a tuk-tuk is a little vehicle designed to carry three people at the most, and even those are in very cramped conditions. You see, my sausage, unlike the Object 730 T-10 tanks you maintained in the Separate Female Tank Regiment, a tuk-tuk has no sides, only three wheels, and a small two-stroke engine. But the one hurtling towards me had four passengers packed in the manner of canned Caspian caviar, plus a man across their laps with his legs hanging out, and, almost beyond belief, on the roof was a crate of chickens. Can you imagine it? Now I will tell you of the divine superintendence on that auspicious day. On the other side of the road, the driver of another tuk-tuk taxi was seeking business, and so when I took out my handkerchief he thought it was to attract him and he swerved across the road toward me. His tuk-tuk collided head-on with the one that seemed destined to kill me. The crash spared my life, my love. Divine superintendence, that's all it could have been. The woman must have been to the Temple and, as a devotee, received the holy water from the Nanumura Mangallaya ceremony. When I delivered her from robbery, it must have rubbed off onto me. It was a miracle.'

'Miraculous!' scoffed Tristan.

'Ah, but this is not the point where the story climaxes, it is but the beginning,' said Dmitriy. 'The two taxis, in trying not to collide, crashed into a watermelon stall. The melons absorbed the impact, saving those in the tuk-tuks from serious injury. The string holding the crates to the roof severed, and they hurtled to the ground. Upon landing there was a great crash, and they disintegrated. The Lord Buddha, seeing the plight of the chickens, provided wings so that they could fly away and gain deliverance from being skewered. Then, my Sweet-sausage, having saved his feathered friends, he blessed me for helping him in their salvation. I am sure you can now see the pattern – how saving the hens and my life with the inadvertent application of holy water was divine superintendence.'

Tristan sneered, 'Divine superintendence! Aerobatic chickens! Are you bonkers? On account of getting an old crone's underarm deodorant on your hand, you destroyed two tuk-tuks putting the drivers and their families into poverty, demolished a roadside greengrocer and a chicken breeder lost his entire clucking flock. That's not divine superintendence, its imbecility.'

'Ah,' said The Venerable Dharma Teacher Lotus Wailing, 'but that is not the full story. What you hear next will amaze you, for it shows how I traversed the path of enlightenment. A man standing next to the watermelon stall, selling genuine branded made-in-China watches from a suitcase, rushed to my rescue and, observing how the thief had made off with my imitation handmade Rolex, offered me one of his at a bargain price. After helping me to gain composure, he suggested I attend his home for tea as, fortuitously, his sister was a nurse who would aid in my recovery from the shock. Was that not providential?'

'Providential!' Tristan laughed. 'You bought a rubbish watch from a dodgy dealer who invites you to his knocking-shop to meet his sister who's a nurse. I tell you this, Dmitriy, I've seen calling cards in telephone kiosks with girls dressed up like nurses, I doubt if a cup of tea was on their table.'

'I have told you a number of times that I am no longer Dmitriy but The Venerable Dharma Teacher Lotus Wailing. You may scoff, but I will continue revealing the amazing story to my wife. Dearest one, I will ignore this ignorant man's scoffing. I asked the watch salesman to take the details of those involved in the accident so that I could compensate them. It was amazing how many injured there were. He made a list of twenty-two at the scene then, after we went by taxi to his modest home for tea, more distressed people came forward, making it in total forty-seven. Many were suffering from post-traumatic stress disorder.'

Sveta interrupted him, 'My love that is a wonderful story, but, as your wife, what must I call you? The Venerable Dharma Teacher Lotus Wailing is such a long name, could we settle upon Veny for short?'

He hesitated, 'You may abbreviate me for the present moment. Now, where am I? Yes, I had arrived at the man's modest home for investigation by his sister, named Chaturi, an off-duty Ayurvedic Nurse Specialist who had left her uniform at the hospital. After they took my details, Chaturi gave me a medical assessment, called Roga and Rogi Pariksha. It took but minutes for her to diagnose my condition as being unbalanced.'

'Hang on a minute,' Tristan cut in. 'You need not be an expert to prove you're unbalanced. No, what I find more interesting is what personal details they desired?'

'Oh, just everyday trivia: health, marital status, employment, petty things. So, I told them I was fit, if somewhat overweight, and sailing the world in my yacht with income from oil, steel and an international property portfolio, and with a wife in London.'

He looked into Sveta's eyes, and said, 'Chaturi, you will recall is a nurse. Well, she diagnosed that I suffered from an ailment called PB and it was that which propelled me out in front of the tuk-tuk, and she said I needed urgent attention with an ACI.'

Sveta reacted with alarm. 'Oh, my dearest love, AC sounds shocking. Please tell me it saved your life and PB won't bring to pass your premature burial.'

'No, my little Sweet-sausage,' he said, laughing. 'It's not AC it's ACI. She diagnosed me as suffering from a Parasitic Bowel for which only one remedy exists, an Ayurvedic Colonic Irrigation.'

'Oh, my dearest treasure, that sounds awful, but you were always brave my dearest one.' She pressed his hand.

'I know,' he said. 'Firstly, they inserted quite a large pipe into my rectum, and then through that they squirted herbs, coffee, and oils. To take my mind off the discomfort I thought of you, my dearest love, but on the whole that part wasn't too painful. It was when they washed my bowels out afterwards that my tears really flowed.'

Sveta stroked his brow, 'Oh my love was it because you were thinking of me?'

'No, dearest one, they used water from the kettle that had only barely stopped boiling.'

Tristan said, 'Now we're getting to the bottom of the story, so let's stop the fiddle-faddle. The long and the short is that they rammed a bouquet garni up your arse, topped you up with a cup of flat white laced with engine oil, then parboiled your piles before knocking the crap out of you. But what's this to do with you walking around London decked in yellow curtains looking like an avant-garde Gandhi?'

Veny glared at Tristan, but held his composure and continued, 'After the treatment, it took time to recover and regain my strength. I felt quite drained.'

'You were, but not deterred from the sound of it,' said Tristan.

'Did you have a lot of discomfort, my cherished one?' Sveta asked.

'Yes it was painful,' he said, 'but as I lay recovering my life flashed before me, and I walked along the path of enlightenment that enabled me to plan my future actions.'

Sveta said, 'I am enthralled with your story, dearest. I recall that when you were with the KGB, your forte was planning. What gems sprang to your mind this time?'

'I vowed to make peace with those from whom in my previous life I'd stolen or harmed because of a medical condition I didn't know that I'd possessed. So, I replaced the two tuk-tuks with Mercedes-Benz taxis and enough money to start the owners off on careers as tour operators. For the fruit stall owner, I purchased and stocked a modest supermarket. The chicken farmer now farms turkeys. I paid compensation to the poor injured souls on Pradeep's list of whom twenty-two were his relatives visiting him on the pavement that fateful day. Everyone was happy, I more than anyone.'

Bewildered, Tristan pondered, 'Right there we have it. Pradeep and the rest of the Sri Lanka nation are happy, you're no longer constipated, you've given away a couple of hundred thousand and are feeling good. What took place next?'

'Well, Pradeep, Chaturi and I then set off in their Diamond Blue Mercedes-Benz to see Pradeep's cousin, called Ranuga. He was the proprietor of a private Buddhist Meditation Centre in the country's south. I told you it was divine superintendence. It was all coming together! They broke-the-news on the drive, for they did not wish to alarm me before, that I had a further medical condition. During the colonic irrigation, Chaturi had observed from the contents of my bowel that the fright I received when stepping off the pavement, had caused my inner being not to work and had blinded my third eye.'

'A third eye up your backside?' Tristan sneered.

'Please do not interrupt me Mr Crooke-Wells. You see, my love, it emerged that Pradeep's cousin could treat me for this condition for he is a deep meditative relaxation therapist.'

'Okay,' said Tristan, 'so you drove south in a Mercedes, let me guess – you bought that for Pradeep?'

'No, it was for his sister, she drove. A long time ago they'd banned Pradeep for dangerous driving.'

'Banned for dangerous driving!' exclaimed Tristan. 'Nobody gets banned for dangerous driving anywhere on the Indian subcontinent unless for stopping at a red traffic light, running over a cow, or driving with their lights on at night. It's the way they're taught to drive, they all motor like maniacs; recklessness is part of the driving test. I've got a suspicion, just a whisper, of the direction we're heading. I fancy they extracted more than crap from you with their coffee-flavoured Ayurvedic Colonic Irrigation, but please continue.'

'The combinations of burns to my bottom, and the bumpy roads, created a tortuous journey, but the wondrous vista that awaited me made every turn of my cheeks worthwhile. For upon arriving I found the centre primitively enchanting. It was most silent – other than for the sound of children and dogs.'

'You mean,' Tristan said, 'it was a ramshackle, rundown, seedy dump in need of complete renovation, full of snotty-nosed kids and scabbed dogs. Tell me, who were the other guests at this holy hovel?'

'There was Pradeep, Chaturi, Ranuga and his cousin's wife, Asheni, a lovely woman, and also fifteen children.'

'Right, so there we have it. Pradeep, Chaturi, Ranuga, Asheni with fifteen kids and twenty-five dogs were in this thriving sanctuary,' Tristan said.

'I think there were more dogs, and also goats,' Veny said. 'And his cousin's mother-in-law was also there.'

'That's most interesting,' Tristan said. 'Now, please correct me if I am wrong, but might I tell you what happened next?' He continued without pausing. 'When you were driving to the Centre from Kandy, they outlined to you how an investment in their Buddhist Meditation Centre would be invaluable to you and to the rest of humanity?'

'Yes.'

'One might imagine they called for you – and you agreed – to invest a prodigious package in their enterprise.'

'No.'

'No! What then did they want?' Tristan asked.

'That I become a Buddhist monk?'

'A monk! Why?'

'I told them of the giant fish and how divine superintendence had led me to their shore. They were then thrilled how far down the path of enlightenment I had journeyed in such a brief time.'

'Let me hazard a guess as to what excited them,' Tristan said. 'It was you being enlightened enough to support the Kraut motor industry by donating three Mercedes-Benz limos – one to the Angel of Mercy and two to the tuk-tuk tourist touts – not to mention a supermarket to the melon merchant and a bloody turkey farm as recompense for fouling up the chicken farmer's business. Let's not forget, on top of those acts of charity you saved the nation's unemployment coffers by taking half the buggers begging off the streets of Colombo. I'm sure they were over the moon. But tell me, The Venerable Dharma Teacher Lotus Wailing, what course did they recommend you follow to become a monk?'

'One usually has to tread a long slow path to reach enlightenment and become a priest...'

Tristan cut in, 'I bet a pound to a pinch of the after-effects of your colonic irrigation that when you arrived at the Centre they had a fast-track special on offer for a limited time?'

'No, it was not limited. It didn't need to be as Pradeep's relative said I had by then travelled far along the path of wisdom and so could take a shortcut. All I needed was topping up, so to speak. Predestination had led me on my path to enlightenment and guided me to meet Pradeep's cousin who turned out to be a priest and his wife a nun. With their help, I completed it in six months instead of three years.' Veny smiled, closed his eyes, assumed the lotus position, and hummed.

'Unless you're practising for a part in a forthcoming performance in the chorus of Madam Butterfly at the Royal Opera House, stop humming please,' said Tristan. 'I'll have a wild stab at the rules to your becoming The Venerable Dharma Teacher Lotus Wailing. It required you to give your oil fields and steel works to the Buddhist Meditation Centre owned by Pradeep's cousin, is that right?'

Veny was ecstatic. 'How wonderful! Yes, you too are on the path of enlightenment. I have given everything to the Meditation Centre and I no longer eat meat or fish and I have consecrated my body.'

Sveta stared. 'What does it mean? What happened when you consecrated your body?'

'No, my love, nothing happened,' he laughed. 'It means that we will no more have sex as I have vowed a life of celibacy, so I will never nudge you at two a.m. Is that not fantastic? I have been back with you for such a short time and already I am steering you down the path of enlightenment.'

Until that point Sveta had gazed into the browless eyes of The Venerable Dharma Teacher Lotus Wailing with love; she was now aghast. Under the circumstances, Tristan was amazed by how steady her voice remained when she finally spoke.

'Despite knowing the joy I found when watching the pumps going up and down, you have given my favourite Volga Ural oil fields to a herd of herbivores. Was it not the oil fields which kept my Bentley Continental filled with petrol? Our steel works in Tula, you have donated to the same grass grazers. Surely the steel works forged the medical-grade stainless steel used for our anniversary cutlery set, the one with the soup spoons which I dreamt of owning for so long? How philanthropic of you!' She stared at him for just a moment. 'If that were not enough, you have given up the only real pleasure you ever provided. How do you presume I will live without sex, or stay in my beautiful London apartment if penniless? Give me a clue, while you sit cross-legged on my English-oak parquet floor humming in the manner of an Aginsky water boatman, stinking like the sewage-disposal tanker I once drove through the back streets of Leningrad. Tell me, what other plans have you to destroy my life?'

A smile lit up Veny's face, 'It never crossed my mind to leave you amid the swarming masses of Mayfair, or any other place, without money, my most prized treasure. I have been also enlightened upon this matter and have a plan. Soon you will be in the same state of enlightenment as I, my dearest love, and will also dance with joy, but not backwards as when we waltzed at the Kremlin balls. We are no longer in bondage, for I have thrown off the shackles of subjugation that both communism and capitalism placed around our necks. You see, my love, we won't live a decadent life here for I have transferred our property portfolio, including this apartment, to the Buddhist Meditation Centre. It is so exciting because, in honour of my, or rather, our gifts, they are to rename the centre as The Venerable Dharma Teacher Lotus Wailing Buddhist Meditation and Ayurvedic Colonic Irrigation Centre. As we speak, they are widening the entrance and seeking a sign long enough so the name will fit.'

She stared at him, speechless.

He continued, 'Dear treasured blossom. The next thing I have to do is to request forgiveness from those whom I have offended in my past life, which is before enlightenment. For this purpose, I will travel to the Kremlin and seek absolution for misappropriating the oil fields, steelworks, and the property portfolio, explaining to my former comrades that I have given everything away to the needy.

'Oh treasured love of my very being, faster than a Tupolev Tu-144 Concordski we will soon take wing to Sri Lanka, repose together in the long grass and meditate. My little lovebird, whose beauty and fragrance humbles that of the scented lotus, I have some even better news. As we speak, Pradeep's cousin's wife, who, you will remember is a nun at The Venerable Dharma Teacher Lotus Wailing Meditation and Ayurvedic Colonic Irrigation Centre, is weaving a reed sleeping mat for when you join the others in the communal dormitory for women. You will then become a nun and won't want sex either. Will that not be splendorous?' Clasping his hands once more in meditative prayer, he hummed.

As a foreshock is to an earthquake, so she spoke, 'Please stop humming.' A saturnine pause hung, as would a fart in a sermon. Sveta said, 'I am sure, Dmitriy...'

He interjected, 'We agreed, my dearest love, for a limited time you'd call me Veny for short.'

'Dmitriy,' she continued, 'it is undeniable your old KGB comrades will welcome your return to Mother Russia seeking forgiveness for robbing them of their oil wells, steel works and property. Without hesitation, they will extend you the hand of love, friendship and forgiveness before ensuring you never again need an Ayurvedic Colonic Irrigation, you blockheaded buffoon.'

Despite the sunshine reflecting upon Veny's bald head, gloom fell faster than a hangman's jerk.

A sullen Sveta continued, 'During the purge, do you recall your affair with the American embassy secretary upon whom you were spying? That stupid expression shows you do. The typist turned out not to be American, but a Soviet secret service agent from the People's Commissariat for Internal Affairs sent to spy on you! For the crime of passing state secrets, they sent us both to the slave labour camp in Siberia. Did I not forgive you for having an internal affair?'

'Yes, my love.'

Tristan marvelled at her calmness as she said, 'Was it not enough I spent those years on my knees tilling frozen soil with only hand tools?'

'Yes, my dearest. I remember you scraping frozen soil from beneath your fingernails before you broke our daily ration of stale bread in the evening, two-thirds for me, one for you.'

'As punishment for stealing a slice of bread for you, was I not sentenced to spending eleven hours a day with a blunt hand axe chopping down Siberian larch in the forest? Were my hands not lacerated sufficiently? Or were the splinters not large enough for your satisfaction? Perhaps the hardest of the woods in Siberia was not rocklike enough: should they have been even more solid? Possibly cracking concrete would have you satisfied?'

Reaching out to touch her hand, which she quickly moved away, he said, 'You worked tirelessly, my darling, and the splinters were horrible. It made me feel quite unwell, just watching you pull them out with the pliers. It was most thoughtful of you to place them on the small fire to give a little extra heat. My angel, you thought only of my comfort.'

Her features were now as frigid as a frozen floe. 'Do you recall, while I dragged felled trees through the ice-covered forest floor you were in a warm classroom being re-educated, but you felt like nodding off?'

'Yes, my love, the heat made it uncomfortable.'

'Let me remind you of the punishment for your crime of apathy. They sentenced me to descend one thousand feet into a coal mine every day for ninety days. There, with a candle stuck to my head with molten wax, I dug for coal with my bare hands. Even from the depths of Hades – which I do not believe in and pray I never go to – I found ways to satisfy you. No doubt you will bring to mind how I smuggled out coal and made a small fire for you at night?'

'Yes, my love, you hid the fuel in your knickers.'

'Were they not large enough? Perhaps the gusset was too weak to carry enough for your liking? Would a roaring log fire have been more enjoyable?'

He smiled, 'I will never forget your face, it was so black with coal dust, my angel. You mustn't blame yourself; it was not your fault your underwear was too small to carry a larger load, but luckily you carried more than I thought possible, but then you had lost a lot of weight so there was a little more space.'

'I will continue,' she said. 'And each evening, after returning from my eleven hours of hard labour, did I not take your cold feet and warm them between my undernourished breasts? Was it not I who gave you not only the thin blanket but also my shrivelled body to keep you warm at night? Did I not do these things for you?' Without waiting for a reply, she continued, 'These things and more I did, when your mind was being enriched in a warm classroom out of the wind and snow.'

Allowing a moment to pass, she said, 'May I mention my right big toenail?'

Veny smiled and nodded, 'Please do so my love, we need to be open with each other if we are to enjoy being jointly enlightened.' He hummed again but, seeing her look, stopped.

'Although I haven't mentioned it before, was it not enough that, because of frostbite, I gave my toenail to the Chief Administration of Corrective Labour Camps? A piece of my body given for you, left forever frozen in the Siberian landscape of The Motherland of The Union of Soviet Socialist Republics. Was that sacrifice insufficient? Would it have been better if it were a toe, the foot, or even my leg?'

Her voice had risen in both pitch and intensity to a scream.

'Not enough losing my toenail – not enough pain – not enough that, even today, it stops me from wearing sandals in the summer? No, I now realise that none of these things were enough because you have compensated me by giving away my oil fields, steel works and property portfolio. You – you stupid, harebrained. . ᾿

As Tristan backed discreetly into the bedroom, he estimated her voice had reached a decibel level on a par to being stuffed head first into a loudspeaker at a Hyde Park rock concert. After rapidly dressing, he collected his few belongings and jammed them into the getaway pack he kept in the corner of a cupboard, ever ready for such an eventuality. Ducking out of the window, he cantered down the fire escape, hearing Mrs Venerable's voice morph into Mrs Wailing's. The screaming and the sound of shattering objects assailed his ears unto the pavement below.

* * *

After doing the runner from Sveta, he was, for a brief time, in-between sheets before slipping between those of a visiting Changchun Circus Contortionist and augmenting his linguistic skills with Cantonese. (Later in life he blamed his lumbago upon the hanky-panky with this charming girl. Luckily, some relief was had using the pelvic undulations learnt from Buthaynah bint Al-Bishi, from Buraydah who, you'll recall, he met in the beit al-share in London's Soho.)

Mandarin was accidental for, whilst escaping from the home of the wife of an expatriate in Southern China, he'd leapt from the balcony into a sampan. The little skiff's sole occupant was a delightful oriental oyster floater whose grip was the strongest he had ever encountered.

Beloved Bibliophile

Tristan's departure did nothing for the fractured relationship of Sveta and Dmitriy, as you will see from the various bits and pieces gleaned from papers, magazines and court records.

Unbeknown to Dmitriy, his Sweet-sausage had secreted a hoard of uncut diamonds and gold nuggets in the reinforced gusset of her mining knickers. Dmitriy had taken it for granted she kept the undergarments, still caked with Siberian coal dust, for sentimental reasons.

Thirty minutes after Tristan had departed the apartment, she journeyed to Hatton Gardens and entered the Da Ville Safe Deposit Company's premises. Although for many years a regular visitor, before being admitted to the private viewing room, off the Class-A vault, she was subjected to a vigorous security check. Two men then brought the largest box the company rented into the private viewing room. Left alone, she placed the knickers on top of the other assets she had squirreled away, thus ensuring poverty would never again be her partner.

Returning to the apartment, she telephoned the police asking to speak to a senior female police officer to report a fatality. They charged her with manslaughter under Section 2 of the 1957 Homicide Act.

At the hearing, the judge, Lady Dorothy Acton, permitted Sveta's right big toe to be Exhibit Five. Sveta's barrister described the lack of a toenail as, 'Mutilation of an otherwise perfect foot.' It distressed several female jury members, while male jurors marvelled at the height to which Sveta had to hoist her skirt to show her foot deformation.

At the end of the two-day hearing, the judge, in her summing up, emphasised the pitiless provocations born by Sveta. Predominantly female, the jury took under twenty minutes to find her guilty of manslaughter by negligence in allowing the heavy ornament to slip twice from her hand onto Dmitriy's shiny head. The sentence meted out was shorter than expected and the press speculated the reason was due to a mainly female court.

After sentencing, Sweet-sausage's solicitor, Annabelle Middleman, stood on the steps of the Court and read a press statement from her: 'I wish to thank Judge Lady Dorothy, my solicitor Annabelle, Inspector Mary Squires from the police and my supporters in the International Women's Collective for their encouragement and love. For nostalgic reasons, I look forward to my brief stay in prison. It will be warmer than my days in Siberia.'

Sri Lanka

The Directors of the twenty-two-million-pound Venerable Dharma Teacher Lotus Wailing Buddhist Meditation and Ayurvedic Colonic Irrigation Centre and, latterly, Luxury Hotel could not find a sufficiently long board for the sign. Instead, a stone mason carved the acronym of its wealthy owners, Chaturi, Ranuga, Asheni and Pradeep into the white Italian marble facade, THE CRAP CENTRE.

It is a resounding success.

Property Pedlar

After the swift exodus from Sveta's embrace, Tristan took no time in joining the cashless society.

What with widows being scantier than the hair on a Peruvian Inca Orchid, and so-called chums turning their backs on him – their wives had taken up different positions – finding a comfortable pillow for his head was impossible. What to do? A pecuniary perquisite had become paramount. There was naught left but to seek employment, which – even the notion of – prompted the shivers.

With no skills other than linguistics under his belt, he answered an advertisement seeking somebody with that talent. He believed the interview had progressed well, and the interviewers said they would post a reply to the address he'd presented – The Kingsway Gentleman's Club, 56, Khartoum Street, Knightsbridge – it was the street address of a newsagent who'd agreed to take in the limited mail he received.

Sifting through the list of the interviewees, and the notes he'd made, the Managing Director read aloud the glowing testimonials that Tristan had flourished, none of which could they follow up: British Military Intelligence Officer in Russia; Interpreter and Adviser to an Arab Potentate, since assassinated; Secondment to the CIA as a Middle Eastern Adviser to US Secretary of State. (Not presented was the glowing recommendation from the US President, Tristan thought it lacked credibility.)

Speaking to the board, the MD gave his assessment. 'It was obvious from the outset that this bilker, Crooke-Wells, is an unqualified charlatan devoid of scruples, principles and morals.' Tossing Tristan's application file on the desk, he continued, 'You can't trust a single bloody word he utters. To be blunt, he's a lying bastard, and – I don't know if you feel the same – I think he'll fit in, like the skin on a chicken.'

They offered him the position of International Clientele Property Consultant, tasked with scouting and touting for the sale of properties worth nothing less than eight million pounds in London, and five million outside the capital. After twenty-one years – upon the incumbent's imprisonment for embezzlement – they appointed Tristan as a senior partner. While the rewards were high, there were many periods that were dryer than a Kalahari snowflake, often consequential of the idiosyncratic client.

A case in point was the ex-GRU Russian agent who, like Dmitriy, had made billions from the privatisation of state companies under Yeltsin's careful watch. For nigh on five years Tristan had hounded Ponomaryov Jaromir Mikhailovich. His tenacity paid off when he hooked a multi-million-pound apartment sale in Mayfair. The day had arrived when they were to sign the required papers and have the Russian transfer almost nine million pounds from his Mauritius offshore account into Tristan's holding company in a Conduit offshore financial centre.

Tristan arrived at Ponomaryov's permanent penthouse suite in a swank London hotel where he stayed with his charming mistress; his wife still lived in their Moscow flat. After the niceties with Ponomaryov and his English solicitor were over, Tristan had chatted to the Ruski's beautiful ladylove, but she showed no interest in his propositioning.

Ponomaryov, who'd been talking to his solicitor, turned and called to his girlfriend, 'We will toast our deal. Natalya, bring vodka for my friends.'

From a serpentine fronted Art Deco sideboard she carried a silver tray containing caviar, raw herring, and smoked fish zazuskis, and a bottle of Beluga vodka, the outside of which dripped with condensation. She placed the tray on a small table.

'Thank you, Natalya. You may leave the room.' Turning to Tristan, he said, 'We will sign the documents after which, we toast the deal.'

The solicitor placed the documents onto the eighteenth-century Louis XV period desk toward which the Russian had moved. Tristan deposited his Swiss fountain pen, a present from a Turkish client – a beautiful woman, particularly when enveloped in only a yashmak – next to the paperwork.

Within seconds of Ponomaryov's posterior touching the cushioned seat, he sprang to his feet screaming in Russian. With his face contorted into a grotesque mask and eyes agape, he fell to the ground. As his body writhed, foam from his mouth dribbled onto the north-west-Persian rug that, only a few moments earlier, Tristan had admired for its high knot count and wonderful dyes.

'Great Scott!' the solicitor said, recoiling in horror. 'What happened? What did he say?'

Tristan translated as he bent next to Ponomaryov's jerking body and checked his pulse, 'He said he felt a prick in his backside. It looks to me as if someone's poisoned the poor sod.'

The events had stunned the solicitor. 'Good heavens! This really is a cock-up. I'll call an ambulance!'

Using his somewhat brief Linseed Lancer tutelage to establish the fact, Tristan announced, 'An ambulance won't help, he's as dead as mutton!'

'Are you sure?'

'Let's just say, there's more life in the eider duck feathers in my duvet than in him. Look old chap, the indications of the permanency of his demise are, there's no pulse, he's not blinking, his false teeth have dropped out, and the deciding factor, he's not breathing.' Tristan's experience in the medical corps enabled him to pronounce, 'He's definitely snuffed it.'

The solicitor said, 'We'd better call the police!'

'Not yet,' Tristan said. 'Don't be too hasty. Let's see if we can get his signature onto the transfer papers while he's still warm and twitching. Otherwise, neither you, nor I, will make a penny out of this balls-up. Have you got his autograph on another form, or letter? If you have, I'll try to guide his hand.'

'That would be most irregular,' the solicitor said. 'But you're right. Not thought of that. Two minutes won't make any difference. Let's see.' He raked through the piles of paper in his briefcase.

'Come on, hurry,' Tristan said. 'I'm sure the blighter's getting colder and the twitching's slowing down.'

'I'm doing my best. Ah, here we are – got it!'

Tristan took the transfer deed and, placing his Swiss fountain pen into the dead man's fingers, he attempted to guide the jerking appendages to replicate the signature.

'Perhaps I can assist,' said the solicitor, bending to help. In his nervousness, he bashed Tristan's arm causing the hand-crafted solid-gold nib to break, thus precipitating a huge black blob to appear in the signature block. Tristan wrenched the pen from the Russian's nicotine-stained fingers.

'You twat,' he said. 'Look what you've done! You've buggered my pen, spattered the paper, botched up everything. Now we'll get nothing out of this mess. And where's that damn girl? Jolly sure she's in on this.' Tristan searched but she'd vanished. Probably an assassin, he thought.

'Poor devil, how unfortunate,' the solicitor said.

'Yes, too bloody true. I've been working on this for yonks and what do I get? Nothing! And my pen's ruined.'

'Not you, I meant my client,' the solicitor responded.

The police later confirmed they had found a poisoned needle in the seat of the gilt-framed Louis XV chair. Luckily it had been skilfully planted without damaging the threads.

In the murky world of money manoeuvring and mansions, Tristan oft dealt with those who had amassed their means by chicanery. However, not all of his clients were villains, plunderers or purloiners; in the sense that most people would describe such crepuscular creatures.

For example, Tristan blessed Lawrence of Arabia for his endeavours in changing the map of the shifting sands of the Middle East for the better. If it hadn't been for Lawrence, the ancestors of his desert-dwelling comrades-in-arms would cuddle their cocks and camels in a desert wadi instead of napping in their Knightsbridge mansions sold to them by Tristan. But even in his dealings with Middle Eastern Royalty, where they measured wealth by the barrel of fossil fuel, things from time to time had gone amiss.

It had taken Tristan over two years of considerable fortitude to find a buyer for the fourteen-million-pound twelve-acre country estate in the south of England. Finally, it was in the bag. An equine-loving Sheikh thought the property, with stabling for ten horses, was perfect for him and ideal for his number one wife and her entourage, during the English flat-racing season.

It had eight bedrooms with en-suites and dressing rooms, all-weather tennis courts, heated indoor and outdoor pools, a twenty-seat cinema and a vast wine cellar. The Sheikh's nags would have more luxury than most of humanity. Their paraphernalia would enable them to plash around in the equine hydrotherapy pool, after which a spell on the equissage machine would set them up for a tan in their own solarium.

Tristan had done his homework and found that, when in Provence Alpes Côte d`Azur, the Sheikha abandoned her burqa in favour of a bikini for frequent waterskiing sessions. So, he believed, the clincher would be the sheltered shoreline of the three-and-a-half-thousand-feet-long and three-hundred-feet-wide purpose-built lake for waterskiing. It would also be somewhere for the Sheikh's eighteen kids, by various wives, to paddle. The only thing left was for his number one to approve the moated mansion with a nod of her head.

At ten thirty on a warm midsummer's Sunday morning, number one wife broke the tranquillity of the pastoral location. As her Bell 407 executive helicopter circled the village church, the downwash from the four blades of the machine caused the six tower-columns of the eight-hundred-year-old flint-cobbled building to vibrate. The clock mechanism began harmonic oscillations, which precipitated its advancement to twelve.

Affluent London weekenders who'd purchased many of the village properties had demanded, ten years before, that the church stop the chimes of the hung dead bell, on the grounds that it breached noise abatement laws. Brigadier Sir Charles Horton-Higgins, Chair of the Parish Council, agreed with them, the chimes played havoc with his hounds, and so they gagged the gong. But the helicopter's rotor-blade vibrations caused the chime-constraining contrivance to break free and the hammer to continuously bash the bell so adding never-ending dongs to the din.

Meanwhile, the congregation of nine – there were two more than normal as it'd been a flower festival week – gave an appearance of wakefulness by staring glassy-eyed at the vicar. The reverend, feeling they ought to get their money's worth, was delivering a sermon concerning the lilies of the fields. Thus far, it had taken thirty-five minutes with three more pages to dispense. When he'd reached the peak of his preachment, his hand-written sermon shook more than was normal. Looking up, he saw the pews shaking, as were the parishioners.

The bell tolled ominously and the door flew open, flooding the dim interior with sunlight and a whirlwind surged through the portal. Marie Minter's flowers flew first, followed by ancient and even more ancient hymnbooks, service sheets and the other floral arrangements.

'Praise the Lord, it's the Second Coming,' the elderly vicar's voice cried out, although it was lost to the racket of the rotor blades and the high-pitched howl of the motor. 'Most unexpected,' he shouted. 'If you are able to, please kneel as we wait to ascend into heaven. Hallelujah!'

His supplications fell upon deaf ears. The churchgoers, to a woman, rushed out of the building as fast as arthritic knees and replacement hips allowed – skirts held down lest their varicose veins became the talk of the village.

After circling the church twice, the chopper screamed and clattered over the cottages to take in the gentle panoramic vista and the lake. In its wake, farm animals and panic-stricken pets frantically charged around fields, paddocks, and gardens. The broken bell thingamajig, having released the hammer to bash the bell, continued its funereal toll.

The wealthy weekenders up from London, who had been enjoying country life by lying leisurely in bed, were oblivious to the helicopter but were cursing the bell. The few stalwart inhabitants who had refused to sell to the odious outsiders emerged from thatched cottages in wild indignation, shaking fists and swearing at the intruder.

Finally, the machine hovered above the estate's house before coming to rest upon the recently manicured lawn; the downdraft sent a stone flying through a drawn glass pane in the Joseph Paxton cast-iron framed glasshouse. Lord Ffrench had installed the greenhouse before the government repealed the window tax in eighteen fifty-one.

With the engine still screaming, an elegant woman dressed in Western attire stepped from the chopper 'How far is it to Fortnum & Masons?' she asked.

Tristan, sensing a problem, told her it was under two, or perhaps three, hours by car, but the village post office stocked groceries and the pub was good for weekend meals, including a once a month carvery with a choice of beef, or pork.

Then all hell broke loose and villagers again blew their stack, waving angry fists as the screaming jet engines and rattling rotors carried her, and the deal, beyond the horizon.

But not all was gloom. A case in point being when, minutes before the artillery battery blasted a North Korean

– condemned for not clapping enough – into fragmented oblivion, his funds were streaked into Tristan's company account.

All's well that ends well.

* * *

The cab's clock indicated he was late… Rodney won't be happy, he thought. Sod him, Mummy and Cuthbert will keep him company.

Dear Reader, the Last of the Brood

Some of you may consider the Crooke-Wells family as somewhat bizarre. If that be so, you may hope to have heard the last of Mummy's little muppets. But no, you are about to rendezvous with another. His name is Cuthbert Upjohn Montgomery Crooke-Wells.

As you know, Mummy had relied upon her gynaecologist, Doctor Ludovic Labuscaigne, a close member within her inner circle, to deliver the first two children. Well, not wishing to end up in court for libel, let me just say a few words about him.

His alleged escapade with Jennifer Winterbottom devastated Mummy. You may have read a little of it in those scurrilous newspapers that thrive on such stuff and nonsense to titillate their readers. But then matters got even worse when Ludo not only skipped bail, but also the country.

Two months after his defection, Mummy had no choice but to seek the help of her friend Sylvie. It was a necessity because Archibald had thrown away the calendar upon which Mummy kept trace of her periodic cycles. So, as she'd felt a bit off-colour, and believed she'd missed two months, she went to Sylvie's obstetrician.

There he put her into a difficult position, then, after an examination, said that it wasn't indigestion and provided an estimated gestational age and confinement date.

If Ludo's casting her off to play ducks and drakes with that bitch Jennifer wasn't bad enough, worse was to come.

She was rushed from a game of bridge into a common hospital with four to a ward because the bloody quack doctor couldn't count.

That experience led Mummy to scream those immortal words echoed by millions of mothers over millennia, 'Never Again!' as Cuthbert entered the world.

The Game Hawkers Hood
is Removed

A tortured rendition of 'Baker Street' delivered by a so-called tenor saxophonist grew ever louder as Cuthbert descended the creaking escalator to the Angel Islington underground station.

To call this reed-licking, duck-honking instrument garrotter a musician would be an insult to any performer possessing a minim of musical mastery. Only the backing track gave Gerry Rafferty's melody an outside chance of recognition.

As he juddered ever closer to the underworld, Cuthbert glanced to his left and saw an advertisement for a new production at a West End theatre. Who would have dreamt that Thomas Lanier Williams III, a Mississippi-born drug-dependent alcoholic, son of a dipsomaniac salesman, would have written such a monumental masterpiece as *Cat on a Hot Tin Roof*? Or that thespians the entire world over would sell their mothers to perform in it. Also, that it would play such a pivotal role in his life.

There being no direct Tube service from Angel to Westminster, he'd have a five-minute trek when changing stations at Bank. With time at a premium, he dashed to platform three. There, the increased air pressure signalled the Northern Line train, that'd rush him head-long toward Mummy's dinner party in the Palace of Westminster, was on the point of emerging from its lair. The flat-fronted cab, with the driver staring trancelike ahead, screeched past. For all intents and purposes, the locomotive had gone loony and was hell-bent on hurtling nonstop into the next pitch-dark void. Then, in the nick of time, the brakes brought the train's silver-and-red carriages to a shuddering halt.

Even before the doors slid completely open the conflict for supremacy began, as those wishing to gain purchase into the overcrowded tube fought with those who sought release from its sanctity. With the help of a good shove he found a foothold, but had to remain standing even though, upon entering the carriage, he'd held his head to one side and limped heavily. This ploy invariably elicited a seat from some elderly person who vacated theirs to appease his 'affliction'. But today there were too many selfish young sods that remained seated, they wouldn't give a monkey's toss even if he were a one-legged ninety-five-year-old pregnant nun on crutches, and so he joined the other straphangers.

Transport London has an amazing conflict-resolution policy, he mused. To observe this in action, one has only to see how, within seconds of entering the carriage, the doors close and those who wished to exit are locked in and those wishing to enter kept out. It seemed a rather democratic process, applicable to other areas of public services. By squashing the washed and unwashed up against each other, the underground is a great leveller of humanity. There's no first, second, or third class, just mankind. Honest, evil, wealthy, impoverished, unhappy, cheerful, all rammed into a pipe.

Buckley's version of *Hallelujah* sounded from an attractive young lady's earphones; she was a fellow straphanger who reminded him of Mary. He preferred

Buckley's version to Cohen's original, finding the songwriter's version too long and dark, even funereal, for his taste. Buckley's he thought tender, and particularly poignant knowing the singer died young in such a mysterious circumstance, and so soon after recording it. It was a travesty, he thought, when performers of Cohen's masterpiece turned it into a religious chorale, losing sight of its poetic secularity.

Glancing at his watch, he thought, Bugger it, I'm late. At least Mummy, Rodney and Tristan will keep each other company. Rodney's invariably angry: he's a mean-spirited stickler for promptness – from others.

He envied his brothers, for they had both done well for themselves. True, he was making money, good money, but the other lucky devils had started a rung, or two, up the ladder compared to him. One at Eton, the other Rugby, while Daddy had dumped him at a third-rate boarding school, Saint Martin's in Faringham. He'd had to work harder than them. Saint Martin's fees told the story. His parents had forked out less than a quarter for his than for his elder brothers' schools. Perhaps one day Mummy would tell him why his education had not been up to the same scratch.

Eton had illustrious Old Boys, such as Sir Reresby Sacheverell Sitwell; Prince Henry, the Duke of Gloucester; HM King Prajadhipok of Siam; and Admiral of the Fleet, Sir Arthur Knyvet Wilson. His school's most distinguished old boy was Reggie Thornton, chosen only once to play cricket for England. The selectors dropped him after he shamefully batted his way for a duck against a team more used to rollicking at rounders than whacking the willow: the USA. One would have assumed the school's name, St. Martin's – the patron saint of beggars – would have given a measure of concern to Mummy and Daddy, but no, it hadn't.

It could have been worse if they'd plonked for the other school on the shortlist – St. Cajetan's in Leicester. That glorified soul had the unenviable task to look after job seekers. Leicester! Why even consider the place? Rumour has it that the council's idea of a theme park, based upon the local hero Thomas Cook, was soon dropped when they learnt that temperance Tom's tours weren't to get tourists in, but to get them clean out of the sin-filled city. Still, desperate to drag tourists off the M1 motorway and into its environs, the City Fathers then boasted they'd found the earliest known remains of a Roman bathhouse, thus asserting the place's value for international travellers. Having endured several visits to the town, Cuthbert had concluded that a Roman Legionnaire may have been the first, but definitely was the last to have had a bath in the borough. As for St. Cajetan, the Leicester layabouts needed not an iota of holy help in their bone idleness.

Never one for the scholarly, he'd found the more erudite subjects at school not only irksome, but, with the abysmal tutelage on offer, beyond him and those with twice his grey matter. The only Latin on the curriculum was of the American ballroom style, as dance lessons had replaced sports after, like state schools, they had sold off the playing fields for housing.

The school's amateur dramatic society was his genuine passion, and where he excelled. With no aptitude for learning lines, backstage had been his forte. They'd adjudged his theatrical accomplishments as the only highlight of his scholarly activities by awarding him Rider Haggard's *King Solomon's Mines* as a prize. The citation within the dust cover read, '*For enthusiastic work as a member of the fly crew*'. He'd operated the curtains. Nanny attended parents evening and, her eyes filled with tears, stood to applaud when he received the presentation.

Most pupils detested Mr Chaplin, but he was the only teacher he liked, and also, the fattest man he'd ever seen. 'Once around me, twice round the Council House' was his favourite self-deprecating joke. Labelled Charlie, he introduced him to Darwin's theory. He remembered it went something like, 'Educating upper-class transmuted twerps, like you, seems insane, for Darwin's abstraction expresses itself as the biological concept of fitness being defined by procreative success. I will put it this way in order there be no confusion: if two large and intelligent rabbits shagged, their offspring would also be big and even brainier; if two millionaires did the same thing, they'd produce twats like you.'

The simplicity of the concept thrilled him. Mr Chaplin had planted the seed for him to consider that there was more to Darwin's theory than a pair of procreating rabbits. Darwin, the wayfaring globetrotter, was himself the product of a wealthy doctor and financier, who was the son of a wealthy doctor and lawyer, who was the son of a wealthy doctor – ad nauseam. While on his mother's side, his grandfather was none other than Josiah Wedgwood, even more staggeringly wealthy, whose father was wealthy, whose father was, it just kept going. Cuthbert reasoned that if Darwin had lost seventy-five per cent of his cash, he would still have been wealthy. Plainly, if, instead of ploughing through the world's oceans puking over the gunwales while searching for the elusive blue-arsed fin-tailed baboon, Darwin had studied the British class system, no seasickness, no cost, and same result.

The survival of the fittest as the predominant factor in humans drew attention to itself every morning when Darwin looked into the mirror. Wealth and privilege were hereditary. All that traipsing around the world, what a waste of money! Heaving his breakfast down the side of the good ship *Beagle*, when the facts were staring him in the face. Obvious – the whole thing was as clear as the bell that tolled upon the ship he sailed.

Darwin and his contemporary, Wallace, needn't have wasted their time. Power comes from wealth, wealth generates power, and power produces wealth: its perpetual motion and therefore only the poor need education to survive and serve. The so-called evolutionary theories of the survival of the fittest was being taught at Eton, Harrow and Rugby aeons before Darwin undertook his all-inclusive cruise; without Thomas Cook's help. Despite having brothers like Tristan and Rodney who made more money than him, Cuthbert felt his birthright to be fortunate and fitted Darwin's doctrine admirably.

As an aptitude for the theatrical had not spanned into the academic, his qualifications within the leaver's certificate were barren. A smattering of potential employers might have considered, '*Did well at Theatrical Work*', of some worth, but Daddy summed it up as, 'Although slightly better than Tristan, you're still a great disappointment.'

In retrospect, St Cajetan's might have been better. His educational encumbrance could have hung over him like a lenticular cloud upon Kilimanjaro, but, although burdensome, it had not shackled him. Anyway, the English public school alumni had, for centuries, provided a network of mutuality which ensured even the most boorish feeble-minded chinless dimwits reached the social strata decreed by their birthright. Maintaining the status quo was imperative for the survival of their class. As no worthwhile alumni had ever studied at St Martin's, Daddy and Rodney secured his connections; Tristan being of no use.

There was no university, as his father refused to add even a penny to educate 'the useless twat', as he expressed his opinion of Cuthbert's capabilities. Daddy knew many people, including Simon Forester, the Chairman of Young-Forester and Partners, who found him a position. The role in marketing handed over a good income that would see him through until the real treasure trove arrived – when he picked up his division of the family fortune.

While establishing himself in the business he'd kept in touch with his passion, by joining the long-established Invictus Amateur Dramatic Society. Compared to the other actors, he was mediocre and received no lead parts and, thankfully, only a few with spoken words and even those he fluffed, but it didn't matter. Being in The Theatre was his passion and the lack of acting talent didn't dampen his devotion; he'd do any task, no matter how menial.

The winter show was *Seven Brides for Seven Brothers*. They cast Mary Evans as Milly, opposite Leander Lovett's, Adam. Cuthbert's role was property master and dogsbody. He was heaving the next bit of scenery into its correct place when the unexpected happened. Mary's rendition of *When You're In Love* fell like silk upon his ears and, in a flash, there were only two people in the universe. Johnny Mercer must have written the song, knowing it would be sung one day by Mary. Borne into paradise, he imagined the two of them floating upon a cloud of joy and happiness: he realised he was in love with Mary Evans.

Wooing her was inconceivable, as many male members were sniffing around and even two, or three, women seemed to have designs on the girl of whom he could only dream. He knew some lusted after her, but, unlike them, his was love, not lechery. Every word she uttered, every breath from her lips or movement of her body, triggered a euphonic symphony within his being; when with her he was tongue-tied and nauseous. Knowing she would never consider him a suitable suitor, he loved her from a distance. There was the occasional mumbled 'hello' – without eye contact over a plastic cup of instant coffee during the break – or 'good evening' upon arrival.

It was a great shock when she made the first move and asked him to be her escort at an award evening given by a local paper. It was the most thrilling moment of his life.

The first date became another, then another, until they were, in modern parlance, an item. Mary continued with her lead roles, growing ever stronger and more confident, and her performances received wild newspaper reviews. Meanwhile, Cuthbert was happy to bathe in her reflected glory and to be the envy of all other members of the group.

He loved Mary with all his heart; there'd been no one else. An engagement came two years later, and one year thereafter Mary Evans became Mrs Mary Crooke-Wells. Although not a fairy-tale marriage, and there were no children, they enjoyed a partnership of tolerance, patience, openness, honesty, and, above all else, love.

When Cuthbert was twenty-eight, Daddy had a chat with the Chairman of the agency which resulted in Cuthbert's promotion to artistic director. While his advancement was reason enough to celebrate, it was also their wedding anniversary. They planned to mark both occasions with an intimate dinner for two, after Mary had finished the penultimate performance of the latest amateur dramatic society's offering, the Rogers and Hammerstein's musical, *Carousel*.

Her role in the all-time favourite was that of Julie Jordan, with Leander Lovett playing her onstage husband, Billy Bigelow. After the first night, the local newspaper reviews raved about her rendition for, beside her amazing singing voice, she had by now developed into an outstanding serious actress. They played the rest of the week to sell-out houses.

Mounting work commitments provided Cuthbert with little time to take part in amateur dramatics, his contentment now being to bask in his wife's glory. Not having to hump scenery was helpful, as sitting in the third row from the front enabled him to watch his adorable wife on stage and hear members of the audience proclaim how good she was. He thought her even better than Shirley Jones, who played the role in the film version. The ovation for *If I Loved You* was so clamorous, they had to encore. Although a duet, it was Mary who bore the audience upon a bewitching journey of love. Without her, they'd have been lucky to get a handclap. He was so proud.

As the curtain closed the audience wildly applauded and, when Mary came to take her bow, they rose as one: cheering, whistling, and even screaming. He had an overwhelming desire to cry out – She's mine, and it's our anniversary and I love her – at the top of his voice. After the show had ended, with hands tingling from clapping, for some time Cuthbert remained seated until Mary entered the auditorium through the door to the right of the stage. He stood to walk over, hug, and celebrate her phenomenal achievement, but paused as a male fan stepped forward to congratulate her. Cuthbert sat and waited. After a minute or two of discussion, the man handed Mary a card which she put into her shoulder bag and, smiling, they shook hands and he departed.

Taking the opportunity, Cuthbert joined Mary, kissed, hugged and told her how wonderful she was, and not just in the show. Her face glowed with excitement, and he found her cheek moist from the theatrical make-up removal cream. It had been a superb performance, perhaps this was how he would remember her when they were old and doddery.

'You were sensational,' a fan waxed lyrical. 'May I have your autograph?' said another. Cuthbert stood aside as, yet more, fans came over to congratulate her; it was her night, her audience and her glory.

He'd booked a table at a local restaurant for their romantic candlelit late-night supper. They chatted as he drove them there in his new Company car; now that he was a higher grade it was much swankier than the last one. Jane Dixon, who played Carrie Pipperidge, and always sang well in rehearsals, was at the forefront of their criticism, for she sang off-key far too often. Then there were several forgotten lines, and not to forget the costume and scenery mishaps – which wouldn't have occurred had he still been in charge.

During a few moments of silence Cuthbert asked, 'Who was that chap?'

'Which one, dear?'

It was true, many had been seeking to congratulate her. 'The one waiting for you by the stage door, he gave you something, you put into your bag.'

'Oh him! He's a theatrical agent, gave me his business card, wants me to call him,' she responded, in a matter-of-fact way, 'Wanted to know if I have a manager, or an agent. Said my performance was good and I have the potential to become a professional.'

'Well, I think you're already a professional. Look at the newspaper reviews, they're always raving about you.'

She snorted. 'Oh, just local rags, they always say gracious things about amateur theatre. They'd never slag off a bunch of hams, or say something's rubbish, they're just being kind.'

'You may be right, but there is a difference between publishing pleasantries and writing the serious stuff that I've read about you. You're already a brilliant actress.'

'No!' She almost laughed, 'Perhaps in an amateur sense, but he's talking about the professional theatre.'

Cuthbert said, 'Professional theatre, gosh we've never considered that, have we?'

'Well, no, well not really,' she said.

'Not really! What does that mean?' he said. 'Either you have, or you haven't?'

'I mean that it had crossed my mind, but not seriously.'

'Oh, so tonight wasn't the first time that it had crossed your mind,' he mimicked. 'I thought we discussed everything. So, tell me why have you kept this secret?'

'It only crossed my mind; it wasn't serious nor a secret and...'

He interrupted, 'Not serious! By following such a career it'd take us to heaven knows where, our lives would be turned upside down, and you say it's not serious. If that's not serious, what the devil is?'

'There's no need for that tone of voice. You don't own me, and I'm allowed to have dreams.'

'Oh, that's it!' He blasted the horn longer than needed at the cat on the pavement. 'So, it was no longer something that crossed your mind and you threw into the gutter, no, now it's become a dream, that's bloody fine for you, isn't it? No thought for me. What have you and your agent cooked up? Where do I fit in to your scheme?'

'I'm telling you it was never serious, and he's not my agent.'

'Never serious! You spend half the night talking to the sodding man and it's not serious! Then, you hide his card away, so I won't see it, and that's not serious?'

'I was talking to him for less than a minute, and he's not my agent, you're being stupid. It's no wonder your father had to get you promoted.'

She wished she hadn't said that, but could think of nothing else to hurt him with, at that moment.

But the curtains were up, unimportant niggles that'd been as safe as dust in a dark corner were as floodlit as the *Carousel* set and magnified into matters that cut to the quick. Their exchange of words became as blistering as the Malayalam Beef Chilli he'd made on their last anniversary when they'd applied butter as balm to each other's lips.

She blamed him for things he'd done and those not done, while he dragged up an equal measure of once worthless wounds. Within the few minutes it took to arrive at the restaurant, they'd run out of painful memories to toss like fireballs into the mêlée, instead descended into silence. Mary leapt out, slamming the door as soon as the brakes brought the car to a skidding halt in the restaurant's car park. Cuthbert was even more forceful, but the internal air pressure meant he had to do it twice.

'A good night this has turned out to be,' she snapped, storming ahead of him.

Cuthbert stomped back to the car. 'What do you want then? Shall we just go home and forget my promotion?

Oh, and our anniversary? Yes, that's what we'll do; we'll go home and celebrate, shall we?'

Mary charged ahead, slamming the restaurant door. Cuthbert, now seething even more at her unreasonable behaviour, followed seconds later. To his dismay, the table next to the one marked 'reserved', upon which had been laid the single red rose he'd ordered, was full of am-dram society members.

'Hello!' they shrieked, in that squeaky, stupid, puerile, feigned, overblown, affected manner adopted by such ilk.

Cuthbert inwardly fumed, thinking: They've not even the savvy to sense that nobody gives a toss about their two-bit acting triumphs.

'Oh, sod it!' he declared and grimaced at Mary. 'You planned this didn't you?'

'No, I didn't! How was I to know?' She glowered at him, while seizing the providential manna of not having to eat in silence. 'Hello darlings,' she called, upping an octave and leaving him standing next to their reserved table, while she traipsed around kissing all and sundry on the cheek making silly 'mwah' noises with each peck. Her feigned charm and good-naturedness belied an angry inner mood. He threw the red rose to the floor and ground it into the carpet with his heel.

'We'll make room, come and join us,' they squeaked and squealed.

The maître d' counted the number of reserve bottles stashed under the counter and kept for such occasions: there were plenty. They'd once contained expensive wine, but he'd refilled them with leftovers and cheap plonk, re-corked and sealed them, using heat shrink foil. He rushed to link the bunch of supercilious twits together.

While the group had shuffled around, Mary grabbed a chair as far from Cuthbert as was possible; they left him standing, and no one offered him a seat. The maître d' rushed over with a chair and seated Cuthbert opposite Leander Lovett, or Billy Bigelow, to Mary's Julie Jacobs in *Carousel*.

Lovett's breath wafted across the table, assailing Cuthbert's nostrils, the odour reminiscent of the dead dolphin in the Cornish cove last year. (Its sleek body and smiling face were being pecked by petrels and had made Mary cry.) Lovett had a spot on his nose that as if by magneto reception attracted Cuthbert's attention. Funny he hadn't seen it when Lovett was on stage, probably covered the pus-sodden thing with make-up.

Engulfed within his solitude of red wine, he brooded upon how long in the love scenes, Julie and Billy – Mary and Lovett – had kissed and, come to think of it, how frequently. Thinking back to the Rogers and Hammerstein movie, he was sure they hadn't kissed so often and certainly not for that length of time. Maybe not at all? Funny, Mary hadn't mentioned Lovett's stinking breath. He recalled reading of an actor who ate garlic to put off the co-stars with whom he smooched on screen. Mind you, he thought, a whole bulb of garlic would have been more acceptable than the open sewerage drain with crooked teeth sitting opposite.

Perhaps Lovett's one of those Stanislavsky actors who aims for a 'complete emotional identification' with the part. Did they practice kissing just to get realism and perfection? They'd say, 'Nothing sexual, nothing like that.' How many times did they rehearse the kisses? He could hear them at it, sniggering and snogging in the wings behind the 'Grand Drapes' – as Lovett would call them in a phoney American accent that wouldn't even fool a child in the audience. Was it only a kiss? In the libretto Julie Jacobs falls pregnant. Did the smarmy rat have to re-enact that as well? He'd read that actors often play out their roles in real life, like an English actor always speaking with an American accent throughout the filming, even at home, and only reverting to the natural Geordie gibberish once 'everything's in the can'.

Had they?

Were they still at it, and did the rest of the cast know? That's why they're laughing, it's at my expense. Am I a cuckold? He was most surprised to see his glass empty again: someone must have drunk it. The maître d' filled it without asking. He recalled Mary had regularly rehearsed the Maine vernacular – large became 'honkin' and the dog became 'numb crittah' when it peed on the floor. She shopped for 'steamers' to make clam 'chowdah' with 'oyster crackers' to go with it, and a glass of 'fat-ass' followed 'suppah'. Oh yes! She'd got into the role all right, but how far had it gone? Let's face it; Julie's a young girl who's seduced by a bounder from a fairground. Had Lovett seduced Julie – no, not Julie, Mary? Did it go beyond a kiss?

He should have taken notice; he'd not sensed the clues. Perhaps he should have and put a stop to it before it got out of hand. How could his wife, whatever her name was, sing *If I Loved You* to that stinking bounder whose impersonation of a New England carousel barker was more like a 'Noo Yawk' cabdriver with a rotten Northern English accent?

It was gratifying to find his small glass was full once more; he must be thirsty, or the glass tinier than he at first perceived.

The boisterous babble had, by now, degenerated into the only common denominator: thespianism. Darling and deary were all they could say. It's as if they're on magic mushrooms, hallucinatory heaven, he seethed. That's it; they're a bunch of magic mushroom munchers. It was a fact proven for, as he peered around, he saw that they were all distorted; some even had three, or four, eyes.

It surprised him to find his glass again empty.

I wish the lot of them would slip on the dribble and snot and break a stupid leg, never mind one leg; I hope they break both legs, and their bloody necks!

It was strange how heavy his head felt, more so than a few glasses ago, and it wouldn't stop falling forward. Nothing about promotion, the new car, or our wedding anniversary, nobody cares, not a dicky. All eyes are on the leading lady regaling her toadying devotees with the sodding agent's tale.

'I may not even bother phoning, such a bore, and quite a tedious little person.'

'Oh, you must, deary, it'd be a loss to the world of art, if you don't,' they screeched, whooped and crowed.

'Please, please do, darling,' Leander Lovett, said, his stinking breath slithering across the table like sulphurous rotten eggs on a funeral march and assailed Cuthbert's whiffer.

The Rhino-horned pustulous pustule was even more pronounced when Cuthbert focused upon it with his left eye closed and head held at an angle.

Thankfully, his glass was, once more, full; it was surprising how quickly it emptied. Moving it closer, he mumbled to the women beside him, 'Drink your bloody own.'

As Mary acquainted the others not only with what the agent had said but also what he meant by what he'd said, Cuthbert became increasingly enraged. How nauseating he found her assertions that she wasn't interested in becoming a professional actress and to declare it had only crossed her mind, but not seriously. Obviously she was interested, the only thing missing from her account of the meeting was the twat's inside leg measurement and the hang side of his crotch. She was interested all right, passing the agent's card around the table for her menagerie's appraisement. It bypassed Cuthbert.

By now, debilitated by the abundance of alcohol, his optical and cerebral cognisance's were such that any comprehension by him was nigh on an impossibility. Nonetheless, he felt that, as the lame-brained narcissistic parasites hanging upon every word his wife uttered had refused to pass the card to him, they were his adversaries. It was obvious for all to see. Mary had never been on such a high – the passion carried her to somewhere unassailable to a mere mortal like him. She'd morphed into a Valkyrie.

In an intoxicated trance, he stared into the empty glass as would a soothsayer a scrying ball: a mere spectator. His resentment was intensifying in proportion to the plentiful wine poured by the maître d' and also what he purloined from the glass of the creature with a flat chest seated on his right and the toss-bag on the other side of the table.

Slumped in the chair, he contemplated the situation.

Julie, or Mary – whatever she wanted to call herself – and this bunch of fop-doodles had cast him adrift like a *Bounty* deckhand. They'd left him to wallow within his own rumination, with only the bare rations of his brainwork as sustainers through the storm. As oil loosens a lock, so Cuthbert's alcohol-liberated larynx projected a full-throated torrent of abuse. His fermented thoughts filled the air.

'Bloody blabbermouths. They're a bunch of stupid pantomime pricks and crap-babbling duck-arsed prats.'

A stunned silence fell like a Balinese Nyepi night.

Mary burst into tears, and, as if she were a maltreated maiden in a Victorian melodrama, collapsed her head onto the table, cradled in folded arms. The four-eyed dick, who'd played the rear end of the donkey in last year's pantomime, stood and offered to take Cuthbert outside for a 'jolly good thrashing', but was held back by the man who'd played the front end.

'You're a bloody arse-sniffing popinjay,' yelled Cuthbert, the insult aimed at the rear end. Then, directing his abuse to the moke's front, sneered, 'And you've got hair like a Poitou Jenny and ears like one too.'

He alone howled with laughter, but then noted that the spotty-nosed gutless wonder, Billy Bigelow, had slunk from his seat and was comforting Julie Jordan. The rotter's arm was around her!

'If that putrid merry-go-round pus-nosed weasel sings again, I'll end his claptrap,' he screamed.

It had been Mary's tireless rehearsals at home that'd perfected her role as Julie. His task had been to read back the other parts with prompts to her lines. The unfolding tear-jerking drama of *Carousel* was as hewn into his head as was 'I Love You' engraved in the wedding ring he'd slipped onto her finger. The wretched crook, Jigger Craigin, had planned a dastardly robbery. Jigger then convinced Billy to be his partner in the heinous crime. Billy's pregnant wife, Julie, pleaded with Billy not to go with Jigger, 'No Billy! Please, no!' she'd called out. But her pleadings fell upon deaf ears for, dismissing his wife's supplications, Billy and Jigger attempted the robbery. It was then Billy met his comeuppance. For it was Jigger's knife that dispatched him to the pearly gates, where a seraphic bouncer, Mr Starkeeper, was not too eager to usher the reprobate into Xanadu.

So, with the aid of bounteous fermentations of a variety of vintages, Cuthbert had by now assumed the persona of that dreadful murderous Jigger Craigin. A determined frenetic frenzied Jigger, aka Cuthbert Crooke-Wells, would assail his rival, the contemptible Billy Bigelow, aka Leander Lovett, who had taken Julie Jordon, aka Mary Crooke-Wells, into his treacherous arms, or, even beyond, into his bed!

At school, the music teacher, Reginald Gracegirdle, had taken his class to see a ballet documentary screened for local schools. Cuthbert had thought the cinema might hurtle off its foundations, it shook so furiously when the orchestra brass section gave Pyotr Ilyich Tchaikovsky's score welly, and then a miracle occurred. A figure flew from the stage as if an eagle borne heavenward upon thermals. At its zenith, the diminutive shape appeared suspended before returning to earth as light as duck-down. He'd witnessed the celluloid image of the great Nureyev dancing as Prince Siegfried. After the film, dancers from the ballet company answered questions. Cuthbert asked how the dancer had seemingly broken the law of gravity by hanging in mid air.

'It's called a grand jeté. It's one of the hardest ballet movements to execute, requiring years of practice to perfect,' the dancer had responded. 'Rather than just answering your question, I will show every move required.'

He'd then carried out an Achilles-flex, a quad-stretch and a grand plié before demonstrating the move. It was breathtaking and, from that moment on, Cuthbert loved ballet. The dancers – no longer a bunch of effeminate guys jumping around in white tights and a padded pelvis – were now athletes telling a story using the fluid movements of their bodies, where every muscle played an integral part.

Through an inebriated mist, he hatched a plan to win back Julie (Mary). It required him to execute a grand jeté, fly through the space dividing him from his adversary, and then to dispatch Billy (Leander Lovett) back to Mr Starkeeper (heaven's gatekeeper) and regain Julie's (Mary's) affection. It was a simple but effective strategy.

He'd astound Mary and the rest of the useless toady tosspots. Proper preparation was the key to preventing a poor performance, and prepared he was. Every detail of the great Nureyev would be emulated; there was no room for error, it had to be perfect. As if projected upon a giant cinema screen in his mind's eye, he saw the frame-by-frame images of Nureyev, his graceful, svelte body bewitching the world.

The Achilles-flex was followed by a quad-stretch and a grand plié. He felt lithe and graceful as he fixed a cold merciless gaze upon Billy (Lovett). As kamikaze pilots took their last glass of saké, so he took a swig from the glass in front of him. Strange, he thought he'd been drinking wine, not beer. Face ashen, vision focused, his mind as clear as the finest high-lead Bohemia crystal, he'd fixed the height and trajectory required to reach Billy and, with preparation complete, he inhaled, ready to take flight. As a raptor's eyes view its prey when the Game Hawkers hood is removed, so Cuthbert's gaze fixed upon the snivelling rat, Billy Bigelow.

Then, in the guise of Jigger – or was it Nureyev? – Cuthbert took flight. The surroundings were but a blur, the faces startled as he spiralled to reach the trajectory from where he'd plummet earthbound, and seek to dispatch the plundering pillager of his passion. Estimating he'd reached the peak of his orbit, he took a deep breath – it was a small, but important, part of the technical technique used by Nureyev to hang in space. With toes pointed and arms extended, Cuthbert executed a perfect grand jeté as he defied gravity and sped towards the spotty-nosed prick.

'Billy Bigelow, you rat-arsed tosspot, I'm on my way. I'll save you Mary, my dearest beloved,' he hollered.

Resigned to his violent demise, Billy Bigelow stood rooted to the spot, open-mouthed, his features contorted with shock, fear, and disbelief.

When viewed with eyes of sobriety, the group saw Cuthbert screaming incoherently as he staggered to his feet. Someone else's glass of beer was streaming down his front as he tried to figure out the position of his mouth. He stood on his chair, but it collapsed which caused him to fall across the table, which disintegrated. A gentleman, whom Cuthbert had described as a donkey's arse, had, as an act of kindness, stepped forward to aid Cuthbert, but received an accidental wallop on the nose and, as the chair splintered, a leg flew up and struck Leander Lovett on his snout. In fear of the crazed psychotic maniac, other guests fought a bloody battle in their dash for freedom, adding to the mayhem by sending tables, chairs, glasses and plates crashing to the floor.

The consequential scene of devastation would have reminded Stavros of a Greek wedding in an Aegean dockyard café: there was not one unbroken plate in sight.

Cuthbert himself had disintegrated into a heap on the floor, screaming something about Prince Siegfried.

Mary fell sobbing into the welcoming, comforting arms of a bloody-nosed smirking Leander Lovett aka, Billy Bigelow.

A Moggie on the Ceiling

The effort required to crowbar his eyes open was greater than he could summon, and the body attached to his thumping head was as stiff as a carcass in a coffin.

Dead, that's what it is, I must be dead. But how can you feel pain if you're deceased? Perhaps I'm not dead, but they think I am, and so they've laid me out in a mortuary awaiting burial or, even worse, cremation. No! Even worse than worse, dissection!

The thoughts staggered through his brain. Attempting anew to open his swollen eyelids, he found they still malfunctioned, requiring a humongous effort from him to lever them apart.

The image of a man standing next to him emerged from a haze. A priest giving him the last rites, or was it God ready to welcome him into life everlasting? He tried to speak, but could manage little more than a rasp through a throat as parched as a stuffed parrot.

A voice boomed, 'Good morning, sunshine! Shall we sit up, sir? I'll be putting a plate of porridge and an enamel mug of tea onto the floor next to your bed.' A few seconds passed, and he heard, 'Feeling any better?' Cuthbert could not utter a word and the voice continued, 'Suppose that'd ask too much.'

After a few minutes he croaked, 'Are you God?'

'No sir. I'm your Duty Custody Sergeant, here to look after your every need. You're in the nick, my boy.'

'In the nick? Prison!' Cuthbert staggered upright, his head bursting. 'Why, why am I here?'

'Now don't get upset, sir. You can stay on your bed for as long as you wish, or at least until the magistrate wants a chat. There's no need for you to get hot and bothered, you're not in prison. You're in a police station custody cell, it's the same as a prison, but they haven't found you guilty. That will come in the due course of time and, while we wait for the guilty verdict, I will look after all of your needs. So, don't fret yourself, sir – at least, not yet.'

'But why am I here?' Cuthbert asked. 'Have I been in an accident?'

The bemused sergeant chuckled, 'Oh no, sir, there was no accident. You have what we in the trade call Alcohol Amnesia. Lots of that goes on around here on a Friday evening, even more on a Saturday night. I can assure you, sir, that without people like you I'd be out of work. Yes, that's what you've got, Alcohol Amnesia. Sir, I don't wish to sound impolite in front of a person of breeding such as yourself, but it's when you get so pissed that it stops you from remembering things.'

Cuthbert asked, 'Remembering what?'

'The restaurant. Can't we remember wrecking the restaurant, injuring a gentleman by punching him on the nose? What about throwing a chair leg that wounded another soul and not to forget puking in the police car, singing that a bint called June was busting out all over, and insisting your name was Prince Siegfried when we arrived here last night, sir?'

Cuthbert sat on the edge of the slab; his pounding head held in shaking hands. 'Oh no! Is Mary here?'

The sergeant seemed perplexed, 'Mary? Is that the rather attractive young lady you called Julie?'

'No. Well, yes, although her name isn't Julie, it's Mary,' Cuthbert responded, feeling even more dejected. Perhaps a ride into a blazing crematorium might have been preferable to what was emerging.

'Ah, I know the young lady you mean. Yes sir, a gentleman who you called Billy, escorted her here and, seeing how distressed she was, accompanied the lady home, sir.'

'Billy! You mean Lovett! What the devil was he doing here?'

'Ah well, you see sir, Mr Lovett was here because he's one of them who's laying charges of assault, together with another gentleman you referred to last night as the arse end of a donkey.'

'Assault! I assaulted no one.' Cuthbert thought long and hard. 'Did I?'

'Well sir, it's like this. In law your wife does not have to be a witness because of your relationship, but she has volunteered to be one of the twenty-seven others who say they saw you lay into Mr Lovett – that's the gentleman you called Billy – and also to the gentleman who you referred to as the arse end of a donkey.'

'Is that bad?' asked Cuthbert.

'Compared to the rest of the charges? No sir.'

'What do you mean, rest of the charges? What other charges are there?'

'Well, there's the restaurant owner, he's got the same witnesses, including your wife, concerning the damage to his property. He estimates, and it's only an estimate because the insurance company has yet to send in an assessor, but his estimate, including the plate-glass window, is ten thousand pounds, sir.'

'Plate-glass window? How. . .?' Cuthbert's voice faltered.

'Well, sir, you threw a chair through that didn't you, or was it a table?' He looked at his papers. 'Must be my age, sir, I'm wrong. It was a chair and a table.'

It was perplexing as he could remember nothing of what was being said. It couldn't be true, and yet even Mary was to witness against him.

The sergeant looked at the papers in his hand. 'Oh dear, and yes, I'm sorry to be the bearer of bad tidings.'

Cuthbert groaned. 'Bad tidings! What could be worse?' Both his body and mind were now feeling as if they were being wrung in a wringer.

The sergeant looked again at the papers. 'Sorry if this shocks you, but as well as the broken tables, chairs, oh – and crockery – we mustn't forget there's compensation for loss of business for which the owner has lodged an estimate.'

'Loss of business! How much is that?'

'The owner's estimate runs into several thousands of pounds. We've got lots of lovely photographs of the damage.' He paused. 'It really was a good night out wasn't it, sir? Would you care to take a peek at the pictures?'

'No, thanks,' Cuthbert said, holding his head in his hands.

'I'm so sorry I've been the bearer of awful news, but you know, sir, in my line of work there's always the lighter moments that lifts the gloom. When I felt low at one o'clock this morning, you brought cheer into my life with your repeated renditions of, *You'll Never Walk Alone*. But, take care if you're ever released back into society, for there are several other gentleman detainees that said they'd do you up, or some such words, when they get out.'

The seriousness of his situation was sinking into Cuthbert's addled brain. 'What happens now?'

'Under the circumstances,' the sergeant sounded jolly, 'when questioned, you may use your own solicitor, or they will appoint one to act on your behalf, if you so wish.'

'A solicitor! Why the devil would I need a solicitor? Can't I pay a little fine?'

The sergeant looked at a piece of paper, 'Well sir, we were quite a naughty fellow, weren't we? The charges: Public Order Act, 1986 section 3, Affray, or disturbing the public peace; Criminal Damage Act 1971, section 4, summary offence of being drunk and disorderly; section 39, assault with intent. You hit Mr Billy Bigelow, aka Mr Leander Reginald Lovett, on the snout with a chair leg and a fellow reveller known to you as arse end of a donkey, aka Mr Solomon Vogelstein, you gave him the old one-two on his beak.'

He checked his notes. 'Sorry sir, I forgot to mention our sovereign's property, as I see by your actions you have involved our monarch in this matter. There is a charge of disgorging the contents of your abdomen upon one of Her Britannic Majesty's car seats, to wit, a police car. She owns every one, a large fleet, and one is now very smelly, so there are the cleaning costs. Really was quite a night out we had, but never mind, sir, not the first time the magistrate will have heard the story.'

As the question left Cuthbert's mouth, he knew it sounded ludicrous. 'Is it serious?'

'I really wouldn't worry about it, sir, unless you have children who'll miss you. We've had worse.' The sergeant thought for a moment before saying, 'Murder is worse but, you know, I wouldn't worry myself if I were you – not just yet, anyway.'

'I'd like to phone my wife.'

'I'm sure you would and if it were in my power to bring you two young people together, I would do my best to make the arrangements. But I am, sad to say, helpless over this matter for, even as we speak, she is giving her statement. The young lady arrived early – she said it was to beat the rush.'

'Beat the rush! It's not a summer sale,' Cuthbert blurted.

'Well, that is true, but the desk sergeant was only saying to the constable, whose leave we cancelled to help with the deluge of eyewitnesses eager to become testators, that he was thinking of issuing numbers to people. You know, like what you get in hospitals because there's a few jumping the queue. Always get them types, champing at the bit, impatient, wouldn't want any fights breaking out in the station, would we? Might have to call a copper,' he chuckled.

'I must have upset many of my wife's friends. I must speak to her, clear things up, perhaps when she's finished giving her statement?'

'I have to say sir, that your actions were troubling to a few souls. As for having a chat with your good lady after she's given her statement, I'm sorry to say that won't be possible. The reason she was first in the queue was that she needed to get away, got an important engagement to attend,' he looked at his papers, 'with Mr Lovett.'

'With Lovett! When did she tell you that?'

'She gave me a message this morning, sir, when she arrived accompanied by Mr Lovett who had a large plaster across his nose. She said she wouldn't be at home to take a call from you today, tonight, or ever.'

Cuthbert sat silently, shocked, as the sergeant continued. 'Well, I must pop off, got more scallywags requiring my ministrations to salve their sufferings without fear, or favour. If I can be of service to you, call me.'

With a smile somewhat akin to that of a shot fox, Cuthbert thanked him, and said he needed to think. The sergeant suggested he would soon have tonnes of time to ruminate and recommended he seek the services of a solicitor who'd endeavour to shorten his penal servitude.

Time passed slowly, and then two hours later the door swung open and a short bald man stood looking over the top of pince-nez around the cell.

'Ah, Mr Cuthbert Crooke-Wells, I presume. I'm from Baumann, Berkovich and Bradshaw, Criminal Solicitors.'

Cuthbert thought the man smiling before him sounded jollier than the circumstances allowed, and asked, 'Which one are you?'

'I'm Avishalom Adelstein, but my friends call me Avi. You may call me Mr Adelstein.'

'Couldn't they send the head honcho? Are you one of the vultures perched outside the cells all day waiting for some poor sod in need of a free solicitor?'

'What do you mean, head honcho? I am he, as you say with such vulgarity. I own the practice. In the trade, they say I am one of the most experienced criminal lawyers in the country. Let me tell you, my boy, there're more convictable criminals strolling the streets because of my accomplishments than are dining on prison dinners. Now let us discuss your predicament.' He surveyed his papers. 'I see the police have twenty-eight witnesses to your shemozzle.'

Cuthbert corrected the doddery tosspot. 'It's twenty-seven, not twenty-eight.'

A look of disdain settled upon the solicitor's face. 'Oy vey! Oy vey! It is abundantly clear that even if you were twice as smart as you are, you'd still be a nitwit. It was twenty-seven, but that was before the lady over the road from the restaurant heard they would charge you. Only then did she feel it her civic duty to tell the police of the violent altercation between you and your wife upon your arrival at the restaurant.'

Cuthbert almost exploded. 'Violent altercation! Violent altercation! We had a slight difference of opinion, a few words in the car, all couples do; we're no different. A lover's tiff, that was all.'

Looking at his papers again, Adelstein responded, 'That must have preceded slamming the vehicle doors and your wife entering the restaurant and shutting the door in your face.' He continued without waiting for a response, 'Now I have a task for you. You will write down everything that you can recall concerning last night. I need to build a picture from your perspective of what happened. Understood?'

Cuthbert sneered. 'If you're so good, why hang around here touting for business?'

'Shmendrik! A duty solicitor I am not. I never carry out publicly funded work, nor do I have need for handouts. Your case I do for your mother, the lovely lady to whom I owe so much.' A wistful smile lingered on his lips. 'I do it for her.'

Cuthbert's alcohol-induced think-tank dome dinger was thankful when Adelstein lowered his voice to almost a whisper. 'It's up to you, but it might upset your mother if you don't use me. I can tell you, my boy, that I am the best in the business and I never act for schnooks and schlemiels but, in your case – ay-yay-yay – I told your mother I make an exception, just for her.'

'I assume Daddy's paying a fat fee for your services and that'll hang over me like a sword of Damocles, so I suppose I must use you.'

'Plotz! I do not help you for pecuniary enhancement. I do it as a dedication to your dear mother who doesn't deserve a bubkes amoretz like you.' Cuthbert thought Adelstein would spit on the floor.

'Also, your dear mother's husband doesn't even enter my thoughts, at least not on this occasion. I do not take money from a man whose pockets are fuller than his brains. This matter is between your mother and me, bless her, and I hope she lives in love. If you wish to walk out of here a free man, then I have a lot of work to do.

'Have your recollections ready by two p.m. Mazel tov, my boy,' he called, as he closed the cell door behind him.

In contemplation, Cuthbert felt a grudging respect for the senile old fuddy-duddy. Although he'd said he was only doing Mummy a favour, he exuded an unusual whiff of warmth. Hopefully, he'd furnish the factors that'd break the chains and tear off the shackles, and grant that short walk to freedom.

He spent the next hour doing his best to remember the sequence of events leading up to his demise of the previous night. It was that stupid theatrical agent who'd started this. He'd put the grand ideas into Mary's stage-struck brain. But he had to accept the role his own jealousy played towards 'Billy Bigelow'.

The lunchtime sandwich was as dry as a tear in daddy's eye, luckily the tea that washed it down was sweeter than the gobstoppers Nanny smuggled him. The cell door swung open. A jubilant Adelstein entered.

'My dear boy, I bring wonderful news. You can stop writing your memoirs.'

Cuthbert sat up to take notice. Not even his father had called him 'dear boy'.

'The first thing is, I have spoken to your wife's theatrical agent, and we have concurred she will withdraw her statement and agrees that there was no argument in your car.'

'But,' Cuthbert said, 'there was a witness. The restaurant's neighbour, she saw it.'

'Ah yes, number thirty-five. We have found out the neighbour at number thirty-five, known as Mrs Hunter, is really Edith Hayes and is *meschugena*, crazy. As I explained to her, the authorities might investigate a woman who at thirty-two had a hysterectomy, and at sixty-eight is drawing child benefit for a five-year-old. Chutzpah!

'After our conversation, she's withdrawn her testimony, so that worry is in the past. There're many crooks in the world so to be certain no other neighbours look to join the mêlée I have agreed the following. Your wife will corroborate that, in the car, you were helping her to rehearse for an upcoming theatrical role in a new West End production. She and you continued the rehearsal when you got out of the car. Slamming the car doors is in act two, scene four and the restaurant door was a substitute for the bedroom scene in act three, scene five.' He smiled, and exclaimed triumphantly, 'Nachas!'

'But that's preposterous! Nobody will ever believe that,' Cuthbert exclaimed. 'She isn't even in a West End production. There was an agent sniffing after her, but there was nothing in the pipeline.'

'Oy vey! Do you think I am stupid? I have spoken to her agent, Hymie Ellenbogen, my wife's cousin by marriage. So, my boy, believe it, and for why not when she starts rehearsals next week? Did I not advise you I was the best? I do this for your wonderful, beautiful mother, for whom I am showing my gratitude. Bless her, may she live a long and healthy life. She always said she could rely on me to be on top and abreast of things.' A faint smile crossed his lips as he said, 'Ah, but that was so long ago.'

'You're a genius,' Cuthbert almost wept.

'Oh please, my boy, you embarrass me. But you are correct, I am just the best there is at my job. Now this is the way things are, after the discussion between me and my wife's dear cousin Hymie, he has offered your wife – and she has accepted – a role as understudy to some West End star, whose name I have never even heard of. She's in a play I cannot say I've seen nor wish to, about a moggie on a ceiling, or something like that. Oy vey, but enough of this, as there are other things we have to discuss.'

'She's in *Cat on a Hot Tin Roof*! She's made it!' Despite his predicament, Cuthbert was proud.

Adelstein continued, 'Yes, they might call it that, but we must continue and not rest on our laurels. When I left you this morning, I recognised several young men waiting to give evidence. One of them was a boy called Solomon, he's the son of Rabbi Izsak Vogelstein. The Rabbi and I together attended yeshiva.

'Upon my return after lunch, he was still in the queue with a large plaster on his nose, and I believe you call him an arse end of a donkey. I confronted him, I said, "Solomon, the maître d' says that you ordered that great symbol of loathing, a gammon steak, with a pineapple slice on top!" He was shamefaced and said it was true. "You should be ashamed eating a disgusting lump of meat that doesn't graze in a field and then try to disguise your misdemeanour as a pineapple. Shmendrik! For why are you, a good Jewish boy, eating swine and swilling it down with alcohol, on a Friday night of all nights? You should've been at home preparing Shabbat, and your father a Rabbi! If you continue with this life, may you lie in the ground and burn bagels!" With this in mind, and knowing that his dear father would not like to hear of his transgression, he had a lapse of memory, as did several friends who all declined to give evidence on the Shabbat.'

Cuthbert looked at his solicitor with a fresh vision of respect. This man knew what he was doing. 'But what about the rest of the witnesses, and the damage?'

'So, what we have is this. Your wife will no longer testify, as she's decided her theatrical career is far more important than frittering her time away on a court appearance and, to be frank, she does not wish to waste her life on you.'

'Waste her life on me? I say, she's my wife!'

'My boy, those were her words. We can talk divorce later because that is also my forte, but for that you will pay. But back to the business in hand, so far we have Solomon and his friends losing their memories. Your wife or, ex-wife, thinks you're such a waste of time and can't be bothered with you. The busybody who saw you slamming the car doors is no longer a testator. So, we now come to the owner of the restaurant who has decided not to press charges.'

'Not press charges! Why?'

'After making a few inquiries from the restaurant owner's accountant, who is a relative of a friend of my cousin Rubin, we found, shall we say, discrepancies. His claim for loss of business does not match his tax return. Oy vey! Oy vey! He is a crook! So, cousin Rubin advised the accountant that I'd seek statements of his accounts, and tax returns, for the past five years as evidence that his claim is fraudulent.'

'And?' Cuthbert said.

'So, we've come to a very reasonable compromise. He has agreed with me that the whole place does not need refurbishment, as he thought. We are now of the same mind that the carpets only need cleaning, that you broke one table and four chairs when you went to the toilet and tripped on a broom he'd left on the floor. You have agreed not to sue him for whiplash, but have acknowledged you will pay for the glassware and dinnerware breakages. He has accepted a five-hundred-pound settlement.'

'What about the plate-glass window?'

'I told you he was a crook. His insurance company says that a stone from a car cracked the window, and they had already agreed to replace it under his policy. The schmo was trying to get the money twice. The restaurant will re-open within two days.' With a look of satisfaction, the solicitor then said, 'There are many crooks in the world, don't you think?'

Cuthbert stared. 'And the other witnesses?'

'My boy, unless you are sure you can kill it, never corner a rat so he fights, always allow an escape route. I am leaving such a route so that the police will have enough evidence to charge you with a minor offence for which they will caution you, but there will be no fine or criminal record. That is my plan.'

So it was. They charged Cuthbert with being drunk and disorderly, for which he received only a caution.

* * *

The train announcement declared the next stop was to be Bank where he'd have to alight and hotfoot it to Monument station. Shoving his way off, he scurried along the platform.

Taking a gander at his watch, he exclaimed, 'Drat! I'm late. Rodney will be bloody livid.'

As the escalator shuddered upwards, he gazed at the plethora of posters plastered on the wall; in the main they were advertising London shows. One stood out from the rest. It was promoting a new play featuring Elspeth Jerome, the famous West End and Broadway star. Universally adored, feted by the rich and perpetually pursued by the paparazzi. He knew her as Mary Crooke-Wells, who ran off, as Julie Jordan, with the fetid-breathed Billy Bigelow, now her husband, the millionaire impresario, Sir Leander Lovett.

'Oh Mary,' was borne on a sigh.

Something Came Up

Rodney didn't bother standing, when he heard, 'Hello old bean.' He raised his eyes and glared at his brothers. 'You're late! Do you think I'm a bloody doormat waiting for you to wipe your feet on?' Although knowing the hour precisely, his assertion as to their time tardiness was authenticated by him glaring at his watch and stating, 'Useless twats.'

'I say, sorry old chap, no need to fly off the handle,' Tristan said. 'Can't help the delay, met Cuthbert in security. Mummy not here yet?'

'Not coming,' snapped Rodney.

'Not coming!' Cuthbert joined in. 'Thought she'd be here keeping you company. What's wrong with the old dear? Not ill?'

'Sent a note saying something came up and a letter to read later,' Rodney muttered, 'but that doesn't let you off the hook. Abominably bad manners, that's what it is, deplorable, there's no excuse. It's taken months for me to organise the blasted dinner. But with Mummy not coming and you late, a bloody fine evening this is turning out to be.'

With the atmosphere as cold as a winter morn brume on Matlock Moors, Tristan broke the silence. 'Marvellous place you've got here,' he said, surveying the beautifully finished, half-wood-panelled walls, fine furniture and deep pile carpets.

'Spiffing,' Cuthbert agreed, and set to work to salve his brother's poisonous pomposity; knowing of no better way than to varnish his vanity. 'I'm really impressed, you must be a big cheese getting us in here for dinner.'

Tristan joined his brother in attempting to end the rancour. 'Really is spot on, thanks Rodney.'

With Rodney's ego now as polished as the Japanese antique lacquered bento box he bought for his birthday, he struck a conciliatory tone. 'Yes, you're right, difficult, but pleased to say chaps, I know the strings to pull to get people like you through the gates. Can't be too lax otherwise the place'd be swarming with even more riff-raff.'

Feeling superior, and having infused sufficient veiled derogatory insinuations within his churlish response to satisfy himself, Rodney sank back into the green-leather chair and snapped at the waiter. 'Move yourself man.'

The waiter stopped polishing the gleaming cutlery. Grabbing the silver Champagne cooler, half filled with ice and topped up to the handles with water, he hurtled toward the table. Just a trifle slopped onto the carpet when his feet skidded to a halt. With a flourish, he added a pinch of salt to the bucket before twisting in another bottle of Champagne, then covered it with a napkin.

Exasperated, Rodney said, 'Get on with it! Seat my guests.'

With difficulty, the waiter held the two chairs, proclaiming, 'There sirs, it is for you a best good seats.'

Rodney looked at the ceiling. 'Useless bugger. I got landed with the twerp at the last minute, was supposed to serve at a dinner for some South American congressmen, but that got cancelled. No doubt the blighters got caught with a pound or two of happy dust. Anyway, we're lumbered with this bloody idiot.' He eyed the waiter. 'Where you from?'

Standing as tall as his five feet, five inches would stretch, the waiter lyrically proclaimed, 'It me, is my name Ramiro. I is Argentino.'

Rodney said, 'No, it's I am from Argentina, not I is Argentino.'

'*Oh Señor, también Argentino, oh cuán maravilloso,*' Ramiro responded.

Rodney spat, 'What the devil are you saying? Speak English!'

'I say it good you also Argentino,' Ramiro said.

'The idiot thinks you're one of them, an Argie.' Tristan laughed, with Cuthbert joining him in the hilarity at Rodney's obvious discomfort.

'One of them! He's deranged,' Rodney said. 'Why would anyone in his right mind want to be one of them?'

The brothers continued chatting as if the waiter were as translucent as a Bohemian brandy snifter.

'Latinos! Damned lazy lot, not worth diddly-squat,' Tristan said, eyeing Ramiro, 'they're all too busy overthrowing governments, dancing the tango, or playing bloody football.'

Cuthbert said, 'I enjoyed Latin American dancing at school, the Argentine tango was my favourite. *La Cumparsita* was the name of the tune we danced to most often, the dance of love and passion.'

Tristan glanced at Ramiro. 'Love and passion! Look at the useless sod, difficult to conceive there could be anything worse.'

'Not so sure,' rejoined Rodney. 'Perhaps Romanians. Never met one that's been of any use, they're a bad lot, no doubt about it.'

'What about the Pols?' Cuthbert said.

'What polls are those? Not seen any polls about Romanians,' Tristan said.

'No, not polls, Pols, you know, Polish Pols, Pols from Poland. Without them bringing their spanners and washers there'd not be a tap turning or a toilet flushing in England.'

'Britain,' Rodney said.

'Well, yes, I meant Britain.'

'I'm not talking about Polish Pols in Britain,' Rodney said. 'I was going to say Britain went to war against the Argies.'

'But aren't they our friends?' Tristan's knowledge of world matters was rather limited.

'Yes,' Rodney said. 'That is until the next occasion. Can't trust 'em, you know, they're a nasty lot.'

After a time of silence, Cuthbert said, 'Not one.'

'Not one, what? What do you mean, not one?' asked Rodney.

'Well, it's just that, isn't it? Name one country in the world with which we've not had a war, just one. The whole point is, if we haven't fought them, they're not worth fighting.'

Rodney retorted, 'What about Switzerland, Bolivia, or Iceland?'

'Don't nit-pick; you know what I mean, proper countries like Germany, France, or even Spain at a stretch. It's those I'm talking about. Can you think of a decent one we've not invaded?'

They concluded there was not a single country on earth worth a tinker's cuss that Britain had not plundered, nor was there one that she hadn't beaten.

They drifted into silence, as each thought of something to say that might add to the pretence of normality and empathy.

It was Rodney's opinion that little was to be harvested from holding any serious deliberations with these half-wits with whom he had nothing in common. The rare occasions when they met he'd found both boring and laboured, and so he turned to the matter at hand. 'It's sad Mummy being unable to make it, but, as I told you, the old dear sent a note to say something came up this afternoon. There's also a letter to read at dinner, apparently explaining everything.'

'No doubt thanking us for the gifts,' Tristan said. 'Just a shame she can't be here. We must make the most of the evening to celebrate her birthday. At least she's with us in spirit, bless her.'

'It all seems a bit strange,' Rodney said. 'A few weeks ago, Mummy agreed to have afternoon tea with me. I phoned when leaving the House to say I was on the way, and it took ages before she answered – not as agile anymore, suspect her joints are seizing up.' He sipped his drink. 'But when she eventually responded, she sounded quite out of breath. I said, Mummy, you sound breathless, are you ill? She said no, but that she'd had to rush to the phone. Then I got the same story: sorry, can't come for tea because something's come up.'

'It would not surprise me,' said Tristan, 'if she's not shielding us from a life-and-death infirmity. We must expect it at her age. She'll soon be languishing in one of those residential places, where they sleep for half the time, and then play bingo and listen to a keyboard entertainer when they're woken.'

'Don't think she's quite ready yet,' Cuthbert said. 'Bound to have difficulties, but, even so, we must try to keep her in her own home for as long as possible before we put her away.'

'Sad to say,' Rodney said, 'you're correct. But, tell you what, plonking her in a geriatric care place would soon pillage our inheritance. It's more expensive to stay in them than in a decent hotel in London, though I accept we must face the fact that it's only a matter of time. Can't be with us forever, we're lucky she's lasted this long.'

Cuthbert looked around the room, 'What's behind the curtains, Rodney?'

'Oh! French doors, they lead onto the balcony overlooking the Thames. After dinner, if it's warm enough, we'll have a brandy and coffee out there. Got the best view in town.'

Flickering candles illuminated Ramiro's smiling face as he dallied by the table. Although his command of the English language prohibited him from comprehending almost anything, he sensed an ambience of peace replacing the rancour of the past few minutes.

His mood now lifted, Rodney asked, 'Care for another drink, chaps?'

'Thought you'd never ask,' they replied.

'Ramiro, get on with it, pour the Champagne.'

Ramiro checked his watch to ensure the bottle had rested for long enough, removed it from the cooler and flourished it with grandiosity. After making a spectacle of feeling the neck and body, he declared the temperature to be correct. Then, with the bottle held in the palm of his hand, he displayed the label to the brothers, seeking their approval – not that they had a choice, for that was Rodney's.

Ramiro gushed with enthusiasm, 'It be a fine wine, 'ave wonderful layers of complexity it...'

'Oh, shut up,' Rodney interrupted. 'Just pour the bloody stuff!'

Showing no sign of petulance at the interruption of his passionate rendition of the wine's victual attributes, Ramiro tilted Cuthbert's bright silvery flute, the wide body curved elegantly inwards, an ideal shape for older complex Champagnes. The luminous pale-golden liquid flowed languidly down the side of the glass, with no overstimulation of the bubbles. Stopping halfway, Ramiro allowed the froth to subside, after which he filled the glass to a little over half of its capacity. Then, with the same care, he filled Tristan and Rodney's glasses. Placing a silver stopper into the bottle, he returned it to the cooler and flamboyantly stepped away from the table. 'Is all or nothing else more, sirs?'

Rodney looked to the heavens, 'As dumb as a box of rocks! No Ramiro, nothing else more. Go and polish the glasses.'

Silently, the brothers sat staring at the table, as the lead crystal glasses refracted the soft candlelight, sending rainbow hues flickering upon the white linen surface.

Ironically, on the day his PA was organising the wine there'd been a discussion in the House where an increase in the minimum wage was being debated. Rodney had stood and declared that any mandatory wage increase was unaffordable to business. His side of the House roared their agreement.

A business luncheon had forced him to raise his head above the parapet and utter those few words. He provided political updates to a company that paid him two thousand pounds a month to apprise them of issues in the offing. They'd sought to discuss a concern with him over lunch. The director had said, 'The board has heard there's to be a government review of the minimum wage. I tell you this Rodney, we can't afford to pay the blighters a penny more.

Look, it's simple. Increasing their take-home won't make an iota of difference to the output. If you double their money, do you think they'll increase their effort? Never! I'll tell you what'll happen, you increase their pay, and we'll get rid of some of them, then the government can pick up their unemployment tab. Not only that, Rodney, and I hope you don't see this as a threat, but we'll reduce our other overheads by getting rid of people like you.'

It was a shock to Rodney, for he needed their two thousand a month. So he assured the director that he'd fight for the company cause, stand up for them, even if he was kicked out of the party. But he was well aware that his input really wasn't necessary, as members on his side of the House, and some on the other, would make sure there'd be no increase. Most had the same interest at heart, which was to keep – for two hours' work – their two thousand a month rolling in, so he and the rest followed the party line and voted against an increase.

'Scrumptious bit of fizz,' Tristan observed. 'I appreciate he's dense Rodney, but that waiter seems to know his onions when pouring bubbly.'

'I should hope so, don't want it all over the place.' Rodney knew each bottle had cost nearly one hundred times the hourly pay of the cellerman who'd earlier picked the three bottles from the client's own rack in the passive cellar.

'Strange Mummy not turning up,' said Cuthbert. 'Not every day she turns seventy. Have you got any clues Tristan?'

Tristan shook his head. 'Tell you what, I recall at least four, maybe five, weeks ago we were going to lunch at that little Italian place she likes. She called and cancelled. Just like you said, Rodney, she referred to something having just come up, and the poor dear was gasping for breath.'

'Strange, don't you think?' said Cuthbert. 'Not a word about breathing problems; hope it's not her heart. Perhaps she just doesn't want us to worry.'

'It's those bloody fleeting clouds,' Tristan said.

'You mean weather related, possibly pollen, that sort of thing?' Cuthbert asked.

'No, not hay fever, cigarettes. Don't you recall those she used to smoke? They had a picture on the packet of a chap in an old-fashioned costume sitting in a chair smoking a clay pipe. Looked like the painting by that Dutch painter, what's his name? Van Dyck, that's him.'

'Ah, I remember, the Laughing Cavalier,' Cuthbert said. 'But it wasn't a clay pipe, he was smoking a cigarette.'

'No,' Tristan said. 'King Charles. Charles the second – or the first, anyway – not the Laughing Cavalier and cigarettes weren't invented then.'

'Passing,' Rodney said.

'Pass what? What can I get for you, old boy?' Cuthbert asked.

'The damned cigarettes.'

Cuthbert looked around the table. 'No cigarettes here, old chap. I thought you only smoked cigars, I'll call the waiter.'

'Not for me, you stupid prat. The cigarettes, they were called Passing Cloud, not Fleeting.'

'Ah yes! Glad you cleared that one up,' Tristan said. 'It'd be buzzing round my ears all night.'

'I recall the painting on the packet was by a Sir somebody Van Dyck,' Cuthbert said. 'But how a Dutchman can be a sir is beyond me.'

Just hearing the word 'sir' stirred a measure of envy deep inside Rodney, who said, 'What the hell is the world coming to? Probably an excellent reason for chopping Charlie's head off, if he went around knighting cheeseheads and their ilk. Bet that wasn't popular.'

'I know that was four hundred years ago, but it still goes on, doesn't it? Tell me Rodney, wasn't Ronald Reagan also knighted?' Cuthbert asked.

'Well yes, the fact is Thatcher needed to cosy up to the Yanks and knew the four magic words needed to make any American drool, "Her Majesty invites you". So, whipping a postcard from her handbag, she writes Ron's name in the box and a lackey trots off, and it's put in the post. When the card pops through the letterbox of 1600 Pennsylvania Avenue, the White House convulses into a tizzy, Ron has his hair dyed and quiff re-concreted, while Nancy buys a new nightie. But, in his rush to start Air Force One's engines, the butler forgets to pack Ronnie's quarter horse's saddle. Upon arrival at Windsor Castle the Queen asks the cowboy if he'd care for a ride. "Can't," he says, "aint got no saddle." So the Queen says, "Not to worry, Ronald," and lends him one her spares.

'We all know that Prince Philip's not the most reticent or slowest pensioner on the pavement so, being aware that his job is to stick close to HM, and seeing her disappearing into a thicket pursued by the Lone Ranger, he grabs the reins of a carriage-and-four. Two secret service men – one disguised as a bowler hat and umbrella and the other as an ill-fitting suit wearing sunglasses – leap into the back of the carriage.

'The prince spots that Nancy's redoing her make-up, again, and he yells, "No time to concrete your creases, jump up woman and be quick about it, bloody colonial."

So Nancy, not wanting to miss the shindig, hurtles up and plonks herself next to Phil.'

The brothers roared. It was rare to see a light-hearted Rodney.

'Now, the second her backside touches the seat, he ups and gives the old grey nag a whip on the arse, the lead horse's I mean. Nancy is then left clinging like a clam, while he takes her on a hair-raising junket around the grounds of the mediaeval edifice in pursuit of Ron and Liz. Meanwhile, because they are unsure that a bevy of Beefeaters parading with pikes, dressed in long red coats, stockings and shoes with flowers on them, are enough of a deterrent for AK47-wielding terrorists, a posse of secret service men mount up, and give chase, whooping like a pack of Apaches. I understand that, afterwards, Nancy tells Phil how much she enjoyed it and that it was not dissimilar to one of her husband's better films, *Sante Fe Trail*. Following a few photo shoots, and a cup of Earl Grey with a bun, the morning out in a theme park that not even the great Walt Disney could emulate, ended.'

'Isn't it marvellous,' said Tristan. 'Americans think there's only one royal family. I mean, ask them about the Queen of the Netherlands and they wouldn't have a clue. They'd confuse it with Neverland, wouldn't even know where the Netherlands is. What I don't like is that the ungrateful wretches tip our tea in the sea to throw off the yolk of imperialism, and then can't stop drooling about our royalty!'

'Yes, but that's it! Maggie understood,' Rodney said. 'That's why the next time he popped over the pond she organised Reagan's Knighthood at Buck House – he felt at home, thought he was on a movie set.'

The brothers chuckled.

Tristan, with his somewhat brief military career to mind, said, 'I enjoy the military aspect of these state things. Soldiers standing for hours, sweating in their red woollen uniforms, cavalrymen in fancy dress, huge horses crapping all over the place, brass bands playing every national anthem under the sun. Can't say what benefits the country gets out of these things.'

'I'll tell you what we got out of the Reagan visit,' Rodney said. 'It was one of the most powerful men on earth becoming an unswerving friend and protector to this country.' He chuckled. 'But, equally amazing, he became someone who liked Margaret Thatcher. That was no mean achievement, and what did it cost us? Almost nothing. The soldiers and the carriages, they're already there, just put 'em in the right place and get the band to learn a new tune. It's easy, gives them something to do. The only cost was a meal, a box of medals and a title he couldn't use because he was unfortunate enough not to have been born British.'

They sat in silence, each trying to think of something to say.

Rodney was first to speak. 'Age, that's why Mummy's not here. Look chaps, we have to face it – she's not getting old, the treasure's already reached decrepitude. What do you think Tristan?'

'You may be correct Rodney, but equally it wouldn't surprise me if she's not up and gone off to one of those women's, things, you know, like, Save the Gherkins campaign.'

'Gurkhas,' corrected Rodney.

'Whales,' said Cuthbert.

'Why would the Welsh concern her?' Tristan asked. 'Didn't know we were trying to save 'em, are they in danger of extinction?'

'No, not the Taffy Welsh, the fish,' Cuthbert said. 'I meant the fish!'

* * *

While the morons maundered their malarkey, Rodney brooded upon the undeniable fact: not an iota of affection bound him to his simpleton siblings.

Being shuffled off to boarding school could be the reason. Lost early-age bonding? They're jealous, he thought, but they always were, even as children. Nanny loved him the most, she always gave him the first lick of her ice cream, and that dug a further ditch between them. It was burdensome and required a monumental effort to be civil. Luckily, they met for only a few hours a year.

* * *

'Mammals, that's what I've been trying to think of,' Cuthbert said.

'Why?' Tristan asked.

'Because whales aren't fish.'

'That's interesting.' Tristan raised his glass, 'Wonderful bit of bubbly-zing. I propose a toast to our dearest Mummy. Happy birthday and long may the darling live.'

'To dear Mummy,' they concurred.

'Couldn't wish for a better mater,' Rodney added.

'God bless her,' Cuthbert pronounced.

'The best, we would never find one finer. . . not ever,' said Tristan.

'As you were late,' Rodney said, still feeling somewhat miffed, 'I had plenty of time to place my order. Will you do so now?' Without waiting for their response, he clicked his fingers to summon Ramiro. 'Come! Dammit, forgotten your name, what are you called?'

'Ees Ramiro, Señor.'

Rodney exploded, 'Señor, Señor! It's, yes sir. Get the menus, my brothers will order now.'

'I sorry, sir, I bring.' He raced to the service table bringing back the large distinctive folders containing the cartes du jour. 'There's sirs, there's sirs, there's sirs,' he repeated, handing one to each brother.

Fixing his gaze on Ramiro, Rodney said, 'Tell me why I need one? I've already ordered. Have you still got my order?'

'Oh! Si, sorry is good, I 'ave your order ees perfecto.' Ramiro took the menu from Rodney with an exaggerated flourish.

'Silly sod,' Rodney muttered.

Cuthbert and Tristan carefully studied the options for a few minutes. Ramiro, meanwhile, with a pencil stub and paper pad at the ready, stood pensively awaiting their choice.

'Ah! For starters, I'll have the butternut squash soup,' said Cuthbert.

Licking the pencil stub, Ramiro muttered as he wrote upon his pad, 'Im e ave sopa de butta nuta.'

Tristan declared, 'Sounds jolly good, I'll have the same.'

'Other eem e 'ave like same as primero persona,' Ramiro wrote, verbalising lyrically as he did so.

Tristan perused the menu. 'It will be the pork escalope and gravy with seasonal roast vegetables for me.'

Ramiro, again intoned, 'Primero eem 'ave pork escalopees en rosta vegetales.'

Then, turning his attention to Cuthbert, said, 'Eet for you sir, what ees?'

'Don't like pork, never have done, can't even stand the look, never mind the smell. Nauseating, I'm going for the shoulder of lamb with red jelly gravy, new potatoes and vegetables.'

'It good! Numero dos e ave lambe en red jelly en new with vegetales,' Ramiro wrote and then asked, 'You 'ave pudding?'

'British cheese board sounds spiffing,' said Tristan. 'Same for me too,' Cuthbert added.

Ramiro wrote onto the pad.

'Better check that the blighter's got it right,' said Rodney. 'Let's see what mess he's made of this lot. Now Ramiro read back what these two have ordered.'

Ramiro stared at his pad, and read back his scribble to Cuthbert. 'Primeramente you ave sopa de butta nuta, and lambe com rosso jelly con vegetables and Inglaterra cheese on wood.' Turning to Tristan he said, 'You ave same sopa, and porke escallope en rosta vegetales, and same cheese on wood.'

'It's unbelievable,' Rodney said. 'We invented English in the fifth century, lost millions of lives in getting nearly two billion beggars to use it and what do we get lumbered with? Tell you what we get: a bloody waiter who lays waste to the spoken word. We need a cryptographer to decode his utterances. Can hardly make sense of a single word the blighter said. Ramiro, now tell me in plain English, what the devil have you written for me?'

'You 'ave uno Terrine de Gooses Leever con Spicy Pineapple wid Gingerbready.' He looked at Rodney, who nodded his acceptance.

Gaining confidence, Ramiro continued, 'Si, ees el plato fuerte one whole lobster thermidor which e come from Cornishland with spicy carroti y lemon verbena.'

Impressed by the stunned looks on Tristan and Cuthbert's faces, he continued with exaggerated gesticulations. 'Eet is for puddings, eet ees I, Ramiro, what at table preparar mia especialidad, crêpes suzette com Grand Marnier con jus lemon, orange y azúcar!'

'Good Heavens, Ramiro. Do I understand you correctly? Did you say you would make my crêpes suzette at the table? I thought the chef would do it.'

He turned to his brothers. 'Can't trust this fool with a flaming pan, might think he's Guy Fawkes!'

'No, not necessary guide a fork, I cook crêpes suzette, no problema,' Ramiro assured Rodney, and studied his notepad. 'It is later you will be seat on the balcony and 'ave a Cognac, I check, it 'as a wonderful floral bouquet. Such good taste.'

'What about my Cuban cigar?' asked Rodney.

'Si, it be in a humidifier at seventy per cent 'umidity and twenty degrees, I check and it has just that nuance of sweet cream, it fantastica.'

'Hard to believe! A complete duffer at everything except for wine and cigars,' was Rodney's view.

'I say,' Tristan sneered. 'It all sounds flash, Rodney. Whole Cornish lobster! Cuban cigars! That lot must cost a mint. Come into ways and means? Fiddled your expenses. . . again?'

'Not to mention the excellent Champagne,' Cuthbert added, gesturing Romero to fill his glass.

'It's absolute tosh!' said Rodney. 'I claim only that for which I'm due. . . or thereabouts.'

'Not what the papers said,' Tristan commented. 'And if it were – as you say – all above board, why did the Parliamentary Standards Authority make you pay it back?'

'It was a minor accounting error,' Rodney stated. 'Anyone could have made it. Invoice just slipped into the wrong column of my expenses by mistake. Have neither of you taken someone to dinner nor, by accident, got the slip mixed up and claimed it as a business expense?'

Tristan laughed, 'I have to confess it has happened, but mixing up a five-thousand-pound invoice for renovations to your lodge in Scotland, and also double glazing your holiday apartment in the Scilly Isles was hardly a luncheon receipt mix-up.'

Cuthbert felt empowered to throw in a zinger. 'Didn't the papers mention holiday flights to Paris as well? That's hardly a dinner with your wife, old boy.'

With a face as florid as when his fly ambushed his dicky, Rodney leapt in. 'Don't you dare, "old boy", me! As soon as I saw the errors in my returns, I galloped off to the powers-that-be for correction. Everyone – except, of course, the tabloid scandal sheets and the slimy turds on the opposition front bench – accepted that I had made a minor error of rule interpretation. It's the pencil pushers in the press; they're to blame for the electorate losing faith in us dedicated public servants. The behaviour of that rabble-rousing bunch that wrung us through the wringer with their scurrilous tripe was nothing less than a load of sanctimonious seditiousness.' He sipped his Champagne, happy that he'd got the better of the stupid sods, but threw in for good measure, 'Lest you've forgotten, the Crown Prosecution Service laid no charges. Clean as a pontifical pondering, minor infringements and, I might add, the PM and the Chancellor also had to pay back tidy sums, far more than me. My conscience is clear; I am a person of uncommonly high principles.'

'So,' Cuthbert said, 'if you've not fiddled your expenses why the slap-up feast?'

With an air of indifference, Rodney explained, 'Oh! Sorry, don't know why I haven't mentioned it before: Mummy's footing the bill. It's all on her.'

With his eyes glued to the menu and, after a moment's hesitation, Tristan declared, 'I'm not sure the waiter got my order correct. I could hardly understand a word he said – put it down to my hearing impairment from gunfire. Tinnitus, that's what it is, voices get jumbled up. Try not to make a big thing about a minor military disability when other fellows are still walking around with holes in 'em.'

Rodney snorted, 'Disability! Gunfire! What unadulterated tosh! If you'd said it was the twanging of bedsprings, screaming climaxes, or the consequences of having your ears bashed by a bunch of cuckolded husbands, that I could believe – but gunfire! Unadulterated rubbish.'

His brother's words stung Tristan more than the hornet had his ear last summer, and he was about to retaliate with spite proportionate to that to which he'd fallen victim, when Cuthbert interjected.

'Did I tell you that I saw a photograph of Mary when I was on the underground? It was advertising a new West End play. Seeing her causes flashbacks, can't help it, even after twenty years. Had one when the waiter was talking, didn't hear a word he said.'

Rodney eyed Ramiro. 'I don't know who's the most useless, you or them. Tell the idiots what they ordered.'

'Si, for starting you has two nuta butter sopa.'

'Sopa! That's soup isn't it? I never ordered soup!' Tristan said. 'Why would I eat such a dish when celebrating Mummy's birthday? Did you order soup?' he asked Cuthbert.

'Not me, old bean,' Cuthbert said, studying the menu. 'Jolly sure I ordered. . . yes! found it. . . Mozambique langoustines piri-piri on a bed of wild rice with a nuance of coconut and a green side salad. Yes, that's what I ordered.'

'Spot on, I agree, my order exactly.' Tristan glared at Ramiro.

'Oh my goodness, it me,' Ramiro said, 'it be my problema! How I am so stupido, I not know!' Studying the menu, he exclaimed, 'Ha, I see! I confuse sopa de nuta butta of day with Mozambique langoustines on a bed of wild rice with a nuance of coconut and a green side salad, in Spanish him sound not same but little bit, how stupido.' He vigorously altered the scribbling on his pad.

'Ask him what's on his list for your main course, Tristan. Wouldn't surprise me if the idiot hasn't muddled it up, you'd better check,' Rodney suggested.

'What have you written for my main course?'

After examining his pad, Ramiro announced, 'Primera, you ave pork escalopees en rosta vegetales.'

'How can mousselline of grouse with pearl barley, Savoy cabbage, pancetta and red wine jus sound like a bloody pork chop, you imbecile?' said Tristan. 'I would never dream of eating pork while Cuthbert was with me, makes him sick.' He turned to Cuthbert, 'Doesn't it?'

'Jolly well does, sick as a seagull. It's unbelievable that anyone, other than this witless creature, could mess up your order. It was very clear, and I agreed to have the same. You better buck up your ideas, my boy, or it'll be back on the banana boat to never-never land for you.'

Upon hearing Cuthbert's harsh words, Ramiro – after his triumphant handling of the Champagne – was crestfallen. 'Oh, I sorry, it be my mind. It not available here tonight, it somewhere elsewhere be.'

'Better check your pudding. Got the rest wrong, bound to have also screwed that up,' said Rodney.

'What is our pudding order?' asked Cuthbert.

Ramiro studied his notes, 'Si, I 'ave 'im somewhere 'er! Ah, I correct this time,' he said as a smile filled his face. 'You no order pudding, you say want cheese on wood.'

'No order pudding? You half-baked dimwit! We said we'd have the same as our brother, crêpes suzette,' Tristan stated.

'And,' Cuthbert added, 'with brandy and cigars on the balcony afterwards.'

'I sorry, sirs,' Ramiro said, hitting his forehead. 'It be my brain, him go to sleep for the night.'

'I will speak slowly Ramiro,' said Rodney. 'Go to kitchen, tell chef what we want for dinner and then come back and give us the time.'

'It be no need for me to ask chef for time.' Ramiro removed a watch from his pocket, and said, 'It be twenty and eight minutes over the six.'

Rodney looked at his wristwatch. 'You're as much use as a saddle without a horse! It's nearly eight o'clock; go tell chef we will eat at eight thirty.'

Ramiro stared at his watch, bashed it on his arm. 'It be he, him stopped turning. My body it be magnetico,' he added, leaving the room despondently.

They sat in silence broken only by the slurp of Champagne until Cuthbert exclaimed, 'Poles apart!'

'Why the devil have we gone back to discussing bloody Pols?' said Rodney.

'No, I didn't mean Polish Pols. No, although it's true we're poles apart from the Pols, were also the poles apart from the rest of the foreigners, all of 'em, we're as dissimilar as night is to day. Think about it: God parted the Red Sea to give Moses and his mob dry ground so they could cross to the Promised Land. In our case, he closed it by giving us the English Channel to keep the Krauts, Frogs and Belgians at bay, the Red Sea parting, but reversed.'

'La Manche!' said Tristan.

'What's that?' Cuthbert asked.

'The English Channel.' Tristan responded. 'That's what the Frogs call it, La Manche. It beggars belief that foreigners feel obliged to alter perfectly good English names.'

'Not just the French,' Cuthbert corrected him. 'It's the Jocks, Taffs and bog-hopping Paddys, they're all at it, mucking up perfectly good names. Absolute nonsense.'

* * *

Rodney sipped the Champagne, delicious – at nigh on a hundred pounds a glass, it should be. It would have delighted Mummy, always had a taste for the finer things in life, he thought. The fizz was the only decent thing the evening had provided, and it had been him who'd seen to the organisation. But never again, it's the last time I dine with these morons, he promised himself. The banality of discussion with these imbecilic lunatics only reinforced his loathing for having to be pleasant to the pair.

* * *

'When I left the army, Daddy wanted me to go to India,' Tristan said.

Rodney nearly choked on his Champagne. 'You didn't leave the army! They bloody chucked you out for screwing the major's wife on the snooker table, you moronic cretin.'

Tristan's fist slamming onto the table caused the cutlery to leap into the air, and at least five pounds worth of Champagne to slop out of the glasses. 'How dare you, you supercilious twit! Sitting there all smug, pretending to be squeaky clean. The big I Am, when you're up to your arse in chicanery and exploitation.'

'Smug you say,' Rodney shot back. 'If I was – and I'm not – at least it'd be so for a good reason. Daddy's idea wasn't to dump you onto an unsuspecting Indian subcontinent to teach English to expat gentry's offspring. Or to send you pulpiting as a missionary, while seeking the source of the Nile. He determined, as did everyone else, that you were fit for nothing more than supervising two, or three, native clerks.'

Tristan flew back, 'You think nobody knows that you're up to no good with your bloody PA. Well, let me tell you, Mr High And Mighty, everyone knows, and also that you're a patronising twat.'

A stony silence fell faster than an iron anchor could descend to the seabed.

Tristan lapsed into a sulk, recalling a Confucius quote, taught to him by Changying, a Chinese consort: Before you embark on a journey of revenge, dig two graves.

After a hostile silence, Rodney resolved that, as the eldest brother, it was his duty to smooth things over, if only for the sake of getting through the evening and get these two packing. 'Let's not spoil Mummy's birthday party by arguing. It's a shame that she's missing it, but I'm jolly sure she's here in spirit and would want us to be, at least, cordial.'

'Quite correct,' Cuthbert said. 'That's what Mummy would want, so come on Tristan, brighten up and put in some effort. Let's all agree to stop this backbiting. She's a wonderful elegant lady, and we all love her, so let's drink a toast to Mummy.'

Although difficult, Tristan crept from beneath his self-imposed sulks to join the others.

'To dear Mummy,' they chorused.

Don't Eat the Bacon

Their confounded sophomoric prattling had angered Rodney and he decided to change the subject. 'Tell you what, we'll discuss the birthday gifts we've each given to the old dear.' Surely neither of their presents could match his, so he'd wait till last. That'd make them feel sick. He chose which moron would go first alphabetically. 'Cuthbert, let's hear what you've handed over for Mummy's birthday.'

'Do you recall what we gave for her fiftieth?' he asked.

From their blank faces, it was obvious they did not. 'The Caribbean cruise, for heaven's sake, we all chipped in. It was a month-long luxury jaunt to share with Daddy. We don't hand out boat trips every day of the week. You must remember?'

'Oh yes, you're right,' said Rodney. 'I'd forgotten, but it was twenty years ago.'

'Didn't we lose Daddy halfway through it?' said Tristan.

'No, not lost,' replied Cuthbert. 'He was alive in Grand Turk and dead when the boat reached Montego Bay, or was it Bermuda? Can't think where it was, but I know the Turks were involved because I thought they'd boarded the wrong boat and ended up in the Mediterranean.'

'Difficult to recall where he expired,' said Rodney, 'but, as it was on board a boat. I'd imagine they wrote his latitude and longitude on the death certificate. Be senseless having a place of death as "the sea".'

Cuthbert thought for a moment. 'The problem is that you might die on a dot on the navigation chart and your body found when they reached another one. Mind you, it'd be worse in a plane, you could be anywhere in a couple of minutes, even seconds – alive above France and expired over Spain – you'd never know where you'd died.'

Rodney tried to look as if he was taking notice, but the bloody fool's waffling drivel would drive anyone over the brink. So, to avoid Tristan joining his brother on the same idiotic wanderings, he'd take the helm and pilot them back as close to sanity as they were capable of journeying. 'Although I can't call up all the details of the voyage, I remember it cost a fortune, and Daddy's perishing in the middle spoilt everything for Mummy.'

'Bound to,' said Tristan. 'I mean to anyone, not just Mummy. There were ten, or maybe even twelve, days of the cruise left and Mummy told me that rather than keep him around, she told the purser she was quite prepared to splash out and have them bury him at sea. A reasonable request. I mean, people marry at sea so why not get buried there? He would have enjoyed that, always fond of the water, and Mummy would have found the remainder of the voyage much easier.'

'I think I know where he died, or at least approximately, I remember seeing the holiday photos,' Rodney said. 'She went into mourning and bought a black bikini when they docked in The Grand Turks, so it must have happened before then. Strange how little details fall into the forgotten box and then pop back.'

'I've got it!' Tristan cried.

'What?' Cuthbert said.

'Cockburn! I've got it, Cockburn.'

Rodney had a disgusted look on his face, 'Can't say I'm surprised, given your lifestyle. Are you getting treatment?'

'No, not a disease, it's a port,' Tristan said. 'I remember now, when Mummy was saying something about Daddy dying she mentioned they were near a place called Cockburn, named by a pirate who'd probably caught a dose of the dogs in Dominica, I wouldn't wonder.'

'I saw it in a film,' Cuthbert said.

'What, a travel programme about cruising? Did the ship call in there?' Rodney said.

'No, it was a war film where they had a burial at sea. All the ship's company in attendance, except the stokers and the steering-wheel man because the ship was still moving. The rest stood to attention on deck blowing whistles and the captain said prayers. Jolly sure it was called *Above Us the Waves*.'

'Don't be a berk,' said Rodney. 'It couldn't have been because *Above Us the Waves* was about a submarine. If you die on a sub, they can't throw you overboard because you're already under the bloody water. No, on submarines they load you into a torpedo tube and shoot you out with gas.'

'If it's the same one I saw,' Tristan said, 'what's-his-name played the part of the skipper. . . I can see him now, standing on the ship's bridge pretending to be in a storm, while stagehands threw buckets of water over him. He looked very melancholic and was muttering something about the atrocious weather. What the devil was it called. . .? Was it, *The Cruel Sea*, and didn't they stitch a dead sailor up in a white sail then...'

Cuthbert interrupted, 'Couldn't have been! That film was about the Second World War, not the Spanish

Armada. They didn't have sails – it was a frigate, or the like, with an engine.'

'That's true. You're quite correct,' Tristan conceded. 'What I meant was they sewed the body of a sailor in a bed-sheet as if it was a sail. Then, they plonked him on a plank and slid the poor begger off the boat covered in a Union Jack, one of his shipmates blew a whistle and the captain read a prayer.' He sipped his Champagne. 'I'm convinced that was the film. I found it moving.'

'Greek,' said Rodney.

'No English,' Cuthbert said. 'There were definitely no subtitles.'

'The ship,' Rodney said. 'I'm sure it was Greek.'

Cuthbert thought back to the film. 'No, definitely not. Did the Greeks have any frigates with English-speaking captains in the Second World War? I'm sure it was English.'

'Not the damned ship in the film,' said Rodney, 'the one on which Daddy died, that was Greek; registered in Greece. Probably had no Union Jack on board and Mummy would never have agreed to Daddy being dumped overboard in a Greek flag.'

'Compressed air,' Cuthbert said.

'What the devil has compressed air got to do with it?' Rodney asked.

'Submarines. You said they use gas, but they don't. They shoot the bodies out with compressed air, just remembered.' Cuthbert sipped his Champagne, elated to have corrected Rodney.

'I recall Mummy saying the captain was Italian,' said Tristan.

'Do you think he knew our father?' said Cuthbert.

'Doubt it, on big boats captains don't get to know the passengers. For them it's photographs, a few dinners with the patrons, dance with some fat old bird and get the steward to lay her, that's all they do. Otherwise, they eat proper food in their cabin, while watching TV.'

Cuthbert snorted, 'I'm not talking about our father, Daddy! It's the other one; the one in heaven I'm talking about, everyone knows Our Father, or maybe another decent English prayer like walking in the shadows of death. When they toboggan someone into the sea, they have to say a prayer, or two.'

Reflective quietude fell upon the siblings.

'It seems to me,' said Rodney, 'that the height of the ship would have been an obstacle. Even twenty years ago, cruise liners were ten to fifteen storeys high. They couldn't hurl him into the sea from the top, much too far from deck to water.'

'Treasure Island,' declared Cuthbert.

'Don't start that damned nonsense again. We've agreed, it was Cockburn where he died,' Rodney said. 'You're going round in senseless circles.'

'No,' said Cuthbert. 'It's the cabin boy I'm talking about, the one in *Treasure Island*. His name was Jim Hawkins and the captain who read the prayers was also a Hawkins.'

'You're right,' said Tristan. 'It was Jack, and he was English. Well done.'

'Can you imagine,' Cuthbert said, 'the colonel and his lady wife lounging on their lower-deck balcony, partaking of mid-afternoon cream scones with strawberry jam when, out of the blue, a body zooms past, like an Egyptian Mummy in an aerobatics display.'

'Or a latter-day superman,' Tristan said, laughing at the notion.

'Downright disrespectful,' Rodney said. 'Terrible taste! No, it's not right; you can't turf bodies over the side of cruise liners, not acceptable.'

'Credit where credit's due,' Cuthbert said. 'I know the crew were a bunch of foreigners but, despite that, one has to say they were superb to Mummy, upgraded her from Silver to a Gold Stateroom. And a partial refund for the unused thirteen days that Daddy missed out on,' Rodney added.

'True,' said Cuthbert, 'but the refund was your doing. If you hadn't got involved, we wouldn't have got a single penny's compensation, or secured recompense for the unused shore trips. I think you did well, don't you agree, Tristan?'

'I don't recall ever getting any money back. What about my share, Rodney?'

'You got your share, I'm sure you did.'

'I'll check my bank statements, don't remember it.' Tristan's distrust of his brother's fiddles was founded on firm foundations dating back to their childhood.

Rodney changed the subject. 'According to Mummy it was the other diners who were cruel and inconsiderate – not because they complained – it was the way they did it. She told me the rumour on the ship was that Daddy was in the fridge lying next to the bacon. And, you know what? Not one person on her table had bacon for breakfast. I ask you! People were whispering – she could hear them – "don't eat the bacon he's still there". She complained, so they moved her, but the new waiter didn't know she was the widow and on the first morning whispered in her ear, I don't recommend the bacon madam, the stiff's still on the slab.'

'Damned shame,' said Tristan. 'I bet they bolted the bacon down when Daddy's body was off and in a mortuary. Most on board were Americans. They're a strange lot.'

'Fine ones to complain, they always take the high ground,' said Cuthbert. 'What about the Waxhaw massacre?'

'Don't you mean the chainsaw massacre?' Tristan queried.

'No, the chainsaw massacre was a horror film. I was talking about a documentary programme I saw. No, it was where an entire army of English soldiers surrendered and the Yanks slaughtered them, to the last man,' recounted Cuthbert.

'Thought the Americans were on our side fighting the Germans,' said Tristan.

'No. Well, yes. The massacre wasn't in the last war, it was during what they call the War of Independence, not the one against Germany,' Cuthbert explained.

'I saw that programme too,' said Rodney, 'and it was the Americans who surrendered and the English slaughtered them.'

'Okay, so Cuthbert finish telling us what you gave Mummy for her birthday,' said Rodney.

'I'm hoping setting sail doesn't bring back unhappy memories of Daddy lying in the fridge,' said Cuthbert.

'A cruise!' said Tristan. 'How thoughtful, a marvellous idea, and I'm sure by now Mummy will have forgotten Daddy died on the last one.' Although such a gift he considered tasteless, and his one far superior.

'Well, it's not exactly a cruise, much better than that. It's a yacht in Cowes.'

'I say, that does sound spiffing,' said Tristan, who – other than a few nights with a delightful girl on a narrow boat moored on the River Cherwell, and the Chinese sampan escapade – had never been boating.

'Not sure Mummy would like yacht racing,' said Rodney, trying hard to hide his glee at such a stupid gift.

'Not a racing yacht. She's a Victorian four-berth forty-foot cutter, got mahogany decks, loads of brass bits, needs a tidy-up, perhaps more a refit, been in dry dock for years, probably needs to be re-hulled, then she'll be good for another fifty years, or more. An old boy in a retirement home overlooking the Solent owned it. He'd been dreaming of navigating the world. If Mummy can't make the odd weekend or two, I'll help her out by popping down and looking after the boat myself, make certain she's clean and in ace condition. These old vessels go to the dogs if they're not used. I hoped the two of you might like to volunteer when she's not in use.'

'Damned thoughtful old boy, I'm ready to help Mummy and you out anytime.' Rodney had been thinking how useful it'd be for him and his PA, even before Cuthbert's suggestion.

'What did you get, Tristan?'

'Well, I know Mummy loves popping off to the continent, so she'll love my gift. It's a four-bedroomed holiday home in the South of France.'

'A four-bed holiday home in France!' Both Cuthbert and Rodney blurted.

'Well, it will be, when converted. At the moment it's called "a rustic barn".'

'I thought you'd purchased a barn in France years ago,' Rodney said.

'Same one, haven't seen it for some time, never got round to its conversion. My frog solicitor signed it over to Mummy. She's got plenty more taste than me, so I thought she'd love transforming it into a luxury holiday home. It's a bit more dilapidated since I got it – roof caved in, so the solicitor says – but, with a dose of cash, it'll transform into a splendid property. Plenty of stabling and it's almost smack in the centre of a tiny village called Les Baux.'

Cuthbert thought back to those wonderful holidays with Mary. 'Know what? I am sure I've been there. It's in a valley and they have a market every Thursday. We purchased a jug of red wine from the back of a pony trap and sat in the cobbled market square, opposite the mayor's office. I recall there's a little fountain with a horse trough. Scorching day, but the wine, cheese and a fresh baguette were excellent. Am I not right?'

'Sounds like the place,' Tristan said. 'The barn's not in the village square though, it's on the hillside looking down onto the centre. When Mummy completes the renovation, there'll be staggering panoramic views from every window. The front door will open onto a pedestrian zone – or rather an unmade track, too narrow and steep for cars – but there's parking at the bottom and the walk's only a few hundred yards. Les Baux is famed for the waterfall that feeds the stream running through a watercourse to one side of the property. Floods from time to time, but I didn't discover that till I bought the place. Engineers say it can be diverted, but when the previous owner tried he came unstuck; you know what the French are like. Apparently, the villagers manned barricades – one woman stood atop with her tit out – and they burnt tyres to stop entry, but the solicitor insisted he can sort it through the courts.'

Rodney joined in the pretence of praising the fool's delusional offering, he knew better than they how to toady up to Mummy. His gift, although smaller, would be much more acceptable. 'It sounds fabulous; bet it's crowded in the summer.'

'Yes, a little, but it's a lovely spot. If Mummy spends enough cash on the place, it'll be spot on and, having four bedrooms, will be ideal for family members to use when she's not there. Tell me, Rodney, what did you get for her?'

Rodney had savoured this moment. He took a sip of Champagne before replying. 'We all know the one thing she has always loved is getting dressed up, so I bought our Mummy darling a wonderful gown.'

His brothers agreed that a gown was an outstanding gift.

'Wish I could claim it was my idea but, sorry chaps, not so: it's my Parliamentary Assistant who gets the accolade. The girl's from an excellent family with a place on the South Downs in Surrey – I've played polo with her father a time or two – also superb at croquet. Anyway, she and I were in Paris – government business – and I said that I couldn't think of a gift, and she said, since we're in Paris why don't you buy her a gown? I thought, that's hunky-dory, a brilliant idea. So, I sent her out to buy one while I chased the paper with the Frogs.

'Toiled day and night wore herself out traipsing around the city. Called upon all the major couturiers, and many smaller ones, before deciding upon Dior. Her entire week was spent taking her clothes on and off, can you believe it? Sheer dedication. Anyone who says the youth of this country are idle hasn't met my PA.'

Cuthbert said, 'A good PA's worth a king's ransom. Sounds as if she spent the week working like the blazes, couldn't do without mine. Problem is, it takes ages getting 'em up to snuff and, before you know it, they're gone. Had mine for three years, took time to get her right, but now, indispensable.'

'Yes, she did, and to say she's only been with me for under a year, it's remarkable.'

'Only a year, gosh, hardly broken in,' said Tristan. 'What happened to the previous one?'

'Foreign affairs,' responded Rodney.

'Does the Foreign Office pay more?' said Cuthbert. 'Would've thought Civil Services all paid the same.'

'No, you misunderstand,' said Rodney. 'She didn't go to the Foreign Office, she had foreign affairs: affairs with foreigners.'

Cuthbert whispered conspiratorially, 'Good Lord, somebody stepped onto your turf. That's not on.'

'No, and it wasn't even a glass of Champagne with a quickie in the office closet. Not a clue it was happening until a poppy from the typing pool dropped the hint. Beautiful girl, Cynthia, she's my new PA.' Rodney took a sip of Champagne before continuing. 'She said apparently half the Russian Embassy was at it for months, but the final straw occurred when I learnt she was pregnant by some Prussian Prince. Couldn't keep her any longer, so depart she had to.'

'What bad luck, old chap, after all you put into her,' said Tristan.

The Champagne bubbles spiralling up Rodney's glass were thinner than at first, but still left their nucleation bunker with enough energy to pirouette to the surface.

'Never can understand these young girls, free and easy, gussets like roller blinds on a widow's window. I mean, call me old-fashioned if you like, but I never considered having sex with my wife before we were married. Did you?'

Cuthbert shook his head, 'Never did.'

'Not that I remember,' Tristan said.

'What do you mean, not that you remember? You've never been married,' Rodney retorted.

'Oh, with *my* wife!' Tristan said. 'Sorry old chap, I misunderstood the question.'

It gratified Rodney that his PA's idea for the gift was unmatched by his brothers'. Mummy would soon see through their little schemes. How well Cynthia had performed in Paris. Must mollycoddle her, can't have her thinking a chargé d'affaires was someone responsible for extracurricular hanky-panky on the desk with a foreign ambassador. Such a pity the last one had no morals: a charming girl who said she was on the pill. Fortuitous that a Kraut fathered the kid, it could have been worse.

He took Mummy's letter from his pocket.

A Commie in the Camp

'Right,' said Rodney, 'I'll read the letter while we wait for dinner. If the profusion of paper is anything to go by, there must be loads of news. Here we go,'

> 'Boys,
>
> *Seventy! Who would ever have dreamt I'd reach seventy! When twenty, I believed I was as evergreen as a Bristlecone Pine, but having passed, and enjoyed, the earlier landmarks, I now realise seventy is another new beginning. Not only do I feel young, but the advancing years have delivered me from the albatross of mediocrity that I had felt descending upon me. I am again a free spirit.'*

'You know chaps,' Tristan interrupted. 'A rare treasure, she brings joy to all. I can't remember an occasion when the word mediocrity and Mummy coexisted. Would you ever have described her in that tone, Cuthbert?'

'Never, no matter the adversity, her love and support have been boundless. Taken everything in her stride, never fallen short. Aren't we fortunate to have a mummy like our Mummy? She's always been our anchor and will be till the cows come home. What think you, Rodney?'

'Must say, a marvel, a real darling. But although it saddens me to bring up the subject. . . how can I put it? Well, chaps, our dearest Mummy is on the cusp of antiquity and close to be being plucked from our bosom by the vulture of time, it's constantly hovering, waiting to swoop. I'll continue,' Rodney said, with a gravity befitting his pronouncement,

> *'Taking cognisance of my progression in*
> *years, I am determined to live every moment*
> *without regret for the past, or present. As*
> *a result, I have decided not to quench the*
> *smouldering fire burning within my breast by*
> *attending another dull-as-dishwater soirée.'*

'I say, dull-as-dishwater soirée!' said Cuthbert. 'A bit over the top, don't you think chaps? It seems whatever keeps coming up has really got her down. Not like Mummy to miss a jolly good bash, and what was it she said. . .? Quench the smouldering fire in her breast? Can't understand what the dear is talking about, quite ridiculous. Do you think she's losing her marbles?'

'It's bizarre,' Rodney said, 'and I don't mind telling you, putting this evening together was easier said than done.'

'Carry on Rodney. We'll soon know if she's lost it,' Tristan said.

> *'I'm awash with news, but first let me speak of*
> *your gifts. Cuthbert, I'll start with yours. Who*
> *else but you could have thought of giving me*
> *a yacht for my birthday?'*

Cuthbert's face lit up, 'I knew she'd love it, always enjoyed doing extraordinary things. Let's hope the pleasure's not too great, don't want her to fly the spinnaker too often and not leave enough time for us. Perhaps I'll give her parachute lessons for Christmas, take her mind off the boat.'

> *'In my youth a myriad of juvenescent nautical types attempted to splice my mainsail with their little playthings whilst boasting about the size of their belaying pins and referring to my bikini top as booby hatches. To be frank, I never gave a toss for their spreaders and struts, or any other accoutrements of which they boasted. I can think of not one prig who ever enticed me to berth below deck. I abhor sailing, you stupid boy.'*

A crestfallen Cuthbert slumped in his chair. 'Not going the way I'd hoped, chaps.'

> *'At seventy, my hanging over the side of a gaff-rigged sailboat trying to keep the damn thing upright whilst regurgitating in the manner of a debilitated seagull, might inhibit me from gaining a full enjoyment, don't you think?*
>
> *As I cannot use your gift, and having given great thought to the situation, I have found an amicable solution.'*

Cuthbert sprang in, 'Never mind, if she gives it back you can chip in, so we can all use it.'

Rodney, having read the next bit while the nincompoop was spouting, gleefully continued,

> *'Knowing you'll love the idea, I have donated it to the Sea Scouts, better than having it lying*

around unused. Perhaps you could become a scoutmaster?'

'Great Scott! Nigh on six thousand smackers down the Solent. Can you believe it? A Victorian sailing boat, and she's given it away to a pack of snotty-nosed dib dib dibbers. How ungrateful,' said Cuthbert.

'Perhaps it was an awful day when she wrote the letter,' said Rodney. 'Don't be too harsh or judgemental of the old dear. Beneath his mollifying manner, he was euphoric that Mummy had given short shrift to the nitwit's gift.

'Let's hear what she has to say regarding what you gave, Tristan,'

> *'Tristan, a holiday cottage in France. Oh, how I love the South and that dear tiny village. I had lunch there with Maurice, oh so many memories ago. We sat outside a bar next to the water pump in the cobbled square on rusty wrought-iron chairs; we laughed as our food and drinks wobbled on the wonky table.*
>
> *The naughty boy drank red wine from my white shoes, it ruined them. An old man wearing a beret and playing an accordion came over to our table; I can even recall the smell of the Gauloises drooping on his lips. Maurice held my hand and crooned 'La Mer'.*
>
> *I was young, he so much older, and experienced. It mattered not, I was but clay to his charm. I still have the shoes; how could I throw them away? He was my first proper lover.'*

Tristan was beside himself with excitement. 'I knew it! I knew my gift would please the old dear. Wonder who Maurice was?'

Rodney was piqued at his brother's elation, but determined to continue reading without giving away his chagrin,

> 'Doubtless you hoped that I'd spend thousands on renovations and then furnish you with a bolt-hole for dallying with the wives of your cuckolded clients, but you're wrong.'

Tristan spluttered, 'Damned cheek.'

Rodney's feeling of intoxication wasn't consequential to his imbibing, but the upshot of seeing his brothers' displeasure at Mummy's slap-in-the-face rejection of their miserable self-centred offerings. Relishing their disquiet, he continued reading, with an ever-increasing inflection of glee that he measured would add more flagellation and discomfiture upon his sorrowful siblings,

> 'When you first bought the property, you showed me the photographs. Rotting roof! No windows or doors! I told you then it was unfit for a donkey, and, since then, you've done nothing.'

'Oh, I forgot she'd seen the pictures,' said Tristan.

> 'Other than its state, what about access? (Don't worry; I am aware of the stream flooding!) I'd have to slither through the quagmire to get down to the village and slide back up on my belly! Are you trying to kill me?

As I would never use it, and knowing how
much you care for the disadvantaged souls of
this sad world, I have donated the property to
a charity that has the wherewithal to convert
it into a refugee centre. I know you would
approve.'

'A damned refugee centre! Housing for a bunch of odious outcasts! She's a raving lunatic. The woman's gone berserk,' Tristan exploded.

Cuthbert agreed. 'There! Now you're on the receiving end. She flung the yacht back in my face with not even a word of thanks. Now you've received the same rotten treatment. Insane! She's insane!'

It was impossible for Rodney to let the splendid moment pass without profit.

'I say, you two, don't be so harsh on the poor dear. Blatantly, neither of you thought of her when purchasing the gifts. Self-centred, that's what you are, and she's seen right through your nasty schemes.'

'Okay Rodney, you think you're so clever,' said Cuthbert. 'Let's see how you fare.'

'Well, as I'm not a cross dresser, I'd hardly buy a Dior gown hoping to get it back. My offertory, although small considering all she's done for me, was a gift demonstrative of my love for her, and given without seeking a trace of recompense. Unlike you two, I had no ulterior motives. Face it chaps, she's seen through your nasty shady offerings. Shall I continue reading the letter?' With a supercilious smirk, he did so, without waiting for a response,

'Rodney, when I saw the gold-embossed name on
the box my youth flashed before me, for when at
society balls I oft wore Dior. Many of the most

> *elegant young – and not-so-young – philandering playboys in London, Paris, Rome, and not least the Riviera, sought after and desired my favours. Life was wonderful. Oh, how I lost my heart to those naughty Rostov Romanovs, I never knew what 'three abreast' meant until one night on a Troika. . . how I fitted it all in, I will never know! How delightful it was to have the memories of those breathtaking, heart-stopping and thrilling times rekindled ...'*

Rodney broke off from reading and eulogised, 'You see chaps. As with the widow and her mite, I'm giving without expecting something in return. Let this be an example of selfless love. My thoughtful gift has opened the floodgates of our dear Mummy's youth; it makes me proud to be her son.'

His brothers, still smarting over the rejection of their gifts, sat silently sullen as he continued,

> *'However, I am a size sixteen and no matter how I tried, I couldn't shoe-horn my body into a size eight destined no doubt for a shapeless bimbo.'*

With his face as grey as the smoke drifting from the smouldering Vuelta Abajo tobacco in his Cuban cigar, Rodney could muster but a strangled utterance, 'The damned thing must still be in Cynthia's wardrobe. The fool wrapped up the wrong frock.'

'I say, that is jolly hard luck old chap, how unfortunate after all you went through.' Tristan's compassionate commiserations masked a deep resentment for his brother's earlier comments. Cuthbert too was deliriously happy at seeing Mummy uncloaking his hypocritical, pompous brother.

'Bloody woman,' said Rodney.

'Come on, old chap,' Tristan smirked. 'Jolly sure you want to hear the rest of Mummy's grateful thanks for your selfless giving.'

Emboldened, Cuthbert joined the fray. 'Yes, tell us more about your offerings, given without any thought of receiving something in return. We're always open to be guided by our elder brother.'

Although ignoring their taunts, Rodney's earlier jollity had departed as he went on reading,

> *'But, thanks to you, "Help the Aged" have benefited, for I delighted them by taking it to their charity shop. It was on their half-price sale rack for barely five minutes before an old lady with a tartan shopping trolley bought it. She's making curtains for her granddaughter's doll's house. It was good luck that I was there, as the shop had no change for the twenty-pound note, so I helped.*
>
> *Silly boy, you left a receipt for 'two' dresses in the package with a note written on it asking a girl called Cynthia to claim them on your Parliamentary expenses.*
>
> *Thoughtless of me, but I shredded it. Never mind.'*

Being the youngest, and seemingly at the tail end of everything, Cuthbert had a measure of resentment towards his siblings, especially Rodney. 'There, Mr High And Mighty, fiddling your expenses MP. You're a bloody crook!'

Rodney snapped back, 'Whatever I do is none of your businesses. But it grieves me to say you are both right, and I am wrong. Something has unzipped her, turned the old bat against her own children.'

'Nutty as a fruitcake, no doubt an age-related medical condition. She's gone gaga, that's what,' Tristan pronounced.

Cuthbert, feeling more charitable, said, 'Have you considered it might be to do with Daddy's demise? I know at the time she got on with life as if nothing untoward had happened, but she may have been bottling his death up all these years – stiff upper lip. Now, just by chance, one of our gifts brought it all flooding back, and she's gone doolally tap.'

Without comment, Rodney continued reading,

> 'I was proud when you became a Member of Parliament. However, in your scramble to the top, you've become like so many of your ilk. You're comparable to a window cleaner in a nudist colony. Looks okay doing the downstairs, but as he climbs the ladder, his more unattractive features are revealed. It saddens me to say, the image that you now flout is not much to look at, from any angle.'

'That's unfair, no cause for that,' Rodney said,

> 'Your life as a parasitic expense-fiddling MP seeking self-gratification within that cesspool of vipers sickens me. With this in mind, I, from now on, will be called Comrade Lady Marjorie Crooke-Wells, for I have joined the Socialist Workers Party.'

It was with astonishment that the brothers stared at each other. Cuthbert was first to speak, 'Comrade! A harebrained commie! Not only deranged, but a crackbrained psychotic pinko, a loony lefty.'

'They're not lefties,' Rodney retorted. 'They're not your *everyday workers of the world unite* Socialist Workers Party. No, she's a born-again rabid red, a Trotskyite.'

'Impossible!' Tristan said. 'Worker of the world! She's never done a stroke of work in her life.'

The return of Ramiro interrupted their consideration of Mummy's mental and political state.

'Chef 'e say you 'ave beginner in the forty minute more, for 'im 'e too much busy.'

'Bugger off,' was Rodney's swift response.

Unconcerned, Ramiro returned happily to his service table where he continued breathing on and polishing the cutlery and glasses.

As had his political idol, Churchill, in times of turmoil, Rodney clasped his lapels and put on his gravest face and inflected his voice to match the moment. 'I thought we'd have a jolly little party, a tête-à-tête, with Mummy, full of the joys of spring, but we've got a nightmare, a catastrophe. Brothers, we have a commie in our camp.'

'You're right,' Tristan said. 'She's made me feel awful and although I hate to hear what other utterances the old crone has exuded, you'd better get on with reading the rubbish.'

> *'The rest of my news I am sure will make you think I have gone insane.'*

'Insane? Insane! Ha! I should say so. Hit the nail on the head there.' Tristan agreed.

'I have fallen in love.'

Looking at his brothers' startled faces, Rodney reiterated what he had read. 'Fallen in love! That's what she says, as mad as a March hare, but that's what she's written. I'll read it again, 'I have fallen in love'. Those are her exact words, in black and white. Off her rocker, not the slightest doubt, stark raving mad. I'll continue reading her drivel, but I fear the worst,'

> *'My years of unsatisfied frustration are at an end, I am released. My life is overflowing with joy and satisfaction. Again a complete woman, fulfilled by adventurous sensual passion, a craving I thought lost forever, an ecstasy I've not enjoyed for many years, I have been recharged.'*

'Adventurous sensual passion!' Cuthbert spluttered. 'Real woman! Been recharged! What the hell is she talking about? Sounds like a clapped-out car battery. Stuff and nonsense!'

'What happened to quilting,' said Tristan, 'and coach trips to the seaside with the rest of the old farts. What think you, Rodney?'

'I can only guess what's happened. She's attended one of those tea dances, waltzed with a toothless, time-expired old goat who had a dizzy spell. He grabs hold of her for support, she thinks he's groping so makes the most of it in case it never happens again. That's it, I'd put my shirt on it. I'll get on reading the rest of her poppycock,'

> *'My loving sweetheart may appear not to be the brightest candle on the Christmas tree, but he is caring and loving. When you meet him,*

*I'm sure you will have the same affection for
him as I. His name is Ramiro.'*

'Ramiro!' The three brothers exclaimed in unison.

The waiter rushed over to their table. 'Si, I sorry if something I forget you.'

It took a few moments before Rodney had recovered sufficiently to say, 'I told you, I'll call you when I want you.'

'Ees good you call, I come. Now you call I come again,' Ramiro said, returning to his table.

'You don't think it's...?' Cuthbert nodded towards the waiter.'

The other brothers looked at Ramiro, who returned their look with a smile.

'Can't be! He's at least thirty years younger than the old bat. She wouldn't, would she? Not our Mummy.' They all voiced an opinion.

With all animosity put aside, they huddled and Cuthbert whispered, 'Carry on, Rodney.'

*'Such a sweet attentive boy, I call him El
Gaucho. He attends to my every need.'*

Rodney stopped reading, stared at his brothers and whispered, 'I know it sounds absurd, but I'm damned sure she's talking about him, that Argentinean carpetbagger! Leave this to me.' Then, with a voice belying his own incredulity at the thought of his mother having anything to do with their bloody worthless waiter he called, 'I say you. . .! Ramiro, come here, I want to have a chit-chat.'

Ramiro picked up a menu, studied it, and walked to the table. 'I sorry but not have chit-chat, they gone, not on menu, it must finish be.'

'No Ramiro,' Rodney said. 'We don't want to order anything. Rather, we are interested to know a little about you.'

'Why you want know?'

'It's just that you are such an interesting little foreign fellow. Do you have a girlfriend? In England, I mean?'

'Si it be I 'ave one.'

'What's her name?' asked Cuthbert, 'Is it Esmerelda? Delores? Evita? Conchita?'

'No, er name that she want me to be call is Cougar.'

The brothers exclaimed, 'Cougar!'

'Si, Cougar, her name be Cougar, and she very much be beautiful.'

'And what does she call you?' asked Rodney.

'She calls me El Gaucho because she say I ride like...'

Tristan interrupted Ramiro's rhetorical and animated gyrations displaying why his girlfriend drew a comparison between him and a bare back rodeo rider. 'Tell me Ramiro, is she ancient and wrinkled, like corrugated cardboard?'

'Ah, si. She little. . . but has mucho gomo.'

His hands showed that it was the size of her breasts of which he was speaking.

'Ramiro, my boy,' said Rodney, 'we won't need you for some time. I want you to go to the kitchen and when we want you to come back, I will ring the bell. Do you understand?'

'Si, I go now talk to chef. When ring bell from you, I come back.' Ramiro tripped lightly from the room.

Dead for a Ducat, Dead

When they were alone, Rodney was first to speak. 'The situation is cataclysmic. That snollygoster is rogering our Mummy. What manner of person would do such a thing to a defenceless old woman? Who would even want to do it with an old hag?'

'A rotten louse, that's the sort!' said Tristan. 'Our Mummy, an old-age pensioner, a sex toy, a common harlot used by a contemptible charlatan.'

As the words passed his lips, he recalled the not-so-young dear Lucy Devine. She was about Mummy's age. Juicy Lucy, an insatiable sex fiend married to a gay banker, but then, thank goodness, she wasn't his mother. Anyway, Mummy could never do the things Lucy did, or at least, it's doubtful, not athletic enough. Cuthbert's barrage of indignation barged into Tristan's licentious cogitations.

'An unethical bounder, that's the breed of person who's taken advantage of an innocent old woman, a rotten cad who needs a jolly good horsewhipping,' said Tristan. 'Tell you what, if I had a cat-o'-nine-tails to hand, I'd thrash the living daylights out of the blighter, and rub salt into the wounds. Bloody foreigners, come here to use our NHS, get cheap housing, and copulate with our women. It's a fact, they all do it, everybody says so.'

'Chaps, it's not just Mummy's feelings the cad's playing with, we have to consider the implications of the whole damned dilemma,' Rodney said. 'It's obvious the blackguard's after the old bat's wherewithal, that's what this nonsense is about. It's not just her body he's after, it's her money. We can't sit back and leave it…. it's madness. Lunacy! He's humiliated us.'

'For once I agree with you,' Tristan said, 'but let's be clear; the money's not hers, it's our inheritance. Daddy worked damned hard to stash the cash, he'd never have dreamt that Mummy would throw it away on a South American bandit, for that's what the scallywag is, he's a rotten bandit here to plunder the old bat, no matter the ignominy it causes.'

'You're right,' said Rodney. 'Every parent's task, including hers, is to safeguard the family fortune, not waste it on an infernal foreigner. Face it chaps, it's fundamental to the preservation of a proper society, and, not least, our future. Wouldn't surprise me if his plan isn't a marriage of convenience; it's the only way blighters like him can stay here since the Home Office cracked down on 'em.'

They sat in silence.

'Can't you get him deported, Rodney?' Cuthbert said. 'You must know someone in the right department. Get him out lickety-split, I say.'

Tristan said, 'Blended. Fly the confounded fool to where they've consigned the rest of 'em, a summer camp in Cuba.'

'It's rendered, like in rendition.' Rodney corrected. 'Impossible, there's no department called Rendition as far as I'm aware. Anyway, it wouldn't work. It's obvious from the tone of the demented doxy's poison pen that she's possessed, probably chain herself to the wheels of the aeroplane transporting him.'

Tristan cracked a joke about becoming a suffragette.

Rodney didn't care for his flippancy. 'This is a serious situation. If you are incapable of adding anything useful, I suggest you bugger off and leave it for Cuthbert and me to handle. Our inheritance is at risk. Oh, and Mummy's welfare. Now, where was I?'

'You were talking about what I think they call extraordinary rendition,' Cuthbert reminded him.

'Ah yes. No, it wouldn't work. She'd be off to wherever they took him, demanding conjugal rights. No, that's no good. Even if I could do something, it wouldn't work and, anyway, the powers-that-be would soon find his link to Mummy and hers to me.'

Thinking a sensible question might redeem him in Rodney's eyes, Tristan asked, 'What about deportation? Know anyone in Deportation, Rodney?'

'I know a few chaps in the Home Office, but you can appreciate what would happen. He'd apply for asylum and our maniacal mother would spend our inheritance assisting his application. Bound to get out, be in the papers in no time. No, that won't work either.'

'So why not get him fired? Out of work and penniless,' said Cuthbert.

'Use your senses man!' Rodney exclaimed. 'That's no good. If he's out of work, they'd spend morning, noon and night pursuing coital contentment. He'd have even more time to turn her against us and hijack our inheritance. To be frank, from her reactions to our gifts, it may have already started. No, if they were at it from morn till midnight, and beyond, she'd be so much worse for wear he'd have no problem getting her to chuck us out of her will and leave him everything.'

'What if we club together,' said Tristan, 'and then pay him off.'

'No, we'd end up in an auction. Mummy would up the offer, using our inheritance, to keep him here. No, we must think of something that's more permanent to get him out of the way.'

They racked their brains in silence.

Cuthbert, while not having wished to play an up-front role in amateur dramatics, had a keen mind for plots and put forward his solution. 'I think we should kill him.'

'Kill him!' his brothers exclaimed, with Rodney adding, 'Having read Mummy's utterances and listening to your stupid thoughts, I am more certain than ever that insanity is congenital.'

'No, no, Rodney. It's not as silly as it sounds,' Cuthbert said. 'I've thought it through, and we could poison the stinker. He deserves it for rogering an old lady like Mummy. What do you think Tristan?'

Tristan thought of Sveta, Sandra, Juicy Lucy, and a myriad of older bed mates, so the propriety of a younger man and older woman was of no concern, but said, 'What poison would we use?'

'I've also worked that out,' said Cuthbert. 'We'll use weed killer. My gardener has a container in his shed. We could spray the rotten devil; he'd wither up and die within twenty-four hours.'

'No, that's ridiculous,' Tristan sneered. 'You can't have him lying here for twenty-four hours withering and dying, that's not the way it's done. I've had experience of a poisoning.'

'What!' Cuthbert exclaimed. 'You poisoned someone?'

'No, I didn't kill anyone. I lost a sale of a London apartment to a Russian oligarch, poisoned the day before completion,' Tristan explained. 'The Russian Secret Service stuffed a poisoned needle up his arse, dead as a dodo in an instant: no mess bar a bit of foam from the mouth. If we poison Ramiro, then we should fill a syringe with a toxin and plunge it into his carotid artery. It'll work even faster than up his backside, and I believe I know where to find the artery.'

'As an ex-medical corps officer,' said Cuthbert, 'I suppose you keep a syringe filled with poison in your pocket, just in case.'

They fell silent, searching Rodney's face, hoping he would volunteer a solution. However, he didn't join in with his brothers' ludicrous discussion, but preferred to sit in preponderant silence.

Cuthbert broke the lull. 'I've got it chaps! I've got another idea even better than the last. We'll use a frog.'

'A Frenchman? A smarmy garlic cruncher,' said Tristan. 'We don't need a foreigner. Hatchet men are ten-a-penny in London, one on every street corner in Soho.'

'No, not a French frog,' Cuthbert protested. 'I mean frog frogs, those that jump.'

Tristan said, 'What's your plan? Fish a frog out of the Thames and beat the blighter to death with it?'

'No,' said Cuthbert. 'Just think about it, Amazon Indians hunt with blowpipes and shoot monkeys out of trees using frog poison on their darts. I've seen it on TV. Nobody would ever suspect a death by frog poison in Parliament, would they?' Sure of his solution, he added, 'We could make a dart out of a toothpick and just scratch him with it, or make a blowpipe.'

Rodney, who'd been racking his brain for a means to disburden them from El Gaucho, couldn't endure his brother's lunacy any longer. 'Look, I have a few questions. Is it your proposition that one of you dimwits trots off to Jean-Baptiste Cuisses de Grenouilles on the

Portobello Road and orders a dozen takeaway sautéed frogs' legs? Then ask for a froggy bag to carry back the live double amputees? Upon your return, is it your intention to transform the infirmed frogs into poison? If that's the master plan, it won't work, you stupid tossers. The amphibians used for poison are special croakers; they don't live in Notting Hill. To make it work, you'd need to break into the London Zoo, get an Amazonian frog and milk the bloody thing, or whatever's done to get the poison out. The notion is so crackpot that it's only worth would be in a psychiatric manual nailing down how to instantly spot a certifiable fruitcake.'

'Pooh-pooh it as much as you like, but it's the best idea so far,' said Cuthbert.

'Of course it's the best! It's the only one you fool,' scoffed Rodney, returning his thoughts to seeking a solution whilst allowing his brothers to fantasise.

'Jolly sure we could find a poisonous frog somewhere in London,' Cuthbert said. 'I have a chum who's got an Amazonian parrot, so why not a frog? Okay, there would be issues to overcome, like how to milk a frog. I mean, where does a frog keep his tits? But nothing's insurmountable.'

'Can't be a *he*, old bean,' Tristan advised. 'Must be a *she*.'

'Well, I don't know, they didn't show how to milk 'em on TV.'

'No, it sounds far too difficult, won't work,' said Tristan. 'Let's forget the idea. You'd never get into the zoo this time of the night and, even if you did, it becomes more difficult when you consider you'd have to sex the sodding thing. You'd be better off stealing a snake or a spider. So, why not simply bash him on the head with this Champagne bottle and heave the rotten duffer into the Thames?'

'Sounds like a jolly good idea to me,' Cuthbert said. 'Bash him on the head and toss him into the wadi. What do you think about that Rodney?'

'No. Doing it that way, there'd be too much noise, not forgetting blood and glass everywhere, can't mess up the carpets. But you're right about drowning the down-and-out scoundrel for taking our Mummy for a ride.'

'Don't know about him taking Mummy for a ride, seems she's enjoying the canter,' Tristan observed. 'So, if whacking him on his noggin with the Champagne bottle is not worth considering, and you don't think poisoning much cop, let's hear how you propose to euthanise the milksop and toss him into the Thames.'

'Look we've agreed to drown him in the river, now we must look for a method,' said Rodney. 'Just stop babbling and think of a way.'

Rodney recalled that Mummy had described Ramiro as not the brightest candle on a Christmas tree. So, how do we make that dim light illuminate a tomb instead? Dunking him in the river was a good idea, but how?

The minutes ticked by in silence.

Rodney leapt to his feet. 'By Jove, I have it! A foolproof plan to liquidate the lecher.'

He crossed the room to the service bell's pull-rope. 'I will ring the bell to call the cur from the kitchen,' he said, while striding to the service table where he picked up a spare tablecloth, and then he crossed the room and stood behind the door. 'Tristan, you will stand in this position whilst you, Cuthbert, will place yourself behind your brother. When the rat enters, I'll distract him and Tristan will hurl this tablecloth over his head and pinion his arms to his sides. Cuthbert, you will wrench the wretch to the ground and the moment he crashes onto the carpet, the three of us will pile on top and remain there until he's lifeless. We then plunge him into the river.'

Tristan clapped his brother on the back. 'Bloody brilliant! Knew we could rely on you. It's a spiffing plan. Well done Rodney, I relish the thought of dumping him in the shake and shiver.'

Although thinking his own idea of frog poison was good, Cuthbert felt, under the circumstances of not knowing how to milk a frog – even if they had one – Rodney's proposed course of action was more workable. 'We must empty the weasel's pockets so there's no identification. By George, it'll serve the blighter right! A well-deserved ignominious departure, not a wisp of a whistle, no Rule Britannia; just let him float back to Argie land. I'm with you, Rodney.'

'I know we're not supposed to put trash into the Thames,' Tristan said, 'but we can't have him do a runner with our inheritance. The blighter deserves to end up carried by the tides for rogering our dear old Mummy and trying to get his hands on her assets.'

'His hands are already on her assets,' Rodney said. 'Not only that, but the swine has twisted her senile senses and transformed her into an insane born-again commie. Never thought I'd say it, but Tristan, he's even more dangerous to a woman than you. Right chaps, man your positions and call *affirmative* when you're ready, then I'll ring the bell.'

The brothers took their position and cried, 'Affirmative.'

'Good, I'm pulling the bell-rope now, and you both know what to do. Remember, it's the duty of every son to save his inheritance, oh, and to look after his Mummy, so let's get the job done.'

As they waited silently for their prey, a sermon note from his ancestral grandfather's diaries came to Rodney's mind. It spoke of King Belshazzar beholding a disembodied hand writing the King's fate upon a wall. Ramiro has no such portent forewarning of his, thought Rodney. And he'll be unaware his name's already upon a metaphorical tombstone: Here rests a rat.

* * *

Earlier, when Ramiro arrived in the kitchen, the patissier had just completed the creation of an enormous croquembouche and had passed Ramiro two pudding bowls with an abundance of chocolate and caramel still clinging to their sides. Such a treat has been a delight for children immemorially, and Ramiro was no exception.

In polite European company, knives, forks and spoons are a social etiquettal need. But such accoutrements are of little use, possibly even an impediment, for such a mouth-watering opportunity of self indulgency. Although fingers and tongues are primordial, they are the only satisfactory way of ensuring baking vessels need little or no washing afterwards.

The bell summoning the hapless Ramiro to his fate did not toll ominously; it was a tinkle from a tiny clapper above a room number. At the time of the unobtrusive ding, he had his face buried inside the larger of the bowls, containing the finest chocolate from Calceta in the Ecuadorian province of Manabi, which had found its way, via Belgium, to his hair and ears. The chef, a kindly man who only screamed and swore when angry, patted Ramiro on the back, pointed to the bell, and suggested he return to the room, while offering to keep the bowls for Ramiro to finish licking later. Laughingly, he pointed out that Ramiro had covered himself with chocolate and caramel.

* * *

Whilst Ramiro busied himself removing the lickings from hands, hair and face, the ambushers awaited their prey, as silent as nocturnal shaggy-bearded wobbegongs concealed upon the ocean floor. Cuthbert turned to Hamlet, 'How now, a rat? Dead for a ducat, dead!'

For Whom the Bell Tinkled?

Cuthbert whispered, 'Keep quiet, chaps. I can hear his footsteps; the stinker's coming.'

As the door swung open, the roar Rodney uttered was louder than intended, and would have startled and wrought fear into the heart of any man. It achieved its intention for Cuthbert leapt leopard-like into action, throwing the tablecloth over their wretched prey. 'Got the vermin – quickly Tristan, bring him down.'

Like a whippet from a trap, Tristan rocketed and encircled the warthog's waist, pinning his arms while wrestling the wretch to the rugs.

Having slammed the door, Rodney launched himself into the scrimmage, finding footage on the fellow's rib cage. 'Quick Tristan! Look lively man, pinion the blighter's legs and stop him kicking, he's making too much of a racket.'

'Got him, hold fast chaps, remember the Falklands,' cried Cuthbert.'

'Forget the Falklands, hang on to our inheritance,' Tristan shouted.

'Who is here so vile that will not love his country?' Cuthbert considered a Shakespearean quote appropriate as he threw himself upon the threshing legs. 'By the Lord, lads, hold the wretch, this blot upon our pride, cry havoc, and let slip the dogs of war.'

Rodney muffled the fellow's cries by clamping the prey's head between the cheeks of his abundant buttocks. It was then but a brief time before the struggling stopped and the brothers relaxed.

'Good! His anchors dropped, he's berthed in harmony harbour,' proclaimed Tristan. 'Well done! Now he's croaked, he'll cause us no more trouble. Let's tie him up in the tablecloth and sink the serpent into the sea.'

'Shush! Shut up!' Rodney cupped his ear, listening intently and said, 'Great Scott, I can hear footsteps, someone's coming. They must have heard us. Quick, back to the table, we'll pretend nothing's happened. Keep calm and follow my lead.'

They sat as nonchalantly as they could, given there was a body prostrated upon the floor wrapped in a tablecloth.

'Yes, you see chaps it works like this,' Rodney raised his voice to emphasise the normality of the situation. 'I'll answer your question as best I can, but it's not simple. When there's a vote in the House of Commons, Mr Speaker shouts "Division! Lock the doors", and nobody may leave the Chamber and then...'

'I sorry I lately come, the chef it be him held up, so am backward in time.'

'Good God!' the brothers exclaimed in unison.

Ramiro looked around the room. 'Not him, it me, Ramiro, I be your waiter, you forget me because I long time, but it not my fault it be chef he talks much.' Pausing, he pointed to the body, 'Who he?'

'Who's who?' Rodney said with shammed indifference, searching the room in every direction other than where the body lay on the floor, his brothers following his lead.

'No, he not there, he be here. There!' Ramiro pointed at the body. 'It be he who lying on the floor, I trip over almost when I come. Who he?'

Whilst Cuthbert and Tristan kept up the pretence of chatting, Rodney followed Ramiro's finger, noting that it had a sticky substance upon it and his face appeared to be shinier and more tanned than before. 'Can't say I've ever seen whatever it is before you mentioned it.' Turning to his brothers, he inquired, 'Sorry to disturb you chaps, but have you ever seen that before, that thing over there?'

'Seen what, old bean?' Tristan asked.

Rodney pointed. 'I believe there's a fellow lying on the floor covered in a sheet. Looks like he's asleep.'

'Can't say I have. Don't recognise him,' responded Cuthbert.

'Nor me,' Tristan said. 'Probably fell asleep waiting for the waiter. Sorry, Ramiro, my good fellow. Before you pointed him out, we'd never even noticed him.'

'Him I not see when leave and go see chef. I go now look see who is him.'

Romero crossed the room and gingerly removed the tablecloth from the inert figure and leapt back. 'Misericordia, ees El Presidente, ees El Presidente, El Presidente. Oh Misericordia.'

Rodney leapt to his feet, grabbed Romero and, shaking him, said, 'Pull yourself together man. We don't have a president.' He looked down. 'Great galloping gonads! It's the Prime Minister!' The chairs were sent flying as the brothers rushed to Rodney's side.

'Great Scott! You're right, it's the PM,' Cuthbert gasped. 'And he's copped it. . . the poor bugger's dead.'

A panic-stricken Ramiro was wringing his hands, 'Ees El Presidente! Esta muerto! He dead! Esta muerto! Misericordia!'

Slapping his face, Rodney snapped, 'Stop wailing man, he's only a prime minister, not a president.'

Ramiro sank to his knees next to the body, 'He dead! He dead! El Presidente muerto. Presidente muerto, he dead, he not here, he be with God.'

'Ramiro, you parasitic psycho, compose yourself. How many times must I tell you? It's not the president, he's the prime minister.' Rodney spoke reassuringly, but his calming words gave no solace as Ramiro knelt beside the body bewailing, 'Esta muerto. El Presidente muerto.'

Rodney whispered, 'Right, back to the table, it's time to talk.'

Replacing the fallen chairs, the brothers sat and Rodney continued, 'How could you make such a mistake? You've killed the wrong bugger. I mean, smothering the PM instead of Ramiro, bloody incompetence.'

'Me! It wasn't me. It was you,' spluttered Cuthbert. 'You said throw the damned tablecloth over him. I didn't know it was the Prime Minister; I only saw the fellow's back. It was your fault, not mine.'

It seemed to Tristan that clobbering the Prime Minister was in itself already an act fraught with danger, but also having the disapprobation of blame meted out by your own brother was, even by Rodney's stinking standards, unprincipled. If it's a shindig he's after, he'll get one, 'It's your fault. We just followed your orders, and the stupid plan that failed was yours.'

Rodney hissed, 'Okay, that's it. You're like the other creatures at Nuremberg, you just followed bloody orders, but remember they still gambolled on the gallows. So, don't worry you two, just stick together. It's my fault, I'll take the blame.'

A palpable enmity descended, with Ramiro's sobs the only solace to the silence.

Rodney recognised that to extricate himself, he'd need the services of the two loathsome turncoats. There'd be time for revenge later. So he said, 'Look, chaps, let's not allot liability, for there'll be no solution found in disunion. Instead remember, it was that sobbing rotter rogering our Mummy that united us, so unified we must remain. It's most unfortunate that the PM had no taste in evening wear. I mean, the man's dinner suit looks no better than that of the wretched waiter and, anyway, there was no time to see the fool's face.'

'Quite a problem we have on our hands,' ventured Tristan.

Cuthbert added, 'More than quite a problem. I'd say it's a can of worms.'

'Quite a problem! A can of worms!' Rodney mimicked. 'You berks, are you off your rockers? Don't you comprehend the enormity of the situation? It's far bigger than big, it's. . . it's. . . it's bloody enormous. . . it's gargantuan.' Once again, he affected a Churchillian voice as befitted the moment. 'Never – other than when we buggered up the Bosch – have we been confronted by a pickle of such magnitude. It's of national, even international importance.'

'Prison!' exclaimed Cuthbert, remembering his night in the cell. 'I couldn't take another stretch in prison.'

'Stretch? It won't be a stretch, other than at the end of a rope,' cried an alarmed Tristan, who'd dangled on a few ropes whilst escaping outraged husbands.

'It's even worse,' said Rodney. 'A general election, and we could lose it, by Jove. We've got a wafer-thin majority in the House and the voters would abandon us if there were an election right now, and if I'm implicated in this fiasco I'd get turfed out by my agent. I'll tell you something, that'll not happen, nor will I go to prison. There's got to be something we can do, but what?'

With Ramiro wailing in the background, they sat thinking until Cuthbert said, 'We should launch them both down the Swanee.'

Rodney considered the proposal. 'No, we can't discharge the PM into the Thames, what if the currents carried him over to France? No, that won't work, consider the repercussions. If a frog fishing boat were to gaff him from the brine, you'd hear the Grimsby trawlermen whining all the way to Westminster that it should've been one of their boats that hooked him.'

Rodney, caring naught for his brothers, was thinking of how to extricate himself from the mess. If he could find a solution, he might get an even bigger majority.

Then it happened. It was as if he were back in his bedroom; Daddy's cigar ash was falling on the bed in slow motion, and smoke rings were rising languidly in the air. Rodney heard his Daddy's voice, *Remember Scrooge, he became a hero.*

'I know what's needed,' said Rodney. 'The PM must come out of this as a national hero, a Westminster Abbey funeral, gun carriages pulled by horses crapping on the Mall, soldiers with shiny armour, muffled drums – all that stuff. Lots of touristy things, you know what I mean? Oh, and at least a knighthood for me,'

'A hero? That's impossible, he is, or at least was, a useless twat,' Tristan said.

'It doesn't matter,' said Rodney. 'Parliamentary history's full of fools. I'll give you an example: the House of Lords is a dumping ground for MPs who've received peerages because they're twats. Screw up a ministry or two and a peerage is your prize. No, being a twat has never been an encumbrance for high political office. All we have to do is to make him look like a hero – you know, smoke and mirrors stuff. Before you know it, we'll have him interred in the Nave of the Abbey. Then, in no time, I'll be kneeling before Queenie getting at least a knighthood.'

Tristan said, 'I stand by my opinion, a complete turd.'

'You're right,' Cuthbert said. 'We'd need a miracle to turn the tosspot into a hero.'

They sat in deep contemplation with the only sound assailing them being that of Ramiro's keening, as would a widow weep. Despite the distraction of the wearisome wailing, a thought sought entry into Rodney's grey matter. At Oxford, he'd attended one of those tiresome altruistic bleeding-heart debates. Staying awake during such tommyrot was unusual for him, but the motion had caught his ear. It was one of many of those stomach-churning, self-satisfying George Washington utterances that went: This House believes, when fighting for your own liberty, you should be cautious not to violate the rights of others.

At the time he considered the proposition stuff and nonsense, but could now kiss George's arse. God Bless America, you've provided the solution. The debate's counter motion – which had won the day – when put into plain English had been, Bugger the others, save yourself.

'Chaps,' Rodney uttered. 'The manifestation of a miracle is upon me. Ramiro! May we have a word, please?' His tone of voice masked the cruel twist of fate he planned to unfurl upon Ramiro's frail frame.

With shoulders heaving in unison with the sobbing tears flowing like the Iguacu Falls down his cheeks, Ramiro moved to the table. 'Si Señor.'

Rodney's frozen stare and staccato voice bayoneted Ramiro to the core. 'Why did you kill our prime minister?'

'Me! I no kill Presidente!'

'I have an eyewitness who swears you killed our democratically elected leader.' Rodney turned to Tristan, saying, 'Are you able to testify to the barbaric attack perpetrated by this man?'

'Me? I mean. . . rather. Oh yes! I saw it all right, you killed him, I saw you. . . you. . . you ne'er-do-well repulsive reptile,' declared Tristan, wiping his eyes with a napkin, thinking that a tear or two added credence to the occasion. 'It was you who assassinated our beloved prime minister.'

'Me! Me no kill El Presedente! It not be me. I have innocence, I have innocence.'

'Um. . . so you're declaring yourself to be pure and blameless. Perhaps one eyewitness is insufficient. I'll seek another unbiased personage willing to step up to the mark as an attestor to this accursed crime and to corroborate that this man is the murderous wretch who carried out the foulest deed.' Rodney turned to Cuthbert.

Cuthbert said, 'Do you mean me, old chap?'

'Well, I'd hardly be calling Lord Lucan, would I? Of course, it's you, you blithering numskull... I know it's unnecessary to remind you of the moral encumbrance upon us all to be certain we have the right person. It's beholden upon us to ensure his due rights, for we don't want a miscarriage of justice. Ramiro, come and stand next to me, and Tristan, stand on the other side of the suspect.' A forlorn Ramiro stood wedged between Rodney and Tristan.

Rodney intoned, 'Whilst recognising the stupidity of the question, Mr Cuthbert Crooke-Wells, are you of sound mind?'

'I am.'

'Good,' said Rodney. 'We'll now conduct an identity parade. Are you, and you must be certain, are you able to identify the person who killed, the Prime Minister,' he pointed to the body, 'that servant of the people? Take your time; you must be free of any doubt. Is the individual who carried out the crime before you?'

Cuthbert traipsed back and forth, eyeing up the three men. Rodney added words of encouragement, 'Be sure, but don't take all night.'

Cuthbert said, 'It's most difficult, everything was so fast.'

Rodney exploded, 'Difficult, you halfwit. There are only three of us and you know which two are innocent, so what's difficult about that? You saw the altercation, you saw the murder, and you saw this moron do it, so just get on with it.'

Cuthbert responded by viewing the suspects a few more times. Then, with a flourish, he thrust out his arm, and said, 'It was that man! I saw that man! It was he who killed our cherished shepherd. For too long I have remained silent, I cannot sustain my silence for one moment longer.' Pointing accusingly at Ramiro, he continued, 'It was he! O villain, villain! Smiling, damned villain!'

'Me! It no me!' cried Ramiro. 'Me no kill Presidente!'

'Thank you, Mr Crooke-Wells.' Rodney placed his arm around the slumped shoulders of his brother. 'Condemning this fellow must have been very difficult.' Turning to Ramiro he declared, 'There, I have two witnesses who, of their own volition and without prejudice, malice or coercion, declare that they saw you kill our prime minister.'

'No! I find El Presidente here,' he pointed to the body. 'It no me, I am innocence.'

Rodney responded, 'Right, I will call my last witness, who will corroborate and swear an oath as to your guilt. No one will disbelieve his evidence.'

'Who he?' Ramiro looked around the room. 'There be no one more, no one see me for I no do it.'

'It's me, I saw it, you rushed at him screaming "Free Malvinas", or some such Jihadi gibberish, and then you struck our prime minister to the floor and leapt upon him. We tried to pull you off, but you were like a wild beast, and by the time we yanked you clear, he was lifeless.'

'I no do!' Ramiro exclaimed, with tears coursing his cheeks, and his lower lip trembling like the strings on the charango with the armadillo-shell back that his father had given him on his twelfth birthday. 'It not is me, I no kill. Me love, not kill.' He slumped to his knees, sobbing. But, as do the morning clouds rise bit by bit above his beloved Aconcagua mountain peak, so Ramiro, little by little, grasped the situation. 'I think you and hims tell a lie. So, if I no kill, it be you. You kill El Presidente. Yes, that be it, you think he me!'

Rodney responded faster than a weasel in a warren, 'Why would I, a worthy Member of Parliament and a representative of the privileged classes, kill this Great Sun of the twenty-first century and risk a buffoon as a replacement? No, my boy, it's not me who's between a rock and a hard place, it's you, and it's you who'll pay the ultimate price for your treachery.'

Tristan joined the condemnation. 'It's the high jump for you and a better world without your sort in it, I'd say. Even the Tower's too good, should ship you off to Australia, or somewhere else at the arse end of the earth. Mind you, that's where you come from, the arse end I mean.'

'I no kill El Presedente,' Ramiro stated, 'so it have to be you.' He looked from one brother to the next. 'I think you kill him because you think he me. . . Why you want kill me? Is because I make mistake with your order? Why you no like me?'

'Because,' Tristan said, 'you're a worthless sewer rat, whose rogering our Mummy.'

It took a moment, and then Ramiro laughed. 'Ah, I understand! Oh, it be so funny.'

'What's so funny,' asked Cuthbert.

'It be funny because you have wrong man. Me not Roger, me Ramiro, me not know anyone called Roger.'

'No we don't have the wrong man,' said Rodney. 'The woman you call Cougar, is our mother, and rogering means you're using her ancient wrinkled body to satisfy your sinful desires.'

'Your mother! I not know Cougar be your mother. She my Cougar, I her Gaucho. She wild, I love...'

Tristan interrupted, 'That's our Mummy you're speaking of, who – despite being a dried-up wrinkled old prune – is still our mother, or at least was until she became a nefarious Bolshevist. We know your game, you pick up a wealthy dilapidated bit of old baggage, make her think it might be the last coming, and when she's in a frenzy, grab the old bag's boodle and cast her out.'

Cuthbert mounted a magniloquent assault he'd heard in some play, 'You're a rotten stinking puke-stocking, don't think for a minute that you can use her cash to set up home in this fortress built by nature for herself, against infection and the hand of war, inhabited by a happy breed of men, this little world, this precious stone set in the silver sea.'

'No understand,' Ramiro said.

'What my lame-brained brother's saying,' said Rodney, 'is that you're a foreign sod, and we'll make sure you don't get a penny of our inheritance. You've used our dear Mummy as one of your sex toys and, although you've pilfered her pantry, you'll not finger her coffer. We'll call security and say that you're an assassin sent by your government to end the life of our PM, yes, an assassin, that's what you are.'

Ramiro's forlorn frame was, in a jiffy, as upright and alert as the pampas deer that'd scented them when his father took him hunting in Bahía Samborombón. It'd been on his tenth birthday, and he'd watched joyously as the graceful creature flew through the tall grass to safety. 'Your Royal Navy! Ha! Argentina have more war boats than you, we will send them up the Thames and blow up your. . . your Biggest Ben, it not have a bong left.'

'Do you hear that, chaps?' said Rodney. 'The dago dog's after another thrashing. Don't threaten me my boy, because my government will...'

A deep moan from the corpse stopped Rodney, and silence fell like the clap from a gloved hand at the opera. All had their eyes fixed upon the body, which, after a few moments, twitched and uttered a further sigh.

Ramiro leapt into action. With outstretched arms, he herded the stunned brothers, as would a llama pastoralist. 'All back, all back, you close too much, give air. It be me, Ramiro, will save El Presidente! I give lips to lips.' Throwing himself down, he locked his lips like a leech upon those of the Prime Minister's.

Tristan was the first to speak. 'I can't see what the blighter's doing, can you?'

'He's giving our PM mouth-to-mouth,' Cuthbert said. 'My bet is – and say if you think I'm wrong – but my bet is that our leader would sooner push up daisies than kiss an Argie. Do you think we should allow it? I mean, it's absolutely disgusting, don't you think? What say you Rodney, Argie lips, or adieu?'

'You're right,' said Rodney. 'There'd be not an Englishman on earth who'd want to live with the shame of that. So lads, give me a hand, and we'll purge the parasite.'

The brothers dived in to remove Ramiro from the Prime Minister. Yanking his arms and legs was to no avail as he held as fast as a tick on a terrier.

Ramiro cried out, as best his locked lips would grant, 'You no stop me, it is I who save El Presidente, me take care of him.' He held on for as long as his body could weather the onslaught from his adversaries, but, unable to breathe, he weakened, and with the sound like an Iberá wetland water lettuce being torn from the swamp by a ravenous gaucho, they wrenched his lips from the PM's.

'You no stop me. . . I give lips to lips,' he cried, sucking air into his bursting lungs, and then, although still weakened, he flung off the brothers and, as if a barnacle on a boat, anchored his kisser to the P.M's.

'Oh no you don't, my boy. That's the job for an Englishman,' said Rodney. The brothers again assailed the struggling limpet's weakened body. Valiantly, he endured the onslaught until they ripped his enfeebled frame from atop the PM.

Writhing and thrashing like a yacare caiman in the jaws of a Jaguar, he screamed, 'Presidente, please, me want save El Presidente.'

So engrossed in their crusade of Ramiro's containment, the brothers didn't catch sight of the PM, but his voice transfixed them. 'I say, sorry chaps, I must have nodded off.'

'Great Scott!' Rodney exclaimed and, with his siblings, lost their grip on Ramiro who fell to his knees, hands clasped in prayer. 'I save him! El Presidente him alive! Gloria A Dios, him alive. Gloria A Dios!'

Rodney took the PM's arm, helping him to his feet. 'Thank heaven you're all right. We've been most anxious, sir.'

'Yes sir,' said Cuthbert. 'Been beside ourselves with worry, were we not, Tristan?'

'Beside ourselves, but pleased to see you're hunky-dory, sir.'

The PM, somewhat confused, inquired, 'What happened? Can't remember a thing. . . felt as if my body was being pulled into eternity, as if someone had plunged me into a deep ocean.'

'Nearly was, sir,' said Tristan, flippantly.

'Nearly was what?' queried the PM.

'What he means, sir,' Rodney sought to explain, 'is that you were nearly bereft of life. Bowled over, prostrated like a flattened frog.'

'Es maravilloso,' proclaimed Ramiro. 'How now you, señor Presidente? It was I, Ramiro, it was I who give you. . . the kiss of the living.'

'I am sorry, sir,' Rodney said. 'We told him not to, but you know these foreigners, wouldn't stop giving you mouth-to-mouth, stubble on stubble like the French, damned revolting.'

With an exaggerated flourish, Cuthbert removed his mobile phone from his pocket. 'Just as you woke up, sir,

I was calling for an ambulance complete with life-saving kit and manned by Englishmen.'

The PM turned to Ramiro, 'But it's you I must thank for saving my life. My dear friend. . . your name again?'

'Is Ramiro, Gonzales, Juan, da Silva, Iglesias, Maria, Ferrari, Presidente.'

'Well, Mr Presidente"

'It be Ferrari you be Presidente.'

'Oh yes, Ferrari. Mr Ferrari, Her Majesty and the party – save for those bastards intent upon stabbing me in the back – and the entire nation, excluding the sixty-five per cent who didn't vote for me, owe you our thanks and gratitude.'

Taking Ramiro's hand, he shook it with oft-practised warmth. Upon its release he removed Rodney's monogrammed Italian silk pocket square from his breast pocket, a snip at ninety-five pounds, and wiped the syrupy residue from the bowls off his mouth, then stuffed it back.

'No, it nothing, I not be a man kisser,' Ramiro said. 'Me prefer Cougar, she has...'

Catching sight that Ramiro's gesticulatory preparations to explain the size of Cougar's gomos were underway, Rodney leapt in to change the subject. 'Sorry Prime Minister, are we delaying you?'

'No, no delay. I'm trying to think of a way of rewarding our dear friend, Mr Lamborghini,' said the PM.

'It be Ferrari,' Ramiro reminded him.

'Quite, Mr Ferrari. You fellows got any ideas?' he asked the brothers.

Cuthbert said, 'A single ticket to Argentina, sir?'

'No,' said the PM. 'I was trying to think of something much more permanent.'

'So were we,' said Tristan, 'much more.'

'In the circumstances, I think a knighthood would be most appropriate. Sir Ramiro Ferrari, that sounds rather spiffing. What think you?' the PM asked.

Rodney convulsed. 'I'm sorry Prime Minister but. . . that's impossible. I mean, sir, he's not even British, never mind English.'

'I'll soon get that fixed. My staff will wake up the Home Secretary at one thirty in the morning, another stinker after my job, and be told to make Mr Ferrari English by nine.'

'If Idi Amin can become the King of Scotland,' Cuthbert said, 'anything's possible.'

From between clenched teeth, Rodney uttered, 'That was a film, you buffoon!'

'As I was saying,' the Prime Minister continued, 'by nine a.m. tomorrow he'll be as British as half the England cricket team. No, not a problem at all, and to give the Home Secretary an even worse night, the Judas can find a Hebridean crofter grandparent.'

Rodney was rarely lost for words, but a knighthood for that Argie rotter rogering Mummy was flabbergasting, and, more than that, diddly-squat for him from the fiasco.

The PM continued, 'What brought me here? I'll check my pager. . . Ah yes! I heard this was where I'd find the Member for Upper Norton. Want a few words with him.'

Rodney said, 'It's me, sir, and I can explain...'

'Explain what? Need none,' said the PM. 'Look, I've been watching you for some time – what's your name again?'

'Crooke-Wells, sir. Rodney Crooke-Wells.'

'Knew your mother before she was married.' Staring at Rodney, he said, 'you don't look like her – handsome, a splendid woman, got great, very great. . . ahem, great potential.'

Rodney said, 'Thank you, sir. I do my best.'

'Not you! Your mother, you blithering fool, but I'm not here to talk about her, as much as I'd like, no, that's not it. Why am I here. . .?' He once again looked at his pager – 'Ha! Yes, got it! I will need a pencil.'

'I 'ave one Presidente.' After licking it, Ramiro handed him the stub.

The PM viewed a printout he'd taken from his pocket. 'I have a few questions, Mr err?'

'Rodney Crooke-Wells.'

'Ah yes, Crooke-Wells. Been watching you for years.' He consulted his printout. 'Old Etonian I see. Do you speak Latin?'

Rodney remembered something to do with a dog called Pluto and said, '*Mus uni non fidit antro.*'

'Ah! *The mouse does not rely on just one hole*, from a play by Plautus the playwright,' the PM translated. 'From time to time we speak Latin in Cabinet; it puts the state schooled upstarts in their place. They say I must have a few there, democratic crap, just tools, they're a means to an end, swings a few votes.' He again looked at his list. 'Went to Brasenose, I see. What subjects?'

'Politics and Media,' Rodney replied, not mentioning his failures.

'Oh, also media!' The PM scribbled on his list. 'Haven't got that one down, jolly useful. Have you useful contacts, at the top, I mean? Know any proprietors?'

'Had Christmas with one last year, sir,' Rodney lied. 'Had a jolly spiffing time, played charades and sang round the Christmas tree, went to church Christmas morning, then shot a partridge on Boxing Day. Splendid fun.'

While scribbling, the PM continued, 'Media contacts, pleased you've got 'em. Most important, never can tell when you need 'em, get you in and out of many scrapes.' He took another look at his list. 'Ah, I see you were a Buller.'

'*Fane non memini ne audisse unum alterum ita dilixisse,*' recited Rodney.

'Ah yes!' said the PM, who then whilst ticking the printout translated the Bullingdon Club motto, 'Truly, none remember hearing of a man enjoying another so much.' He looked up and said, 'Bet you wrecked a few restaurants, I know your father did.'

'Yes sir, I mean, no sir. I was there, but it was the other chaps who did the damage. Some of them sit in the House. I can give you their names if you like, sir.' Rodney grovelled, as he thought back to the incident when, after a splendid evening dining out with the Club, they had wrecked a seventeenth-century inn's lounge bar. They reimbursed the landlord for the damage, adding a fee for silence.

'No need for that, I know their names already. Have to ask you, because it's on the list, but do you know Shakespeare?'

Rodney showed off a little. '*Hic et ubique.*'

'Ah, Hamlet! So, you also know that Shakespeare, but I meant Sir Percy Shakespeare, the Chief Whip,' said the PM, and Rodney agreed he knew him. The PM looked at his list again. 'Look, Crooke-Wells, this has all gone splendidly, quite splendidly, killed two birds with one stone.' He ticked the list twice, intoning, 'Acquainted with Percy and the classics.' Then he said, 'You enjoy going abroad, don't you?' he glanced at the sheet, 'I see you enjoy Paris.'

Oh, no! Rodney's mind hurtled back to the Paris hotel where he and his PA had stayed, that's why he was being interrogated. Just the thought of his French exploits seeing the light of day drew sweat to his brow. It was an episode he'd intended to keep forever shrouded in a Cimmerian shade. How the devil had the PM found out? It must be a scurrilous Sunday tabloid threatening to spill the beans, to publish a lurid article full of half-truths, or even worse, the full truth, about his Paris trip. Possibly his face was to be on their front page this Sunday. Now it's clear why the PM had asked about newspaper owners, it needed powerful men to stamp on the story.

* * *

Day one in Paris had been irksome. The garlic-sodden diminutive French host had insisted on their taking a casse-croûte. That so-called 'snack' lasted three hours with the know-it-all Napoleonistic midget consulting his well-thumbed pocket wine-tasting guide, sending the wine back thrice. Then the runt had the audacity to discuss the nouvelle cuisine menu with the chef, in French, although knowing that he wasn't picking up the tab. (The consequential bill had made expense manipulation that much more challenging.)

After lunch, the junior minister insisted on a visit to the boring Palais Bourbon and, if that wasn't bad enough, ended the day careering around Paris in the half-pissed prat's personal Citroen DS with a steering wheel over which the maniac could hardly see. It had been most frightful as the dimwit had been even more demoniacal than the rest of the Parisian lead-footed psychopathic bedlamites. Thankfully, blue lights and wailing sirens from behind gave notice that the cops were in pursuit. One of the cavalry drew level; it was an officer of the Gendarmerie Nationale astride a blue Yahama. The rider looked through the window at the midget motorist, spoke on his radio, and rocketed ahead to set up a roadblock. Then a blue light moved to within inches of the rear bumper, accompanied by a siren wailing in that idiosyncratic French manner. But, unconstrained, Napoleon was evidently up for a bit of action, even showing contempt by holding the steering wheel with his knees whilst cranking his Transfo Flameless Cigarette Lighter to ignite yet another Gitane. The speedo read one hundred and ten kph, and climbing. Although he'd never been a prayerful person, like many an atheist on the *Titanic* he'd muttered a word or two of hope.

Then it'd become obvious, the cops had pulled the other Parisian road hogs into the side of the boulevard to give the maniac a clear run. There was a policeman at every intersection blowing whistles and saluting. When the car screeched to a stop outside his hotel, Rodney reeled out of the vehicle – as one only can from the low-slung DS with hydro pneumatic suspension –telling boozed up Boney precisely what he could do with himself for the rest of his short life. With a mood darker and murkier than a mausoleum, and having had the garlic-sodden luncheon swilled around in a superabundance of fermented grape juices during the demoniacal journey, he'd decided '*menu du diner*' was not on the cards. His own pre-planned repast was of much more interest.

When booking the hotel, his PA had requested two rooms with an interleading door. The hotel staff had assured her of their compliance. But, as the French do best, they failed to execute the simplest of biddings, so it was arranged that she'd pop into Rodney's room at around ten p.m. for a spot of rompy-pompy.

At the appointed time, a knock declared her arrival. Whilst an enchanting girl, she could be endearingly irresponsible, for she stood at the threshold of his room wearing a silly latex fetish outfit, with handcuffs, whip, and mask. He, dressed only in body-matching white underpants, pulled her into the room, and then stepped into the corridor to satisfy himself it was devoid of human life.

After a paltry admonishment for her rashness, the evening had been most jolly.

The next morning she toddled off to reception to complete the check-out, but rapidly returned in quite a dither. She'd seen a cluster of staff behind the reception huddled around a monitor screen. One viewer turned, saw her, and said something to the others, they also gaped, and some even making rude gestures. She'd said the pictures showed her standing outside his door and him pulling her inside and then him in his underpants in the corridor. Upon hearing the news, he rushed and checked, and to his horror spotted several cameras. Calling the head of security, he'd offered a sizeable sum to erase the recordings but, after taking the cash, was told it wasn't possible as they were tamper-proof. But the so called '*chef de la sécurité*' assured Rodney the secret would be safe if he coughed up another thousand euros.

* * *

The Prime Minister's voice brought Rodney back to the here and now, 'Well, do you or don't you like Paris?'

Rodney thought it better to come clean. 'Sir, the reason my PA was in the hotel corridor wearing a rubber fetish outfit was because I needed papers and it was ten o'clock at night, so I phoned to ask her to bring them. Well, you see sir, the poor girl – from a delightful family, went to a superior convent school, sir...' Rodney scrambled for an explanation. 'She was tired, jet lag – London to Paris – not used to flying – so when I phoned her, to bring the papers, she had to get dressed. It was dreadful luck that the room lights had failed, forcing her to delve into the wardrobe in the dark. The poor girl didn't know the earlier occupant was a Miss Whiplash who'd left behind articles of clothing. My PA put on an outfit, thinking it was her suit. When I mentioned what it was, she became hysterical, got an allergy to latex, and I was trying to...'

'Don't waste time, all sounds most innocent,' the PM said. 'It could happen to any of us, especially in France.' He studied his list. 'But that's not on my printout; I'll make a note for future reference. Never know when these things come in useful.' Glancing sideways at Rodney, he spoke as he wrote, 'Paris, PA, hotel, fetish gear. One never knows, might prove to be of use one day. Crooke-Wells, the question is simple: do you, or do you not, enjoy foreign travel?'

Rodney replied, 'Yes, sir. Yes, I do.'

'Sounds good so far, won't take much longer.' The PM ticked his list, and continued, 'Have you ever had a proper job?'

'Good heavens no, never even considered it, sir. No, not at all, went off to Eton, Oxford, and then Parliamentary Assistant before being elected to the House. Work! No sir,' Rodney said. 'Never considered working, hadn't crossed my mind. Do you think I should have?'

'No not at all,' said the PM. 'Excellent thing not to have had your mind sullied and warped by work.' He looked at his list again. 'I see you've never voted against a government policy, but it's noted you did very nearly walk through the No Door in a division. Why?'

'I think the matter you're referring to could be the evening Sir Richard Cunningham-Hastings took a tumble in the bar, sir. We all thought it'd be his usual one too many, but no, he was lifeless. As they stretchered him out, we were raising a toast to his departure and – blow me down – Speaker called a division. So, what with the body being removed, and a division, I can tell you sir, there was some confusion. With no clue what I was voting for, nearly went wrong, but The Whip helped me through the correct door. No sir, I assure you I'd never dream of straying from party lines – whatever they are – never crossed my mind.' Knowing the PM enjoyed both smoking and foxhunting he added, 'Also against restrictions on smoking and the prohibition on bloodsports, and we're spending too much on welfare benefits.' Remembering the PM's father sat in the Lords, 'And, I'm in favour of hereditary peers, sir.'

'Now, I have just one final question, but think before you answer.' The PM stepped closer and eyeballed Rodney. 'I repeat, reflect before you answer my next question. Are there any skeletons secreted in your cupboard, just waiting to be exposed by one of those unsavoury left-leaning rags? You know what I mean, don't you? Is there anything at all? Out with it, man, is there anything you need to tell me? Better say it now, can't have it popping out like a jack-in-the-box.'

Rodney was at a loss for words.

'Come on,' the PM demanded. 'I don't have all night. Are there any lefties, illegitimate children, financial irregularities, rent boys, or drugs waiting to be headlined by a tabloid?'

'He's as clean as a whistle, sir,' Tristan said. 'Just shy at blowing his own trumpet.'

Cuthbert also acclaimed his sainted brother to be, 'As pure as a vestal virgin.'

At last Rodney spoke, 'Prime Minister, sir, I have searched my conscience for I did not wish to speak with any falsehoods upon my tongue. I have nothing to hide.'

'Good man, need more like you,' the PM said. 'An old Etonian, Bullingdon, Brasenose, never worked, enjoys foreign travel, always follows party lines, Christmas with a newspaper baron, speaks Latin, no skeletons, you're perfectly qualified.' He beamed and tucked the list into his pocket, shook Rodney's hand and said, 'Congratulations, my dear fellow.'

'For what, Prime Minister? For what am I perfectly qualified?'

'Why the devil do you think I left an excellent dinner to come here and talk to you? Have you not read tonight's press statement? I've announced my full confidence in the Foreign Secretary. That must have told you he was on his way out. Damn it! The odious backstabbing rotten stinker's going next week. Are you up for the job? If you don't want it, say so, got lots on the list.'

'Me, Foreign Secretary? Oh, Prime Minister, may I say, sir, what an honour! Oh, yes, thank you, sir, thank you. I didn't realise that full confidence meant getting the sack.'

'No thanks needed. Out with the old, in with the new. Got my chaps to run the computer and your name popped out. Technology, that's the way the world's going you know. Soon we'll all be redundant.'

Rodney was rapturously intoxicated. 'Oh, Prime Minister, I don't know what to say. Oh, sir, I'll do my best, sir.'

'No, you damned well won't!' the PM snapped. 'Listen to what I say, Crooke-Wells as I won't repeat it. You don't do your best. That's the job of the Civil Servants. You'll let them do their best, they run the country, don't get in their way. Your task is to listen when they explain the problem, pretend to understand, ask for their advice and accept it. If it works you'll get the credit, if it fails you'll send a junior minister in front of the cameras – use someone nobody's ever heard of – and then fire the sod for incompetence. You see, Crooke-Wells, the most incompetent civil servant will be infinitely better than you. Live on a different planet, they have a language of their own. It's a code; you may understand the words, but their meaning is unintelligible. Your job, above all other matters, is to keep me in office. Do you understand?' Rodney nodded. 'You vote the way I tell you and when I tell you – by doing so you'll keep your ministerial car. Play Judas and you're back on your bike, do you understand?'

'Yes, Prime Minister.' Rodney bowed his head in the best display of servile bootlicking he could muster.

'Sorry chaps,' said the PM, checking his watch. 'Tempus fugit.' He turned, taking Ramiro by the hand. 'Sir Ramiro, I'll see you at the Palace for your investiture.

'And for your information Crooke-Wells, the headline in this Sunday's edition of a certain newspaper has already been crafted. It reinforces the press rumours of an unfortunate dollop of slimy scandal about the present incumbent of your new position. The latest leak will have emanated from an unknown government source and will send the gutter press to his front door baying like bloodhounds. After a sleepless night with his wife beating the shit out of the double-crossing sneak, they'll emerge hand in hand proclaiming undying love and a determination to fight the slander through the courts.

'On Monday at ten a.m., I will issue a statement telling the world what a fine fellow he is and reiterating my full support and confidence in the craven rat, that's sure to nail his coffin lid. Late on Monday afternoon, but in time for the evening papers, a compromising photograph will find its way onto an Editor's desk, providing a firm foundation for the unfounded rumours.

'On Tuesday at nine-hundred hours, he'll slither into my office where we will view other documents that have emerged from my safe, and the turncoat will then tender his resignation. I will, reluctantly, accept his departure whilst declaring him a splendid chap who wishes to spend more time with his wife and children. The backbiting double-crossing weasel has had this coming for a long time.

'Now we turn to you, Crooke-Wells. At twelve p.m. my deputy principal private secretary, Sir Tarquinius St John Cholmondeley-Fetherstonhaugh, will telephone you. He's a good man who'd go far if anyone could understand what the devil he was saying, mouth problems, assaulted as a child.' Rodney gulped, Tarquinius? The name rang a bell. 'Here's what he'd tell you if he could, you're being summoned to Downing Street. You will walk to Number 10 with a supercilious smug look upon your face, speak to no one – you may smile at the press – then after our meeting you'll leave in a ministerial car. On Wednesday you'll be on the front bench for PM's questions, is that understood?'

'Yes, Prime Minister.'

'And, Crooke-Wells, for good order's sake, I will have the name of your Paris hotel and the name of your PA on my desk by Monday morning, understood?' Rodney nodded.

As the PM turned to leave, Ramiro asked, 'Can I 'ave my lead please?'

'Sorry, Sir Ramiro, there you are.'

After the door closed, Ramiro asked, 'What him mean, I am sir?'

'It means, you greasy Argie Gaucho, that we have to call you Sir Ramiro,' Rodney sneered.

Ramiro rushed from the room. 'Must telephonee Cougar, she be happy.'

Llamedos

The durian stench of Mummy's entanglement overpowered the sweet whiff of Rodney's imminent rise to international fame, leaving them all crestfallen.

It was Tristan who cut into the stillness. 'Well, congratulations Foreign Secretary! Who'd have thought it? It'd be spot on, except for the Mummy situation, rather takes the shine off everything, don't you agree?'

'Imagine chaps,' said Rodney, 'can you comprehend the plethora of opportunities available? Okay, it'll need a bit of fancy footwork and a few fiddles, but it's worth a fortune. I mean, how many directorships are waiting? Write a book or two, give a few lectures, a knighthood, Chancellor of a university, and then it'll be into the Lords.' He sat back for a few moments in silent contemplation before continuing, 'But that. . . that damned prairie dog and his Jezebel! It could easily get out and ruin everything. I'd end up as an out of work MP! Laughing stock, that's what I'll be, no, not just me, all of us, we'd end up as fair game for every scandal sheet.'

'Revolting,' Cuthbert said. 'But other than the situation ruining what we've got already, we mustn't forget our inheritance. It's odds on the scallywag is already spending our money.'

'You're right,' said Tristan. 'The rat'll up and dump the trollop once he's pocketed our mazuma, the sneaky double-crossing opportunistic ne'er-do-well flimflammer that he is. He'll be awash with our wherewithal, and we'll get zilch. Nothing! We've been waiting for our birthright all these years, not forgetting Daddy had to die for it, and for what? Nothing! What say you, Rodney?'

'Well chaps, I'll admit I was relying upon our legacy to see me through. I need the inheritance, been spending it for years never considering there was any doubt. Guaranteed, like an insurance policy, but no, the hag's squandering it on that scoundrel! I tell you what, Cuthbert, my guess is you don't make a fortune telling people what beans to buy, and so you'll also need the cash.'

'You're right, Rodney, I was relying on it. But what really riles me is thinking about all those years Daddy spent slogging in the City to turn an honest penny, then to have it squandered on a fresh-off-the-banana-boat vagrant. If they hadn't incinerated him, Daddy would turn in his bloody grave at the thought of his years of hard labour being converted into dinero, or whatever they use for money in Argie land.'

'We must slay the slimy serpent again, but this time there'll be no mistakes,' said Tristan. 'The stinker must die! Have you read the entire letter, Rodney?'

'No, there's more. I'll get on and finish her ramblings, but I agree, he must be liquidated. Well, here goes,'

> *'My dear Ramiro is so much like his lovely
> father.'*

The brothers exclaimed, 'Father!' Rodney continued reading with a measure of incredulity in his voice,

> *'Oh yes, his father Ricardo was a charming
> man, dark, handsome and gallant. I met him
> when he worked as a waiter in a London*

restaurant. We flirted as he served the tomato soup; it splattered onto the back of Daddy's jacket. He was aware I saw him do it and winked, I smiled, and within a few days we became lovers.

Daddy never knew of our dalliance and whenever he departed on business, his plane was not the only thing to go up, for my spirits rose as heaven fell.

I was young and savoured every second of our togetherness. Joy and happiness filled our lives as we curled upon the red long-haired shaggy rug in front of a roaring gas fire. It was so romantic. We oft lay there sharing a glass of Burgundy wine, our lips touching over the rim. It was in those moments Ricardo told me of his past life.

He was a foundling, abandoned on the steps of a convent in Buenos Aires. With not a soul in the world willing to adopt him, he spent his childhood scrubbing the convent flagstone floors and washing the nuns' knickers.

At fifteen, they threw him into the gutter because a noisy trainee sister of mercy woke up the rest with her panting and ear-popping squeals. Mother Superior found the novice had graduated under Ricardo.

Life on the streets was hard, and one day he was slashed by a knife. A doctor, a little older than Ricardo, sat him on a bar and sewed the wound up with a needle and thread supplied by the bar owner's wife. The doctor had an Irish name, Lynch, but you will know him as Che Guevara.

That naughty anarchist and Ricardo became firm friends, so it's easy to see why he grew to be a communist. His political views, and his penchant for blowing up railway lines, put Ricardo at odds with the military government, and so he escaped to London.

It's sad, but even the best things end, for after we'd been lovers for several months, one day he didn't arrive for our tête-à-tête, nor the next: he'd vanished. I was never to feel his tender touch nor hear his whispers again. Daddy never knew why I loved that shaggy rug so much, or how many tales it could tell. It was there that I conceived Ricardo's son, one of you!'

Tristan was the first to vocalise the mind-blowing information. 'Conceived one of us! Conceived on that bloody shaggy rug. I used to play on it! To think, they'd been, well – you know what I mean – copulating on the carpet. Disgusting, but even worse than that, the harridan's saying their carnal procreations produced one of us. . . one of us is Ramiro's brother.'

'No, half-brother, an Argie half-brother,' Rodney almost spat the words. 'A string of affairs I could get away with, even a rent boy or two, but, as Foreign Secretary, with one of you an illegitimate son of an Argentinean communist jailbird, not at all good, not good at all. Couldn't survive that.'

Tristan joined the scrimmage. 'You might be onto something, Rodney, but it can't be me, never could master Spanish. But, Cuthbert, don't you enjoy Latin dancing, and isn't the tango one of your favourites?'

'I say, you're going too far. I enjoy the Viennese waltz, but I don't climb mountains, yodel, or eat strudel. It could be you, dammit.'

They fell silent for a moment or two.

'Conceived on a shaggy rug, how apt,' Rodney observed.

'I don't even remember a shaggy rug,' Cuthbert announced.

'You wouldn't remember anything at conception,' Tristan retorted.

'I'm sure,' Cuthbert said, 'I read something about precognitive memory being attached to your DNA. That might give a clue as to who's his son. Do either of you enjoy having sex on shaggy rugs?'

'That's stupid,' Rodney said. 'We'd all savour sex on a shaggy rug in front of a warm cosy fire with a bottle of red wine, you berk.'

'Well, no, that's what I'm saying,' Cuthbert responded. 'I've never thought of having sex on a shaggy rug and I can't even imagine what it would be like. So, it's not in my DNA, old bean. What about you, Tristan?'

'I've never considered it either, so if Rodney's the only one who can imagine it, then it must be him: he's the love child. Ramiro's half-brother.'

'You stupid twats! Anyone would enjoy sex on a shaggy rug,' Rodney said. 'Find me anyone who wouldn't. It's nothing to do with precognitive memory. Our Mummy threw her honour to the wind and copulated with a commie whilst poor Daddy flew around the world keeping us in house and home. And now, what do we hear? Not only did Ricardo plunder passion valley, but his rotten son's safaried there! Is nothing sacred?'

'There was no plundering,' Tristan corrected. 'She wasn't press-ganged, she was a volunteer: ready, willing and able.'

'Exactly,' Rodney said. 'It wasn't an invasion, it was more a fraternisation: a capitulation! She's behaved no better than a lop-eared rabbit on heat.'

'Spot on the mark,' Tristan said. 'We should read the rest of the letter. We're her sons, her rightful heirs, and are not responsible for her shenanigans. We shouldn't squabble between ourselves. We must stick together under these dire circumstances and combine our efforts to float that blighter down the river and save our cash. Come on Rodney, let's get it over with. Read the rest of the old biddy's babblings.'

> *'What a surprise it must be for you boys*
> *to know I have again found happiness. The*
> *sweetness of Ramiro's passion has whisked*
> *away my aches and pains, and the wrinkles*
> *are now laughter lines. It is my dearest wish*
> *for you to be happy for me.'*

'Happy for her!' Rodney roared. 'Sweetness of passion! Laughter lines! The wrinkled bag is a disgrace to the proud name of Crooke-Wells.' He continued reading,

> *'But just in case you're mindful of vengeance*
> *I have taken precautions. My solicitor has a*
> *letter telling the world of my dalliance with*
> *Ramiro's father, complete with details of the*
> *consequential birth of the one of you. Also, he*
> *has your offshore banking details that you left*
> *in my safe, Rodney.*

*Oh, and I nearly forgot to mention, the
paternity of at least one other of you might be
in question!'*

'Another one? What does the Jezebel mean by that?'
Cuthbert asked. 'Are there two of us related to Ramiro,
do you think?'

'Sounds like another bounder was having his way behind
Daddy's back,' Cuthbert said, scanning his memory for
any small clue, anything that could be a pointer, anything.
What about the solicitor sent by his mother? What had he
said. . .? He owed Mummy a favour. What favour, or even
favours? For what was Mr Avishalom Adelstein repaying
Mummy? He recalled thinking, in one of the darkest
hours of his life, that Adelstein was more like a father to
him than his actual father. Perhaps his father wasn't his
proper father. Was it, could it be, was Avishalom Adelstein
his father?

He felt confused and, placing his hand into his pocket,
sought comfort as he so often did. Great Scott! The clue
was on hand. He was the only brother circumcised, and
he hated pork, even the thought of bacon made him feel
sick. It fitted together like the hora at a Bar Mitzvah. 'Oy
vey iz mir,' he uttered, but seeing the others look at him,
said, 'Great Scott, what made me say that? Just something
I once heard.'

Simultaneously, Tristan recalled his confab with Colonel
Piss-Horn – as he pronounced it. Had the colonel's influence
provided the key to his entry as a gentleman cadet through
the ceremonial gates of Sandhurst? Why would anyone
pull more than a few strings to get him in, and then what
about the court-martial? Why did he intercede? Had it
been because he felt shame toward a son he'd abandoned?

One of fourteen million tadpole-like sperm fighting off the competition to battle a passage through Mummy's womb, never mind the later fallopian tube ordeal it had undergone. Was his conception a consequence of a rearguard action, a flanking manoeuvre, a full-frontal assault, or – heaven forbid – an ambush? Perhaps there were no rules of engagement and the colonel had just galloped in for regular guerrilla skirmishes on the shaggy rug of shame.

Rodney interrupted his brothers' thoughts by continuing reading,

> 'To embarrass you even further, lodged with
> my solicitor are some photographs of me in
> my Cami Suspender Set with Matching Net
> Stockings and Black Thong. I'm sure you
> wouldn't want those photos in the papers.
> Imagine the headline, 'Argie Beds Margie!' Oh,
> how delightful! But not good for any of you.'

'Damn the woman,' Rodney said. 'This could end my political career. Insufferable! She's a devious deviant. We'd never live down the shame. Depraved, that's what she is. Depraved.' He continued reading,

> 'As my darling Ramiro and I are upping sticks
> to live in Argentina, tonight's dinner was
> to have been my fond farewell treat. Upon
> reflection, I'm sure Rodney won't mind picking
> up the bill.'

The revelation poleaxed the brothers.

Cuthbert was the first to speak. 'Who'd believe it? Live in Argentina on our inheritance! A Marxist nymphomaniac corralling cows on the prairie with the son of a communist mastermind of the revolution.'

'It's as clear as a flute,' said Rodney. 'Ramiro won't want her after he's got his filthy finger on the funds. The besotted bat will relinquish life glued to a stool in a dingy dago bar drooling over a glass of pisco sour. Her curtain will fall with a drunken accordionist pumping out *La Cumparsita* on his stomach-Steinway while Ramiro trots the tango with a local strumpet. Chaps, she's got us by the short and curlies, we're trapped in the quagmire of her deceit and treachery. It's not sounding good for a new Foreign Secretary, but sorry to say, there's more to come. I'll get on and read it.'

> 'Ramiro's father never knew we had a son, but then I would never have told him even had the opportunity arisen.
>
> When the dear man died, a condition of his Will stipulated Ramiro should seek me out to tell me of his father's demise, and to follow a list of things that he had done in his youth. Included in the list was being a waiter in London for six months.
>
> Ricardo had loved being a waiter. He told me how we would never have met were it not for the tomato soup. I surmise he wanted to open Ramiro's eyes to the real world.'

'Open his flies more like it,' Tristan remarked. 'Disgusting!'

> 'There is no doubt you always thought we were rich. Well, the reality is your father squandered everything. Did you ever consider why you didn't go to a better school, Cuthbert? When it was your turn, we had

little money and very few assets left. He'd
mortgaged the house to the hilt, and I was
unaware of the dire situation.

When Daddy died, I wasn't concerned about
the mountain of debts, as I knew I could carry
on living as I always had and rely upon you
boys to pay off everything and support me in
my old age.'

'Strewth,' said Tristan. 'She's broke.'

'Good heavens,' said Cuthbert, 'there's no inheritance, and we've been buggered. The philandering fossil's a disaster. Mountains of debt that she believes we'll pay off and then support her until she croaks.'

'This is an absolute calamity. As soon as Ramiro discovers there's no cash he'll dump her,' Rodney declared, and continued reading,

'I feel a need to tell you a little about Daddy's
death. The cruise you gave for my fiftieth
was lovely – the suite was so tasteful and
the balcony had a beautiful sea view. But
Daddy didn't die in our cabin on a luxury
mattress containing thousands of coil springs
and an aerify levity system, topped with a
Hungarian goose-down duvet. He expired on
a slab of plastic foam in a lower-deck inside
berth, below the waterline where the poor
people bunk, and drown if the boat sinks.
The coroner, we later became good friends,
recorded death by accidental asphyxiation.

The reality was a cleaner found an obese
American woman lying on top of him. In her

statement, the trollop said she'd fallen asleep from boredom. The coroner's verdict was that your father hadn't the strength to hoist the heifer off and was accidentally smothered. He died a bankrupt weakling.'

Rodney briefly added, 'It's no wonder she wanted him dumped overboard.'

'Now, back to Ramiro, I never thought for a moment that Ricardo had left me on his own volition, we were too much in love, and Ramiro proved me right. The reason Ricardo didn't turn up for our tête-à-tête was that the British government had him arrested and deported to Argentina. Upon arrival, the Military junta threw my love into prison, and although they tortured him, he survived.

When they released him, Fidel, the Cuban one whom he'd earlier met through Che, who was by then dead, helped him set up a cigar factory in Argentina.

It is said that the finest cigars in the world are rolled on the sweaty thighs of plump Afro Cuban ladies. So, along with the gear came a few Torcedoras, that's what cigar-rolling ladies are called, to jump-start the business – must have been right up Ricardo's street, always a leg man. His cigars were acclaimed, mainly for their distinctive aroma, and made him millions.

Later, he sold the factory and bought some lucrative vineyards and, pandering to his pet hobby, a cattle ranch. Although becoming very wealthy, he always remembered his humble beginnings and never forgot me.

Sadly, he died last year leaving everything to his only living relative, Ramiro.

I know my lover is not very bright, but then why should he have to be, with others to run everything for him?

Ricardo's dying desire was that Ramiro seek me out and, if he found me alive, make sure my life ends in the lap of luxury. He found not only me, but also love, and it took us no time to decide to live in the Uco Valley on one of his wine estates.'

'Strewth!' Rodney exclaimed. 'A multimillionaire half-brother who'll look after the harlot. Chaps, I remember Nanny reading a story about a little reed bending to the force of the wind and then standing upright again when the storm had passed, whilst the gale felled an enormous oak tree.'

'What's that to do with our situation?' asked Tristan.

Rodney explained. 'We don't have to like the blighter but needs must when the devil drives. So, let's blow with the wind, let's grin and bear it. I do not intend to give my cash for that withered strumpet to diddle away on a Maoist mission. If we don't want to fund the trollop, we need the Argie to do it and save our own cash. I say if it means she sits swilling wine from a barrel all day, it's up to her. At least she'll be out of sight and out of mind.'

'So, my understanding is, we sacrifice Mummy's honour for our good,' Cuthbert said. 'If that be it, I agree.'

'Honour? You're joking! From the sound of it, the old bat lost that many a year ago,' Rodney retorted.

'Well,' Cuthbert said, 'her being stuck in a vineyard at the arse end of the world sounds very beneficial.'

Rodney pulled the bell-rope. 'In which case, chaps, if we don't want any vacillation, we'll treat him – and I hate using the word, but – we'll treat him as a brother. Must make sure he financially supports her.'

'What's your plan, Rodney?' Tristan asked.

Rodney quoted a Tom Fuller ditty, '"We never know the worth of water till the well is dry". I'd say ours has evaporated chaps, so when the rat returns follow my lead and remember that flattery's free, but he'll pay a high price for our indignity, and for rogering Mummy. I can hear him coming.'

Ramiro put his head around the door, but, on spotting Rodney hastening towards him, drew back in alarm. Rodney lost no time in heading off his flight.

'Ah, Ramiro,' he said, putting an arm around his shoulder.

Ramiro's eyes darted from one brother to the other, and trembling said, 'What I do wrong?'

'Wrong! Why nothing. What in the world would make you conclude such a thing, my dear and valued friend?' Rodney gushed.

'None dearer,' concurred Tristan. 'Or more valued,' Cuthbert agreed.

'Or more treasured,' said Rodney. 'Now, my fine fellow, in the short time we have known you...'

Ramiro interrupted, 'I not know why I be a fine fellow. Why you try to kill me? What I do wrong?'

Rodney's reptilian tongue slithered from its dank den, 'Wrong? You did naught wrong, my valuable truncated slice of a nobody. You are so funny. Now, I understand that you love Cougar?'

'Si, I have much love her.'

'Well, I also love Cougar,' Rodney said. 'But my brothers made me fearful for her future. It was their fault. They said you were going to – how shall I say? – use Mummy and then jettison the poor dear as one would a tissue in the lavatory. My duty as her eldest son is to safeguard the darling. My worthless brothers are but silly fussbudgets, and they misled me. No, my dear Ramiro, you're my cherished chum whom I have learnt to love. You are a fine fellow and I know you will not only look after Mummy, but also provide her with the bounteous life she deserves.'

'A crackerjack,' Cuthbert added. 'A paragon,' Tristan said.

Rodney patted Ramiro on the back. 'With the greatest pride, we welcome you into the bosom of our family.'

Ramiro's face lit up with joy. 'Ah, no understand any of what you say, but know you speak of Cougar, and she has mucho gomo,' his hand gesticulations again showing the size of Mummy's bosoms.

'No, my dear fellow, I am not referring to Mummy's mamillae. What I mean is, we welcome you to our family, or something along those lines.' Rodney embraced Ramiro and even plonked a kiss on his cheek. He wiped his lips on his handkerchief and then rinsed the taste of sticky pudding from his mouth with Champagne. 'Cuthbert, pull up a chair for Sir Ramiro, come on, and get on with it. Tristan, lay the table for two, and make it smart!'

Flicking off imaginary dust and crumbs with a napkin Tristan carried out his brother's orders.

'The service here is abysmal, Ramiro,' Rodney said. 'It's the English, you know, a nation of scobberlotchers – that's to say, they're a slow, lazy lot, not used to hard work, most of 'em on benefits, you know.'

'Champagne, sir?' asked Tristan.

'Is Blanc de Blancs?' Ramiro asked.

'It is,' Rodney responded. 'Only the best for you, my dear friend – get on with it, Tristan! Ramiro, I would be more than honoured if you joined me for dinner. Cuthbert, hurry man, hand Sir Ramiro a bill of fare.'

While studying the menu, Ramiro asked, 'Rodney, how you say oldee boy in English?'

'My dear chap, oldee boy is perfectly correct. I am amazed at your command of the language. Few master it, as have you, in such a short time. There's many a lout born here far less capable – get cracking, Tristan, take Sir Ramiro's order.'

'May I have your pencil please, sir?' Tristan asked.

Ramiro licked the lead, and passed it, together with the dog-eared pad.

'Get a move on,' Rodney said. 'I am so sorry, Ramiro. I'm sure you can now understand why we welcome foreign nationals to our shores. It's the only way of getting decent service.'

Tristan stood at the ready, pencil poised.

'I 'ave uno Terrine de Gooses Leever con Spicy Pineapple con Gingerbready.'

Rodney nodded his approval.

'It be followed by Cornishland Lobster Thermidor com spicy carroti y lemon verbena.'

'You could have chosen nothing better,' said Rodney.

'For puddings it be crêpes suzette con Grand Marnier con jus lemon, orange a sugar.'

'Sir, it will be my pleasure. I will prepare them myself at your table,' Tristan said.

Rodney snapped, 'No, you damned well won't. You'll get the chef to do that.' Turning to Ramiro, he continued, 'The problem is, Ramiro, one can't trust the fool with a flaming pan. He'll burn down the place. Might I suggest you join me on the balcony for cognac and a cigar after dinner?'

'Si, is good,' Ramiro said. 'I 'ave Cognac, also I 'ave a cigar, Cuban, put in the humidifier at seventy per cent 'umidity and twenty degrees, comprendo?'

Tristan wrote the order.

A hovering Cuthbert said, 'More Champagne, Sir Ramiro?'

'Pour it and push off,' said Rodney. 'Ramiro and I have much to catch up on.'

Both siblings left to fulfil their separate duties, while Rodney continued being cringingly smarmy. 'Precious fellow, my understanding is that you and our dear Mummy are off to live in the Uco Valley.'

'Si, is correct,' Ramiro responded.

'Tell me, dear and valued friend, do you have any brothers, sisters, aunts, uncles, or cousins?'

'No, not have, only have me. I only one.'

'Most interesting,' commented Rodney. 'I am sure you understand. . . my brothers and I have only our dearest Mummy's interests at heart.'

'Si,' Ramiro nodded.

'Tell me, what are your intentions toward our beloved Mummy?'

'How mean you, "intention"? No understand.'

Rodney's unctuous ophidian tongue set about its calling, 'Well, my cherished chum, my brothers and I are seeking to understand the plans you have for our Mummy. She is a woman whom we love very much, always been there, forever be our pride and joy. It's our wish to know what you have planned. Will you be plighting your troth? Will you marry our Mummy?'

'Marry!' Ramiro blurted out. 'No, she much too old. Me love, but no marry, we live together, we not marry.'

'Just as I expected, this miserable muppet's got no plan to marry Mummy,' Rodney called to his brothers.

'No, oldee chappee,' Ramiro enthused. 'It is Cougar – she says love but no marry. I ask, she say no. She says she too old and house on estate ees enough, not want to marry.'

'Oh, I see. You are telling me Mummy wishes to live with you, but not to marry you?'

'Si ees correct. I unhappy, but she says no marry,' said Ramiro.

Rodney paused and considered the implications before responding. 'But what will transpire when the dear lady's wrinkles become even more corrugated than they now are? Look, we are both men of the world, we know about these things. What I am trying to say is this, if you no longer want her, what stops you from throwing her out to forage in a Buenos back alley, a used woman walking the streets, trying to sell a body that's seen better days? I tell you what, at her age she has little hope of making anywhere near enough to live on. It's intolerable, we will not allow it!'

'Why Cougar walk street? I not understand what you say. I take care, look after Cougar.'

'But for how long? I can see the poor dear girding her loins in anticipation of being plundered by the bosun and his mates on grab-a-granny night in a sleazy bordello. Just the thought of her molestation by a bunch of matelots brings me near to tears,' Rodney said, wiping his eyes.

'No, it cannot be, we could never countenance our closest and dearest one being out on her neck with her poor, tired, moth-eaten old body deflowered by the ship's company. The facts are that even in a full swing bob-a-job, she'd be earning only a pittance. No, our Mummy's destiny is not to end her life decrepit and destitute.' Rodney felt another sob was proper. 'Dearest darling Mummy, we'll protect you,' he mumbled, wiping his eyes once more.

Cuthbert thought Rodney's performance merited a standing ovation. 'Bravo! Bravo!' he exclaimed. Then, recalling the last time he had attended a performance that merited such an ovation was for Mary in *Carousel*, he slipped back into silence.

With his head bowed, Rodney felt Ramiro's warm sticky hand upon his – thankfully he'd remembered to put the sanitiser into his pocket – another sob seemed proper. 'Dear Mummy, we'll protect you,' he said, wiping his eyes and then holding his hands in prayer.

'No, my oldee chappee friend, it be never can be happen. Cougar, she live on one of my wine estates until she goes to visit God. Will be happy, have plenty money.'

'No, it's too risky, she can't go,' Rodney stated.

'But why? Cougar, she be happy. Not big estate, but it be good, have small, how you say, rooming house where Cougar live.'

'Oh, I see! Like a little bed-and-breakfast?'

'Si, 'ave wonderful breakfast.'

'You mean you are expecting our dearest Mummy to get up every morning and cook bacon and eggs for a bunch of antipodean hyponasaled backpackers in a boarding house and then spend the rest of the day treading grapes?'

Ramiro laughed. 'You not understand oldee chap, others what do the work.' He laughed again. 'It too big for Cougar to cook, it 'as ten suites, very discreet luxury for rich peoples. There is breakfast, dinner, lunch, or whatever you want, any time day or night. It is for millionaires to stay with lovers and – 'ow you say? – boyfriends. It 'as airstrip and pad for helicopters.'

'Do you mean it's a hotel for the rich to bring their bits on the side? Mistresses? So, it's a high-class knocking-shop where the rich entertain their lovers,' Rodney said.

'Ah si, correct. Hotel, it be very discreto. It be called Los Moulin Rouge, many politicians who leave wife at home.'

'Now, my dearest friend – to whom I am warming ever more as the moments pass – how large is the wine estate?'

'It be little, but wonderful wine for the connoisseur. It do only five thousand cases a year, but it sell for high price, at auction.'

Rodney addressed his brothers, 'Hear that chaps?' Turning back to a very relaxed Ramiro, he said, 'Let me make sure I understand how you plan to look after our greatest treasure, Mummy, or should I say Cougar with rather large gomos, she will stay rent free?'

'Si, gratis.'

'Right,' Rodney said. 'So, she will also have her own suite and receive an income for life, is that right?'

'Si!'

'What happens if you cease to live?'

'No understand.'

'What if you were to get killed, say trampled by a herd of llamas, what will become of our beloved Mummy? Will they kick her out?'

'It not happen. I 'ave no one, no one kicks her out, I 'ave no relative, I even not know I 'ave mother. If I die,

Cougar 'ave hotel and wine estate, it say so in my will. Mr Adelstein, he makes paper and say it be waterproof,' Ramiro said.

Adelstein's name spurred Cuthbert to slip his hand into his pocket, and, upon finding his faithful comforter, heave a sigh of thanks.

'Ah, I see. Ramiro, my dearest friend,' Rodney enthused, 'just to be sure, let me explain how I understand what you have said. That in your will, if you die first, Cougar with the mucho gomos gets to keep the small estate and the little hotel? You also have more wine estates, plenty more money, and did I hear something about a cattle ranch?'

'Si, is right!'

'Oh, and – not that it's important – but how much money was it you were planning to leave our dearest one?' Rodney asked, with feigned indifference.

'Mr Adelstein 'e say two million dollar be good,' Ramiro responded.

'Make it five million,' Rodney shot back, 'and we'll draw up an addendum to your will tonight.'

'No, make ten be good, no problem, if dead no need,' Ramiro stated.

In nothing flat, Rodney wrapped Ramiro in a warm hug. 'Welcome to our family,' he said, as his guileful cerebral cogs clicked into gear, searching for the chicanery required of him to bag his bundle of Argentinean boodle.

Unaware of the treachery shrouded within the warm embrace, Ramiro smiled blissfully.

* * *

Meanwhile, Rodney sought to make sense of the story he'd gleaned about his mother and the sower of the seed who had produced the gullible weasel enfolded in his embrace.

His take on the story was that an empty-headed harlot rids herself of the idiot's father, Ricardo, in a Buenos Aires gutter. A Good Samaritan, traipsing through the whiffy backstreets, comes upon the dross and plucks the snipe from the drain just before he's submerged in the sewer. The do-gooder junkets off to the Bleeding Heart Convent, jettisons the jetsam in the lost property office and throws away the ticket. Like so many unwanted dogs in a pound, the ragamuffin's left unclaimed with no known kith and kin in the sublunary world.

Mother Superior, believing many unpaid hands makes cash for the convent, raises the wastrel. When the blighter can grasp the smallest brush, in nothing flat, he's set to work scrubbing the holy flagstones. Over time, the ex-guttersnipe finds a new pursuit for his pecker, and he's caught having nooky with a noisy novice nun. So, saying a fond farewell to the flagstone floors, he's reacquainted with the sewerage system.

With nowhere to lay his head, Ricardo takes to the streets to join the rest of the ragamuffins. As kids do, he gets into a few fights, and whilst playing Gauchos and Amerindians he gets sliced. A young physician, Dr Ernesto Lynch, is in a local bar as pissed as a newt, and so lays the hero on the counter and stitches him together. The sawbones, aka Che Guevara, then takes him under his care and teaches him that the Hippocratic Oath of 'do no harm' doesn't apply to South American medics by demonstrating that gelignite is far superior to 'leaves on the line' at bringing a train to a grinding halt.

Under Che's tutelage, he becomes a Marxist guerrilla fighter and sets about detonating a few bangers himself, only to discover he's addicted to dynamite and using it to stop trains is such a caper that he'll make it his career.

Then, with the military junta on his tail, by an unexplained means he finds his way to Tilbury docks and, with the rest of the vermin, gallops down the gangplank swapping the Buenos Aires feculence for that flowing beneath the litter-strewn streets of London. Later he drags himself from the drain and morphs as a waiter. The degenerate then gives the old bird a wink, pours soup over Daddy's jacket and thereafter plunders the wanton woman. Just when he thinks he's on top, and not knowing he's seeded Mummy, he gets his just deserts when he's hauled off to spend time in a South American hellhole with accommodation inferior even to that provided by the Mother Superior. After bashing boulders, Ricardo gets out of the slammer and impregnates another wretch, who inflicts Ramiro upon an unsuspecting world and vanishes.

Meanwhile, a mate of Che's, Mr Castro – the bewhiskered Cuban Comrade – takes pity on the jailbird and helps him to become filthy rich by providing a slather of sweaty black thighs upon which to roll cigars. Then, after a passage of time enjoying the fruits of his labours, garnering grapes and corralling cows, the Great Master of the Revolution goes the way of all flesh, checks into a cosmic commie commune and surrenders his terrestrial trappings to this moronic muppet.

* * *

How unjust life is, Rodney mused, can't rely on an inheritance to end my days, and even worse – a hammer slammed a thought into Rodney's brain – what if Mummy dies before Ramiro? One has to face the facts: he's fit and forty, riding the old nag as if he's mounted a flat racer, so she's likely to breathe her last from prostrated exhaustion.

If that happens, everything reverts to the idiot and I'm saddled with a monumental albatross of debt.

Can't trust Tristan, he's an irresponsible useless sod, and Cuthbert's not only clueless, but has nowhere near the cash to pay his fair whack. The old London home must be worth millions by now, but Daddy pawned it, so there's no bricks and mortar. If we want to be sure Mummy gets the cash, we have to dispatch Ramiro. But, if there's any suspicion of my involvement in his demise, the hag's solicitor sends my offshore account to the revenue services, and her horrible picture's published.

If there's no suspicion of my involvement, she'll get the ten million and the wine estate. Manifestly, I must plan for the bounty to abide in my bank, and bugger my brothers.

Now, what if the lunatic leaves life as an unfortunate casualty in a tragic accident far from these shores, where I patently can have no involvement? As Foreign Secretary, I must be able to get my PA to find at least one, or even two, assassins. Then, with no Argentinean heirs and assigns to his estate, and thanks to our lascivious mother, one of us – being the imbecile's half-brother and heir – would get the boodle.

He smiled over Ramiro's shoulder at his brothers.

And if it's me, those useless sods will get nothing. They won't see a penny. The problem is – with lunacy being hereditary – Cuthbert or Tristan could well be his brother. But, if either of them inherited the cash and thereafter has a fatal accident, Mummy would be the beneficiary, in which case Mummy would get everything and then, if something happens to her. . . that's an interesting thought.

But what if Mummy is wrong and Ramiro relates to none of us? The baggage was probably being bedded by a bevy of debauchers and could have been inseminated by anyone, a squadron of Dragoon Guards for all we know. If that were so, there would be no DNA matches. Mummy would still get her inheritance. However, there'd be nothing for me. Unless, let's say, hypothetically, she survived long enough to get the boodle but short enough not to spend it, or give it to a home for displaced rats.

Having considered all eventualities, Rodney knew what was required of him. Sod 'em all.

Hugging the dimwit even more warmly, he said, 'Ramiro, my dear and valued friend, that all sounds admirable. A wine estate, a hotel and ten million dollars.' Plucking a few loose hairs from the idiot's shirt and placed them into a dry glass on the table. 'I say chaps, bring paper and a pencil, oh, and clean glasses for a Champagne toast'.

'If luck is a matter of preparation meeting opportunity, I feel good fortune drawing nigh.'

Rodney's smile grew wider, as his unprincipled morals set his thought processes journeying through a labyrinthine thoroughfare of deviation. Noting which brother drank from which glass he said, 'Daddy taught me an old Welsh toast for occasions such as this, Llamedos, to Mummy and Ramiro, and also to you my brothers, for as long as you all shall live.'

Buenos Aires

The raucous laughter and resonating long reeds of the German seventy-one-button bandoneon almost drowned out the ringing telephone. The battered squeeze box, and vibrating strings of the violin, had just joined forces with the double bass and piano to strike up a melancholic milonga. It was two in the morning in the dockside bar El Tiburón, or The Shark. The barman nodded at, and passed the receiver to Ricardo.

Taking the grubby handset, he moved away from the noise, as far as the short, curly cord allowed. With cupped ear, he listened, with increasing excitement, to the detail of Ramiro's London success.

The news confirmed that, as he had forecasted, Lady Marjorie's voracious sexual appetite hadn't diminished, so enabling his son's charms to overwhelm any doubts she might entertain.

It was regrettable that Marjorie had declined the proposal of marriage. Their plan for her departure in the arrival hall at the Ezeiza International Airport, he thought, was perfect. They would arrange a new accident. Canoeing too close to Cataratas del Iguazú, sounded perhaps even better. Nasty occurrences often take place around the largest waterfalls in the world.

The newspaper reports that he'd get written would detail how Ramiro was himself close to drowning, whilst dragging her almost lifeless body to the shore. That should make the headlines. He'd find a few witnesses to the incident. Oh yes, and he knew a priest to hear her supposed whispered confessions, where she'd praise Ramiro, and confirm him as her sole heir. Mustn't forget the last rites.

The ink on the new death certificate, detailing the circumstances of her demise, will have barely dried by the time it lays alongside the forged will confirming the truth of her last utterances.

Saving the life of the prime minister was an act of genius. A police investigation would have undone the whole thing. Yes, his son had carried out the task to perfection.

Returning to the stool, the handsome seventy-year-old returned to sit next to one of his accomplices, Gagita.

Carrying on stroking the gossamer blonde hairs on her leg, he said, 'There now, my little pussycat, that was Ramiro. Everything's gone well, we'll soon be rich.'

The news was thrilling, for it was her income that had covered the cost of the sting. Although she doled out her favours freely to both father and son, there were wealthy clients aplenty willing to refill her pot, if the needs be, but better a life as a rich lady.

Ricardo beamed as the girl took his hand and led him toward her room for a celebratory freebie.

The Truth in a Nutshell

Ricardo's rendition to Marjorie of his past life as a guerrilla friend of Che was pure cock-and-bull, romanticised to enhance his allure.

(Ramiro's version of his father's extradition from England was just as deceitful, but driven by even darker designs.)

After only a few months as Mummy's lover, the police arrested Ricardo for shoplifting trinkets in a Pound Shop. Finding out he was an illegal immigrant, they deported him back to Argentina. There, he faced a jail term imposed in absentia for robbery with violence.

While incarcerated in the prison named Caseros, aptly a converted orphanage, he'd encountered many political prisoners held under the Junta's *Guerra sucia* policy. They'd barked up the wrong tree when sharing with Ricardo their left-wing beliefs, and accounts of torture. Any harboured hopes he would pass their plights on to anxious families were in vain.

In the cell, built for three but housing ten – before the strangulation there'd been eleven – he befriended a notorious forger, Gervaso Panicucci and a corrupt but brilliant attorney, Enrique Martinez.

Their association was, at first, an alliance for mutual preservation. The hellhole was a hive of *asesinos* willing to slip a knife into any unsuspecting back to steal the most trivial possession.

It overjoyed Ricardo when they chucked out common jailbirds to make space for thousands of political prisoners.

The Western World considered the plight of the left-wing detainees a trade hampering irritant, but, for him, their bind was a bounteous blessing. Rounding up communists gave the police less time to pursue petty criminals.

Now, more skilled in the art of villainy than when he'd entered the slammer, he set about his felonious endeavours with greater confidence, but bagged only modest rewards.

Ramiro's mother, with whom he'd enjoyed a brief dalliance, had worked in a dockside bar. She'd skedaddled after meeting a Brazilian sailor and tangoing to the Portuguese sea shanty Canção do Marinheiro, leaving Ricardo holding their baby.

Unschooled himself, and with a sparsity of pesos to shell out, Ricardo felt there'd be no benefit in having his son educated, so oversaw that he followed in his footsteps.

It was Ramiro who, using his father's reminiscences of a besotted titled English lady, had banded an idea requiring him to play the role of a multi-millionaire. He and Ricardo, who'd warmed to the notion, employed an Internet café computer to determine that she still lived at the same address. They'd also gleaned from online newspapers and magazines, that she was a widow enjoying an opulent lifestyle.

They put together a team, comprising Gervaso, the brilliant forger, Enrique Martinez, the crooked attorney, and Gargita. She, as well as funding the treachery, was their common girlfriend and a lady of the morning, noon, and night.

The gang concocted a perfect plan for plundering Marjorie Crooke-Wells' riches.

The forger and crooked attorney had penned documents detailing the assets purportedly left to Ramiro by his supposedly dead father. Flawless proof, if need be, that her wealth was of no account.

Training his son as a waiter was, his father found, irksome, for he was not an easy student. But, all-in-all, the whole thing had gone swimmingly.

A Knight Races to the Rescue

Fourteen days before, Marjorie had told her close friend and confidant, Major General Pishorn rtd, of her relationship with a forty-year-old Argentinean multimillionaire called Ramiro, and that he'd asked her to marry him and trot off to Argentina.

In a wink, the odour of a rotten rat had overpowered Pishorn's whiff of Marjorie's Jardin d'Amalfi fragrance.

That evening, he instructed his nephew, Reginald Merryweather, to enlist the aid of the son of an old friend in the Agencia Federal de Inteligencia, Argentina.

Reggie was the head of MI5's elite group of senior agents and he could order the extermination of persons considered dangerous to the state.

Bartolo Alvarez, the number two of SIDE, the equivalent of Reggie's MI5, seized the opportunity to help, having in mind a reciprocal favour his department needed.

The news came back faster than a jararaca pit viper's strike; Ramiro and Ricardo were stone-hearted villains capable of the most heinous skulduggery. The underworld gossip of Buenos Aires was that an English lady millionaire was to be duped into coming to Argentina. At the airport terminal, before reaching customs, she would die in an unfortunate accident involving a runaway luggage trolley, and that Ramiro was to be the sole benefactor of her cornucopia of cash. Bartoli said, 'My end will deal with the matter, if you wish.'

Reggie lost no time in telling Marjorie of the sad saga. She found the information most upsetting, for, as always, she was a romantic and clung for almost a full minute to the fairy tale fed to her by Ramiro. But, upon considering the number of tears she'd shed for Ricardo and what a fool his son had made of her, she felt quite revengeful.

To think not only was her erstwhile lover, and father of her child, still alive, but he, and his offspring, planned to kill her! The very thought caused the sluice gates of her lacrimal glands to spring open and a deluge of tears to course down her cheeks. Reggie mollified her malaise, and Marjorie thanked him in the manner she knew best. Whilst recovering from coition exhaustion, he swore to revenge her honour.

Together with Marjorie, Pishorn and Adelstein, he laid plans that'd dupe Ramiro and Ricardo into thinking she'd go along with their ghastly undertaking. Furthermore, Marjorie's sons, who had for some time been acting like opportunistic scavenging hyenas waiting for her to drop, and thereby get their fangs into her extensive wealth, would be left thinking she was a penniless widow.

Ramiro's Destino

Ramiro considered serving at the brothers' table was the devil's own luck. Only good fortune prevented the fluke from derailing the plan.

However, his knighthood wasn't forthcoming, for, later the following day, he was bundled into the back of an unmarked car. Thereafter, at Bournemouth International Airport, on England's sleepy South Coast, he'd been palletised, and loaded onboard an ancient Boeing 707 converted freighter.

The following day, at the crack of dawn, the plane rolled along the runway bound for Latin America.

In its long life, the craft had performed a whole slew of tasks for umpteen owners. She was now employed trafficking weapons, drugs, and hauling nefarious cargoes for several crooked regimes. Western government agencies, not wishing to be seen sullying their hands, shrouded its use by classifying them as National Security. The latter role was so valuable to the 'democratic' authorities that they turned a blind eye to the villainous acts the owners called upon it to do.

It was on the cards that Ramiro, being tied up and deposited in a cardboard box for the long journey, was going to find the trip uncomfortable. But, the idiot handling agent had added insult to injury by inverting the 'This Way Up' logo, resulting in Ramiro's buttocks facing the now unused 'Fasten your seatbelt' signs.

After nigh on fourteen hours, the first officer called Bogota's el Dorado air traffic control, 'We have a low oil indication in number two engine and request priority approach into el Dorado'.

'Roger,' said the Colombian controller, who was awaiting the pre-arranged call, 'emergency acknowledged, expect vectors for priority approach runway three one right.'

The plane frequently suffered *'problems'* requiring diversion to the Colombian airport. Their boss had many friends in this international drug centre.

The bumpy landing woke Ramiro. He hoped this was where they'd re-invert him.

They taxied the 707 to an isolated apron in the vast cargo area, and, after parking, the crew, with little formality, departed for their hotel.

It was not long thereafter, that Ramiro felt his cardboard box moving and heard Spanish speaking voices conversing with an accent he couldn't place.

Unbeknown to him, he'd been moved by a forklift onto the back of a seemingly dilapidated ex Colombian military lorry.

Next to his box were four similar sized cartons that had arrived from Argentina just hours before.

The truck's v8 supercharged F-150 engine roared as it hurtled the modified lorry in the direction of Norte de Santander. Despite its dilapidated condition, the vehicle, like the aircraft, was kept in top-notch mechanical condition.

It was there, on the Venezuelan border that el Hombre Caimán, the nickname of the local drug baron, would find a skilled forger for his export documentation, a clever attorney and a girl for the brothel, all great assets. The two unskilled workers, he'd accepted them as a favour to his Argentinean SIDE friend, would toil in the fields.

Bloomsbury, London

Lady Marjorie gazed up at the ceiling-mounted mirror. It was a wee bit bigger than her king-sized circular bed. Barbara da Vechia, the boutique owner friend, now a widowed countess, had overseen its creation by a master artisan. His studio was near her chateau overlooking the Venetian Lagoon on the island of Murano.

The multifaceted design echoed the Tolkowsky cut diamond given to Marjorie by one of the Rostov Romanovs. She'd forgotten which one, for, as they were identical twins, it was inconsequential.

The flat *table facet* portrayed the brothers in the guise of Greek Satyrs, frolicking with a naked nymph on a horse-drawn Troika; mummy had modelled as the sylph, Arethusa.

With the mirror maker's skilled use of the ancient technique known as *gelatine verre églomisé*, he'd created a modern masterpiece.

Her lovers, and she, had enjoyed the shaggy rug. Not only while youthful, but up to not so long ago. She'd given it up in favour of using a bed after losing her dignity by having to be helped to her feet by Charlie Althorn, five years her senior and using a stick. He'd only dropped in for tea and hadn't brought his Viagra, so settled for a shot of bremelanotide which Marjorie's American friend, Caroline, had left behind last time she popped over the pond to shop.

Other than making his flatulence worse than normal, it was not a success.

In terms of comfort, the foam mattress far outweighed dear old shaggy's performance. Mummy had balked when told it carried a nomenclature of memory foam. (She hoped it could hold its memoirs as mute as had the rug.)

She had instructed a trendy young resin sculptor, Pietro Pisani, to shape the telephone, standing on her bedside table, in-the-form-of her beloved Italy. The instrument's six ring tones simulated the bells of the Canpanièl that had deafened her and Barbara da Vechia when visiting the Basilica di San Marco in Venice.

That morning, as was her usual daytime routine, she'd set it to number *six*, the full toll, before immersing herself in the bath. The hydro massage clear glass whirlpool, in which she luxuriated at least twice every day, was also the artisan's creation.

After wallowing for an hour in the heat regulated water, and without forethought, she'd pressed the button labelled *Maleficio*. Mediaeval magistrates used that single knell as an invitation for citizens to stuff their bread and watered-down wine into a sack and enjoy an execution – or, if it be their good fortune, a torture or two.

Oft, she would lie gazing up at the reflections in the Rostov mirror with joyous remembrances.

Tonight, over Reggie Merryweather's shoulder, the sixteen bezel and star facets reflected a plethora of a fifty-something pink posteriors bobbing in the manner of a tailor's treadle.

The telephone's striking bell interrupted her observation. But, he being shorter than her, had his ears nestled between mummy's ample mammaries so muffling his hearing, she received no respite from his wobbling cheeks.

Stretching out her arm, she grasped the receiver between Pescara and Rome and lifted it from its Sardinian base. Pressing Turin to her ear, she spoke into Palermo, 'Lady Crooke-Wells.'

A faint foreign voice said, 'Tell Señor Reggie it be done.'

Before the handset landed beside the bed, the SIDE agent, seated in his second-floor room on Ave. 25 de Mayo, Buenos Aires, had his ears filled with Marjorie's excited squeals.

She hadn't realised what a relief that message would muster. Whooping with delight, she flipped Reggie over like a spaghetti frittata, and shocked him with a ride that played havoc with the electrical impulses of his newly installed cardiac resynchronisation pacemaker.

Lightning Source UK Ltd.
Milton Keynes UK
UKHW021533151221
395708UK00016B/82